By the same author

FICTION

Shadow of a Sun
The Game
The Virgin in the Garden
Still Life
Sugar and Other Stories
Possession

CRITICISM

Degrees of Freedom: The Novels of Iris Murdoch
Unruly Times: Wordsworth and Coleridge in Their Time
Passions of the Mind

ANGELS & INSECTS

ANGELS
&
INSECTS

Two Novellas

A. S. Byatt

Random House
New York

All rights reserved under International and Pan-American
Copyright Conventions. Published in the United States by Random House,
Inc., New York.
This work was originally published in the United Kingdom by Chatto &
Windus Ltd, London, in 1992.

A signed first edition of this book has been privately printed
by The Franklin Library.

Library of Congress Cataloging-in-Publication Data

Byatt, A. S. (Antonia Susan).
Angels and insects : two novellas / A. S. Byatt.—1st ed.
p. cm.
ISBN 0-679-40512-7
I. Title.
PR6052.Y2A83 1993
823'.914—dc20   92-56806

Book design by Michael Mendelsohn

Manufactured in the United States of America

98765432

For Jean-Louis Chevalier

CONTENTS

Morpho Eugenia

'You must dance, Mr Adamson,' said Lady Alabaster from her sofa. 'It is very kind of you to sit by me, and fetch glasses of lemonade, but I really do think you must dance. Our young ladies have made themselves beautiful in your honour, and I hope their efforts will not have been in vain.'

'I think they are all delightful,' said William Adamson, 'but I am out of practice at ballroom dancing.'

'Not much dancing in the jungle,' stated Mr Edgar Alabaster.

'On the contrary. There is a great deal of dancing. There are religious festivals—Christian festivals—which occupy weeks together with communal dancing. And in the interior there are Indian dances where you must imitate the hops of woodpeckers, or the wriggle of armadillos, for hour after hour.' William opened his mouth to say more, and closed it again. Didactic rushes of information were a great shortcoming in returning travellers.

Lady Alabaster moved some of her black silk rolls of flesh on the rosy satin of her sofa. She persisted. 'I shall ask Matty to find you a pretty partner, unless you can pick one out for yourself.'

The shimmering girls whirled past in the candlelight, shell-pink and sky-blue, silver and citron, gauze and tulle. A small orchestra, two fiddles, a flute, a bassoon and a cello scraped and shrilled and boomed in the minstrels' gallery. William Adamson felt constricted, but composed, inside a dress suit borrowed from Lionel Alabaster. He remembered a *festa* on the Rio Manaquiry, lit by lamps made of half an orange-skin filled with turtle oil. He had danced with the *Juiza,* the lady of the revels, barefoot and in his shirtsleeves. There, his whiteness itself had given him automatic precedence at table. Here he seemed sultry-skinned, with jaundice-gold mixed into sun-toasting. He was tall and naturally bony, almost cadaverous after his terrible experiences at sea. The pale people in the soft light polka'd past, murmuring to each other. The music stopped, the partners walked away from the floor, clapping and laughing. All three Alabaster daughters were being conducted back to the group round their mother. Eugenia, Rowena, and Enid.

They were all three pale-gold and ivory creatures, with large blue eyes and long pale silky lashes visible only in certain lights and shadows. Enid was the youngest, still with a trace of childish plumpness, wearing blush-pink organdie trimmed with white rose-buds, and a wreath of rosebuds and a net of rosy ribbons in her hair. Rowena was the tallest, the one who laughed, with richer colour in her cheeks and lips, with the coil of hair in the nape of her neck studded with pearls and blush-tipped daisies. The eldest, Eugenia, wore white tarlatan over a lilac silk underskirt, and had a cluster of violets at her breast, and more violets at her waist, and violets and ivy woven in and out of her sleek golden head. Their brothers, too, had the gold and white colouring. They made a charming and homogeneous group.

'Poor Mr Adamson had no idea we were having a Ball at the beginning of his visit,' said Lady Alabaster. 'Your father wrote immediately to invite him when he heard how he had been rescued at sea after being cast away for fifteen days, very terrible, in the Atlantic. And your father, naturally, thought more of his eagerness to see Mr Adamson's specimens than he did of our own projected entertainment. So Mr Adamson arrived to find the whole house in turmoil and servants running hither and thither in the greatest possible disorder. Fortunately he is much of a height with Lionel, who was able to help with the suit.'

'I should have had no dress suit in any event,' said William. 'All my earthly belongings are burned, or drowned, or both, and they never included a dress suit. During my last two years at Ega I had not even a pair of shoes.'

'Well, well,' said Lady Alabaster easily, 'you must be possessed of immense resources of strength and courage. I am sure they will be equal to a turn around the dance floor. You must do your duty too, Lionel and Edgar. There are more ladies than gentlemen here. There always are, I do not know how it comes about, but there are always more ladies.'

The music struck up again, a waltz. William bowed to the youngest Miss Alabaster, and asked if she were free to dance. She blushed, and smiled and accepted.

'You look at my shoes with a new consciousness,' said William, as he led her out. 'You are afraid not only that I shall dance clumsily but that my unaccustomed feet will stumble into your pretty slippers. I shall endeavour not to. I shall try very hard. You must help me, Miss Alabaster, you must take pity on my inadequacies.'

'This must seem very strange to you,' said Enid Alabaster, 'after so many years of danger and hardship and solitude, to take part in this kind of entertainment.'

'It is quite delightful,' said William, watching his feet, and gaining confidence. The waltz was danced in certain kinds of society in Pará and Manáos; he had whirled around with olive-skinned and velvet-brown ladies of doubtful virtue and no virtue. There was something alarming in the soft, white creature in his arms, at once so milky-wholesome and so airily untouchable. But his feet were confident.

'You know very well how to waltz,' said Enid Alabaster.

'Not so well as your brother, I see,' said William.

Edgar Alabaster was dancing with his sister, Eugenia. He was a big, muscular man, his blond hair crimping in windswept, regular waves over his long head, his back stiff and straight. But his large feet moved quickly and intricately, tracing elegant skipping patterns beside Eugenia's pearly-grey slippers. They were not speaking to each other. Edgar looked over Eugenia's shoulder, faintly bored, surveying the ballroom. Eugenia's eyes were half closed. They whirled, they floated, they checked, they pirouetted.

'We practise a lot in the schoolroom,' said Enid. 'Matty plays the piano and we dance and dance. Edgar likes horses better of course, but he likes any kind of movement, we all do. Lionel's not so good. He doesn't let himself go in the same way. Some days, I think we could dance forever, like the princesses in the story.'

'Who wore their slippers out secretly every night.'

'And were exhausted in the mornings, and no one could understand it.'

'And refused to marry because they loved dancing so much.'

'Some married ladies still dance. There is Mrs Chipperfield, look, in the bright green. She dances *very* well.'

Edgar and Eugenia had left the floor and returned to their positions beside Lady Alabaster's sofa. Enid went on talking to William about the family. As they passed the sofa again, she said, 'Eugenia used to be the best of all, before she was unhappy.'

'Unhappy?'

'She was to be married, you see, only Captain Hunt, her fiancé, died quite suddenly. It was a terrible shock, poor Eugenia is only just recovering. It is like being a widow without being married, I think. We don't talk about it. But everyone knows of course. I'm not tittle-tattling, you know. I just thought—since you are to stay here a little time—it might be helpful to you to know.'

'Thank you. You are very kind. I shall not now say anything unwittingly foolish. Do you think she would dance with me, if I asked her?'

'She might.'

She did. She thanked him gravely, with a slight lift of her soft lips and no change in her deep, distant eyes—or at least that was how he saw them—and put up her hands gracefully to take his. Her presence within his grasp—that was how he thought of it—was lighter, more floating, less springing than Enid's. Her feet were deft. He looked down from his height at her pale face and saw her large eyelids, blue-veined, almost translucent, and the thick fringes of white-gold hairs on their rims. Her slender fingers, resting in his, were gloved and only faintly warm. Her shoulders and bust rose white and flawless from the froth of tulle and tarlatan like Aphrodite from the foam. A simple row of pearls, soft white on soft white with a shimmering difference, rested on her collarbone. She was both proudly naked and wholly untouchable. He guided her round the floor, and felt, to his shame and amazement, unmistakable stirrings and quickenings of bodily excitement in himself. He shifted himself inside Lionel's dress suit, and reflected—he was, after all, a scientist and an observer—that these dances were designed to arouse his desire in exactly this way, however demure the gloves, however sweetly innocent the daily life of the young woman in his arms. He remembered the palm-wine dance, a swaying circle which at a change in rhythm broke up into hugging couples who then set upon and danced round the one partnerless scapegoat dancer. He remembered being grabbed and nuzzled and rubbed and cuddled with great vigour by women with brown breasts glistening with sweat and oil, and with shameless fingers.

Nothing he did now seemed to happen without this double vision, of things seen and done otherwise, in another world.

'You are thinking of the Amazon,' said Eugenia.

'Are you gifted at thought-reading?'

'Oh no. Only you looked far away. And that is far away.'

'I was thinking of the beauty of everything here—the architecture, and the young ladies in their gauzes and laces. I was looking at this very fine Gothic fan vaulting, which Mr Ruskin says is like the ancient imagination of trees in a forest, overarching, and I was thinking of the palms towering in the jungle, and all the beautiful silky butterflies sailing amongst them, high up and quite out of reach.'

'How strange that must be,' said Eugenia. She paused. 'I have made a beautiful display—a kind of quilt, or embroidery almost— out of some of the earlier specimens you sent my father. I have pinned them out very carefully—they are exquisitely pretty—they give a little the effect of a scalloped cushion, only their colours are more subtle than any silks could be.'

'The natives believed we were collecting them as patterns for calico. That was the only way they could explain our interest to themselves, since the butterflies are not good to eat—indeed, I believe many are poisonous, feeding on poisonous plants. And it is those who are the brightest, and sail about slowly and proudly, flaunting their colours as a kind of warning. They are the males, of course, making themselves brilliant for their brown mates. The Indians resemble them in that. It is the men who dress in brilliant feathers and coloured paint and stones. The females are quieter. Whereas here we men wear carapaces like black beetles. And you ladies are like a flower garden in full flight.'

'My father was so sorry to hear you had lost so much in the terrible shipwreck. For your sake, and for his own. He was eager to add to his collection.'

'I managed to save one or two of the rarest and most beautiful. I kept them in a special box by my pillow—I liked to look at them—and so they were there to hand to be snatched up, when we saw that we must abandon ship. There is pathos in saving a dead butterfly. But one in particular is a rarity—I shall say no more now—but I believe your father will be glad to have it—and you too—but it is to be a surprise.'

'I hate people who tell me I am to have a surprise and will not tell me what it is.'

'You do not like suspense?'

'No. No, I don't. I like to know where I am. I am afraid of surprises.'

'Then I must remember never to surprise you,' he said, and thought he sounded foolish, and was not surprised when she did not answer. There was a little crimson stain, the size of a medium ant, where her round breasts met, or parted from, each other, where the violet shadow began. There were blue veins here and there in the creamy surface, just under the skin. His body pulled at him again, and he felt dirty and dangerous. He said, 'I feel privileged to be allowed to be a temporary part of your happy family, Miss Alabaster.'

She looked up at him, on this, and opened the large, blue eyes. They were washed with what looked like unshed tears.

'I love my family, Mr Adamson. We are very happy together. We love each other very much.'

'You are fortunate.'

'Oh yes. We are. I know that. We are very fortunate.'

Since his ten years in the Amazon, and even more since his delirious days afloat in a lifeboat in the Atlantic, William had come to see clean, soft English beds as the heart of some earthly Bower of Bliss. Although it was well after midnight when he retired to his room, there was a thin, silent housemaid waiting to bring him hot water, and to warm his sheets, whisking past him with downturned eyes on noiseless feet. His bedroom had a small carved bay window, with a stained glass roundel depicting two white lilies. There were modern comforts within its Gothic walls—a mahogany bed, intricately carved with ivy leaves and holly berries, spread with goosefeather mattress, soft woollen blankets, and a snowy bedspread embroidered with Tudor roses. He did not, however, climb immediately between the sheets, but carried his candle to his desk and got out his journal.

He had always kept a journal. When he was a young man, in a village outside Rotherham in Yorkshire, he had written a daily examination of his conscience. His father was a successful butcher and a devout Methodist, who had sent his sons to a good local school, where they had learned Greek and Latin and some elementary Mathematics, and had required them to go to chapel. Butchers, William had observed, categorising even then, tend to be well-fleshed men, outward-looking and with strong opinions. Martin Adamson, like his son, had a mane of dark, shining hair, a long, solid nose, and sharp blue eyes under straight brows. He took pleasure in his craft, in anatomising the slain, in delicate knifework and artistry with sausages and pies, and he was dreadfully afraid of Hell Fire, whose flames flickered at the edge of his daily imagination and consumed his dreaming nights. He provided prime beef for mill owners and mine owners in their places, and scrag end and faggots for miners and factory workers in theirs. He was ambitious for William, but without specificity. He wanted him to have a good trade, with possibilities of expansion.

William trained his eye in the farmyard and amongst the bloody sawdust of the slaughterhouse. In the life he finally chose, his father's skills were of inestimable value in skinning, and mounting, and preserving specimens of birds and beasts and insects. He anatomised ant-eaters and grasshoppers and ants with his father's exactness reduced to microscopic scales. In the days of the butchery, his journal was full of his desire to be a great man, and his self-castigation for the sins of pride, of lack of humility, of self-regard, of sloth, of hesitation in pursuing greatness. He tried schoolmastering and supervising wool-carders, and wrote in his journal of his distress at his success in these tasks—he was a good Latin teacher, he saw what his students did not see, he was a good supervisor, he could detect laziness and ameliorate real grievances—but he was not using his unique gifts, whatever they were, he was *going* nowhere, and he meant to go far. He could not read those circular and painful journals now, with their cries of suffocation and their self-condemnatory periods, but he had them in a bank, for they were part of a record, of an accurate record, of the development of the mind and character of William Adamson, who still meant to be a great man.

The journals had changed when he began collecting. He had taken to long walks in the countryside—the part of Yorkshire where he lived consisted of foul black places amongst fields and rough land of great beauty—and he had at first walked in a state of religious anxiety, combined with a reverence for Wordsworth's poetry, looking for signs of Divine Love and order in the meanest flowers that blew, in bubbling brooks and changing cloud formations. And then he had begun to take a collecting-box, bring things home, press them, categorise them, with the aid of Loudon's *Encyclopaedia of Plants*. He discovered the Crucifers, the Umbellifers, the Labiates, the Rosaceae, the Leguminosae, the Compositae, and with them the furious variety of forms which turned out to mask, to enhance the underlying and rigorous order of branching families, changing with site and climate. He wrote for a time in his journal of the wonders of divine Design, and his self-examination gave way insensibly to the recording of petals observed, leaf forms noted, marshes, hedges and tangled banks. His journal was for the first time alive with a purposeful happiness. He began also to collect insects, and was amazed to discover how many hundreds of species of beetle existed in a few square miles of rough moorland. He haunted the slaughterhouse, making notes on where the blowflies preferred to lay their eggs, how the maggots moved and chewed, the swarming, the pullulation, a mass of mess moved by an ordering principle. The world looked different, and larger, and brighter, not water-colour washes of green and blue and grey, but a dazzling pattern of fine lines and dizzying pinpoints, jet-black, striped and spotted crimson, iridescent emerald, sloppy caramel, slime-silver.

And then he discovered his ruling passion, the social insects. He peered into the regular cells of beehives, he observed trails of ants passing messages to each other with fine feelers, working together to shift butterfly-wings and slivers of strawberry-flesh. He stood like a stupid giant and saw incomprehensible, purposefully intelligent beings building and destroying in cracks of his own paving stones. Here was the clue to the world. His journal became the journal of an ant-watcher. This was in 1847, when he was twenty-two. In that year, in the Mechanics' Institute at Rotherham, he met a fellow amateur entomologist who showed him the reports of Henry Walter Bates in the *Zoologist,* on Coleoptera and other matters. He wrote to Bates, including some of his own observations about ant societies, and received a kind reply, encouraging his work, and adding that Bates himself 'with my friend and co-worker in the field, Alfred Wallace' was planning an expedition to the Amazons in search of undiscovered creatures. William had already read Humboldt and W. H. Edwards' highly coloured account of the wild luxuriance, the frolicking and joyous coatis, agoutis and sloths, the gaudy trogons, motmots, woodpeckers, chiming thrushes, parrots, manakins and butterflies 'the bigness of a hand and of the richest metallic blue'. There were millions of miles of unexplored forest—it could lose in its brilliant virgin depths another English entomologist beside Wallace and Bates. There would be new species of ants, to be named perhaps adamsonii, there would be space for a butcher's son to achieve greatness.

The journals began to intermingle a rapt, visionary note with detailed practical sums for outfitting, for specimen boxes, with names of ships, with useful addresses. William set out in 1849, one year later than Wallace and Bates, and returned in 1859. Bates had given him the address of his agent, Samuel Stevens, who had handled and sold the specimens shipped back by all three collectors. It was Stevens who had introduced William to the Reverend Harald Alabaster, who had inherited his baronetcy and his Gothic mansion only on the death of his childless brother in 1848. Alabaster was an obsessive collector, who wrote long letters to his unknown friend, which arrived at infrequent intervals, and asked about the religious beliefs of the Natives as well as the habits of the hummingbird hawk-moth and the Saüba ant. William wrote back to him, the letters of a great naturalist from an untrodden wilderness, spiced with an attractive self-deprecating humour. It was Harald Alabaster who had told him of Wallace's calamitous fire at sea in 1852, in a letter that had taken almost a year to reach him. William had somehow supposed that this was a statistical insurance against another naturalist being wrecked on the return voyage, but it had not been so. The brig, *Fleur-de-Lys,* had been rotten and unseaworthy, and William Adamson, unlike the vaguer Wallace, had not been properly insured against the loss of his collection. He was still full of the survivor's simple pleasure in being alive when Harald Alabaster's invitation reached him. He packed up what he had saved, which included his tropical journals and the most valuable butterflies, and set off for Bredely Hall.

His tropical journals were much stained—by the paraffin in which their box had once been doused to prevent their being eaten by ants and termites, by traces of mud and crushed leaves from canoe accidents, by salt water like floods of tears. He had sat alone under a roof woven of leaves in an earth-floored hut, and scribbled descriptions of everything: the devouring hordes of army ants, the cries of frogs and alligators, the murderous designs of his crew, the monotonous sinister cries of the howler monkeys, the languages of various tribes he had stayed with, the variable markings of butterflies, the plagues of biting flies, the unbalancing of his own soul in this green world of vast waste, murderous growth, and lazily aimless mere existence. He had peered into these pages by the light of burning turtle oil, and had recorded his solitude, his smallness in the face of the river and the forest, his determination to survive, whilst comparing himself to a dancing midge in a collecting bottle. He had come to be addicted to the written form of his own language, which he spoke hardly at all, although he was fluent in Portuguese, the *lingoa geral* spoken by most of the natives, and several tribal tongues. Latin and Greek had given him a taste for languages. Writing gave him a taste for poetry. He read and reread *Paradise Lost* and *Paradise Regained,* which he had by him, and an anthology of *Choice Beauties of our Elder Poets.* It was to this he turned now. It must have been one in the morning, but his blood and his mind were racing. He was not ready for sleep. He had bought a new notebook, an elegant green with marbled covers, in Liverpool, and now opened its first blank page. On this he copied out a poem by Ben Jonson which had always intrigued him and had now suddenly taken on a new urgency.

> Have you seen but a bright lily grow,
> Before rude hands have touched it?
> Have you marked but the fall o' the snow,
> Before the soil hath smutched it?
> Have you felt the wool o' the beaver?
> Or swan's down ever?
> Or have smelled o' the bud o' the briar?
> Or the nard i' the fire?
> Or have tasted the bag o' the bee?
> O so white! O so soft! O so sweet is she!

That was what he wanted to set down, exactly. O so white! O so soft! O so sweet, he wanted to say.

Beyond that was unknown territory. He remembered a sentence from a fairy story of his childhood, a sentence spoken by a Prince of Araby about the lovely Princess of China, brought briefly to him in her sleep by mischievous spirits. 'I shall die if I cannot have her,' the Prince had said, to his servant, to his father and mother. William poised his pen above his paper and wrote,

' "I shall die if I cannot have her." '

He thought for some time, pen in hand, and then wrote again, under the first line,

' "I shall die if I cannot have her." '

He added,

Of course I shall not die; that is absurd—but that old statement from an old tale seems best to reflect the kind of landslide, or whirlpool-gulf, that has taken place in my soul since this evening. I believe I am a rational being. I have survived, retaining my sanity and cheerfulness, near-starvation, prolonged isolation, yellow fever, treachery, malice, and shipwreck. I remember as a little boy, on reading my Fairy Book, a premonition of terror rather than delight about what human love might be, in that sentence, 'I shall die if I cannot have her.' I was in no hurry for love. I did not seek it out. The rational plan I had made for my life—the romantic plan no less, which now coincides with the rational, both implying a return, after a reasonable rest, to the forest—left no space for the search for a wife, for I believed I felt no particular need for one. In my delirium in the boat, it is true, and earlier under the ministrations, or torments, of that filthy *hag* in whose house I cured *myself* of the fever, I did dream from time to time of a kindly female presence, as something deeply needed, unreasonably forgotten, as though the phantom were weeping for me as I was weeping for her.

Where am I taking myself? I am writing in almost as high a delirium as I experienced then. Conventional wisdom would be shocked that I even allowed the idea of union with her to enter my mind—for in conventional wisdom's eyes, our stations are unequal, and more than that, I am penniless and with no prospects. I would not be swayed by such wisdom myself—and have no respect for artificial ranks and places, which are supported by inbreeding of stock, and by time-wasting frivolous pursuits—I am as good a *man,* take me for all in all, as E. A. and have, I dare swear it, used my intelligence and my bodily courage to greater purpose. But how would that consideration weigh with any such family, constructed exactly to reject any such intr . . .

The only rational course is to forget the whole matter, suppress these inopportune feelings, make an end.

He thought for a moment, and then wrote for a third time, ' "I shall die if I cannot have her." '

He slept well, and dreamed that he was pursuing a flock of golden birds through the forest, which settled and preened and allowed him to approach, and then rose and wheeled away, crying in high voices, only to settle again, just out of reach.

Harald Alabaster's study, or den, was next to Bredely's small chapel. It was hexagonal in shape, with wood-panelled walls and two deep windows, carved in stone in the Perpendicular style: the ceiling too was carved stone, pale grey-gold in colour, a honey-comb of smaller hexagons. There was an unusual roof-light at the centre of this, reminiscent of the Lantern of Ely Cathedral, under which the large Gothic desk was imposingly set, giving the room the appearance of a chapter house. Round the walls were both tall, arched bookcases full of polished leather, and deep-drawered cabinets. There were also three free-standing hexagonal, glass-topped display cabinets, in lustrous mahogany, inside one of which reposed, on their pins, several of William's earlier captures, the Heliconeae, the Papilionidae, the Danaidae, the Ithomiidae. Above the cases hung texts, written out with careful penmanship in Gothic script, and bordered with charming designs of fruit, flowers, foliage, birds and butterflies. Harald Alabaster pointed them out to William Adamson.

'My daughter Eugenia takes pleasure in working these designs for me. I think they are very pleasing—prettily penned, and carefully executed.'

William read aloud,

'There be four things which are little upon the earth, but they are exceeding wise:
The ants are a people not strong, yet they prepare their meat in the summer;
The conies are but a feeble folk, yet make they their houses in the rocks;
The locusts have no king, yet go they forth all of them by bands;
The spider taketh hold with her hands, and is in kings' palaces.
                                                Proverbs 30, 24–8'

'It is Eugenia who made this elegant arrangement of the Lepidoptera also. I fear it is not done upon quite scientific principles, but it has the intricacy of a rose window made of living forms, and does show forth the extraordinary brilliance and *beauty* of the insect creation. I am particularly taken with the idea of punctuating the rows of butterflies with the little iridescent green scarabs. Eugenia says she got the idea from silk knots in embroidery.'

'She was describing the work to me last night. She obviously has a very precise hand in handling specimens. And the result is very fine, very delightful.'

'She is a good girl.'

'She is very beautiful.'

'I hope she will also be very happy,' said Harald Alabaster. He did not sound, William thought, listening for every nuance of meaning, *entirely* convinced that this would be the case.

Harald Alabaster was tall, gaunt, and slightly stooping. He had a bony, ivory version of the family face, the blue eyes a little watery, the lips buried in the fronds of a patriarchal beard. The beard, and his abundant hair, were largely white, but the original blond lingered here and there, giving the white a stained, brassy look, a paradoxical tarnish. He wore a clerical collar and a black loose jacket over baggy trousers. Over this he wore a kind of monkish gown, black and woollen, with long sleeves and a sort of cowl. This could have had a practical purpose—the far reaches of the hall were bitterly cold, even with fires lit in all the fireplaces, which they mostly were not. William, who had corresponded with him for many years, but was now meeting him for the first time, had imagined a younger, more substantial man, solid and cheerful like the collectors he had met in London and Liverpool, men of business and intellectual adventure together. He had brought down his salvaged treasures, which he now laid out on Alabaster's desk, unopened.

Harald Alabaster pulled a kind of dangling bell-rope by his desk, and a soft-footed servant came in with a coffee tray, poured the coffee, and went out.

'You are fortunate to have escaped with your life; we must give thanks for that—but the loss of your specimens must have been a very severe setback. What will you do, Mr Adamson, if you do not think it impertinent to ask?'

'I have hardly had time to think. I had hoped to sell enough to be able to stay in England for some time, write about my travels perhaps—I kept extensive journals—and earn enough money to equip myself to return to the Amazon. We have barely begun to pick up twigs, Sir, those of us who have worked there—there are millions of unexplored miles, unknown creatures . . . I have particular problems I propose to solve—I have come to be particularly interested in ants and termites—I should like to make a prolonged study of certain aspects of their life. I believe for instance that I may have a better explanation for the curious habits of the leafcutter ants than that put forward by Mr Bates, and I should like also to find the next of the army ants—the Eciton burchelli—which has never been done. I have even wondered if they are perhaps perpetual travellers who form only *temporary encampments*—this is not the nature of the ants we know—but these forage so extensively, so ferociously, it may be that they *must* be perpetually on the move in order to survive. And then there is the interesting problem of the way in which—and this would reinforce the observations of Mr Darwin—certain ants that inhabit certain Bromeliads appear to have affected the form of the plants over the millennia, so that the plants actually seem to build chambers and corridors for their insect guests in the natural process of growth. I should like to see if this can be demonstrated; I should like—I am sorry, I am talking disjointedly on and on—I forget my manners. You have been so kind in your letters, Sir, the receipt of which was one of the very rare moments of luxury in my time in the forest. Your letters, Sir, came with necessities like butter and sugar, wheat and flour which we never saw—and were more welcome. I rationed the reading, so as to savour them longer, as I rationed the sugar and flour.'

'I am glad to have given so much pleasure to anyone,' said Harald Alabaster. 'And I hope I may be able to help you now in more material ways. In a moment we will examine what you have brought back—I will give you a good price for anything I require, a good price. But I wonder if . . . I ask myself . . . would you care to make a part of this household for a period of time sufficient to . . .

'Had your specimens survived, I take it you would have spent a considerable time identifying and cataloguing everything—it would have been a considerable labour. Now I have in my out-houses—I am ashamed to admit it—crate upon crate I have enthusiastically purchased, from Mr Wallace, from Mr Spruce, from Mr Bates and yourself, but also from travellers in the Malay peninsula, in the Australias, in Africa—I had quite underestimated the task of setting these in order. There is something very wrong, Mr Adamson, in plundering the Earth of her beauties and curiosities and then not making use of them for what alone justifies our depredations—the promotion of useful knowledge, of human wonder. I feel like the dragon in the poem, sitting upon a hoard of treasure, which he makes no good use of. I could offer you employment in setting all that to rights—if you would accept—and this might give you time to resume your own path in whatever way seemed to you best on reflection . . .'

'That is an extremely generous offer,' said William. 'It would give me at once a roof over my head, and work I am fitted for.'

'But you hesitate—'

'I have always had this clear vision—a kind of picture in my head—of what I must do, of how my life should be—'

'And you are not sure your vocation includes Bredely Hall.'

William hesitated. His mind's eye was occupied by a picture of Eugenia Alabaster, her white bust rising from the lacy sea of her ballgown like Aphrodite from the foam. But he was not going to say that. He even enjoyed the duplicity of not saying that.

'I know I must find some means of fitting out another expedition.'

'Perhaps,' said Harald Alabaster carefully, 'I might, at some future date, be of help in that regard. Not only as a buyer of specimens, but in some more substantial way. May I suggest that you make an extended visit here—and at least *look over* what I have in store—I would of course pay you some agreed salary for that work, I would put things on a professional basis. And I would not expect to take up your complete attention with these tasks—oh, no—so that you would have time also to set your ideas for writing in order. And then, in due course, a decision might be made, a ship might be found, and I might perhaps hope that some monstrous toad or savage-seeming beetle in the jungle floor might immortalise me— Bufo amazoniensis haraldii—Cheops nigrissimum alabastri—I like that, do not you?'

'I do not see how I can refuse such an offer,' said William. He was unwrapping his specimen box as he spoke. 'I have brought you something—something very rare—which already, fortuitously, takes a name from this house into the virgin forest. Here I have a most interesting group of Heliconine and Ithomiine butterflies, and here are several very rich Papilios—some red-spotted, some dark green. I hope to discuss with you some significant variations in the *forms* of these creatures, which do suggest the species may be in the process of modification, of change.

'But here—here is what I think will particularly interest you. I know you received the Morpho Menelaus I sent you; I went in pursuit of its congener, the Morpho Rhetenor—which is of an even brighter, more metallic blue, and over seven inches across. I do have *one* Morpho Rhetenor, here—not a good specimen—a little torn, and missing a leg. They fly in the broad, sunny roads in the forest, they float very slowly, occasionally flapping their wings, like birds, and they almost never come down below twenty feet, so they are almost impossible to catch, though exquisitely beautiful to see, sailing in the greenish sunlight. But I employed some agile little Indian boys to climb up for me and they were able to bring me a pair of a related species *equally* rare and in its way equally lovely, though not blue—here, look—the male is a lustrous satiny-white, and the female is a quieter pale lavender, but still exquisite. When they were brought to me, in such perfect condition, I felt the blood rush to my head, truly felt I might faint with excitement. I did not know then how appropriate they were to add to your collection. They are related closely to Morpho Adonis. And to Morpho Uraneis Batesii. They are Morpho Eugenia, Sir Harald.'

Harald Alabaster looked at the dead, shining creatures.

'Morpho Eugenia. Remarkable. A remarkable creation. How beautiful, how delicately designed, how wonderful that something so fragile should have come here, through such dangers, from the other end of the earth. And very rare. I have never seen one. I have never heard tell of anyone who has seen one. Morpho Eugenia. Well.'

He pulled his bell-rope again, which produced, in the room, only a faint creaking sound.

'It is hard,' he said to William, 'not to agree with the Duke of

Argyll that the extraordinary beauty of these creatures is in itself the evidence of the work of a Creator, a Creator who also made our human sensibility to beauty, to design, to delicate variation and brilliant colour.'

'From our spontaneous response to them,' said William carefully, 'I feel instinctively drawn to agree with you. But from the scientific viewpoint I feel I must ask what purpose of Nature's might be fulfilled by all this brilliance and loveliness. Mr Darwin, I know, inclines to think that the fact that it is very preponderantly *male* butterflies and birds that are so brilliantly coloured—whilst females are often drab and unobtrusive—suggests that perhaps there is some advantage to the male, in flaunting his scarlets and golds, which might make the female select him as a mate. Mr Wallace argues that the drabness of the female is *protective* coloration—she may hang under a leaf to lay her eggs, or sit in the shades on her nest and melt unseen into the shadows. I have myself noticed that the brightly coloured male butterflies wheel about in huge flocks in the sunlight whilst the females seem timid, and lurk under bushes and in damp places.'

There was a knock at the door, and a footman came into the study.

'Ah, Robin, find Miss Eugenia if you can—and all the young ladies—we have something here to show them. Tell her to come as soon as she may.'

'Yes, sir.' The door closed again.

'There is another question,' said William, 'which I ask myself often. Why do the most brilliant butterflies bask with open wings on the upper surfaces of leaves, or fly in a slow, flapping motion, not rapidly? The Papilios, for instance, are also known as pharmacophages, or *poison-eaters,* because they feed on the poisonous aristolochia vines—and they seem to know they may flaunt themselves with impunity, that predators will not snap them up. It is possible that their gaudy display is a kind of defiant *warning.* Mr

Bates has even suggested that certain inoffensive species *mimic* these poisonous ones in order to share their immunity. He has found some Pieridae—whites and sulphurs—indistinguishable from some Ithomines, to the casual eye, or even the careful observer, without a microscope . . .'

Eugenia entered the room. She was wearing white muslin, with cherry-red ribbons and bow, and a cherry-red sash, and looked delightful. When she came up to Harald's desk to be shown the Morpho Eugenia, William felt confusedly as though she carried with her an atmosphere of her own, a cloud of magic dust that at once drew him in and held him off, at precisely the distance of the invisible barrier. He bowed politely to her, and thought at once of his drunken, clear-eyed journal entry, ' "I shall die if I cannot have her" ', and of a ship in flight, with the green water churning away from the bows, and the spray racing. He was not afraid of danger, but he was shrewd, and took no relish in the thought of shrivelling in a fruitless fire.

'What a lovely creature,' said Eugenia. Her soft mouth was a little open. He could see the wet, evenly milky teeth.

'It is Morpho Eugenia, my dear. Not named for you, but brought *to* you, by Mr Adamson.'

'How delightful. What a beautiful glittering white she is—'

'No, no, that is the male. The female is the smaller one, the lavender.'

'What a pity. I prefer the white satin. But then I *am* a female, so that is natural. I wish we could display them in flight. They seem a little stiff, like dead leaves, whatever you do to make them natural. I should like to keep butterflies as we keep birds.'

'It is perfectly feasible,' said William. 'In a conservatory, if the larvae are cared for properly.'

'I should take great pleasure in sitting in the conservatory in a great cloud of butterflies. It would be most romantic.'

'I could procure you such a cloud, with the greatest of ease. Not, of course, Morpho Eugenia. But blue, and white, and golden, and black and red damask, native kinds. *You* would be Morpho Eugenia. It means beautiful, you know. Shapely.'

'Ah,' said Eugenia. 'The opposite of amorphous.'

'Exactly. The primeval forest out there—the endless sameness of the greenery—the clouds of midges and mosquitoes—the struggling mass of creepers and undergrowth—often seemed to me the epitome of the amorphous. And then something perfect and beautifully formed would come into view and take the breath away. Morpho Eugenia did that, Miss Alabaster.'

She turned her liquid gaze on him to see if she had detected a compliment, as though she had a special sense for those. He met her eyes and smiled, briefly, ruefully, and she smiled briefly back, before dropping her lashes over the blue pools of her eyes.

'I shall make a special glass box for them, Mr Adamson, you will see. They shall dance together forever, in their white satin and lavender silk. You must teach me what to paint into their background, what leaves and flowers—I would wish to get it right, naturally.'

'I am yours to command, Miss Alabaster.'

'Mr Adamson has consented to stay here for a little while, my dear, and help me to organise my collections.'

'Good. Then I shall be able to command him, as he suggests.'

Understanding daily life in Bredely Hall was not easy. William found himself at once detached anthropologist and fairytale prince trapped by invisible gates and silken bonds in an enchanted castle. Everyone had their place and their way of life, and every day for months he discovered new people whose existence he had not previously suspected, doing tasks of which he had known nothing.

Bredely was built like a mediaeval manor house, but with new money. In 1860 it had been completed only thirty years, and had been long in the building. The Alabasters were an ancient and noble family, who had always been very pure-blooded, and had never wielded very much power, but had tilled their fields and collected books, horses, curiosities and poultry. Harald Alabaster was the second son of the Robert Alabaster who had built Bredely, with the money brought to him by his wife, the daughter of an East India merchant. The house had been inherited by Harald's elder brother, also Robert, who had also married a rich woman—the daughter of a minor earl—who had borne him twelve children, all of whom had died in infancy. Harald, a conventional second son, had taken Holy Orders, and had had a living in the Fens, where he had spent his spare time on botany and entomology. He had been poor in those days—Robert the first's wealth was tied up in Bredely, which had gone to Robert the second. Harald had married twice. His first wife, Joanna, had borne him two sons, Edgar and Lionel, and died in childbed. Gertrude, the present Lady Alabaster, had married him immediately after his widowing. Gertrude Alabaster, too, had brought along a fat dowry—she was the granddaughter of a mine owner who was given to charitable benefaction and also to shrewd investment. She had survived maternity with repetitive complaisance. William had initially supposed that the five children he met were all there were but discovered that there were at least three more in the schoolroom—Margaret, Elaine and Edith, and twins in the nursery, Guy and Alice. Also part of the community were various dependent spinsters of various ages, relatives of the Alabasters, or of their wives. A Miss Fescue was always at meals, chomping her food very loudly, never speaking. There was a thin Miss Crompton, usually known as Matty, who, although not the governess—that was Miss Mead—nor the nursery nurse—that was Dacres—seemed to be in some way employed in the care of the younger members of the family. There were visiting young men, friends of Edgar and Lionel. Then there were the servants, from the butler and housekeeper to the scullery maids and boot and bottle boys in the dark depths behind the servants' door.

His days began with morning prayers in the chapel. These took place after breakfast, and were attended by those members of the family who had risen, and a varying gathering of quiet servants, maids in black dresses and spotless white aprons, menservants in black suits, who sat at the back, men on the right, women on the left. The family occupied the front rows. Rowena came often, Eugenia rarely, the children always, with Matty and Miss Mead. Lady Alabaster came only on Sundays, and had a tendency to drowse in the front corner, purple in the light of the stained-glass window. The chapel was very plain, and not very warm. The seating was hard oak benches, and there was nothing to look at except the high windows, with their glassy blue grapes and creamy lilies, and Harald. In the early days of William's presence, Harald would preach succinct little sermons. William was interested in these. They bore no relation at all to the threats and ecstasy of the religion he had grown up in, the red caverns of eternal fire, the red floods of spilt sacrificial blood. Their note was kindly, their subject matter love, family love, as was appropriate to the occasion, the love of God the Father, who watched the fall of every sparrow with infinite care, who had divided His infinity into Father and Son, the more to make His love comprehensible to human creatures, whose understanding of the nature of love began with the natural ties between the members of the family group, the warmth of the mother, the protection of the father, the closeness of brothers and sisters, and was designed to move outwards in emulation of the divine Parent and embrace the whole creation, from families to households, from households to nations, from nations to all men, and indeed, all living beings, wondrously made.

William watched Harald's face attentively during these addresses. When Eugenia was present, he watched her face, when he dared, but her eyes were always modestly cast down, and she had a great capacity for stillness, sitting with her hands quiet in her lap. Harald changed aspects. At times, with his head up, and the white fronds of his beard catching the light, he had a look of God the Father himself, piercing-eyed, white as wool, ancient of days. At others, speaking quietly, almost inaudibly, and looking at the black-and-white chequered floor beneath his feet, he had almost a bedraggled look, to which the slightly musty, frayed quality of his gown contributed. And at others still, he reminded William briefly of Portuguese missionary friars he had met, out there, with feverish eye and ravaged faces, men who failed to comprehend the incomprehension of the placidly evasive Indians. And this analogy in turn would make William, sitting in the English stonelight on his hard bench, remember other ceremonies, the all-male gatherings to drink *caapi,* or *Aya-huasca,* the Dead Man's Vine. He had tried it once and had seen visions of landscapes and great cities and lofty towers as though he were flying, had found himself lost in a forest surrounded by serpents, and in danger of death. Women were not allowed to taste these things, or to see the drums which summoned the participants, the *botutos,* on pain of death. He remembered the fleeing women, faces covered, sitting amongst the decorous English family, men on one side, women on another, watching Eugenia's pink tongue moisten her soft lips. He felt he was doomed to a kind of double consciousness. Everything he experienced brought up its contrary image from *out there*, which had the effect of making not only the Amazon ceremonies but the English sermon seem strange, unreal, of an uncertain nature. He had smuggled away a *botuto* under blankets, in a canoe at night, but it was lost with all his other things, under the miles of grey water. Perhaps it had brought him ill-luck.

'We must never cease to be thankful to the Lord for all his many mercies to us,' said Harald Alabaster.

A workshop was set up for William in a disused saddle-room, next to the stables. This was half-full of the tin boxes, the wooden crates, the tea-chests of things Harald had purchased—apparently with no clear priority of interest—from all over the world. Here were monkey skins and delicate parrot skins, preserved lizards and monstrous snakes, box upon box of dead beetles, brilliant green, iridescent purple, swarthy demons with monstrous horned heads. Here too were crates of geological specimens, and packs of varied mosses, fruits and flowers, from the Tropics and the ice-caps, bears' teeth and rhinoceros horns, the skeletons of sharks and clumps of coral. Some packages proved to have been reduced to drifting dust by the action of termites, or compacted to viscous dough by the operation of mould. William asked his benefactor on what principle he was required to proceed, and Harald told him, 'Set it all in order, don't you know? Make sense of it, lay it all out in some order or other.' William came to see that Harald had not carried out this task himself partly at least because he had no real idea of how to set about it. He felt moments of real irritability that treasures for which men like himself had risked life and health should lie here higgledy-piggledy, and decay in an English stable. He procured a trestle-table and several ledgers, a series of collecting cabinets and some cupboards for specimens that would not lie flat and slide conveniently in and out of drawers. He set up his microscope, and began to make labels. He moved things from day to day from drawer to drawer as he found himself with a plethora of beetles or a sudden plague of frogs. He could not devise an organising principle, but went on doggedly making labels, setting up, examining.

His saddle-room was dark, and stone-cold, except where the light came in from the window, which was high up, too high to look out of. He worked amongst the noise and smells of the grooms mucking out the stables, the steaming scent of dung, the ammoniac whiff of horse-piss, the plod of leather boots, the swish of hay on a fork. Edgar and Lionel were both keen horsemen. Edgar kept an Arab stallion, a gleaming chestnut with a silky-muscled, arching neck and eyes that rolled white in the half-dark of his box, where he paced, baring his teeth. His name was Saladin. Edgar's hunter was Ivanhoe, huge, iron-grey, full of oats and a great leaper. Edgar was always accepting challenges to jump impossible objects on Ivanhoe, who always rose to the occasion. The two of them were in some ways alike, rippling with muscle, standing tall, somehow strutting with pent-in force, not flowing, like the confined Saladin, like the mares and foals in the paddock, like Rowena and Eugenia. William could hear Edgar and Lionel coming in and out from rides as he worked, the quick clatter of iron on stones, the scrape of horses wheeling and dancing. The young women sometimes went out with them too. Eugenia rode a pretty and docile black mare, and wore a blue riding habit that matched her eyes. William tried to manage to come out of his cavern to watch her mount, her neat little foot in the groom's hands, her own gloved hands on the reins, her hair bound in a blue net. Edgar would watch William from the height of Ivanhoe's saddle. William sensed that Edgar did not like him. Edgar treated him as he treated the intermediate folk between the family and the invisible, speechless servants. He offered him the time of day, a nod on meeting, and no encouragement to converse.

Lady Alabaster spent her days in a small parlour, with a view over the lawn. This room was a lady's room, and had dark pomegranate-red wallpaper, sprinkled with sprigs of honeysuckle in pink and cream. It had thick red velvet curtains, often partially drawn against the sun: Lady Alabaster's eyes were weak, and she frequently had the headache. There was always a fire lit in the hearth, which at first did not strike William, who had arrived in early Spring, as anything unusual, but brought him out in sweat under his jacket as Summer advanced. Lady Alabaster appeared to be immobilised, by natural lethargy more than by any specific complaint, though she waddled, more than walked, when she progressed along the corridors to eat luncheon or dine, and William formed the impression that under her skirts her knees and ankles were hugely, maybe painfully, swollen. She lay on a deep sofa, under the window, but with her back to it, oriented towards the fire. The room was a nest of cushions, all embroidered with flowers and fruit and blue butterflies and scarlet birds, in cross-stitch on wool, in silk thread on satin. Lady Alabaster had always an embroidery frame by her, but William never saw her take it up, though this proved nothing—she might have laid it aside out of courtesy. She did, in her fading voice, point out to him the work of Eugenia, Rowena and Enid, Miss Fescue, Matty and the little girls, for his admiration. She had several glass cases of dried poppy-heads and teazles and hydrangeas, and several little footstools, over which guests and servants stumbled on their way into the dimness. She seemed to spend most of her day drinking—tea, lemonade, ratafia, chocolate milk, barley water, herbal infusions, which were endlessly moving along the corridors, borne by parlourmaids, on silver trays. She also consumed large quantities of sweet biscuits, macaroons, butterfly cakes, little jellies and dariole moulds, which were also freshly made by Cook, carried from the kitchen, and their crumbs subsequently removed, and dusted away. She was hugely fat, and did not wear corsets except for special occasions, but lay in a sort of voluminous shiny tea gown, swaddled in cashmere shawls and with a lacy cap tied under her many chins. Like many well-fleshed women, she had kept some bloom on her skin, and her face was moony-bland and curiously unlined, though her pale eyes were deep in little rolling pits of flesh. Sometimes Miriam, her personal maid, would sit by her and brush her still lustrous hair for half an hour at a time, holding it in her deft hands, and sweeping the ivory-backed brush rhythmically over and over. Lady Alabaster said that the hair-brushing eased her headaches. When these were very bad, Miriam would apply cold compresses, and wipe her mistress's eyelids with witch hazel.

William felt that this immobile, vacantly amiable presence was a source of power in the household. The housekeeper came and went for her instructions, Miss Mead brought the little girls to recite their poems and tables, the butler carried in documents, Cook came and went, the gardener, wiping his boots, brought in pots of bulbs, little posies, designs for new plantings. These people were often ushered in and out by Matty Crompton, and it was Matty who came to seek William in his stable for what turned out to be his instructions.

She stood in the shadows in the doorway, a tall, thin dark figure, in a musty black gown with practical white cuffs and collar. Her face was thin and unsmiling, her hair dark under a plain cap, her skin dusky too. She spoke quietly, clearly, with little expression. Lady Alabaster would be glad if he would take a cup of tea with her when his work was finished. He had undertaken quite a labour of love, it appeared. What was that he had in his hand? It looked quite alarming.

'It has become detached from whatever specimen it was attached to, I think. Several parts of several specimens have become detached. I keep a special box for the most puzzling. This hand and arm obviously belong to some fairly large quadrumane. I see you might suppose they were those of some human infant. I can assure you they are not. The bones are far too light. I must look to you as if I were practising witchcraft.'

'Oh no,' said Matty Crompton. 'I did not mean to make any such suggestion.'

Lady Alabaster gave him tea, and sponge fingers, and warm scones with jam and cream, and said she hoped he was comfortable, and that Harald was not overburdening him with work. No, said William, he had a great deal of spare time. He opened his mouth to say that it had been agreed that he should have some spare time, to write his book, when Matty Crompton said, 'Lady Alabaster expressed the hope that you might be able to spare a little time to help Miss Mead and myself with the scientific education of the younger members of the family. She feels that they should profit from the presence amongst us of such a distinguished naturalist.'

'Naturally, I should be happy to do what I can—'

'Matty has *such* good ideas, Mr Adamson. So ingenious, she is. Tell him, Matty.'

'It is nothing much really. We already go on collecting rambles, Mr Adamson—we fish in the ponds and brooks, we collect flowers and berries, in a *very* disorganised way. If you would only accompany us, once or twice, and suggest a kind of *aim* for our aimless poking about—show us what is to be discovered. And then there is the schoolroom. It has long been my ambition to set up a glass-sided beehive, such as Huber had, and also some kind of viable community of ants, so that the little ones could observe the workings of insect societies with their own eyes. Could you do this? Would you do this? You would know how we should set about it. You would tell us what to look for.'

He said he would be delighted to help. He had no idea how to talk to children, he thought to himself, and even believed he did not like them, much. He disliked hearing their squeals when they ran out over the lawn, or through the paddock.

'Thank you so very much,' said Lady Alabaster. 'We shall truly profit from your presence amongst us.'

'Eugenia likes to come on our nature rambles,' said the quiet

Matty Crompton. 'She brings her sketchbooks whilst the young ones go fishing, or collect flowers for the press.'

'Eugenia is a good girl,' said Lady Alabaster vacantly. 'They are all good girls, they are none of them any trouble. I am much blessed in my daughters.'

He went on nature rambles. He felt coerced into doing this, re-minded of his dependent status by the organisation of Miss Mead and Matty Crompton, and yet at the same time he enjoyed the outings. All three elder girls sometimes came and sometimes did not. Sometimes he did not know whether Eugenia would make one of the party until the very moment of setting out, when they would assemble on the gravel walk in front of the house armed with nets, with jam-jars on string handles, with metal boxes and useful scissors. There were days when his morning's work became almost impossible because of the tension in his diaphragm over whether he would or would not see her, because of the imagination he lavished on how she would look, crossing the lawn to the gate in the wall, crossing the paddock and the orchard under the blos-soming fruit trees to the fields which sloped down to the little stream, where they fished for minnows and sticklebacks, caddis grubs and water-snails. He liked the little girls well enough; they were docile, pale little creatures, well buttoned up, who spoke when they were spoken to. Elaine in particular had a good eye for hidden treasures on the undersides of leaves, or interesting bore-holes in muddy banks. When Eugenia was not in the party he felt his old self again, scanning everything with a minute attention that in the forests had been the attention of a primitive hunter as well as a modern naturalist, of a small animal afraid amongst threatening sounds and movements, as well as a scientific explorer. Here the pricking of his skin was associated not with fear, but with the invisible cloud of electric forces that spangled Eugenia's air as she strolled calmly through the meadows. Perhaps it was fear. He did not wish to feel it. He was only in abeyance, until he felt it again.

One day, when they were all occupied on the bank of the stream, including both Eugenia and Enid, he was drawn into speaking of his feelings about all this. There had been a great fall of spring rain, and various loose clumps of grass and twigs were floating along the usually placid surface of the stream, between the trailing arms of the weeping willows and the groups of white poplar. There were two white ducks and a coot, swimming busily; the sun was over the water, kingcups were golden, early midges danced. Matty Crompton, a patient huntress, had captured two sticklebacks and trailed her net in the water, watching the shadows under the bank. Eugenia stood next to William. She breathed in deeply, and sighed out.

'How beautiful all this is,' she said. 'How *lucky* I always feel to live just here, of all spots on the earth. To see the same flowers come out every spring in the meadows, and the same stream always running. I suppose it must seem a very *bounded* existence to you, with your experience of the world. But my roots go so deep . . .'

'When I was in the Amazons,' he answered simply and truthfully, 'I was haunted by an image of an English meadow in spring—just as it is today, with the flowers, and the new grass, and the early blossom, and the little breeze lifting everything, and the earth smelling fresh after the rain. It seemed to me that such scenes were *truly* Paradise—that there was not anything on earth more beautiful than an English bank in flower, than an English mixed hedge, with roses and hawthorn, honeysuckle and bryony. Before I went, I had read highly coloured accounts of the brilliance of the tropical jungle, the flowers and fruits and gaudy creatures, but there is nothing there so *colourful* as this is. It is all a monotonous sameness of green, and such a mass of struggling, climbing, suffocating vegetation—often you cannot see the sky. It is true that the weather is like that of the Golden Age—everything flowers and fruits perpetually and simultaneously in the tropical heat, you have always

Spring, Summer and Autumn at once, and no Winter. But there is something inimical about the vegetation itself. There is a kind of tree called the Sipó Matador—which translates, the Murderer Sipó—which grows tall and thin like a creeper and clings to another tree, to make its way up the thirty, forty feet to the canopy, eating its way into the very substance of its host until that dies—and the Sipó perforce crashes down with it. You hear the strange retorts of crashing trees suddenly in the silence, like cracks of gunshot, a terrible and terrifying sound I could not for some months explain to myself. Everything there is inordinate, Miss Alabaster. There is a form of the violet, there—see, here are some—that grow to be a huge tree. And yet *that* is in so many ways the innocent, the unfallen world, the virgin forest, the wild people in the interior who are as unaware of modern ways—modern evils—as our first parents. There are strange analogies. Out there, no woman may touch a snake. They run to ask you to kill one for them. I have killed *many* snakes for frightened women. I have been fetched considerable distances to do so. The connection of the woman and the snake in the garden is made even out there, as though it is indeed part of some universal pattern of symbols, even where Genesis has never been heard of—I talk too much, I bore you, I am afraid.'

'Oh no. I am quite fascinated. I am glad to hear that our Spring world in some sense remains your ideal. I want you to be happy here, Mr Adamson. And I am most intrigued by what you have to say of the women and snakes. Did you live entirely without the company of civilised peoples, Mr Adamson? Among naked savages?'

'Not entirely. I had various friends, of all colours and races, during my stay in various communities. But sometimes, yes, I was the only white guest in tribal villages.'

'Were you not afraid?'

'Oh, often. Upon two occasions I overheard plots to murder me, made by men ignorant of my knowledge of their tongue. But also I met with much kindness and friendship from people not so simple as you might suppose from seeing them.'

'Are they really naked, and painted?'

'Some are. Some are part-clothed. Some wholly clothed. They are greatly given to decorating their skins with vegetable dyes.'

He was aware of the limpid blue eyes resting on him, and felt that behind her delicate frown she was considering his relations with the naked people. And then felt that his thoughts smutched her, that he was too muddied and dirty to think of her, let alone touch at her secret thoughts from his own secret self. He said, 'Those floating grasses, even, remind me of the great floating islands of uprooted trees and creepers and bushes that make their way along the great river. I used to compare those to *Paradise Lost*. I read my Milton in my rest-times. I thought of the passage where Paradise is cast loose, after the Deluge.'

Matty Crompton, without lifting her eyes from the stream surface, provided the quotation.

> 'then shall this mount
> Of Paradise by might of waves be moved
> Out of his place, pushed by the horned flood,
> With all his verdure spoiled, and trees adrift,
> Down the great river to the opening gulf,
> And there take root an island salt and bare,
> The haunt of seals, and orcs, and sea-mews' clang.'

'Clever Matty,' said Eugenia. Matty Crompton did not answer, but made a sudden plunge and twist with her fishing net and brought up a thrashing, furious fish, a stickleback, large, at least for a stickleback, rosy-breasted and olive-backed. She tipped it out of the net into the jar with the other captives, and the little girls crowded round to look.

The creature gasped for a moment and floated inert. Then it could be seen to gather its forces. It blushed rosier—its chest was the most amazing colour, a fiery pink overlaid, or underlaid, with the olive colour that pervaded the rest of it. It raised its dorsal fin, which became a kind of spiny, draconian ridge, and then it became an almost invisible whirling lash, attacking the other fish, who had nowhere, in their cylindrical prison, to hide. The water boiled. Eugenia began to laugh, and Elaine began to cry. William came to the rescue, pouring fish from jar to jar until, after some gasping on grass, he had managed to isolate the rosy-waistcoated aggressor in a jar of his own. The other fish opened and closed their tremulous mouths. Elaine crouched over them.

William said, 'It is very interesting that it is only this very *aggressive* male who has the pink coat. Two of the others are male, but they are not flushed with anger, or elation, as he is. Mr Wallace argues that females are dull because they keep the nests in general, but this father both makes and guards his own hatchery until the fry swim away. And yet he remains an angry red, perhaps as a warning, long after the need to attract a female into his handsome house has quite vanished.'

Matty said, 'We have probably orphaned his eggs.'

'Put him back,' said Elaine.

'No, no, bring him home, let us keep him awhile, and put him back when we have studied him,' said Miss Mead. 'He will build another nest. Thousands of fish eggs are eaten every minute, Elaine, it is the way of Nature.'

'*We* are not Nature,' said Elaine.

'What else are we?' asked Matty Crompton. She had not thought out her theology, William said to himself, without speaking out loud. Nature was smiling and cruel, that was clear. He offered his hands to Eugenia, to help her up the bank of the stream, and she took hold with her hands, gripping his, through her cotton gloves, always through cotton gloves, warmed by her warmth, impregnated by whatever it was that breathed from her skin.

It was difficult to know what Harald Alabaster did all day. He did not go out, as his sons did, though he was occasionally to be observed taking a solitary twilight stroll amongst the flower-beds, his hands clasped in the small of his back, his head down. He did not appear to occupy himself with what he had so assiduously, if indiscriminately, collected. That was left to William. When William went to the hexagonal studium to report progress, he was given a glass of port or sherry, and listened to intently. Sometimes they spoke—or William spoke—of William's projected work on the social insects. Then one day Harald said, 'I do not know whether I have told you I am writing a book.'

'Indeed you have not. I am most curious to know what kind of book.'

'The kind of impossible book everyone now is trying to write. A book which shall demonstrate—with some kind of intellectual respectability—that it is not impossible that the world is the work of a Creator, a Designer.'

He stopped, and looked at William under his white brows, a canny, calculating look.

William tried silently to weigh up the negative: 'it is *not impossible*'.

Harald said, 'I am as aware as you must be that all the arguments of force are upon the other side. If I were a young man now, a young man such as you, I would be compelled towards atheistic materialism by the sheer beauty, the intricacy, of the arguments of Mr Darwin, and not only Mr Darwin. It was all very well *then* for Paley to argue that a man who found a watch, or even two interlocking cogs of a watch, lying on a bare heath, would have presumed a Maker of such an instrument. There was then no other explanation of the intricacy of the grasp of the hand, or the web of the spider, or the vision of the eye than a Designer who made everything for its particular purpose. But now we have a powerful, almost entirely satisfactory explanation—in the *gradual* action of Natural Selection, of slow change, over unimaginable millennia. And any argument that would truly seek to find an intelligent Creator in His works must take account of the beauty and force of these explanations, must not sneer at them, nor try to refute them for the sake of defending Him who cannot be defended by weak and *partial* reasonings . . .'

'I believe you are quite right in that, Sir. I believe that would be the only way to proceed.'

'I do not know your own views on these matters, Mr Adamson. I do not know if you hold any religious beliefs.'

'I do not know myself, Sir. I believe not. I believe I have indeed been led by my studies—by my observations—to believe that we are all the products of the inexorable laws of the behaviour of matter, of transformations and developments, and that is all. Whether I *really* believe this in my heart of hearts I do not know. I do not think that such a belief comes naturally to mankind. Indeed, I would agree that the religious sense—in some form or another—is as much part of the history of the development of mankind as the knowledge of cooking food, or the tabu against incest. And in that sense, what my reason leads me to believe is constantly modified by my instincts.'

'That sense that the idea of the Creator is as natural to man as his instincts will play an important part in what I hope to write. I am in a great puzzle about the relations between instinct and intelligence in all the creatures: does the beaver *design* the dam, does the bee understand—or in any way *think*—the intricate hexagonal geometry of her cells, which always are adapted to their space, however that is formed? It is our own free intelligence, Mr Adamson, that leads us to find it impossible to conceive this infinitely wonderful universe, and our own intelligence within it, looking

before and after, reflecting, contriving, contemplating, reasoning—
without a Divine Intelligence as source of all our lesser ones. We
cannot conceive of it, and there can be only two reasons for this
incapacity. One, because *it is so,* the Divine First Cause is intelligent, and IS. Two, the opposite, which has been better and better
argued of late—that we are limited beings, like any arthropod or
stomach-cyst. We make God in our image, because we cannot do
otherwise. I cannot believe that, Mr Adamson. I cannot. It opens
the path to a dark pit of horrors.'

'My own lack of faith', said William hesitantly, 'comes partly
from the fact that I grew up amongst a very different sort of
Christian from yourself. I remember one particular sermon, on the
subject of eternal punishment, in which the preacher bade us imagine that the whole earth was merely a mass of fine sand, and that
at the end of a thousand years, a grain of this sand flew away into
space. Then we were told to imagine the slow advance of ages—
grain by grain—and the *huge* time before the earth would even
appear to be a little diminished, and then thousands of millions of
millions of aeons—until the globe was smaller—and so on and on
until at last the final grain floated away, and then we were told that
all this unimaginable time was itself only *one grain* in the endless
time of infinite punishment—and so on. And we were given a
horribly lively, exceedingly imaginative picture of the infinite torment: the hissing of burning flesh, the tearing of nerves, the piercing of eyeballs, the desolation of the spirit, the unceasing liveliness
of the response of body and soul to pure pain, which never dulled
nor failed through all those millennia of ingenious cruelty—

'Now *that* I think is a God made in the image of the worst of
men, whose excesses we all tremble at, yet,' in a lower voice, 'I
think I have perceived from time to time that cruelty too is instinctive in some of our species at least. I have seen slavery in action, Sir
Harald, I have seen a little of what ordinary men may do to men
when it is permitted by custom—

'I felt cleansed when I rejected that God, Sir, I felt free, and in the clear light, as another man might feel upon suffering a blinding conversion. I know a lady who was driven to suicide by such fears. I should add that my father has completely cut me off and rejected me, in consequence. That is a further reason for my present poverty.'

'I hope you are happy here.'

'Indeed I am. You have been most kind.'

'I should like to propose that you assist me also with the book. No, no—do not mistake me—not with the writing. But with debate from time to time. I find I need conversation, even opposition, to try out, to clarify my ideas.'

'I should be honoured, whilst I am here.'

'You will be eager to be off again, I know. To return to your travelling. I hope to be of very material assistance to that end, in due course. It is our duty either to seek out Nature's secret places and ways, or to support and encourage those who are able to do so.'

'Thank you.'

'Now, Darwin, in his passage on the *eye,* does seem, does he not, to allow the possibility of a Creator? He compares the perfecting of the eye to the perfecting of a telescope, and talks about the changes over the millennia to a thick layer of transparent tissue, with a nerve sensitive to light beneath, and he goes on to remark that *if* we compare the forces that form the eye to the human intellect "*we must suppose that there is a power always intently watching each slight accidental alteration in the transparent layers.*" Mr Darwin invites us to suppose that this intently watching power is inconceivable—that the force employed is blind necessity, the law of *matter*. But I say that in matter itself is contained a great *mystery*—how did it come to be at all—how does organisation take place—may we not after all come face to face in considering these things with the Ancient of Days, with Him who asked Job, "Where wast thou when I laid the foundations of the earth? Declare if thou hast any knowledge.

When the morning stars sang together, and all the sons of God shouted for joy?" Darwin himself writes that his transparent layers form "a living optical instrument as superior to one of glass, as the works of the Creator are to those of man." '

'So he does. And it is easier for us to imagine the patient attention of an infinite watcher than to comprehend blind chance. It is easier to figure to ourselves shifts and fluctuations in transparent jelly with the image of the floating grains from the world of sand in the sermon—one may *almost* come at the imagination of blind chance in that way—grain by random grain—infinitesimal yet cumulative . . .'

Matty Crompton reminded William of the promise she had extracted about the glass hive and the formicary. The glass hive was constructed under William's direction, the width of the comb of honey, with an entrance hole for the bees cut in the nursery window, and black cloth curtains placed over its walls. The bees were procured from a tenant farmer and inserted, buzzing darkly, into their new home. For the ants, a large glass tank was carried from the nearest town, and set up on its own table on a green baize cloth. Matty Crompton said that she herself would accompany William in search of the ants themselves. She had observed trails of several sorts of ants in the elm coppice last Summer. They set out together with two buckets, various jars, boxes and test-tubes, a narrow trowel and several pairs of tweezers. She had a quick step, and was not given to conversation. She led William straight to what he immediately saw to be a very large Wood Ants' nest, the work of generation upon generation, backed up against an elm-stump, and thatched with a high dome of twigs, stalks and dry leaves. Little ragged chains of ants could be observed entering and leaving.

'I have attempted to keep these insects myself,' said Matty Crompton, 'but I have a deathly touch, it appears. No matter how beautiful a house I build, or how many flowers and fruits I offer, the creatures simply curl up and die.'

'You probably had not captured a Queen. Ants are social beings: they exist, it appears, only for the good of the whole nest, and the centre of the nest is the Queen ant whose laying and feeding the others all tend ceaselessly. They will kill her and drag her away, it is true, if she ceases to produce young—or abandon her, when she will rapidly starve, for she is unable to fend for herself. But they exist to lavish attention on her when she is in her prime, on her and her brood. If we are to make a mimic community, we must capture a Queen. The worker ants lose their will to live without the proximity of a Queen—they become immobile and listless, like young ladies in a decline, and then give up the ghost.'

'How shall we find a Queen? Must we break open the city? We shall do a great deal of damage . . .'

'I will look about and try to find a fairly recently established nest, a young community that can be transferred more or less entire.'

He paced up and down, turning over leaves with a stick, following small convoys of ants to their cracks and crannies in roots and earth. Matty Crompton stood watchfully by. She was wearing a brown stuff dress, severe and unornamental. Her dark hair was plaited around her head. She was good at keeping still. William felt a prick of pleasure at the return of his hunting, scanning self, which had been unexercised inside the walls of the Hall. Under his gaze the whole wood-floor became alive with movement, a centipede, various beetles, a sanguine shiny red worm, rabbit pellets, a tiny breast feather, a grass smeared with the eggs of some moth or butterfly, violets opening, conical entrance holes with fine dust inside, a swaying twig, a shifting pebble. He took out his magnifying lens and looked at a patch of moss, pebbles and sand, and saw a turmoil of previously invisible energies, striving, striving, white myriad-legged runners, invisible semi-transparent arthropods, button-tight spiderlings. His senses, and his mind attached to them, were like a magnetic field, pulled here and there. Here was a nest of Jet-black Ants, Acanthomyops fuliginosus, who lived in small households inside the interconnected encampments of the Wood Ants. Here, on the edge of the coppice, was a trail of slave-making ants, Formica sanguinea. He had always wanted to study these in action. He said so to Matty Crompton, pointing out the difference between the Wood Ants, Formica rufa, with their muddy-brown heads and blackish-brown gasters, or hind parts, and the blood-red sanguinea.

'They invade the nests of the Wood Ants, and steal their cocoons, which they rear with their own, so that they become sanguinea workers. Terrible battles are fought by raiders and defenders.'

'They resemble human societies in that, as in many things.'

'The British slave-makers appear to be less dependent on their slaves than the Swiss Formica rufescens observed by Huber, who remarks that the workers of this species do no other work than capturing slaves, without whose labour their tribe would certainly become extinct, as all the child-rearing, and the food-gathering, are done by slaves. Mr Darwin observes that when these British Blood-red Ants migrate, they *carry* their slaves to the new home—but the more ferocious Swiss masters are so dependent, they require to be carried helplessly in the jaws of their slaves.'

'Maybe they are all perfectly content in their stations,' observed Matty Crompton. Her tone was neutral, so extraordinarily neutral that it would have been impossible to detect whether she spoke with irony or with conventional complacency, even if William had been giving her his complete attention, which he was not. He had found a meagre roof of thatch which he was ready to excavate. He took the trowel from her hands and removed several layers of earth, bristling with angry ant-warriors, littered with grubs and cocoons. A kind of seething attack accompanied his next moves, as he cut into the heart of the nest. Miss Crompton, on his instructions, gathered up the workers, grubs and cocoons in large clods of earth, interlayed with twigs and leaves.

'They bite,' she observed tersely, brushing her minute attackers from her wrists.

'They do. They make a hole with their mandibles and inject formic acid through their gaster, which they curve round, very elegantly. Do you wish to retreat?'

'No. I am a match for a few justifiably furious ants.'

'So you could not say with the Fire Ants or the tucunderas in the forest, who made me suffer torments for weeks when I unwarily stirred them up. In Brazil the Fire Ant is King, they say, and rightly. It cannot be kept down, or diverted, or avoided—men leave their houses to escape its ravages.'

Matty Crompton, tightlipped, picked individual ants out of her cuffs and scattered them in the collecting boxes. William followed a tunnel, and came upon the brood-chamber of the ant Queen.

'Here she is. In her glory.'

Matty Crompton peered in.

'You would not suppose her to be of the same species as her rapid little servants—'

'No. Though she is less disproportionately gross than the termite Queens, who are like huge inflated tubes, the size of haystacks compared to their docile little mates, who are in attendance in the same chamber, and the workers, who clamber all over them, cleaning and repairing and carrying away the endless succession of eggs as well as any debris.'

The Queen of the Wood Ants was only half as large again as her daughter-workers/servants. She was swollen and glossy, unlike the matt workers, and appeared to be striped red and white. The striping was in fact the result of the bloating of her body by the eggs inside it, which pushed apart her red-brown armour-plating, showing more fragile, more elastic, whitish skin in the interstices. Her head appeared relatively small. William picked her up with his forceps—several workers came with her, clinging to her legs. He placed her on cottonwool in a collecting-box and directed Miss Crompton in the collection of various sizes of worker ants and grubs and cocoons from various parts of the nest.

'We should also take a sample of the earth and the vegetable matter, from which they have made their nest, and note what they appear to be eating—and the little girls may usefully experiment with their preference in foods, if they have patient natures, when they are in their new home.'

'Should we not search for male ants also?'

'There will be none, at this time of the year. They are only present in the nest in June, July and possibly August. They are born sometimes—it is thought—from eggs laid by unfertilised workers—a kind of parthenogenesis. They do not long survive the mating of the Queens in the Summer months. They are easy to recognise—they have wings and hugely developed eyes—and they do not *appear* to be in any way able to fend for themselves, or build, or forage. Natural Selection appears to have favoured in them the development of those skills which guarantee success in the nuptial dance, at the expense of the others—'

'I cannot help observing that this appears to be the *opposite* to human societies, when it is the woman whose success in that kind of performance determines their lives—'

'I have thought along those lines myself. There is a pleasing paradox in the bright balldresses, the *floating* of young girls in our world, and the dark erectness of the young men. In savage societies, as much as in birds and butterflies, it is the males who flaunt their beauty. But I do not know that the condition of the Queen here is much happier than that of the swarms of useless and disregarded suitors. I ask myself, are these little creatures, who run up and down, and carry, and feed each other lovingly, and bite enemies—

are they truly individuals—or are they like the cells in our body, all parts of one whole, all directed by some mind—the Spirit of the Nest—which uses all, Queen, servants, slaves, dancing partners— for the good of the race itself, the species itself—'

'And do you go on, Mr Adamson, to ask *that* question about human societies?'

'It is tempting. I come from the North of England, where the scientific mill owners and the mine owners would like to make men into smoothly gliding parts of a giant machine. Dr Andrew Ure's *Philosophy of Manufacturers* wishes that workers could be trained to be co-operative—"to renounce their desultory habits of work, and to identify themselves with the unvarying regularity of the complex automaton." Robert Owen's experiments are the bright side of that way of thinking.'

'That is interesting, but it is not the same question,' said Miss Crompton. 'The will of the mill owners is not the Spirit of the Nest.'

William's brow furrowed as he thought this out. He said, 'It might be. If you were to suppose the mill owners in their machine-making to be equally in fact obeying the will of the Spirit of the Hive.'

'Ah,' said Matty Crompton with a kind of glee. 'I see where you are. A modern Calvinism by the back door, the nest door.'

'You think a great deal, Miss Crompton.'

'For a woman. You were about to add, "for a woman", and then refrained, which was courteous. It is my great amusement, think-ing. I think as bees sun themselves, or ants stroke aphids. Do you not think we should provide an artificial ant-paradise with aphids, Mr Adamson?'

'Indeed we should. We should surround it with plants beloved of aphids if it can be contrived. If their presence can be tolerated in the schoolroom.'

*   *   *

The little girls gathered to observe the ants with mingled squeals of fascination and repulsion. The ants set about excavating and organising their new home with exemplary industry. Miss Mead, an elderly soft-faced person with thinning hair and sprouting hairpins, made little speeches to the little girls about the *kindness* of the ants, who laboured for the good of each other, who could be observed greeting passing sisters with little drinks of nectar from their stored supply, who caressed each other, and nursed their unborn sisters in the egg, or in their larval form, with loving care, moving them from dormitory to dormitory, cleaning and feeding with unselfish devotion. Margaret jabbed Edith in the side with a quick elbow and said, 'See, you are a little grub, you are just a little *grub*.'

'You are all three grubbier than you should be,' said Matty Crompton. 'You have spread the earth much further than necessary, well beyond your pinafores.'

Miss Mead, who was obviously accustomed to ignoring small tiffs, embarked in a dreamy voice on the story of Cupid and Psyche.

'Ants, my dears, have been seen as human helpers since the remotest antiquity. The story of the unfortunate Princess Psyche illustrates this. She was so beautiful, and so beloved of all who saw her, that the Goddess of Beauty, Venus, grew jealous of her, and told her son Cupid to punish the beautiful girl. The King, her father, was told that he had offended the gods, and must be punished by the wedding of his lovely daughter to a terrible flying serpent. He must dress her as a bride and carry her to the top of a terrible crag to await her monstrous bridegroom.'

'Someone will come along and kill the dragon,' said Edith.

'Not in this story,' said Matty Crompton.

Miss Mead rocked herself to and fro in her chair, eyes part-closed, and continued.

'So there the poor girl was, up on a cliff, in all her laces and flowery wreaths and pretty pearls. She was very unhappy, but after a time she noticed that all her garments were being moved by the gentle breezes, which finally lifted her and carried her far away to a lovely palace, with marble halls, and silk hangings, and golden cups and delicious fruits to eat, and *no one to be seen anywhere*. She was all alone in the rich luxury. But she was waited on by unseen hands, and heard unseen musicians playing, and did not need to lift a finger for herself—her very wishes were instantly answered. When she finally came to rest for the night, a voice of great sweetness and gentleness told her that he was her new husband, and would try to make her happy, if she would only trust him. And she knew she *could* trust him, so beautiful a voice could not belong to anything harmful. So they were happy together and her husband warned her that this could only continue if she obeyed instructions, which were above all *never to try to see him*.

So she stayed there, in bliss, until she thought she wished to see her family, and expressed this wish to her gentle husband. This made him sad, for he knew harm would come of it, but he could refuse her nothing. So her family were quite suddenly whisked into her presence by the West Wind, and very marvellous they found it. Only her sisters were a little jealous, my dears—as sisters are—and though they were glad she had not been devoured they did not quite like to see her so blissful. So they asked her how she knew her husband was *not* a monstrous serpent—one had been seen, they said, swimming in the river—and they suggested she should take a candle in the night, when her beloved was sleeping, and look to see what he was. So she did as they said, which was foolish of her, and the candle flame illuminated not a serpent but the most beautiful golden-haired young man she had ever seen. And some drops of wax from the candle fell on his skin and woke him, and he said sadly, "Now you will never seen me again," and spread his wings—for he was winged Cupid, the God of Love—and flew away.

Now Psyche was a resourceful girl, as well as unhappy, so she set off to wander the world in search of Love. And Venus heard of her wanderings, and put it about that she was a runaway servant-girl of her own, and Psyche was captured, and dragged into the presence of the angry goddess. And the goddess set her to perform various impossible tasks, and if she failed, she would be cast out, and never see her husband or her friends again, but become a mere slave and work for her living.

And one of these tasks was the sorting of seeds. The goddess threw together a whole heap, a *mountain* of mixed seeds—wheat, barley, millet, lentils, beans, and the seeds of poppy and vetch— and told the poor girl she must sort the different kinds by the evening. And Psyche sat and wept, for she did not know where to begin. And then she heard a very small, scratchy, whispering voice from the floor, asking what was the matter. And the speaker was one little ant—a tiny mite, quite insignificant.

"Maybe I can help you," it said. "I do not see how you can," Psyche replied, "but I thank you for your kind intentions." But the ant would not be denied, and summoned its friends, and relations, and neighbours, thousands and thousands of ants, in great waves—'

'My skin pricks,' said Matty Crompton to William, 'at the idea of these benevolent armies.'

'And *I* am made nervous by the idea of sorting a mountain of mixed seeds or anything else. I am reminded that I am neglecting my work—'

'It is odd, is it not, how *sorting* so often makes a part of the impossible tasks of the prince or princesses in the tales. There are a great many frustrated lovers who are set to sorting seeds. Do you think there is a good anthropological explanation?'

'No doubt. But I do not know it. I have always supposed those tales to be about the sagacity and usefulness of the creatures, of the ants. I may be biased by my interest in ants. Tropical ants are *not* easy to live with. I have tried it—I lived for some time in a room with an earthen floor where there were two huge mounds of earth reared up by the Saüba ants. That was where I also found a *modus vivendi* with several nests of large brown house-wasps. They make the most ingenious houses, like inverted goblets that hang from the rafters. I flattered myself that they knew I was the owner of the house in which their houses hung—certainly they never stung me, though they did attack roaming strangers. I felt we *co-operated*—though this may have been an illusion—they were very fierce in keeping down large flies and cockroaches, which they slaughtered with terrible precision. I came to admire them for their beauty, ingenuity and heroic ferocity. I made quite a study of their work, both as builders and butchers.'

'Our Wood Ants must seem a little tame after those wild creatures.'

'I am very happy here. I am useful, and every one is most kind.'

'I hope your *sorting* may be completed to everyone's satisfaction,' said Matty Crompton. He decided later he had imagined something knowing in her tone.

He had moments, as Spring ripened into early Summer, when he began to weary of his task of sorting. He figured it to himself, in some sense, as a labour of love, but he could see no reward at the end of it. What reward could there be? Eugenia was not for him. He was more and more relegated to a kind of between-world, a companion of the little girls, a companion and assistant for the old man. The young people went in and out constantly amongst a growing number of friends, both male and female. There was one young man, Robin Swinnerton, who could often be seen lifting Eugenia down from the back of her black mare, Dusk, his hands about her waist, his laughing face turned up to hers. Confusion coiled round William Adamson when he saw this, confusion composed of a vicarious pleasure in the imagined grip on her young muscles, a stab of blind envy, a reasonable cold voice that told him it was best if she were soon spoken for, for then he could go free.

Now he could go free, for all the hope he had, he answered himself, but he could not listen. He traced on his own lips with one finger the perfect arch of hers, as it would be, if touched.

He was used to solitude; he had no idea how to gossip, or to listen to gossip, though he was aware, as one is aware of clouds of pollen drifting from great trees on warm days, that speculation was in the air. Then one day he was making his way along the cloister-passage to the hexagonal studium, when he met Robin Swinnerton hurrying the other way. He was a chestnut and russet, curly young man, with a pleasant smile, which on this day stretched from ear to ear and took in William Adamson. He nearly knocked William over, and stopped to apologise, shake his hand, and break into laughter. 'I am on a happy errand, Sir, I was preoccupied—'

'That young man', said Harald Alabaster, when William had entered, 'wishes to marry my daughter. I have given permission, and he says he already knows what she will say—so you must wish me joy.'

'I do indeed.'

'The first fledgling out of the nest.'

William turned to look out of the window. He said, 'The others must soon follow, in the course of things.'

'I know. They must. I worry about Eugenia, I must confess. I feel this news is not calculated to increase *her* happiness—though perhaps I underestimate her.'

It took William what seemed like hours to make sense of this pronouncement.

'Then it is not—not Miss Eugenia Alabaster—who is to be married?'

'What? Oh no. I had almost said, oh no, alas. It is Rowena. It is Rowena who is to marry Mr Swinnerton.'

'I thought Mr Swinnerton showed signs of becoming attached to Miss Eugenia.'

'My wife too—was of that opinion—but it turns out to be

Rowena. Eugenia may not like Rowena to be married first. She was engaged herself, you know, but the young man died in a tragic accident. And since then—I do not know how it is—she has had many suitors, very many, considering the limitations of the neighbourhood—but she has not—I do not know whether she herself displays coldness—or whether—she is a *good* girl, William, she bore her grief very well, she did not go into decline, or repine, she was docile as ever—but I fear the life went out of her, to some extent, and has not come back.'

'She is so beautiful, Sir—so very beautiful—and—and—*perfect*—that she cannot be long without finding—some worthy partner.'

'So I believe, but her mother is concerned. I think her mother will not be best pleased if Rowena goes first—it isn't right—but I do not see how Rowena's happiness can or should be prevented. Indeed, it is wrong of me to burden you with my concern for Eugenia when it is to be such a happy day for Rowena that should be uppermost in our thoughts.'

'I think your concern for Eugenia is very natural—is thoughtful, as you always are—it is not my place—I too—' he was about to add 'care for Eugenia', but caution overtook him.

'You are a good young man, and a sympathetic presence,' said Harald Alabaster. 'I am very glad you are staying here with us. Very. You have a good heart. That is the most important thing.'

William watched Eugenia with a new sharpness, when he saw her, searching for signs of unhappiness. She appeared to be quite as serene as ever, and he would have thought her father was mistaken, if he had not one day been witness to a curious little scene in the saddle-room. He was going quietly past there, to his workplace, when he noticed, glancing through the window, that Eugenia was in there, talking to someone he could not see from his spying place, and her manner was agitated, even tearful. She appeared to be pleading. Then he heard quick footsteps and ducked out of sight, and Edgar Alabaster strode past him, his face set in anger, towards the house. A moment or two later Eugenia came out into the yard and stood stockstill for a moment or two before walking away rather unsteadily towards the paddock and the ha-ha. He knew, because he loved her, that she was blinded by tears, and he guessed, because he had studied her, because he loved her, that her pride would be hurt if she thought her tears had been seen. But he followed her, because he loved her, stood beside her on the grass, looking on to the pit of the ha-ha, the barrier between the house and the outside world, invisible from the yard. It was late afternoon: the poplars cast long shadows across the meadows.

'I could not help seeing you were in distress. Can I be of help? I would do anything to help, if I can.'

'There is nothing,' she said dully, but without making a movement to repulse him.

He could not think what to say next. He could not reveal his knowledge of her circumstances, which did not come from herself. Nor could he say, 'I love you: I want to comfort you because I love you,' though his body throbbed with desire that she should turn to him and weep on his shoulder.

'You are beautiful and good—you deserve to be happy,' he said foolishly. 'I cannot bear to see you weep.'

'You are very kind, but I cannot be helped, I am beyond help.' She stared, unseeing, at the long shadows. 'I wish I were dead, to speak truly, I wish I were *dead,*' she said as the tears ran faster. 'I ought to be dead,' she added wildly. 'I ought to be dead, as Harry is dead.'

'I know of your tragedy, Miss Alabaster. I am very sorry. I hope you may be comforted.'

'I don't think you *do* know,' said Eugenia. 'Not at all. No one can.'

'That must be so. You have shown great courage. Please don't be unhappy.' He tried to think what to say. 'So many people love you, you cannot be unhappy.'

'Not really. Not truly. They think they do, but they cannot. They cannot. *I cannot be loved*, Mr Adamson, I am *not able to be loved*, it is my curse, you don't understand.'

'I *know* that is not true,' he replied heatedly. 'I know of no one more worthy to be loved, no one. You must be aware—I am not in a position—if my life were different, my position in life—in short—I would do anything for you, Miss Alabaster, you must know that. Women do know these things, I find.'

She gave a little sigh, almost of solace, he thought, and dropped her head from its marble stare across the ha-ha.

'It is you who are good and kind,' she said, with a new gentleness. 'And brave, even though you don't understand. You have been kind to everyone, even the little girls. We are lucky to have you here.'

'And *I* would feel lucky—and honoured—if you would feel you could let me be your friend—despite the differences between us— if you could trust me a little. I don't know what I am talking about—why *should* you trust me? I want so much to be able to do something for you. Anything at all. I own nothing in the world, as you know. So it is all folly. But please command me if I can help in the least way, ever.'

She was drying her eyes and face with a lacy handkerchief. Her eyes were slightly pink round the rims, and swollen. He found this touching and arousing. She gave a little laugh.

'You have given the little girls a glass anthill and a glass hive. You once promised me a cloud of butterflies. That was a pretty idea.'

She held out her little hand—always gloved—and he brushed it with his lips, a butterfly-kiss that nevertheless stung his senses and beat in his veins.

He resolved that she should have her butterflies.

*　　*　　*

It changed his relation to her, to have seen her so unhappy. A new sense of protectiveness mingled with what had been pure worship, making him notice new things: Edgar's brusquenesses towards her, the way in which her sisters chattered eagerly to each other about wedding plans and she moved about at a distance, either left out, or reluctant to join in, he was not sure which. He began collecting caterpillars of various kinds from various places, and enlisted Matty Crompton and the little girls, without revealing why he wanted the creatures. He gave instructions: they were always to be brought with their food plants, with whatever leaves they were found on. He borrowed rabbit hutches and dove cages, in which, as the caterpillars made themselves cocoons, he placed them to hatch. It turned out to be difficult to co-ordinate a *cloud,* but he persevered, and managed to hatch several small blues, a large collection of whites, some red admirals, tortoiseshells and fritillaries, along with one or two greenish woodland butterflies and a collection of moths, buff ermines, footmen, goat moths and other nocturnal fliers. Only when he thought his hatchings contributed as much of a *cloud* as he was likely to manage did he ask Harald for permission to release the creatures in the conservatory—'I shall see they do not damage the plants there, there is no danger of an invasion of ravenous larvae. I promised Miss Alabaster a *cloud of butterflies* and now I think I have one.'

'You have been very assiduous, I can see. They are certainly more beautiful in flight than on pins. She will be enchanted.'

'I wanted to—to make her smile—and had nothing to offer—' Harald looked at William Adamson and brought his white brows together.

'You are concerned about Eugenia.'

'I gave the little girls a glass hive and a glass anthill. I promised her, in a foolish moment, a cloud of butterflies. I hope you let me give her this—ephemeral—gift. It will only live a few weeks, Sir, if that, as you know.'

Harald had a way of looking piercing and benign, as though he read thoughts. He said, 'I imagine Eugenia will be delighted. So shall we all, we shall share her moment of magic. Magic is not a bad thing, William. Transfiguration is not a bad thing. Butterflies come out of the most unpromising crawling things.'

'I do not hope—'

'Say nothing. Say nothing. Your feelings are to your credit.'

The butterflies were released very early one morning, before any of the household was up. William, running downstairs at six, found a very different population from the daylight one—a host of silently hurrying, black-clad young women, carrying buckets of cinders, buckets of water, boxes of polishing tools, fistfuls of brooms and brushes and carpet beaters. They had come like a cloud of young wasps from under the roof of the house, pale-faced and blear-eyed, bobbing silently to him as he passed. Some were no more than children, hardly different from the little girls in the nursery, except that the latter were delicately swathed in petticoats, and frills, and soft festoons of muslin, and these were for the most part skinny, with close-fitting, unornamental bodices and whisking dark skirts, wearing formidably starched white caps over their hair.

The conservatory joined the library to the chapel cloisters on the far side of the chapel from Harald's study. It was solidly built of glass and wrought-iron, with a high domed roof and a fountain on the wall side, surrounded by mossy stones with a little statue of a marble nymph holding a pitcher to the water. There were goldfish in the shallow bowl into which the water fell. The vegetation was abundant, and in places vigorous—a series of wrought-iron grilles, in the form of ivy leaves and twining branches, supported a mixture of creeping and climbing plants, making a series of half-hidden bowers, inside which hung huge wire baskets, always full of flowering plants, brilliantly coloured, delicately scented. Palm trees stood here and there in gold-gleaming brass tubs, and the floor was tiled in shiny black marble, giving the impression, from certain angles in certain lights, of a deep dark lake with a reflecting surface.

William carried in his boxes of somnolent insects, and placed them all carefully on the moist earth, in the baskets, among the leaves. The gardener's boy looked on dubiously and then became enthusiastic as one or two larger butterflies, warmed by the rising sun, floated lazily from basket to basket in the roof. William charged him to keep the doors closed, and the family, on any pretext, out, until the sun was high and the butterflies in motion; butterflies feed on light, butterflies dance when warmed by the sun. When they were dancing, he would bring Eugenia. 'I told Miss Eugenia I would make her a cloud of butterflies,' he said.

The boy said stolidly and expressionlessly, 'She would like that, Sir, I am sure.'

He waylaid her on the stairs after her breakfast. Since this was late, the sun was now high and rising. He had to say her name twice: she looked preoccupied, and very serious. She answered with some impatience, 'So what is it?'

'Please come with me. I have something to show you.'

She was wearing a blue dress, trimmed with tartan ribbons. There was a bad moment when it looked as though she meant to refuse, and then her face softened into a smile, and she turned, and came with him. He led her to the conservatory door.

'Come in quickly, and close the door.'

'Am I safe?'

'With me, quite safe.'

He closed the door behind her. At first, in the sunny green and glinting glass, he thought he had failed, and then, as though they had been waiting for her, the creatures came out of the foliage, down from the glassy dome, darting, floating, fluttering, tawny orange, dark and pale blue, brimstone yellow and clouded white, damask dark and peacock-eyed, and danced round her head and settled on her shoulders, and brushed her outstretched hands.

'They take your dress for the sky itself,' he whispered. She stood very still, turning her head this way and that. More and more butterflies made their way through the air, more and more hung trembling on the blue sheen of the cloth, on the pearly-white of her hands and throat.

'I can brush them off,' he said, 'if you find them disagreeable.'

'Oh no,' she said. 'They are so light, so soft, like coloured air—'

'It is *almost* a cloud—'

'It is a cloud. You are a miracle-worker.'

'It is for you. I have nothing *real* to give—no pearls, no emeralds, I have nothing—but I wanted so much to give you something—'

'Life,' she said. 'They are *alive*. They are living jewels, or better than jewels—'

'They think you are a flower—'

'So they do, they do.' She turned slowly round about, and the creatures rose and settled in undulating patterns.

The vegetation belonged to no place on this planet, and in some sense to all. English primroses and bluebells, daffodils and crocus shone amongst evergreen luxuriant tropical creepers, their soft perfumes mingling with exotic stephanotis and sweet jasmine. She turned round and round, and the butterflies circled, and the captive water splashed in its little bowl. He thought he would always remember her like this, whatever happened to her, to him, to them, in this glittering palace where his two worlds met. And so he did, from time to time, for the rest of his life: the girl in the blue dress with pale sunny head, amongst creepers and Spring flowers, and the cloud of butterflies.

'They are so terribly fragile,' she said. 'You could hurt them by just touching, one careless pinch would be enough. I would never hurt one of those. Never. How can I thank you?'

He engaged her to come back in the evening, when instead of the butterflies, the moths would be flying, with their subtle hues, chalky and ghost-like, soft lemons, buffs, silver plumes. All day the little girls ran in and out of the conservatory exclaiming, crying out at the colours and motions. He did not extend the evening invitation to them. He hoped to be able to sit alone with her in the dusk for a short time, companionably. This was the reward he had promised himself, which shows how things had changed a very little, how he had changed towards her. He even once or twice went over Harald's remarks, so full of some kind of charge of meaning, so ambivalently impenetrable. 'Say nothing. Say nothing. Your feelings do you credit.' Which feelings? His love, or his respect for her difference, her station? What would Harald say if he said, 'I love Eugenia. I must have her or die'—no, not that, that was ridiculous—'I love Eugenia; it is painful for me to stay in her presence, unless I may hope where I cannot expect to hope—' *What would Harald say?* Had he imagined a paternal benignity in his gaze? Would paternal ire and outrage take over if he spoke? Did Harald respect his patience or his discretion?

When evening came, he had a newly hatching large cocoon, which he took along with him to the conservatory; watching it would be a kind of reasonable employment, whilst he waited to see if she would come. He sat on a low bench, overhung with trailing vines and a wandering passionflower. The glass wall was cold against his back in the night air. Here and there it reflected the shimmering halo of the lamps hidden amongst curtains of leaves. Here and there it was transparent and he could see dark, colourless grass, the empty sky and the thin silver paring of the moon. The moths were moving—a little cloud was round each lamp, which he had protected in cages of netting. It was not part of his plan to shrivel his flock. The colours were lovelier than he expected. Grass-green, paper-white, creamy-yellow, luminous grey. The large moth—it was an Emperor Moth, the only British Saturniid,—was working its way free, splitting the pupa, shaking out crumpled wing-tissue, staring with huge eyes and weakly fluttering plumed antennae. William never overcame his sense of pure wonder at this process. A complete, lively caterpillar, bright green, banded with brown streaks and yellow hairy warts, vanished inside the cocoon and became a kind of formless custard. And out of the custard came the Emperor Moth, with eyes inscribed on brown velvet and a fat body of mouse-coloured fur.

He heard the door click open, and heard her listening for him inside it. Then he heard her feet on the marble, slippered and soft, and the swish of her skirts. And then she was there, in a silvery evening gown, whose underskirt was lilac—Morpho Eugenia. The dark took from her face even the colour it normally had.

'There you are. You always do what you say you will. Your moths are trying to perform suttee.'

'As you see, I have netted the lights to protect them. I do not know why they are so driven to make burned offerings of themselves. I do not know if it can be explained as a function of any normally life-protecting strategy made null by our interfering habit of setting up bright artificial light. I have wondered if they navigate by moonlight and mistake candles for very bright heavenly bodies. I don't find that an entirely satisfactory hypothesis. Won't you sit down, and see if the moths think *you* are the moon, as the butterflies took you for flowers and the sky?'

She sat beside him on the bench, and her presence troubled him. He was *inside* the atmosphere, or light, or scent she spread, as a boat is inside the drag of a whirlpool, as a bee is caught in the lasso of perfume from the throat of a flower.

'What is that?'

'A newly hatched Emperor Moth. A female. In a little time, when she is strong, I will take away her cage and release her.'

'She seems very weak.'

'It requires great force to break out of the pupa. The insects are all at their most vulnerable at the moment of metamorphosis. They can be easily snapped up by any predator.'

'There are none here, I hope.'

'Oh no.'

'Good. How lovely it is, in the moonlight, with the moths going about so peacefully.'

'This is what I promised myself for making your cloud of butterflies. This little time, sitting here quietly, with you. That is all.'

She bowed her head, as though studying the Emperor Moth intently. A moth blundered repeatedly against the pane, trying to get in, it appeared, and was joined by another. The tremulous female quivered and shook her wings.

'Don't answer this—and don't think I speak to alarm you, or upset you—I only want to say, you cannot know how much these few moments can mean to me—how I shall remember them always—your closeness—your calm. If things were only different, I might say—quite different things to you—but I know how the land lies, I am reasonable, I have *no hopes*—except perhaps to be able to speak briefly and honestly to you, for I do not see how that can hurt you—'

Large insects were advancing along the the black floor, their wings outspread. More could be seen forcing themselves through a small hole in the pane of the conservatory door. More still sailed down from the roof, hurtling blindly forwards in the semi-dark. The small concussions of the creatures on the glass walls and roof increased in number and volume. They advanced, a disorderly, driven army, beating about Eugenia's head, burring against her skin, thirty, forty, fifty, a cloud, the male Emperors propelling themselves out of the night towards the torpid female. More came. And more. Eugenia tried to push them off, she brushed her skirts, she plucked at those lost in her sleeves, in the crevices of her dress. She began to cry.

'Take them away. I don't like these.'

'They are the male Emperors. They are drawn by the female in some mysterious way. I will carry her to the other end of the conservatory—there—see—they follow her, and leave you—'

'There is another, trapped here in my lace. I shall scream.'

He came back through the crowd of blindly struggling males, and put his fingers inside her lace collar to remove the intruder.

'It must be scent—'

Eugenia was weeping. 'It was *terrible,* like bats, like ghosts, it was foul—'

'Hush. I didn't mean to frighten you.'

He was trembling. She put her arms about his neck and her head on his shoulder and hung there letting him bear her weight.

'My dear—'

She wept.

'I didn't mean—'

She cried out, 'It isn't *you*—you tried to help. It is everything. I am so unhappy.'

'Is it because of Captain Hunt? Do you still grieve for him so much?'

'He didn't want to marry me. He died because he didn't want to marry me.'

William held her close while she wept.

'That must be nonsense. *Any* man would want to marry you.'

'It wasn't really an accident. That is only what they say. He did it because he didn't—want—to—marry—me.'

'Why didn't he?' asked William, as one might question a child who sees an imaginary bogeyman where nothing is.

'How should I know? Only, it is so. It is just clear to me—that he didn't want—the wedding was arranged—the clothes, I had all my clothes, *everything* was bought, the bridesmaids' dresses, the flowers, everything. And he—couldn't bear—'

'You torture me, saying this. My dearest wish in the world—*as you must know*—would be to be able to ask you to be my wife. Which I can never do, because you have a fortune, and I cannot support a wife, or even myself. I do know that. But it is unbearably painful to me to hear you speak in this way and *not* be able—myself—'

'I do not need to marry a fortune,' said Eugenia. 'I have one of my own.'

There was a long silence. Several more single-minded male moths blundered past and joined the pulsing carpet of male bodies in the wire walls of the female's cage.

'What are you saying?'

'My father is a kind man, and he believes in Christian fellowship, in the equality of everyone in the sight of God. He believes you are a man of great intellectual gifts which he thinks are very valuable, as valuable as lands and rent and things. He has said so to me.'

She looked at him with the same pink, swollen, vulnerable eyes.

'There could be a double wedding,' said Eugenia. 'I should not be married *after* Rowena, not if I am to be married at all.'

He swallowed. A moth brushed his hot forehead. He smelled the ghosts of jungle smells and the sweet, thick breath of gardenias. A small moth, a Rosy Footman, was perched on Eugenia's shining hair, under his chin. His heart thudded.

'Shall I speak to your father? Tomorrow?'

'Yes,' said Eugenia, and put up her mouth to be kissed.

William had supposed that Harald's attitude to himself would change sharply the moment he raised the question of marrying Eugenia. Harald had been vaguely kind, and had appeared at times almost surprisingly grateful for William's conversation and attention. Now, he told himself, this would change. The patriarch would brandish the protecting sword. He would be made to feel the presumption of his own lack of prospects and breeding. He would almost certainly be ejected. Eugenia's total confidence that this would not be so only reflected her innocent trustfulness. He found himself divided against himself. I shall die if I cannot have her, his blood cried on its one note. And yet he dreamed dreams reminiscent of those induced by the *caapi*-spirits, dreams of flying fast over forests, of sailing at speed over the sea in a high wind, of fighting the rapids on the upper reaches of the Amazon, of beating his way through creepers with a machete.

He told Harald that he had long and silently loved Eugenia, and that it had only been revealed to him by accident that she returned, might return these feelings. He had not meant to go behind her father's back, he had meant to say nothing, but now it appeared he must ask, and if he was refused he must go away. 'I know most painfully that I have nothing to offer that could weigh against my lack of prospects.'

'You have courage, and intelligence, and kindness,' said Eugenia's father. 'All families stand in need of these qualities if they are to survive. And you have Eugenia's love, apparently. I must tell you, I would give a great deal to see Eugenia happy. She has had great troubles and I had almost given up hope of her finding the power actively to seek her own happiness in this. She has her own fortune—which is entailed and will remain in her own hands—'

It might have been a fault of courage in William Adamson, or it might have been a proper delicacy or tact that he did not then raise any question about settlements, about arrangements for living, about his own prospects. It seemed worse than vulgar, being male, and bringing nothing, to ask what, if anything, he might receive. Harald talked on, easily, vaguely, making warm, imprecise promises. William was shrewd enough to see their imprecision, but he had no will, indeed no reason, to cavil or press for clarity.

'You could remain here,' Harald said, 'amongst this family, for the present, you and Eugenia, so that when, as you may well wish to do, you make another voyage, she is among her own people. You will naturally not wish to make changes immediately, you may be very happy here, I think. I hope you will make journeys later, if you wish. I hope you will. I hope I may be of substantial help to you in that. And I hope in the meantime you will consent to give me your time in conversation with the generosity you have shown so far. I do hope so. I find I can make my way much better through the tangles of thought about ourselves and the world we are in, with the benefit of the clarity of your mind. We might even write down our discussions as a kind of philosophical dialogue.'

He was to pay, he saw, with his thoughts. That was something he could easily afford, something he could do as he breathed air, or consumed meat and bread. And during the time between Eugenia's acceptance of him, and their wedding, which was as short as it could be, so that Rowena's marriage should not be delayed, giving time just for the making of bride-clothes, William talked to Harald Alabaster. He himself had given up his father's religion of torment, suffering and promised bliss with a sigh of relief—Christian's sigh of relief when the burden fell from his shoulder after the Slough of Despond. But Harald was partly sunk in the Slough. His thoughts were a torment to him, his own intellectual rigour a source of deprivation and pain.

He talked often of the folly of those who argued unconvincingly for the existence of God, or the truths of the Bible—and this damaged their own cause. How *dare* William Whewell argue that the lengths of the days and nights were adapted to the duration of sleep of Man? asked Harald. It was painfully and gloriously clear that the whole Creation lived and moved in a rhythm of response to the heat and light of the Sun and to its withdrawal: the sap rose in trees, flowers opened and shut, men and beasts drowsed or hunted, Summer followed Winter. We must not put ourselves in the centre of things unless we could truly perceive we *were* there. We must not make God in our own image, or we made ourselves look fools. It was because he hoped, hoped sometimes beyond belief, that a Divine Creator would be proved beyond reasonable doubt, that he could not abide arguments about male nipples and the rudimentary tail of the human embryo, which saw that Creator as a fumbling craftsman who had changed his mind in mid-work. A man might behave thus, a God could not, if they but thought clearly, unclouded by emotion, for a moment. And yet there were arguments from the analogy between the Divine Mind and the human mind which he accepted, which supported him, which he did not discard.

'What do you make of the argument from beauty?' he asked William.

'What form of beauty, Sir? Beauty in women, beauty in forests, beauty in the heavens, beauty in creatures?'

'In all these. I would wish to argue that our human ability to love beauty in all these things—to love symmetry, and glorious brightness, and the intricate excellence of leaf-forms, and crystals, and the scales on snakes and wings of butterflies—argues in us something disinterested and spiritual. A man admiring a butterfly is more than a brute beast, William? He is more than the butterfly itself.'

'Mr Darwin believes the beauty of the butterfly exists to attract his mate, and the beauty of the orchid is designed to facilitate its fertilisation by the bee.'

'I retort—neither bee nor orchid has our exquisite sensation of joy at seeing the perfection of the colours and forms of these things. And we may imagine a Creator who created the whole world out of delight in his making the variety of species, of stones and clay and sand and water, may we not? We may imagine such a Creator very precisely because we ourselves have an indwelling need to make works of art which can satisfy no base instinct of mere survival, or perpetuation of the species, but are only beautiful, and intricate, and food for the spirit?'

'A sceptic, Sir, would retort that our own works—as you speak of them—are not unlike Paley's watch, which he said would lead anyone to deduce a Maker, were he ever to find two interlocking cogs. Maybe the sense of wonder at beauty—at form—you speak of, is no more than what makes us human, rather than brutes.'

'I believe, with the Duke of Argyll, that the superfluous brilliance of the birds of Paradise is a strong argument that perhaps in some sense the original world *was* made for the delight of man. For they cannot delight in themselves as we delight in them.'

'They dance for their mates, as do turkeys and peacocks.'

'But you do not feel your own sense of wonder corresponds to something *beyond* yourself, William?'

'I do indeed. But I also ask myself, what has this sense of wonder to do with my moral sense? For the Creation we so admire does not appear to have a Creator who cares for his creatures. Nature *is* red in tooth and claw, as Mr Tennyson put it. The Amazon jungle does indeed arouse a sense of wonder at its abundance and luxuriance. But there is a spirit there—a terrible spirit of *mindless striving* or apathetic inertia—a kind of vegetable greed and vast decay—which makes a mindless natural force much easier to believe in. For I think you will not accept the old deists' arguments that tigers and strangling figs were designed to prevent the miseries of old age in deer and of rotting in tree trunks, any more than you accept Whewell's ideas about day and night.'

'The world has changed so much, William, in my lifetime. I am old enough to have believed in our First Parents in Paradise, as a little boy, to have believed in Satan hidden in the snake, and in the Archangel with the flaming sword, closing the gates. I am old enough to have believed *without question* in the Divine Birth on a cold night with the sky full of singing angels and the shepherds staring up in wonder, and the strange kings advancing across the sand on camels with gifts. And now I am presented with a world in which we are what we are because of the mutations of soft jelly and calceous bone matter through unimaginable millennia—a world in which angels and devils do not battle in the Heavens for virtue and vice, but in which we eat and are eaten and absorbed into other flesh and blood. All the music and painting, all the poetry and power is so much illusion. I shall moulder like a mushroom when my time comes, which is not long. It is likely that the injunction to love each other is no more than the prudent instinct of sociability, of parental protectiveness, in a creature related to a great ape. I used to love to see paintings of the Annunciation—the angel with his wings dipped in the rainbow, of which the butterfly and the bird of Paradise were poor, imperfect echoes, holding the white and gold lily and going down on his knee to the thoughtful young girl who was about to be the Mother of God, love made flesh, knowledge given to us, or lent. And now all that is as it were erased, and there is a black backcloth on an empty stage, and I see a chimpanzee, with puzzled eyes and a hanging brow and great ugly teeth, clutching its hairy offspring to its wrinkled breast—and is *this* love made flesh?

'I know my answer—it *is*—if God works at all he works in the ape towards Man—but I cannot measure my loss, it is the pit of despair itself. I began my life as a small boy whose every action was burned into the gold record of his good and evil deeds, where it would be weighed and looked over by One with merciful eyes, to whom I was walking, step by unsteady step. I end it like a skeleton leaf, to be made humus, like a mouse crunched by an owl, like a beef-calf going to the slaughter, through a gate which opens only one way, to blood and dust and destruction. And then, I think, no brute beast could have such thoughts. No frog, no hound even, could have a vision of the Angel of Annunciation. *Where does it all come from?*'

'It is a mystery. Mystery may be another name for God. It has been well argued that mystery is another name for Matter—we *are* and have access to Mind, but Matter is mysterious in its very nature, however we choose to analyse the laws of its metamorphoses. The laws of the transformation of Matter do not explain it away.'

'Now you argue on my side. And yet I feel all these arguments are *nothing,* the motions of minds that are not equipped to carry them through.'

'And there too is hope, as well as dread. Where do *they* come from, our minds?'

Away from the hexagonal stadium, much attention was being paid to the mysteries of the mundane and the material. Eugenia and Rowena, and the other girls too, for there was to be a bevy of bridesmaids, were always undergoing fittings. A steady stream of dressmakers, milliners and seamstresses wove their paths in and out of the various nurseries and boudoirs. Odd glimpses could be had of the young ladies standing still, cocooned in silk, whilst the neat, self-effacing little attendants, their mouths bristling with pins and their hands busily snapping scissors, went round and round them. New bedrooms were in preparation for William and Eugenia. She occasionally brought him patterns of silk twill or damask to approve. He had no sense that *disapproval* was possible, and in any case was indifferent enough to his creature comforts to be mildly amused by all this industry and tastefulness, though he was less delighted to find himself the object of the attentions of Lionel Alabaster's tailor and valet, who made him a wardrobe consisting not only of his wedding-suit, but of suitable gentlemen's country wear, breeches, jackets, boots. As time drew on, the kitchens began to smell delightfully of the baking of batches of cakes and jellies and puddings. William was expected now, as he had not quite been before, to sit in the smoking-room with Edgar and Lionel and Robin Swinnerton and their friends, whose conversation had only two topics, the mysteries of breeding horses and hounds, and the laying of bets and taking of dares. After several glasses of port, Edgar would, invariably, begin to recount the high moments of his life. The time he and Sultan had flown over the wall into the Far Paddock, where they had almost broken their necks. The time he had jumped Ivanhoe in through the window of the Hall for a bet, and skidded the length of it on a Turkey carpet. The time he had swum the river in flood on Ivanhoe, and nearly been swept away.

William liked to sit quietly in his corner during these relations, invisible, he hoped, in a cloud of smoke. The veins stood out on Edgar's temples and down his neck. He had both brute strength and a nervous spirit, like his horse. His voice varied between a deeply melodious mumble and a kind of strangled shout that was painful to hear. William judged him. He thought he was likely to die of an apoplexy in the not too distant future, and that this would be of no consequence, since his existence was entirely without aim or value. He imagined the poor horse, snorting and sliding on the Hall floor, its silk haunches twisted with stress. And the man, laughing as he laughed in action, *making* it dance on stone, as it would never have done in nature. William had not entirely thrown off his father's censorious religion. He judged Edgar Alabaster in the eye of the God he no longer believed in, and found him wanting.

One evening, only a week before the wedding, he became aware that Edgar judged him, too. He was sitting back invisibly whilst Edgar told a tale of driving a gig through narrow gaps in seven hedges, and must have allowed his thoughts to appear on his face, for he found Edgar's hot, red face disagreeably close to his own.

'*You* must not have the nerve or the strength to do that, Sir. You sit there and smile fatuously, but *you* could not bring such a thing off.'

'No doubt I could not,' said William pacifically, his legs stretched in front of him, his muscles relaxed, as he knew they should be, faced with such aggression.

'I do not like your attitude. I have never liked it. I believe you sneer in your heart.'

'I do not mean to sneer. Since we are to be brothers, I hope I would not give such an appearance. It would be most wrong.'

'Ha. *Brothers,* you say. I don't like that. You are underbred, Sir, you are no good match for my sister. There is bad blood in you, vulgar blood.'

'I do not accept either "bad" or "vulgar". I *am* aware that I am no good match, in that I have few prospects and no fortune. Your father and Eugenia have done me the great kindness of overlooking that. I hope you may come to accept their decision.'

'You should wish rather to fight me. I insulted you. You are a miserable creature without breeding or courage. You should stand up, Sir, and face me.'

'I think not. As for breeding, I count my father as a good man, and an honest man, and a kind man, and I know no other *good* reasons for respect except his high achievement. As for courage, I think I may claim that to have lived ten years in great hardship on the Amazon, to have survived murder plots and poisonous snakes, and shipwreck and fifteen days on a lifeboat in the mid-Atlantic may reasonably compare with driving a poor horse into a house through a window. I think I know what true courage is, Sir. It does not consist in fisticuffs as a response to insults.'

'Well said, William Adamson,' said Robin Swinnerton. 'Well said, my fellow bridegroom.'

Edgar Alabaster clawed at William's coat collar. 'You shall not have her, do you hear? She is not for such as you. *Stand up.*'

'Please do not breathe in my face. You resemble an angry dragon. You will not provoke me into disgracing a house and family I hope to belong to.'

'*Stand up.*'

'In the Amazons, the young men of the tribes who make themselves stupid with spirits behave as you do. They often end by killing each other inadvertently.'

'I should not care if you were killed.'

'No. You would care if you were. Eugenia might care deeply if I were. She has already—'

He had not known where he was going. He was appalled that his tongue, even in anger, had run as far as Eugenia's dead lover. The effect on Edgar of even that half-allusion, choked off, was startling. He went white, drew himself up awkwardly and dusted down his trousers repeatedly with heavy hands. William thought, Now he will really try to kill me, and waited for the blow, turned to avoid it, to leap sideways to kick at the groin. But Edgar Alabaster merely made an incoherent, choking sound, and went out of the room, still beating his clothes with his hands. Lionel said, 'I beg you not to—not to make too much of Edgar. He is wild in his cups, and he is quiet after, he often does not remember what has passed. It was the drink insulted you.'

'I am happy to accept that explanation.'

'Good man, fellow bridegroom. Civilised man. We are not armed warriors now, are we? Civilised men in smoking jackets, we are, who stay seated as we should. I admire you, William. Edgar is an anachronism. You didn't think I knew such a word, I'll be bound.'

'On the contrary. Thank you for your kindness.'

'We must see each other often through our marriages.'

'With great pleasure.'

He found it hard, afterwards, to remember the exact emotions of his wedding day. It was his observation that all ceremonies brought with them, besides a sense of deeply coloured significance, a heightened sense of unreality, as though he were a watcher, not a participant. He thought this sense of *watching* might derive from the absence of simple belief in the Christian story, the Christian world, as Harald had so movingly described it to him. Irrelevant analogies poked their way through the curtains of his inner eye, even in these most sacred moments, so that, as he stood beside Robin Swinnerton, under the booming organ of the parish church of Saint Zachariah, and watched Eugenia and Rowena advancing along the aisle on the arms of Edgar and Lionel, he thought of the religious festivals at Pará and Barra, the puppet-images of the Virgin, decorated in laces and silk floss and silver ribbons, smiling perpetually on their way to the church, and beyond that to the dances in Indian villages, where he was dwarfed by masked beings with the heads of owls, or ibises, or anacondas.

And yet it was a very English, a very bucolic wedding. Eugenia and Rowena were dressed like sisters, but not like twins, in white silk dresses with long lace trains, one trimmed with pink rosebuds all over, and one—Eugenia's—with cream and gold. Both wore crowns of the same rosebuds, and pearl necklaces. Both carried mixed lilies and roses—the scent dizzied him as the procession reached the place where he stood to receive her. Behind them was a bevy of little girls, with ribbons and streamers in pink and gold, wearing dresses of white net with satin sashes, and carrying baskets of rose petals to throw. The church was packed: the absence of any friend or family of his own was more than made up for by the ranks of Alabasters and Swinnertons and local friends and connections, all nodding in flowers and ribbons. Rowena was flushed with excitement, and Eugenia was wax-white, most colourful in the gold of her downcast lashes, her lips pale, her cheeks smoothly, evenly, colourless. They made their vows before Harald, who married both his daughters with sonorous pleasure in the repeated phrases, and spoke briefly about the moving nature of a double wedding which made it more than usually clear that a family was being enlarged by additions, rather than anyone being taken away. For Rowena would remain in the parish, and Eugenia for the time being in her home, now William Adamson's home, which was a matter for rejoicing.

He should have been conscious, he thought, of two souls speaking their vows together, but he was not. He was conscious of all the soft finery surrounding Eugenia's body, and the scent of the flowers, and the perfection and clarity with which she spoke her responses, as opposed to Rowena, who tripped, and stumbled, and put her hand to her mouth, and smiled at her husband for forgiveness. Eugenia looked straight in front of her, at the altar. When he took her hand, to put on the ring, he had to push, to manoeuvre, as though the finger had no will or life of its own. And he thought, standing there in the church, on the circumference of her skirts, Will she be so numb in the bed tonight, what shall I do? And then he thought how many men in his position must have thought such secret thoughts, all of them unuttered and unutterable. And he thought, as they progressed back through the church, between the respectable ladies in their florid bonnets, and the dark gentlemen in their silky cravats, between the modestly clad servants in their straw hats and the few farm labourers at the very back, that everyone at the wedding had a secret thought about him and her, those two, how would they be when left alone together? Everyone's imagination tickled and pricked and clutched at him, he sensed, as he went by them. *She* was too innocent to know, he thought. He tried to imagine Lady Alabaster imparting information to Eugenia, and could not. She was there in the front row, smiling benignly in glistening mauve.

Everyone *does* survive their marriage night, he thought, coming blinking out into the daylight of the churchyard, and the chatter of birds in the trees and the shrill squeals of the little girls. The species is propagated, it goes on, innocent girls become wives and mothers, everywhere, every day. Eugenia's hand was very still in his, her face white, her breathing faint. He had no idea what she was thinking or feeling.

The little girls pelted them with petals which a sudden gust of wind lifted into the air like a cloud of wings, rosy, gold and white. They swarmed around the two couples, making their shrill noise, and hurling their soft missiles.

The day passed in eating, and speeches, and running on the lawn, and finally in dancing. He danced with Eugenia, who remained white and silent, gravely watching her steps. He danced with Rowena, who laughed, and with Enid, who chattered about his coming to the house as a shipwrecked stranger. He saw Eugenia go past, in Edgar's arms, and then in Lionel's, and then in Robin Swinnerton's, and everyone seemed to twirl dizzily even when the music stopped. When, finally, the young Swinnertons drove off and the Alabasters began to make preparations for the night, he was uncertain where to go, and no one offered him guidance. Edgar and Lionel lounged in the smoking-room and he did not think he would be welcome even if he wanted to be there, which he did not. Harald passed him in the corridor and stopped him, and said, 'God bless you, my boy,' but offered him no advice. Lady Alabaster had retired early. His things had been moved from his little attic room to his new dressing-room, which opened out of the new bedchamber prepared for him and Eugenia. He made his way up there, nervous and lonely—Eugenia had already gone up—unsure of what, if any, ceremonial was required.

In his dressing-room, a valet was turning down his bed and warming the sheets, an exercise that might surely be deemed to be unnecessary. A new nightshirt had been laid out for him, and new silk slippers, embroidered by Eugenia. The valet, a thin, black-coated creature with long white hands and soft russet whiskers, poured water from a blue jug into his washbasin and handed him soap and a towel. He indicated the new hairbrushes, ivory-backed, a present from Eugenia, and bowed himself out of the room, softly, quickly. William walked across to the connecting door, and knocked. He had no idea how she was, what state she was in, what he should do. He vaguely believed they might consult with each other.

'Come in,' said the clear voice, and he opened the door, to find her standing in the furled, crushed circle of the dress, its lace spread all over, her shoulders rising white out of her petticoats, marble and untouchable as he had seen them on that first evening. Her head-dress was cast on her dressing-table, and had begun to wilt. Her maid was unpinning her hair. It fell in crimped runnels over her shoulders. The maid, a thin girl, in a black stuff gown, was brushing out this hair, stroke by silky stroke. It lifted electrically to meet the brush, and clung here, ballooning, before the next stroke began. It crackled.

'I am sorry,' he said. 'I will go back.'

'Martha has just to unhook me, and finish the brushing—I need at least two hundred strokes every evening if my hair is to have any life in it. I hope you are not too tired?'

'Oh no,' he said, standing in the doorway. She was white all over. Even her nipples must be white. He remembered Ben Jonson. 'O so white! O so soft! O so sweet is she!' He felt an intruder then, in all his clothes, in front of Martha the maid, who shared his embarrassment, who turned her head away and brushed and brushed and brushed more intently.

Eugenia was not embarrassed. She stepped out of the ring of her discarded lace trains and floating silks. She said, 'As you see, we are nearly finished. Attend to these laces, Martha, leave off brushing until these things are away. I do not think all this can be quite as you expected to find it? Do you like your rooms? I paid special attention to the colours you seem to prefer—a kind of green, with touches of crimson here and there. I hope all is to your liking.'

'Oh yes. It is all most beautiful, most comfortable.'

'Don't pull, Martha. Unhook me, here and here. I shall be only a very little time, William, now.'

It was his dismissal. He went back into his dressing-room, leaving the door ajar, and put on his own nightshirt and the pretty slippers. Then he waited, standing in the candlelight, with the moonlight behind it, a curious sheeted figure, attentive to small sounds. He heard the maid run to and fro, he heard the bed creak as Eugenia climbed in. And then he heard the maid at his door, knocking softly, opening. 'Madam is ready for you now, Sir. If you would care to come in, everything is ready.'

And she held the door for him, and made a bob, and turned back the corner of the sheet and whisked out of the room on silent feet, with downcast eyes.

He was afraid of hurting Eugenia. He was also, more obscurely and more urgently, afraid of smutching her, as the soil smutched the snow in the poem. He did not come to her pure. He had learned things—many things—in the raffish dancing places in Pará, in the sleep-time after dancing in the villages of the mulattoes, which it was better not to remember here, though the knowledge might have its uses. He saw her sitting up in the bed, which was huge, and curtained, and piled high with goose-feather quilts, and white-lace-trimmed pillowcases, and soft bolsters, a soft nest in a severely frowning box. How the innocent female must fear the power of the male, he thought, and with reason, so soft, so white, so untouched, so untouchable. He stood there, with his hands at his sides.

'Well,' said Eugenia. 'Here I am, you see. Here we are.'

'Oh my dearest. I cannot believe my own happiness.'

'You will catch cold, if you cannot believe it enough to come— to come in.'

She was wearing a nightgown in broderie anglaise, and the well-brushed hair fanned over her shoulders. Her face danced before his eyes in the candle flames, around which a single moth was dancing and darting, a buff ermine. When he approached her, slowly, slowly, in fear of his own wrongful knowledge and power, she gave a little laugh, suddenly blew out the candle, and plunged under the bedclothes. When he found his way inside she held out her invisible arms to him and he reached for her softness, discovering it by touch. He held her to him strongly, to still the trembling, his and hers, and said into her hair, 'I have loved you from the first moment I saw you.'

She answered with a series of soft, wordless, moaning sounds, half-frightened, half like a bird settling. He stroked her hair, and shoulders, and felt her arms twine round him, surprisingly strong and certain, and then the flicker of her legs against his. Down and in, she plunged and pulled, into the dark, warm nest, almost suffocating, its heat increasing, and with it a sprouting damp, on his skin, and hers, between them.

'I don't want to hurt you,' he said, and her little moans and cries and intimations of pleasure and invitation increased in urgency as she twisted, laughing, first against him, then away. He followed her for a little, meeting her hot little hands with his, gathering courage to touch her breasts, her belly, the small of her back, and she answered with little sighs—of fear, of content, he did not know. And when, finally, his own urgency overcame him, and he went into her with a shivering cry, he felt her sharp little teeth on his shoulder, as she took him in, throbbing, aching and falling away.

'Oh,' he said, in the warmth and the wet, 'you are honey, you are so *sweet,* my dearest.' He heard a strange chuckle, something laughing and weeping together, in her throat. He thought of the mysteries of knowledge, of what men and women, no less than the creatures, could do if they followed their instinct, unafraid. She was darting her hot face, the cold white Eugenia, into his neck, and kissing him repeatedly where his vein pulsed. Her fingers were wound in his hair, her legs were wound in his, and this was Eugenia, of whom he had said he would die if he could not have her.

'Oh my beloved,' he said, 'we are going to be so happy, we are going to be so happy together, it is *overflowing*.'

And she chuckled, and rolled on her back, and pulled at him, and asked for more. And when they slept, uneasily, he woke in the dark dawn to see her huge eyes fixed on his face, and found her hands touching his private places, and the little sobbing sounds starting again, asking for more, and more, and still more.

And then the maid knocked at the door, with the hot water and the morning tea and biscuits, and Eugenia rolled away, quick as a lizard on a hot stone, and disposed herself, immobile, a sleeping beauty, her rosy face peaceful under her hair.

And so he lived happily ever after? Between the end of the fairy story with its bridal triumph, between the end of the novel, with its hard-won moral vision, and the brief glimpse of death and due succession, lies a placid and peaceful pseudo-eternity of harmony, of increasing affection and budding and crowing babes, of ripe orchards and heavy-headed cornfields, gathered in on hot nights. William, like most human beings, expected this in some quiet corner of his emotions, and, although he would not have said so, if asked, he would have been properly cautious about the unknown future. Certainly he expected some kind of intimate new speech to develop between himself and his wife, and expected her, vaguely, to initiate it. Women were expert in emotional matters, and much of what preoccupied him—his ambition, his desire to make discoveries, his wish to travel—seemed inappropriate subject matter for such delicate explorings. For the first few weeks of his marriage he felt that their bodies spoke to each other in a kind of fluttering bath of molten gold, a kind of radiant tent of silky touch and shimmering softness, so that long, tender silences were a natural form of communion during the mundane grey daylight. Then one afternoon, his wife came to him with downcast eyes and said in a composed whisper that she believed she was with child; that she believed they could expect a happy event. If his first emotion was a stab of fear, he was quick to hide it, to caress and congratulate her, to turn her laughing around and tell her that she looked quite different, a new creature, wonderfully mysterious. She smiled quickly and briefly to herself on this, and then said that she did not feel quite herself, that she was a little peaked, somewhat nauseous, no doubt quite naturally. And as quickly as the door to his bliss had opened, it snapped shut again, the golden garden of the nights, the honey and the roses. He slept alone, and his wife slept alone in her white nest, and swelled slowly, developing large breasts and a creamy second chin, as well as the mound she carried before her.

With her pregnancy, Eugenia disappeared into a world of women. She slept a great deal, rising late, and retiring again during the afternoons. She busied herself on making little lacy clothes, gossamer shawls, ruched bonnets, and tiny stockings. She sat for hours staring into her mirror at the creamy round of her face, whilst behind her her maid brushed and brushed out her hair, which grew sleeker with every long stroke. Her ankles swelled; she lay upon sofas, an unopened book to hand, staring into vacancy. In due course the waiting came to an end, the doctor was summoned, and Eugenia retired to her bedroom in a crowd of nurses and chambermaids, one of whom, after a period of almost eighteen hours, announced to William that he was the happy father of not one, but two living infants, both female, both doing well. Busy women slid past William as he took in this information, carrying buckets of unidentifiable slops, and baskets of soiled linen. When he went in to see Eugenia, she was lying back on freshly starched pillows, her hair dressed with a soft blue ribbon, her body below the chin hidden under pristine coverlets. His daughters lay beside her in a basket, like two eggs in a box, bound up like tiny mummies, small faces with fleeting stains of red and ivory and slate-blue crumpled under pinned hoods. There was a smell of lavender, from the sheets, and all sorts of suppressed, furtive-seeming birth-smells, milky and bloody, still lingering. William bent to kiss his wife's cheek, which was cold, though there were beads of sweat in her hairline and along her upper lip. Eugenia closed her eyes. He felt huge, dirty, bloated, *wrong* in that room, amongst those odours. Eugenia gave a little sigh—no words.

'I am very proud of you,' William said, feeling his male voice croak and rasp in the layered softnesses.

'You must go now, she is exhausted,' the midwife told him.

The babies were named Agnes and Dora, and christened by Harald in the chapel. By then they had faces. Identical faces, identical mouths opening at identical moments, identical cheekbones and blue eyes. They resembled Harald himself, they had bred true to stock. They had a faint white down on their pulsing little heads. 'Like cygnets,' William said to Eugenia, when he found himself, unusually, sitting beside her in the parlour when the nursemaid brought the babies down for their daily visit to their mother. 'You are like swansdown and they are like cygnets. They don't seem to resemble me at all.'

Eugenia, muffled in silk shawls, put out a hand from amongst them and took his.

'They will, you know,' she said, with a new matronly wisdom. 'I've seen ever so many babies, they change from week to week, even from day to day. Resemblances run across their little faces like clouds, papa today, grandpapa tomorrow, Aunt Ponsonby on Tuesday and great-grandmama at Friday dinner-time. It's because they're so *soft,* the dears, so plastic, you'll suddenly see your own chin on Agnes and one or other of your grandmothers smiling out of Dora's eyes, if you're patient.'

'I'm sure you are right,' said William, noticing with surprise and pleasure that the little round hand was still in his, that the soft fingertips were still in his palm.

The little girls were being suckled by a wetnurse, Peggy Madden, who did not resemble William's fantasies of such a person, which were of someone Junoesque and everywhere abundant and generous, with ample arms and ample lap, as well as the capacious bosom. Peggy Madden was a thin creature, with a long neck like a crane, and wiry arms. She wore an earth-coloured dress, buttoned to under her chin, under a dark blue apron, in general. Her breasts under this discreet, unobtrusive cloth could be seen to be disproportionate, prominent globes, unrelated to her trim waist and slight shoulders. The sight of these gave William an uncomfortable consciousness of corresponding swelling in his own body. However, the existence of Peggy had restored Eugenia's body to use, and William, on retiring, found the door into her bedchamber invitingly open, and a warm fire flickering beyond. He stepped into its glow, and was received into the bed, with the same cosy nuzzlings, the same flaring ecstasy, the same little cries as before, only that the skin was softer and more stretched, that the breasts where he laid his triumphant head were larger and sugar-sweet, that the centre lay softer and more enfolded. And the whole pattern was played out again, the brief weeks of pleasure, the long months of expansive and exclusive languor, the nest-making, the birth of his son, another white-headed cygnet, and again, exactly the same, until he had a second pair of twin daughters, Meg and Arabella. Eugenia said that the boy's name must be Edgar, and that was the only time he demurred, or tried to assert himself. There was an Edgar in every generation of Alabasters, Eugenia said, her lips pushed firmly out, her capacious chin tucked in. William said that his son was not an Alabaster but an Adamson, and that he would wish to give his child a name from his own family, however undistinguished.

'I do not see why,' said Eugenia. 'We do not see your family, or speak, or seem likely to do so. Your family does not come here, and Edgar will not know them, I suppose. *We* are your family, and I think you must own we have been good to you.'

'More than good, my dear, more than good. Only—'

'Only?'

'I should like something *of my own*. And my son is my own, in some sense.'

She brooded over this, puzzled. Then she said pacifically, 'We could call him William Edgar.'

'Not my name. My father's. Robert. Robert is a good English name.'

'Robert Edgar.'

It seemed ungracious to dispute the Edgar, after that. And the child was known as Robert, and sometimes William thought he saw his own alert look on the little creature's face, though mostly the child, like all five children, was an Alabaster, a pale, clean-cut, nervous creature. Five in three years was, even in those days, a large and rapid family, a mass of tumbling child-flesh like a litter of puppies, William once caught himself thinking. For he was not happy. He had perhaps never been exactly happy, though he had had what he desired, what he had written in his journal he had desired.

He was unhappy for many reasons. Most of all, and every day, he worried that he had lost his sense of purpose, even vocation. He could not ask Harald to help him make another expedition, when his children were so new and so small—it looked ungracious. He did go back to the cataloguing of Harald's collection, and put in hours and days and weeks of work in mounting specimens, inventing ingenious forms of storage, even comparing, under the microscope, African ants and spiders with those from Malaya and the Americas. But the collection was so random, so intermitted, that he was frequently discouraged. And such work was not what he had been made for. He wanted to observe *life,* not dead shells, he wanted to know the processes of living things. He made the analogy, sometimes, almost bitterly, between Harald's collection of wing-cases and empty ribcages, elephant's feet and Paradise plumes, and Harald's interminably circular book on Design, which rambled on from difficulty to difficulty, from momentarily illuminated clearing to prickling thicket of honest doubt.

The more the two of them looked at fur and teeth and flower and beak and proboscis the more he himself became aware of a huge, inexorable random constructive force, not patient, because it was mindless and careless, not loving, because it was remorseless in its discarding of the ineffectual or the damaged, not artistic, because it needed no wonder to fuel its subtle and brutal energies, but intricate, but beautiful, but terrible. And the more he delighted in his own observations of its gradual workings the more vain and pathetic he felt Harald's attempts to throw a net of theology over it, to look into its working and churning for a mirror of his own mind, to demand of it kindness, or justice. He would sometimes argue almost fiercely with Harald—he always felt some kind of inhibition about saying with complete clarity what he believed, because he felt indebted to the older man, deferential, and also protective. And he was arrogant enough to believe that if he *said* all he truly thought, he would cast his patron and father-in-law into complete despair. And he had enough human kindness in him to shrink from that.

But this holding back added to the loneliness that was his other problem. He had been lonely in the Amazon forests. He had sat by a fire in a clearing, listening to the howling monkeys, and the buzz of wings, and had thought to himself that he would have given *anything* to hear a human voice, a conventional question, 'How are you?', a bland comment on the weather, or the monotonous taste of the food. But he had also a sense of himself, there—a thinking being, living by sharpened wits, a mind in a fragile body, under the sun and the moon, bathed in sweat and river-steam, punctured by mosquitoes and biting flies, senses alert for snakes and creatures on which he could feed. Here, in the midst of the enclosed and complicated society of the country house, he was lonely in a different way, though he was hardly ever exactly alone. He had no place inside the female society of kitchen, nursery, or pretty parlour. His little ones were passed from hand to hand, from wetnurse, to nanny, to nursemaid, they were wheeled in perambulators and fed with bottles and spoons. His wife dozed and sewed and her attendants fed and groomed her. The other girls were away doing this and that, they dressed and undressed and played complicated games in the evenings with spillikins and alphabet cards, with boards and dice. The young men were not often there, and when they were, were smoky and noisy. He liked Robin Swinnerton, who seemed to like him, but relations between Eugenia and Rowena had cooled since Rowena had remained childless whilst Eugenia bred, and the Swinnertons were often away on journeys to the Lakes, or to Paris or the Alps.

The servants were always busy, and mostly silent. They whisked away behind their own doors into mysterious areas into which he had never penetrated, though he met them at every turning in those places in which his own life was led. They poured his bath, they opened his bed, they served his meals and removed his dishes. They took away his dirty clothes and brought back clean ones. They were as full of urgent purpose as the children of the house were empty of it. Once, rising at five-thirty because he could not sleep, he had gone through a door towards the kitchen, intending to slice himself some bread and walk down to the river, to watch the dawn on the water. He had surprised a kitchenmaid, a diminutive little black sprite with a mob cap, carrying a broom and two large buckets, who gave a little cry on seeing him unexpectedly, and dropped one bucket with a clang. Catching the signs of movement he looked into this bucket and saw a seething mass of black beetles, several inches deep, stumbling and waving legs and feelers, slimed with something glutinous.

'What *are* you doing?' he had said.

'I have been emptying the traps,' said the child. She was no more than a child. Her mouth trembled. 'When I come down, the scullery's arun with the creatures, Sir. I have to set traps at night, Miss Larkins showed me how, you put molasses in one of them deep tins, and they fall in and can't right themselves. And then I have to take them out and pour boiling water on them. You'd be amazed, Sir, how they come back, no matter how many of 'em you boil to death. I hate the smell,' she said, and then, as though afraid of this human statement, snatched up her bucket. 'I beg your pardon,' she said, vaguely, sure she was somehow in the wrong.

The idea flashed across his mind of making a study of these beetles, which were so plentiful and so unwanted.

'I wonder if there's a way of observing how they breed. Could you procure me two dozen large, healthy specimens, do you think—for a consideration, of course—'

'They eat just about anything,' she said, 'I do suppose. Those are disgusting creatures, they crack under your feet in the early morning. I *don't* think Miss Larkins'd like me to collect any alive if it's all the same to you, she wants 'em boiled, and fast, before the gentry gets out of bed. I'll *ask* her for you, but I don't suppose it'll be liked.'

Her breath had a faint taint discernible from some distance. Both the molasses and the struggling, crackling insects had a sharp, sickly smell. He backed away, forgetting his bread. She picked up the buckets, her muscles tightening above her frail shoulders, along her thin neck. Her back had a curve in it. She was a poor thing. He could not begin to imagine her life, her habits of mind, her hopes and fears. She became confused in his memory with her imprisoned Coleoptera, struggling and hopeless.

If he had a place, it was in the spaces between the cushioned family softnesses and the closed-away servile hierarchies in the attics and cellars and back rooms. In the schoolroom, for instance, where he found himself sometimes idly observing the inhabitants of the glass hive and the inverted glass anthill, both successfully established and busily at work. He went there when he knew the children were out playing or walking, and there occasionally he would find Matty Crompton, whose status in the household, he sometimes ruefully thought, had the same uncertainty as his own. They were both poor, both semi-employed, both, now, relations of the masters but not masters. He did not say this to Miss Crompton, who was more guarded with him since his marriage, and addressed him with punctilious respect. He did begin to wonder how she spent her days, as he began also to notice the hard work of creatures like the beetle-boiling sprite, and came to the conclusion that Matty Crompton was required to 'make herself useful' without any demeaning named post. Women were better at making themselves useful, he supposed. Houses such as this were run for and by women. Harald Alabaster was master, but he was, as far as the whirring of domestic clocks and wheels went, a *deus absconditus*, who set it all in motion, and might at a pinch stop it, but had little to do with its use of energy.

It was a chance suggestion of Matty Crompton's, however, that put him in the way of purposeful activity again. He found her, one late spring morning, sitting at the table in front of the ant heap with a china saucer of fragments of fruit and cake and meat, and a large notebook, in which she was busily writing.

'Good morning. I hope I don't disturb you.'

'By no means. I am conducting experiments upon the behaviour of these fascinating creatures. You will no doubt find my researches crude—'

He demurred, and asked what she was studying.

'I have been putting various foods upon the surface of the earth in the tank and counting the number of ants who hurry to avail themselves of the food and how rapidly they dispose of it, and in what way. Come and look—they are greatly attracted to fragments of melon and grapes—it has taken half an hour almost exactly for this scrap of sweet fruit to become no more than a living pincush-ion. They always begin in the same way, by biting into the fruit and absorbing it—burying their bodies in it if it can be done—from *below,* and sucking it slowly dry. Whereas small scraps of ham are lifted bodily—by several ants at once—and inserted into the nest through cracks in the surface—where they are handed to other ants. You cannot but admire the spirit of co-operation. You cannot but admire the way in which they communicate to each other the existence of the melon or ham, the number of ants needed to suck or transport it. Their processes appear to be random but are so purposeful—all this *swarming* I do believe can be translated into messages given and received. I do hope my formica prima is not drowned in juice. She has not stirred for quite ten minutes.'

'You are at the point of recognising individual ants?'

'For some hours together I can follow one—if ever I have *some hours*—but can think of no method of marking one so that I would know it again. I have, I think, observed that some ants are consider-ably more *active* than others, they stir up others to act, they change task or direction. But I can never stay long enough at one time.'

'If we were to stain one with cochineal—its fellows might reject it—'

'That would be a way, possibly—but would the colour *appear*—?'

'May I see your book?'

He looked at her incisive, careful drawings, in pencil, in Indian ink, of ants feeding, ants fighting, ants rearing up to regurgitate nectar for each other, ants stroking larvae and carrying cocoons.

'You put me to shame, Miss Crompton. I have been secretly worrying myself about the—the cutting-short of my hoped-for researches into insect life in the Amazon basin—by present good fortune—and here are you, doing what I should be doing, observ-ing the unknown world which is to hand.'

'My sphere is naturally more limited. I look naturally closer to hand.'

He felt her glance surveying him, assessing him. She said, 'If you were to wish to make a study of the great ant heap from which this colony originated—for example—I am sure both I and the children could be co-opted as humble helpers, and counters—'

'I have noticed nests of both Acanthomyops fuliginosus and of the slave-making Formica sanguinea near our original citadel. A comparative study might yield much interest—'

'We cannot see what goes on *inside,* as here—'

'No, but we can devise ways and means of seeing very much. I am grateful to you, Miss Crompton.' He was about to say, 'You have restored me to a kind of hope,' but realised in time that this was inappropriate, even faintly disloyal.

This conversation took place, as far as he could later remember, in the spring of 1861, shortly after the birth of Agnes and Dora. He had been at Bredely almost exactly a year. Later, he was to see the conversation as the origin of the increasingly ambitious study of the ant communities, and to a lesser extent the beehives in the Hall grounds, which was to be conducted over the next three years by himself and a team of helpers—the schoolroom children and Miss Mead, the gardener's boy and his little brother, and the watchful and efficient Matty Crompton herself. Ants are seasonal creatures, who live intensely in the Summer months and sleep through the cold days. William was beginning to discover in 1861 that his own life was to be subject to such seasonal fluctuations. Eugenia's renewal of interest in him, after the little girls were safely in the nursery with Peggy Madden and her full-blown breasts, thus coincided with the events in the field to which Miss Crompton was inviting him to pay attention. Eugenia the young matron was no longer ready to join in any communal saunter along the river bank, let alone grubbing about in the earth of the Elm Copse, but she did appear there once or twice, delicious and vulnerable in white muslin, with sky-blue ribbons, and a little white parasol, and stand, waiting, for his attention, which she rewarded with a slow, secret little smile. Mostly she would then turn away and make her slow way back to the house, knowing that he must follow, that he would drop his trowel and hurry to join her, that his permitted hand would rest lovingly on her blue sash as, with a certain consciousness, they made their way indoors, into their own rooms. Nevertheless, in a somewhat haphazard way, in that first year, several nests were found and named.

There was the Mother Nest, with a six-foot mound and an estimated four-foot underground city, nicknamed irreverently Osborne Nest, for Queen Victoria's Summer retreat, by the vivacious Margaret. There were its satellites or colonies, Elm Tree Bole, Bramble Patch Colony and Stonewall Nest, and one that had fallen into disuse, named by Miss Mead, who had a poetic touch, The Deserted Village. It was Miss Mead, too, who was responsible for the Elm Tree Bole, an accurate description of the site of the thriving young nest in the tree stump, but also a reference to Robert Browning's poem 'Home Thoughts from Abroad' describing the expatriate nostalgia for an English Spring which William had felt so strongly in the seasonless warmth of the Tropics.

> Oh, to be in England
> Now that April's there
> And whoever wakes in England
> Sees, some morning, unaware,
> That the lowest boughs and the brushwood sheaf
> Round the elm-tree bole are in tiny leaf,
> While the chaffinch sings on the orchard bough
> In England—now!

It was not until the subsequent Spring, in 1862, that his contrary yearnings for the tropical smells, and the howler monkeys and the space of the river and the easy-going people he had known, were to begin to work with their own energies. In 1861 he told Miss Mead and Matty Crompton how much this poem had meant to him, how the tiny leaves had become etched on his imagination, the spring freshness, and they said how interesting it all was. The Mother Nest and its satellites were all cities of the Wood Ants, Formica rufa. Cities were also discovered of the Jet-Black Ants—Acanthomyops fuliginosus, the Yellow Lawn Ants, Acanthomyops umbratus, and the Blood-red slave-makers, Formica sanguinea. Miss Mead wanted to name the citadels of these last Pandemonium, after Milton's city of demons, and stood in the clearing, her spectacles shining in the sunlight, and recited *Paradise Lost*.

> '. . . but chief the spacious hall . . .
> Thick swarmed, both on the ground and in the air
> Brushed with the hiss of rustling wings.'

'Those were *bees*,' said Matty Crompton. 'It goes on,

> As bees
> In spring time, when the sun with Taurus rides,
> Pour forth their populous youth about the hive
> In clusters; they among fresh dews and flowers
> Fly to and fro, or on the smoothèd plank,
> The suburb of their straw-built citadel,
> New rubbed with balm, expatiate and confer
> Their state affairs: so thick the aery crowd
> Swarmed and were straitened; till, the signal given,
> Behold a wonder! They but now who seemed
> In bigness to surpass earth's giant-sons,
> Now less than smallest dwarfs, in narrow room
> Throng numberless, like that pygmean race
> Beyond the Indian mount; or faery elves,
> Whose midnight revels, by a forest-side

Or fountain, some belated peasant sees,
Or dreams he sees, while overhead the moon
Sits arbitress, and nearer to the earth
Wheels her pale course; they, on their mirth and dance
Intent, with jocund music charm his ear;
At once with joy and fear his heart rebounds.

'We should rename the *beehive* Pandemonium if we are to have Miltonic references.'

William observed that Milton was accurate about his bees, and that Miss Crompton knew her Milton extraordinarily thoroughly.

'I was made to commit that passage to memory as an example of heroic comparison,' said Miss Crompton. 'I cannot say I am sorry—it is very beautiful—and I cannot claim the learning was difficult. I have a quick and retentive memory. But if we call the beehive Pandemonium, what name shall we give to the home of the Blood-red slave-makers?'

'It is a horrible trade,' said Miss Mead, with unexpected vehemence. 'I have never wept so over a book as I wept over *Uncle Tom's Cabin*. I pray nightly for the cause of President Lincoln.'

The first shots had just been fired in the war between the states. Opinions were divided in Bredely about the issue—much of the family money came from the Lancashire cotton trade—which was therefore not on the whole discussed. William told Miss Mead that he had seen slavery at work on the Brazilian rubber plantations, and agreed that it was evil, though it worked differently in that country where few of the population were racially pure, either white, black or Indian.

'Several of my own most agreeable companions there', he said, 'were liberated Negroes, men of strong principles and kindly dispositions.'

'How interesting,' said Matty Crompton.

'And there is a law forbidding the Portuguese to enslave the

Indians by buying them as infants from the chiefs of the tribes. This has led to a curious euphemism used by the Portuguese traders in human flesh. They use the word "ransom"—*resgatar*—to mean that they purchase people. The Manáos tribe are very warlike and enslave their captives, who are then "ransomed" from them by the Portuguese and taken into slavery. So that *resgatar* is the general word for child-purchase along the river. And the concept of ransom—in both the theological and humane sense—is thereby debased.'

'How very terrible,' said Miss Mead. 'And you saw these things.'

'I saw things I should not dream of telling you,' said William, 'for fear of giving you nightmares. I also saw inconceivable human kindness and good fellowship, especially amongst those of black and mixed race.'

He felt Miss Crompton's keen look again. She was like a bird, sharp-eyed and watchful. She said, 'I wish you would tell us more. We should not live in ignorance of the rest of the world.'

'I will save my traveller's tales for the Winter firesides. Now, we must name the Blood-red Ants' nest.'

'We might call it Athens with perfect justice,' said Miss Crompton, 'since the Greek civilisation we so much admire was founded on slavery, and I daresay could not have shone so brightly without it. But its architecture—if it can be called architecture—is less glorious.'

The small inhabitants of the place hurried beneath and between their feet, nervous and irritable, carrying scraps and threads of this and that.

'I propose Red Fort,' said William. 'That sounds warlike enough, and brings in the colour of the sanguinea.'

'Red Fort let it be,' said Matty Crompton. 'I shall embark on its geography and history, if not *ab urbe condita* then from *our* discovery of it.'

*   *   *

And once or twice more he found her diligently at work, recording episodes in the lives of hive and city. The Wood Ants all over that part of Surrey chose Midsummer Day for their nuptial flight. No one was prepared for this in 1861—indeed, the young adults and the schoolroom inhabitants were all partaking of a strawberry picnic on the lawn when the swarming began, and hundreds of frantic, tumbling winged creatures, male and female, dropped out of the sky into the cucumber sandwiches and the silver cream jugs, scurrying away in attached pairs, drowning in strawberry juice and Orange Pekoe, scrambling across spoons and lace doilies. Eugenia was much put out, and plucked various errant males out of her collar with a fastidious pout of disgust, helped by William, who brushed the clinging feet from her hair and her sunshade. The little girls ran up and down squealing and flapping. Miss Crompton took out her sketchbook and drew. When Elaine tried to peep at her drawings she snapped the book shut and put it away in her basket, turning her attention to the battle between Alabasters and ants, shaking out the tablecloth with a forceful crack and putting away the butter. The dead and dying lay in stiff silky heaps of silver and black. The cook was sweeping them from the kitchen windowsill with a broom. As the servants hurried in with the picnic things, William caught another glimpse of his little beetle-sprite, trotting grimly across the grass with the heavy tea urn. Miss Crompton, relieved of the responsibility, took out her sketchbook again. William—it was the end of his second honeymoon—followed Eugenia indoors to change her dress, to make sure no swarming creature was caught in any frill or fold of starched cotton.

In the Winter, fretted by cold, both human in Eugenia and climatic, William had his first real argument with Harald Alabaster. The cold was not good for Harald, either. The studium was as far from the kitchen and its heating appliances as it could be, to preserve the master of the house from cooking smells and smoke, but it was therefore, even with a fire burning in its grate, cold to work in. Winter brought liveliness to the younger men in the house. Edgar and Lionel were always out, shooting or hunting, coming back with heavy burdens of bleeding creatures, feathers and fur spattered with blood, and blood often on their hands and clothing, too. Their liveliness made their father's isolation appear greater. He seemed almost confined to his studium and almost invisible if he took walks along the corridors, or hovered in the doorway of his wife's hot little nest. He sent a servant to ask William to come and look at a new passage he had put together on evidences of divine providence.

'I thought you might care to look this over, the more because it has certain arguments in it—certain illustrations—which fall very much in your province. I have come at the argument from the direction of *mystery* and the certainty of *love*. Perhaps you will be so good as to look it over.'

He held out his pages, written in a tiny, precise script, just beginning to show evidences of the shakiness of elderly hands, the weakening of nerves and muscles. The paper had been much worked and reworked, and resembled a kind of stitched patch-work, with paragraphs crossed out with black bars, reinserted higher or lower, circled and divided. William sat down in his father-in-law's chair and tried to make sense of it, with mounting irritation. It was a new rehearsal of old arguments, some of which Harald had already, in conversation, rejected as untenable.

'I will praise thee,' cries the author of the 139th Psalm, 'for I am fearfully and wonderfully made: marvellous are thy works; and that my soul knoweth right well.' And the Psalmist continues quite as if he were aware of the current debates about the origin of living creatures and the development of embryos. 'My sub-stance was not hid from thee, when I was made in secret, and curiously wrought in the lowest parts of the earth. Thine eyes did see my substance, yet being unperfect; and in thy book all my members were written, which in continuance were fashioned, when as yet there was none of them. How precious also are thy thoughts unto me, O God! how great is the sum of them! If I should count them, they are more in number than the sand: when I awake, I am still with thee.'

We have all had these intuitions, these breathings, of awe at *being fearfully and wonderfully made,* and it is our natural instinct to assume a *maker* of such intricacy, which our developed minds may hardly believe to have come about by blind chance. The Psalmist here forestalls the theorists of development by his knowledge of the *perfection of substance* and the *continuous fashioning* which goes to make living beings. He writes earlier of God's loving care of the unborn infant, in verse 13, 'For thou hast possessed my reins: thou hast covered me in my mother's womb.' It is not unreasonable to ask in what way such a Deity differs from that force which Mr Darwin calls Natural Selection, when he writes, 'It may be said that natural selection is daily and hourly scrutinising, throughout the world, every variation, even the slightest; rejecting that which is bad, preserving and adding up all that is good; silently and insensibly working, whenever and wherever opportunity offers, at the improvement of each organic being . . .''

Is not this watchful care another way of describing the providences through God's grace in which we have traditionally been taught to believe? Might we not indeed argue that Mr Darwin's new understanding of the means by which these providential changes are brought about is in itself a *new providence* contributing both to human advance and development, and to our capacity to wonder at, to know, to further and repair those forces which God has set in motion, and which Mr Richard Owen has described as the 'continuous operation of ordained becoming'. Our God is not a *Deus Absconditus,* who has left us darkling in a barren waste, nor is He an indifferent Watchmaker, who wound up a spring and looks on without passion as it slowly unwinds itself towards a final inertia. He is a loving craftsman, who constantly devises new possibilities from the abundant graves and raw materials he gave to them.

We do not have to be Pangloss to believe in beauty and virtue and truth and happiness and above all in fellow-feeling and in love, human and divine. Clearly all is not for the best in the best of all possible worlds, and it is the height of folly, of wishful thinking, to attempt to deduce God from the joyful skipping of spring lambs, or the brightness of buttercups, or even the promise of the rainbow in a thunderous sky, though the writer of Genesis does offer all men the image of the bow set in the cloud as a promise that while the earth remaineth, seed-time and harvest, and cold and heat, and summer and winter, and day and night shall not cease. The Bible tells us that the earth is accursed, since the Fall of Man, the Bible tells us that the curse is lifted, in part, after the Flood, the Bible tells us that our own destructive natures may be redeemed, *are* redeemed by the ransom paid by our Lord, Jesus Christ. The face of the earth does not always laugh, even if it speaks God to us through the mouths of stones and flowers, tempests and whirlwinds, or even the lowly diligence of ants and bees. And we may discuss, if we wish, an *amelioration* of our own cursed natures, working itself out in our daily lives, with many a setback, many a struggle, since the day when Our Lord bade us 'Love our neighbours as ourselves' and revealed Himself as God of Love as well as of Power and of special Providence.

Let us, like Him, speak in parables. His parables are drawn from the mysteries of that Nature, of which, if we are to believe His Gospel, He is Maker and Sustainer. He speaks to us of the fall of sparrows and the lilies of the field who toil not, neither do they spin. He speaks to us—even He—of that wastefulness of Nature which so appals the Laureate, in His parable of the seeds which fell among weeds or on stony ground. If we consider the humble lives of the social insects I think we may discern truths which are *riddling paradigms* for our own understandings. We have been accustomed to think of *altruism* and *self-sacrifice* as human virtues, essentially human, but this is not apparently so. These little creatures exercise both, in their ways.

It has long been known that amongst the nations both of the bees and of the ants, there is only *one* true female, the Queen, and that the work of the community is carried on by barren females, or nuns, who attend to the feeding, building, and nurturing of the whole society and its city. It has also long been known that the insects themselves seem able to determine the sex of the embryo, or larva, according to the attention they pay to it. Chambers tells us that the preparatory states of the Queen Bee occupy 16 days; those of the neuters 20; and those of the males 24. The bees appear to enlarge the cell of the female larva, make a pyramidal hollow to allow of its assuming a vertical instead of a horizontal position, keep it warmer than other larvae are kept, and feed it with a peculiar kind of food. This care, including the shortening of the embryonic condition, produces a true female, a Queen who is destined, in the noteworthy words of Kirby and Spence 'to enjoy love, to burn with jealousy and anger, to be incited to vengeance, and to pass her time without labour'. Mr Darwin has confessed to his distress at the savagery with which the jealous Queens watch over, and murder, their emerging sisters in the beehive. He questioned whether this murder of the new-born, this veritable slaughter of the innocents, did not argue that Nature herself was cruel and wasteful. It could conversely be supposed that a special providence lay in the survival of the Queen best fitted to provide the hive with new generations, or the swarm with a new commander. Be that as it may, it is certain that the longer development of the worker produces a very different creature, one, again in Kirby and Spence's words 'zealous for the good of the community, a defender of the public rights, enjoying an immunity from the stimulus of sexual appetite and the pains of parturition; laborious, industrious, patient, ingenious, skilful; incessantly engaged in the nurture of the young, in collecting honey and pollen, in elaborating wax, in constructing cells and the like!—paying the most respectful and assiduous attention to objects which, had its ovaries been developed, it would have hated and pursued with the most vindictive fury till it had destroyed them!'

I do not think it is folly to argue that the society of the bees has developed in the patient nuns who do the work a primitive form of altruism, self-sacrifice, or loving-kindness. The same is even more strikingly true of the sisterhood of ant-workers, who greet each other with great shows of affection and gentle caresses, always offering sips from their chalices of gathered nectar, which they are hurrying to carry to the helpless and dependent inhabitants of their nurseries. The ants too are able to determine, how is not known, the sex of the inhabitants of their nurseries, so that the community is replenished by desirable numbers of workers, males or fertile Queens at various epochs. Their care of their fellows might itself be thought to be a special Providence, if it were thought to be conscious, or a true *moral choice*. Much labour has been expended on attempts to distinguish the voice of authority in these communities—is it the Queen, or the workers, or some more pervasive Spirit of the City, located everywhere and nowhere, that determines these matters? *What* dictates the coherent movement of all the cells in my body? I do not, though I have Will, and Intelligence, and Reason. I grow, I decay, according to laws which I obey and cannot alter. So do the lesser creatures on the earth. How shall we name the Force that directs them? Blind Chance, or loving Providence? We churchmen have always in the past given one answer. Shall we now be daunted? Scientists attempting to 'explain' phenomena such as the growth of the ants' embryos have resorted to the idea of a '*forma formativa*', a Vital Force, residing perhaps in infinitely numerous gemmules. May we not reasonably ask, what lies behind the forming power, the Vital Force, the physics? Some physicists have come to speak of an unknown x or y. Is it not possible that this x or y is the Mystery which orders the doings of ants and men, which moves the sun and the other stars, as Dante recorded, across the Heavens—the Spirit, the Breath of God, Love Himself.

What is it that leads Mankind to yearn for the Divine Reassurance, the certainty of the Divine Care and the organising hand of the Divine Creator and Perpetuator? How should we have had the wit to *devise* such an aweful concept did not our own small minds correspond to some true Presence in the Universe, did we not dimly perceive and even more crucially N E E D such a Being? When we see the love of the creatures for their offspring, or the tender gaze of a human mother bent on her helpless infant, which without her loving watchfulness would be quite unable to survive a day of hunger and thirst, do we not *sense* that love is the order of things, of which we are a wonderful part? The Laureate puts the terrible negative questions squarely in his great poem. He allows us to glimpse the new face of a world driven aimlessly by Chance and blind Fate. He presents, with plaintive singing, the possibility that God may be nothing more than our own invention, and Heaven a pious fiction. He gives the devil-born Doubt its full due, and makes his readers tremble with the impotent anxiety which is part of the Spirit of our Age.

> Oh yet we trust that somehow good
> Will be the final goal of ill,
> To pangs of nature, sins of will,
> Defects of doubt, and taints of blood;
>
> That nothing walks with aimless feet;
> That not one life shall be destroyed,
> Or cast as rubbish to the void,
> When God hath made the pile complete;
>
> That not a worm is cloven in vain;
> That not a moth with vain desire
> Is shrivelled in a fruitless fire,
> Or but subserves another's gain.
>
> Behold, we know not anything;
> I can but trust that good shall fall

At last—far off—at last, to all,
And every winter change to spring.

So runs my dream: but what am I?
An infant crying in the night:
An infant crying for the light:
And with no language but a cry.

In the next poem, Mr Tennyson writes even more strongly of
Nature's cruelty and carelessness, she who cries, 'I care for nothing, all shall go,' and of Poor Man:

Who trusted God was love indeed
And love Creation's final law—
Though Nature, red in tooth and claw
With ravine, shrieked against his creed—

And how does he answer this terrible indictment? He answers
with the *truth of feeling* to which we must not be impervious,
though it may seem childishly simple, naive, almost impotent.
Can we accept this truth of *feeling* from the depths of our natures,
when our intellects have been stunned and blunted by difficult
questions?

I found Him not in world or sun,
Or eagle's wing, or insect's eye;
Nor through the questions men may try,
The petty cobwebs we have spun:

If e'er, when faith had fallen asleep,
I heard a voice 'believe no more'
And heard an ever-breaking shore
That tumbled in the Godless deep;

A warmth within the breast would melt
The freezing reason's colder part,

And like a man in wrath the heart
Stood up and answered 'I have felt.'

No, like a child in doubt and fear:
But that blind clamour made me wise;
Then was I as a child that cries,
But, crying, knows his father near;

And what I am beheld again
What is, and no man understands;
And out of darkness came the hands
That reach through nature, moulding men.

Was it not a true leading that enabled Mr Tennyson to
become again as a little child, and *feel* the Fatherhood of the Lord
of Hosts? Was it not significant that the *warm organised cells* of his
heart and his circulating blood rose up against the 'freezing
reason'? The infant crying in the night receives not enlighten-
ment, but the warm touch of a fatherly *hand,* and thus believes,
thus *lives* his belief. We are fearfully and wonderfully made, in
His Image, father and son, son and father, from generation to
generation, in mystery and ordained order.

Harald had put up the cowl of his gown against the cold. His long
face, on its scrawny neck, peered at William as he read, assessing the
flicker of the other's eyes, the compressions of his lips, the odd nod
or shake of the head. When William had finished, Harald said,
'You are not convinced. You do not believe—'

'I do not know how I can believe or not believe. It is, as you
most eloquently say, a matter of *feeling*. And I cannot feel these
things to be so.'

'And my argument from love—from paternal love?'

'It is resonant. But I would answer as Feuerbach answers, "*Homo
homini deus est*", our God is ourselves, we worship ourselves. We

have made our God by a specious analogy, Sir—I do not mean to give offence, but I have been thinking about this for some years— we make perfect images of ourselves, of our lives and fates, as the painters do of the Man of Sorrows, or the scene in the Stable, or as you once said, of a grave-faced winged Creature speaking to a young girl. And we worship these, as primitive peoples worship masks of terror, the alligator, the eagle, the anaconda. You may argue anything at all by analogy, Sir, and so consequently nothing. This is my view. Feuerbach understood something fundamental about our minds. We need loving kindness in *reality;* and often we do not find it—so we invent a divine Parent for the infant crying in the night, and convince ourselves all is well. In reality, many cries remain unheard in perpetuity.'

'That is not a refutation.'

'In the nature of the case, it cannot be. It leaves the matter exactly where it first stood. We desire things to be so, and so we create a tale, or a picture, that says, we are so and so. You might as well say, we are like ants, as that ants may develop to be like us.'

'Indeed I might. We are all one life, I believe, shot through with His love. I believe, I hope.'

He took back his papers with careful hands, in which the papers shivered. The hands were ivory-coloured, the skin finely wrinkled everywhere, like the crust on a pool of wax, and under it appeared livid bruises, arthritic nodes, irregular tea-brown stains. William watched the hands fold the wavering papers and was filled with pity for them, as for sick and dying creatures. The flesh under the horny nails was candlewax-coloured, and bloodless.

'It may be an emotional deficiency in myself, Sir, that I cannot feel the strength of the argument. I have been much changed by the pattern of my life, of my work. My own father was very much in the image of a terrible Judge, who preached rivers of blood and destruction, and whose own profession was bloody too. And then the vast disorder—the indifference to human scale and preoccupations—in the Amazon—I have not been left with a propensity to find kindness in the face of things.'

'But I hope you have found it here. For you must know that *we* must count your coming as a special Providence—to make a new life for dear Eugenia, and now for your little ones—'

'I am most grateful—'

'And happy, I hope, contented, I hope,' the tired old voice insisted in the sharp air, hanging there in a question.

'Very happy, of course, Sir. I have all I wished for, and more. And when I come to think about my future—'

'That shall be provided for, as you richly deserve, have no fears. There can be no thought of leaving Eugenia as yet—you would not so disappoint her—her happiness is young—but in due course, you will find all your needs can be answered, amply so, have no fears. I regard you as my dear son, and I intend to provide for you. In due course.'

'I thank you, Sir.'

There was frost on the inside of the windows, and watery tears, involuntary damp, round the red rims of the clouded eyes.

William was not invited to join in the amusements of Lionel and Edgar, though Eugenia did ride out to the Meets, in a velvet habit, and come back flushed and smiling. There was a tacit conspiracy, he could almost have called it a conspiracy, to assume that, not being a pure gentleman, he would not have the skill or bravery for these gentlemanly pursuits, however resourcefully he had endured the Amazon. He went on long country walks, most frequently alone, sometimes with Matty Crompton and the schoolroom young. He was expected also to join in the evening games, in the drawing-room, where Lady Alabaster liked to play dominoes, or spillikins, or Black Maria, and where charades were occasionally organised, very ambitiously. He caused a great deal of laughter once, by likening these to the village feasts of the Indians, where everyone was fantastically dressed, and he had once met a dancing brown figure in a red-checked shirt and straw hat with a net and a box whom he recognised as a parody of himself. Great gales of laughter were aroused too by a particularly witty enactment of AM A ZON, in which AM was represented by Lionel as Abraham hearing the Voice of God out of the burning bush, a wonderful creation of yew boughs and red silk and tinsel made by Matty Crompton, A was represented by the children and Miss Mead, enacting a schoolroom alphabet lesson, in which apples were plucked from a paper tree, bees flew from a hive, and an animated Crocodile snapped at everyone's heels. ZON was a love scene in which Edgar, in full evening dress, pinned a beautiful silver girdle (zone) around Eugenia's waist—she was wearing a new silver and lemon ballgown, and her appearance aroused a huge round of applause. AMAZON was William himself, paddling a canoe made from an upturned bench behind paper reeds and dangling woollen vines, observed by a tribe of feathered and painted Indian children led by Matty Crompton in an imposing cloak painted with feathers, and a mask painted like a hawk. Tissue-paper butterflies danced in the hothouse plants stacked on the stage, and colourful snakes made of string and paper hissed and wriggled dramatically.

William congratulated Miss Crompton on the scenery of this *tour de force,* when he met her next day, winding up the crimson ribbons and folding the tinsel of the Burning Bush.

'It was easy to see whose was the inventive mind behind all these beautiful objects,' he said.

'I do what comes to hand, as well as I can,' she said. 'Such activities stave off boredom.'

'Are you often bored?'

'I try not to be.'

'That is not an answer.'

'I suppose we all feel we have greater capacities than are called for in our daily lives.'

She gave him her sharp look as she said this, and he had the uncomfortable feeling that she had only answered his intrusively personal question in order to draw him out. He was beginning to be a little afraid of Matty Crompton's sharpness. She had never treated him other than very benevolently, and had never put herself forward in any way. But he sensed a kind of suppressed fierceness in her which he was not wholly sure he wanted to know more about. She had herself very much in her own control, and he thought he preferred to leave things that way. However, he answered, because he needed to speak, and he could not speak to Harald or to Eugenia on these matters. It would be wrong. Wrong now, at least, wrong at this juncture.

'I do feel something of the kind myself, from time to time. It is strange that in the Amazons I woke daily from a dream of mild English sunshine, of simple and wonderful things such as bread, and butter, instead of endless cassava. And now I wake from dreams of the forest curtain, of the movement of the river, of my *work*, Miss Crompton. I do not have my work, my own work here, though my life could not be more pleasant, nor my new family kinder.'

'You work, I believe, with Sir Harald, on his book.'

'I do, but I am not really *needed,* and my views—in short, my views do not wholly agree with his. He desires me to play *advocatus diaboli* to his arguments, but I fear I distress him and add little to the advancement of the work—'

'Perhaps you should write your own book.'

'I have no settled opinions to advance, and no wish to convert anyone to my own rather uncertain views of things.'

'I did not mean *opinions.*' There was a possible curl of contempt—he could not decide—in the incisive voice. 'I meant a book of facts. A book of scientific facts, such as you are uniquely qualified to write.'

'I have meant to write a book of my travels—such books have been very successful, I know—but all my detailed notes, all my specimens were lost in the shipwreck. I have not the heart to invent, if I could.'

'But nearer to hand—nearer to hand, lie things you could observe and write about.'

'You have suggested this before. I am sure you are right—I am most grateful to you. I do intend to begin a close study of the Elm Copse nests just as soon as they return to life in the Spring—but a scientific study will take many years, and much rigour, and I had hoped—'

'You had hoped—'

'I had hoped to be able to set out again on another foreign journey to collect more information about the untravelled world—I wish to do that—Sir Harald suggested, more or less promised, that he might be sympathetic—'

Matty Crompton closed her sharp mouth tightly. She said, 'The book I should like to see you write is not a major scientific study. Not the work of a lifetime. It is a book I think might prove useful—and dare I say it—*profitable* to you, in the quite near future. I believe if you were to write a *natural history* of the colonies over a year—or two years, if you were to feel the need was absolute— you would have something very interesting to a very general public, and yet of scientific value. You could bring your very great knowledge to bear on the particular lives of these creatures—make comparisons—bring in their Amazonian relatives—but told in a *popular* way with anecdotes, and folklore, and stories of how the observations were made—'

She looked him in the eye. Her own dark eyes gleamed. He caught at her idea.

'It might be interesting—it might be fun—'

'Fun,' said Miss Crompton. 'The children could be usefully employed. I myself would be proud to assist. Miss Mead would do what she could. I see the children as characters in the drama. There absolutely has to be drama, you know, if the work is to appeal to the general public.'

'You should write it yourself, I think. It is all your idea, and you should have the credit.'

'Oh no. I have not the requisite knowledge—nor the spare time, though it is hard to say where my days go to—I do not see myself as a writer. But as an *assistant*, Mr Adamson, if you would accept me. I would be honoured. I can draw—and record—and copy if necessary—'

'I am quite extraordinarily grateful. You have transfigured my prospects.'

'Hardly. But I do believe it may answer. With good will and hard work.'

In the Spring of 1862, then, around the time of the birth of Robert Edgar, the organised ant-watch began. The city and its satellite suburbs were mapped and all their entrances and exits carefully recorded. Drawings were made of the way in which the gates of the city were closed at night with barricades of twigs behind which the watchers slept. Maps were made of the paths of the foraging ants, and judicious investigations were made of the nursery chambers, the eggs, grubs and cocoons which formed both the city's population and its living treasure. A kind of census was taken of guests and parasites in the community. There was a thriving population of aphid 'cattle' in the Elm Tree Bole, assiduously stroked and petted by their ant-keepers to induce the secretion of drops of sweet honey-dew, eagerly sipped and stored. There were a great many wandering guests, whose presence was encouraged or tolerated— the beetle, Amphotis, who would solicit sips of nectar from returning workers, but who, in turn, appeared to secrete some marvellous manna which its hosts energetically scraped and licked from its wing-cases and thorax, another beetle, Dinaida, which seemed to lie quietly around the corridors, gulping up a few eggs when no one was watching. The whole process of cleaning the nest was observed and documented, as convoys of ants flowed out to the huge rubbish mound bearing mouldered foodstuffs, unsavoury droppings and the corpses of their dead or dying sisters. Many of the internal processes of the nest—the Queen's industrious parturition, the workers' perpetual grooming and nourishment of her, their carrying-off and nursing of eggs, their shifting of eggs and larvae to nurseries that were warmer or cooler—could be seen in the glass-sided nest in the schoolroom, where the young girls, in good moods, would be set to document a nursery, or the Queen, for an hour or two together. William made a study of the foodstuffs brought into two particular entrances over the whole period, and thought he discerned distinct seasonal variations in what was chosen, and offered, depending on the needs of the larvae for secretions, or later for insect-flesh, and the lessening needs, in the latter part of the year, to provide for these myriads of dependent mouths. William and Miss Crompton together began to construct a military history of the whole society, which turned out to bear a remarkable resemblance, in some ways, to human warfare, with sudden invasive attacks by one army on the neighbouring stronghold of another community. They observed both successful sieges and fights which resulted in stalemates and simultaneous retreats. Matty Crompton made some very spirited drawings of battling formicae; she sat on a grass hummock whilst William lay full-stretch on the earth identifying the waves of attackers and defenders.

'How anything can *survive* with a hair for a waist, puzzles me,' she said. 'They seem so vulnerable, with their bristling little feet and their delicate antennae, and yet they are armed with stings and savage jaws, they can slice and pierce as well as any knight in armour, and they are armoured moreover. What would you say to a few cartoon-like illustrations for your text—here, I have drawn one with a stiletto, and there with a staring helmet and a kind of heavy *wrench*.'

'I should think it might add greatly to the human interest', said William. 'Have you observed how they can sever antennae and legs and cut each other in half so very quickly? And have you observed how many of the combatants advance to meet an adversary with several helpers clinging to their legs? Now, what possible advantage can such assistance be? Is it not rather an *impediment*?'

'Let me see,' she said, dropping to her knees beside him. 'Why, so they do. How endlessly *interesting* they are. See this poor soul bend round to sting an adversary who has a terrible vice-grip on her head. They will both die, like Balin and Balan, I should think.'

She was wearing a brown cotton skirt, and a striped shirt, the sleeves rolled up to her elbow. Her face was shadowed by a rather ragged straw hat, with a limp crimson ribbon, which were her usual ant-watching garments. He knew all her wardrobe by now; it was not extensive; two cotton skirts, a Sunday dress, in Summer, in navy poplin, with a choice of white starched collars, and perhaps four different shirts, in various fawns and greys. She was thin and bony; he found himself abstractedly studying her wristbones, and the tendons on the back of her brown hands, as she drew. Her movements were quick and decisive. A flick, a sweep, a series of little hooks and curves, and there was an exact diagrammatic rendering of ant-jaws crunching ant-legs, ant-thorax and ant-gaster contorted either in pain or in effort to inflict it. Beside these informative images trotted tiny anthropomorphised ant-warriors, with swords, bucklers, tridents and helmeted heads. She was absorbed in her work. William found himself suddenly sharply inhaling what must have been her peculiar smell, a slightly acid armpit smell, inside the cotton sleeves in the sunlight, mixed with a tincture of what might be lemon verbena, and a whiff of lavender, either from her soap, or from the herbs in the drawer where her shirts were laid up. He breathed more deeply. The hunter in him, now in abeyance, had a highly developed sense of smell. There were jungle creatures whose presence he sensed with all sorts of senses undeveloped in urban Englishmen, he supposed—a pricking in the skin, a fluctuation in the soft nasal lining, a ripple in the scalp, a perturbation of his sense of balance. These had tormented him in London streets, where they had over-responded to fried onions and sewage, to the garments of the urban poor and the perfumes of ladies. He sniffed again, secretly and quietly, the scent of Miss Crompton's outdoor identity. Later in Eugenia's bedroom, when she had reclaimed him, and he was buried in the smells of her fresh sheets and her fluid sex, her hot hair and her panting mouth, that sharp little smell returned briefly like a ghost of the outdoors, and he puzzled for a moment, as he pressed Eugenia into the plump mattress, over what it could be, and remembered the severed feelers and Matty Crompton's busy wrists.

Matty Crompton gave a name, at least a first name, to the child he thought of as his beetle-sprite, whom she recruited to keep an eye on the nest of the Blood-red Ants, on her afternoons off. Her name, it turned out, was Amy, and Miss Crompton asserted that it would do her good to get a bit of fresh air, having no family and nowhere to go, and to earn a few extra pennies. She sat with the gardener's boy, who had to be dissuaded from dropping stag beetles down her neck, but was observant. It was these two who alerted William and Miss Crompton to the change in the activities of the slave-makers. Tom said he had noticed several of the red ants, as he put it, '*prowling around* like', near the Stonewall Nest, and one day, sent by Tom, Amy came running across the lawn crying, 'Come quick, come quick, Tom says the Bloody Ants are coming up in a fizzing great army, he says, he says, come quick something is up, he says. I saw them mysen, they are like gravy boiling, do come.' She was still a thin, bowed, pinched little thing, but the project, and Tom, had put some colour into her cheeks, and she was developing a bird-like prettiness of which she was wholly unconscious.

William and Matty sallied forth, armed with camp-stools and notebooks, and were there in time to observe the slave-makers' forces, after a great deal of excited waving of antennae and legs and apparently inane running-about, suddenly get out, purposefully, led by an advance guard of particularly excited scouts, across the thirty yards or more that separated their smaller mounds from the Elm Tree Bole. They poured out in various regiments, accompanied, as William duly noticed, by a sizeable force of Wood Ant slaves, whose behaviour appeared to be identical to that of their masters.

William wrote up what they observed, and read it aloud later to Matty Crompton and the rest of the inhabitants of the schoolroom.

The great Slaving Raid took place on a hot June day, when the temperature had been rising steadily for some time, and with it the activities of the Blood-red Ants, as reported to our historians by our spies and pickets. We were led to speculate whether slave-raids, like other large exoduses and population changes, are instigated by the heat of the Sun. Ants do not move in cool weather, and sleep at night, even in the balmiest Summer days; they are cold-blooded, and need external warmth to get their desires and designs in motion. Be that as it may, the approach of Midsummer roused the Blood-red citizens to an increasing hum of conversation and activity. Messages came in more and more speedily and frequently. More and more scouts could be seen spying on the peaceful foraging of the Wood Ants, or busily trampling out trails between their nest and that of their unsuspecting victims.

Finally, at some signal, awaited eagerly by the gossiping and seething crowds who had rushed in readiness to the *agora* on their hill-top, the red armies divided into four parties, which set out in direct lines across the terrain—following well-mapped routes, used, we suspected, on previous raids. When the four regiments had taken up their positions around the Elm Tree Bole Nest, the leaders of all four could be observed like little Napoleons rushing excitedly along the ranks, stirring up valour and determination with strokes of their antennae and agitated bodily movements. Suddenly the 1st Sanguine Troopers moved into concerted action, storming their way towards the entrances—so carefully barricaded at night, now gaping open to the incitatory sunlight. The 2nd, 3rd and 4th Regiments patrolled the positions they had taken up, with increasing forcefulness and ferocity.

The Wood Ants sallied forth bravely to beat off the thieves and kidnappers. Waving their antennae, hurrying furiously, they bit at the legs and heads and feelers of the busy Bloody Ants, attempting, often with success, to grasp the invaders and sting them to death. We observed that the Sanguine Ants did not retaliate unless they were wholly impeded from progress. They had one purpose only—to snatch the unhatched infants from the Nursery, and to bear them back, in their fine jaws, to their own fortress. Whilst the martial Wood Ants battled to delay them, the tenders of the helpless young snatched up their infant sisters and tried to bear them away to safety. Most strange was to see Wood Ants, identical in appearance to the inhabitants of Elm Tree Bole, rushing forwards into the corridors of the castle, seizing cocoons and bearing them, not to safety, but out again to the ramparts and the waiting, protective corps of *sanguinea* who would be the rearguard for their safe passage back to the Red Fort. We were sufficient in numbers, as observers, to make quite sure, from repeated trackings of individual *sanguinea* and Wood Ants, that the residents of Elm Tree Bole did not distinguish between the ruddy foreigners, and their slaves of their own race, attacking both impartially.

It was all over remarkably quickly. There were very few casualties. The Blood-red Ants had not come to slaughter, and had moved so swiftly, so single-mindedly, that the Wood Ant defenders—retaliating as they would to aggressive territorial invasions by their own kind—had been baffled and bewildered, and had allowed their attackers to make their limited assault without very effective opposition. Back streamed the victorious invaders, carefully bearing the captured nestlings whose fate was to live and die as *sanguinea,* not as true Wood Ants, to feed and nourish little *sanguinea,* to respond to the Summer sun by massing to attack their forgotten parents and sisters. They do not appear to have depleted the nursery inhabitants so severely as to disrupt the way of life of the Elm Tree Bole, which resumed, after the excitement, much as it had been. They did not, as human soldiers do, rape and pillage, loot and destroy. They came, and saw, and conquered, and achieved their object, and left again. It is believed that slave-making raids are made not more than once a year, so we were lucky to have—as the Red Ants themselves did—good spies to alert us to this interesting event.

The English slave-makers are not so specialised as certain other larger slave-makers are. These are known as the Amazons, though they do not originate in the Amazon basin but are commonly found in Europe and North America. The Amazona—for example *Polyergus rufescens*—never excavate nests nor care for their young. Their name is probably bestowed because like the classical Amazon warriors, who were all women, led by a fierce queen, they have substituted belligerence for the delicate domestic virtues associated with the female sex. Unlike the Blood-red Ants, the Amazons have developed such powerful tools and weapons of fighting and thieving that they are unable to perform any other function, and depend entirely on their slaves to feed them and polish their ruddy armour. Their jaws cannot seize prey; they have to beg their slaves for food; but they can kill, and they can carry. It might be argued that Natural Selection has perfected these creatures as fighting machines, but in the process has rendered them irrevocably dependent and parasitic. We may ask if there are not lessons to be learned by ourselves from this curious and extreme social state.

'Nature does indeed teach us,' said Miss Mead. 'A terrible war is being waged at present across the Atlantic, to secure not only the liberation of the unfortunate slaves, but the moral salvation of those whose leisure and enrichment are sustained by their cruel labours.'

'And we are urged', said Matty Crompton, 'to fight on the side of the slave-makers, to preserve the work, that is the daily bread, of our own cotton-mill workers. And our own philanthropists, in turn, seek to rescue those *machine-slaves* from their specialised labour. I do not know quite where these thoughts may lead us.'

'Analogy is a slippery tool,' said William. 'Men are not ants.'

Nevertheless, in the hot days just after Midsummer, when they increased their vigilance in order to observe, if possible, the nuptial flight of the Queens and their suitors, he was hard put to it not to see his own life in terms of a diminishing analogy with the tiny creatures. He had worked so hard, watching, counting, dissecting, tracking, that his dreams were prickling with twitching antennae, advancing armies, gnashing mandibles and dark, inscrutable complex eyes. His vision of his own biological processes—his frenzied, delicious mating, so abruptly terminated, his consumption of the regular meals prepared by the darkly quiet forces behind the baize doors, the very regularity of his watching, dictated by the regularity of the rhythms of the nest, brought him insensibly to see himself as a kind of complex sum of his nerve-cells and instinctive desires, his automatic social responses of deference or required kindness or paternal affection. *One* ant in an anthill was neither here nor there, was dispensable, was nothing. This was intensified, despite his recognition of the grimly comic aspect of his reaction, by the recording of the fate of the male ants. This passage he did not read aloud to the whole team of researchers; he showed it in the Winter, after several rewritings, to his chief collaborator, Matty Crompton.

We were fortunate also, in 1862, to be able to observe the spectacle of the wedding dance of the thousands of winged Queens and aspiring suitors, who swarmed on the Osborne Nest and the Elm Tree Bole as if at a given signal, a trumpet-sound, or the resonant hum of a gong. Vigilant young eyes had observed young males attempting to leave the nest some days earlier, and being held back by determined guardians until the appointed time. We had had some idea when that might be, for we had noted the exact date of the nuptial ceremonies during the previous Summer, when the whirling couples had plummeted, like so many Icaruses or falling angels, to a creamy suffocation, or death by drowning in a steaming cauldron of fragrant Mysore in the midst of our own strawberry picnic. The appointed day in 1862 was the 27th June, and the ball-guests emerged in clouds of gauze and took to the air in fragile spires. Many ants consummate their unions in flight, embracing each other high above the earth. The Wood Ants appear to mate in fact on the earth—the males of this species are nearer in size to the Queens than in many others, where the Queen may exceed her consort by twenty times or more in bulk, and can easily transport her lover through the empyrean. We were unable on this occasion to observe whether the Wood Ant Queen practises polyandry, though other species of ants are known to do so—we hope to be able to observe more closely next year. We did observe heaps of fiercely struggling and battling black bodies, wrapped in their diaphanous veiling, each Queen fought for by ten or twenty determined suitors, who will hang fiercely on to each other's legs, to get a purchase anywhere at all—more like a battle in Rugby Football than the elegant minuet for which their silky robes might seem fitted. The little workers stand by and observe, occasionally pulling at one or other of the actors in this passionate drama. We might imagine them feeling a certain complacency at their immunity from the terrible desire, both murderous and suicidal as well as amorous, which drives the winged sexual creatures. They appear also to feel a certain organising interest in things going well, and will give a pull or a push or a tweak to one or other of the embracing combatants—we could not ascertain the purpose of these interventions, though in other breeds of more primitive ant, where mating takes place in the nest, the workers are known to control the access of the males to the Queens, choosing which shall be admitted to their presence and which shall be kept at bay with jaws and sting.

How busy, how festive, how happy the dancing seemed! How tragic its outcome for almost all of the participants! The nuptial flight of the Wood Ants offers a supremely moving example of the inexorable secret work of Natural Selection, so that anyone observing it must be struck by how completely Mr Darwin's ideas might seem to explain it. The males struggle mightily to possess the winged Queens; they must prove their strength of flight, their combative skills, their powers of attracting and gaining the trust of the wary female, spoiled as she is by choice of an almost infinite number of pressing lovers. And the Queens themselves, who emerge in their hundreds of hundreds, must possess strength and skill and cunning and tenacity to survive more than a very few moments after successful fecundation, let alone to start a nest. The time in the blue sky, the dizzy whirling in the gauzy finery lasts only a few hours. Then they must snap off their wings, like a young girl stepping out of her wedding veils, and scurry away to find a safe place to found a new nest-colony. Most fall prey to birds, other insects, frogs and toads, hedgehogs and trampling humans. Few indeed manage to make their way again underground, where they will lay their first eggs, nourish their first brood of daughters—miserable dwarfs, fragile and slow, these early children—and in due course, as the workers take over the running of the nursery and the provision of food, they will forget that they ever saw the sun, or thought for themselves, or chose a path to run on, or flew in the Midsummer blue. They become egg-laying machines, gross and glistening, endlessly licked, caressed, soothed and smoothed— veritable Prisoners of Love. *This* is the true nature of the Venus under the Mountain, in this miniature world a creature immobilised by her function of breeding, by the blind violence of her passions.

And what of the males? Their fate, even more poignantly, exemplifies the remorseless random purposefulness of Dame Nature, of Natural Selection. It is believed that early males of primitive ants were also in some sense workers, members of the community. But as the Societies of insects became more complex, more truly interdependent, the sexual forms of the creatures involved became more and more specialised. It is not generally known that worker-ants can and do, upon occasion, lay eggs, from which, it appears, only male children will emerge. But they appear to do this only if the Queen is ailing, or the nest is threatened. In general the Queens mother the whole society, and have changed in body to be able to do so, swollen with eggs, enough eggs fertilised from this one matrimonial encounter for a whole generation. Changes in bodily form according to function exist throughout the insect societies. There are ants whose heads exactly fit to plug the holes in the stems of plants where they live, which when not plugged are entrances and exits. There are ants known as Repletes, hung up in cellars like living wineskins, bloated with stored nectar. And the males, too, have become specialised, as factory-hands are specialised *hands* for the making of pin-heads or brackets. Their whole existence is directed *only* to the nuptial dance and the fertilisation of the Queens. Their eyes are huge and keen. Their sexual organs, as the fatal day approaches, occupy almost the whole of their body. They are flying amorous projectiles, truly no more than the burning arrows of the winged and blindfold god of Love. And after their day of glory, they are unnecessary and unwanted. They run hither and thither, aimlessly, draggle-winged. They are beaten back for the most part from the doors of their home nests, and driven away to mope and die in the cooling evenings of late Summer and early Autumn. Like the drones of the bee-hive they toil not, neither do they spin, though like the drones too, they are pampered in the early stages of their lives, tolerated pretty parasites, who dirty and disturb the calm workings of the nest, who must be fed on honey-dew and cleaned up after in the corridors. The drones, too, as Autumn approaches, meet with a terrible fate. One morning in the hive a mysterious Authority arms and alerts the worker-sisters, who descend on the sleeping hordes of velvet slugabeds, and proceed to tear them limb from limb, to pierce, to sever, to blind, to bundle bleeding out of doors, and remorselessly to refuse readmission. How profligate is Nature of her seeds, of her sons, making thousands that *one* may pass on his inheritance to sons and daughters.

'Very eloquent,' commented Matty Crompton, drily. 'I am quite overcome with pity for these poor, useless male creatures. I must admit I had never seen them in that light before. Do you not think you may have been somewhat *anthropomorphic* in your choice of rhetoric?'

'I thought that was our intention, in this History. To appeal to a wide audience, by telling truths—scientific truths—with a note of the fabulous. I have perhaps overdone it. I could tone it down.'

'I am quite sure you should not—it will do *excellently* as it is—it will appeal greatly to the dramatic emotions—I have had an idea of writing some real fables of my own, to go with my little drawings of mestizo fairy-insects. I should like to emulate La Fontaine—the tale of the grasshopper and the ant, you know—only more *accurately*. And I have been making a collection of literary citations in a commonplace book, which I thought might be placed at the head of your chapters. It is important that the book be *delightful* as well as profound and truthful, is it not? I found a wonderful sonnet by poor mad John Clare, which, like Milton's Pandemonium-bee-hive, seems to suggest that our idea of fairies may be only an anthropomorphising of insects. I like your Venus under the Mountain. She is related to the Little People under the Hill of all British fairy lore. I am convinced that many of the flying demons on church walls are inspired by stag beetles with their brows. How I go on! Here is the Clare. Tell me what you think. Rulers and labourers alike were men to him, you will see.'

> What wonder strikes the curious, while he views
> The black ant's city, by a rotten tree

Or woodland bank! In ignorance we muse:
Pausing, annoyed, we know not what we see,
Such government and thought there seem to be;
Some looking on, and urging some to toil,
Dragging their loads of bent-stalks slavishly;
And what's more wonderful, when big loads foil
One ant or two to carry, quickly then
A swarm flock round to help their fellow-men.
Surely they speak a language whisperingly,
Too fine for us to hear; and sure their ways
Prove they have kings and laws, and that they be
Deformed remnants of the fairy-days.

She was keen, she was resourceful, William thought. He half-wished he could confide in her about his own drone-nature, as he increasingly perceived it, though that, of course, was impossible for all sorts of reasons. He could not betray Eugenia, or demean himself by complaining of Eugenia. Moreover, to complain in this way would make him look foolish. He had yearned for Eugenia, and he *had* Eugenia, and he was bodily in thrall to Eugenia, as must, in this confined community, be apparent even to a sexless being like Miss Crompton.

It interested him, that he thought of her as sexless. That thought itself might have arisen out of some analogy with the worker ants. She was *dry,* was Matty Crompton. She did not, he was coming to see, suffer fools gladly. He was beginning to think that there were all sorts of frustrated ambitions contained in that sharp, bony body, behind those watchful black eyes. She was determined and inventive about the book. She was fiercely intent, not only on its production, but on its success. Why? He himself had an unspoken, almost unacknowledged vision of making enough money to be able to set out again for the Southern Hemisphere independent of Harald and Eugenia, but Miss Crompton could not want that, could not know that *he* wanted that, could not want him to go, when he added so much to the interest of her life. He did not think she was so altruistic a being.

The end of the Summer made him think rather sourly of the fate of the drones, not only in terms of himself and the ants, but in terms of other male members of the household. Harald was enmeshed in the problems of instinct and intelligence and his powers of thought seemed paralysed. Lionel had cracked his ankle jumping over a park wall for a dare, and was laid up on the terrace, on a rattan chaise longue, complaining loudly of his immobility. Edgar went riding, and paid long visits to various neighbouring squires. Robin Swinnerton and Rowena were back in the neighbourhood, still childless. Robin invited William to ride with him, and said that he envied him his luck: 'A man feels a fool, you know, if an heir doesn't put in an appearance in due course—and unlike Edgar, I don't have little love-children all over the county to show I can father them if I choose.'

'I know nothing about Edgar's private life.'

'A veritable centaur, or do I mean a satyr? A man of *appetites*—no girl is safe, they say, except the most unimpeachably respectable young creatures, who innocently set their caps at him and whom he avoids like the plague. He likes a rough and tumble, he says. I don't think a man should behave as he does, though there's no denying plenty do, maybe most.'

William, about to be righteously indignant, remembered various golden, amber and coffee-skinned creatures he had loved on hot nights—and smiled awkwardly.

'Wild oats,' said Robin Swinnerton, 'according to Edgar, are stronger and more savoury than the cultivated kind. I always meant to save myself, to commit myself—to one.'

'You have not been married long,' said William uncomfortably. 'You should not lose hope, I am sure.'

'I do not,' said Robin. 'But Rowena is downcast, and looks

somewhat enviously at Eugenia's bliss. Your little ones are very true to type—veritable Alabasters.'

'It is as though environment were everything and inheritance nothing, I sometimes think. They suck in Alabaster substance and grow into perfect little Alabasters—I only very rarely catch glimpses of myself in their expression—'

He thought of the Wood Ants enslaved by the *sanguinea,* who believed they *were sanguinea,* and shook himself. Men are not ants, said William Adamson to himself, and besides, the analogy will not do, an enslaved Wood Ant looks like a Wood Ant, tho' to a *sanguinea* it may smell Blood-red. I am convinced their modes of recognition are almost entirely olfactory. Though it is possible they navigate by the sun, and *that* is to do with the eyes.

'You are dreaming,' said Robin Swinnerton. 'I propose a gallop, if you are agreeable.

Early one morning, that Autumn, a disagreeable incident revealed the centaur or satyr in Edgar to William. William had risen early and was making his way to the stable yard when he heard a kind of choking sound in a scullery at one side of the corridor and turned aside to investigate. Inside the scullery was Edgar, bending over the sink, his back to William. In Edgar's grasp, William saw slowly, was his little beetle-sprite, Amy, whose curls had become brighter and thicker over the Summer, though her face remained white and pointed. Edgar had bent her backwards, and had one hand over her mouth and one thrust into her bodice. His buttocks swelled behind him: his genitals were pushed up against Amy's skirts. William said, 'Amy?'

He wondered if he should retreat. Amy made an inarticulate cry. Edgar said, 'I didn't know you had an interest in this little thing.'

'I don't. Not a personal one. In her general wellbeing—'

'Ah. Her general wellbeing. Tell him, Amy. Was I hurting you? Were my attentions unwelcome, perhaps?'

Amy was still bent back over the sink. Edgar withdrew his arm from her clothing with the deliberation of a trout-tickler leaving a trout stream. His fingermarks could be seen on Amy's skin, round her mouth and chin. She gasped. 'No, sir. No, sir. No harm. I am quite well, Mr Adamson. *Please*.'

William was not clear what the plea meant. Perhaps she was not clear herself. In any case, Edgar stepped back, and she stood up, head hanging, hands nervously rearranging her buttons and waistband.

'I think you should apologise, Sir, and leave us,' said Edgar coldly and heavily.

'I think Amy should run away,' said William. 'I think she would do best to run away.'

'Sir?' said Amy in a very small voice, to Edgar.

'Run off then, child,' said Edgar. 'I can always find you when I want you.'

His large pale mouth was unsmiling as he said this. It was a statement of fact. Amy ducked a vague obeisance at both men, and scuttled away.

Edgar said, 'The servants in this house are no concern of yours, Adamson. You do not pay their wages, and I'll thank you not to interfere with them.'

'That little creature is no more than a child,' said William. 'And one who has never had a childhood—'

'Nonsense. She is a nice little packet of flesh, and her heart beats faster when I feel for it, and her little mouth opens sweetly and eagerly. You know nothing, Adamson. I have noticed you know *nothing*. Go back to your beetles, and your creepy-crawlies. I won't hurt the little puss, you can believe. Just add a bit of natural spice. Anyway, it's none of your business. *You are a hanger-on*.'

'And I have yet to learn what use *you* are to the world, or anyone in it,' said William, his temper rising. Surprisingly, Edgar laughed at this, briefly, and without a smile.

'I told you,' he said. 'I have noticed you know *nothing*.'
And he pushed past William and went out to the stables.

The book was put together in a provisional way during the Winter of 1862. Its final title was to be

THE SWARMING CITY
*A Natural History of a Woodland Society,
its polity, its economy, its arms and defences,
its origin, expansion and decline.*

William worked on it fairly steadily, and Matty Crompton read and revised the drafts, and made fair copies of the final versions. It had always been their intention to devote one more Summer to the checking and revision of the previous Summer's observations. Two years' data were better than one, and William wrote off with queries about comparative observations to various myrmecological parts of the world. The project of a publishable book was, by tacit consent, shared only by William and Miss Crompton: there was, in fact, no ostensible reason why this should have been so, but they both behaved from the beginning conspiratorially, as though the family should think of the ant-study as a family educational amusement, a gentleman's use of leisure time, whilst *they,* the writers, knew differently.

The book took shape. The first part was narrative, a kind of children's voyage of discovery into the mysterious worlds that lay around them. Chapter 1 was to be

THE EXPLORERS DISCOVER THE CITY

and William wrote sketches of the children, of Tom and Amy, of Miss Mead and her poetical comparisons, though he found himself unable to characterise either himself or Matty Crompton, and used a narrative voice that was a kind of royal or scientific We, to include both of them, or either of them, at given points in time. Miss Crompton brightened this passage considerably with little forgotten details of friendly rivalry between the little girls, or fragments of picnics carried off by the foraging ants.

The second chapter was

THE NAMING AND MAPPING OF THE COLONIES

and then followed the serious work of describing their workings:

Builders, sweepers, excavators.
The nursery, the dormitory, the kitchen.
Other Inhabitants: Pets, pests, predators,
temporary visitors and ant-cattle.
The Defence of the City: War and Invasion.
Prisoners of Love: The Queens, the Drones,
the Marriage flight and the Foundations
of new Colonies.
The Civic Order and Authority: What is the source
of power and decisions?

After this, William planned some more abstract, questioning chapters. He debated with himself on various possible headings:

Instinct or Intelligence
Design or Hasard
The Individual and the Commonwealth
What Is an Individual?

These were questions that troubled him, personally, as deeply as the questions of Design and the Designer troubled Harald Alabaster. He debated with himself on paper, not quite sure whether his musings were worthy of publication.

We might remark that there is a continuing dispute amongst human students of these interesting creatures as to whether they possess, singly or collectively, anything that can be called 'intelligence' or not. We might also remark that the attitude of the human student is often coloured by what he would *wish* to believe, by his attitude to the Creation in general, that is, by a very general tendency to see every other thing, living and inanimate, in anthropomorphic terms. We wonder about the utility to men of other living things, and one of the uses we make of them is to try to use them as magical mirrors to reflect back to us our own faces with a difference. We look in their societies for analogies to our own, for structures of command, and a language of communication. In the past both ants and bees have been thought to have kings, generals and armies. Now we know better, and describe the female worker-ants as slaves, nurses, nuns or factory-operatives, as we choose. Those of us who conclude that the insects have no language, no capacity to think, no 'intelligence', but only 'instinct' tend to describe their actions as those of automata, which we picture as little mechanical inventions whirring about like clockwork set in motion.

Those who wish to believe that there is a kind of intelligence in the nest and the hive can point to other things besides the marvellous mathematics of the hexagonal cells of the bees, which recent thinkers have decreed to be a function simply of their building movements and the shape of their bodies. No one who has spent long periods observing ants solving the problem of transporting an awkward straw, or a bulky dead caterpillar through the interstices of a mud floor, will feel able to argue that their movements are haphazard, that they do not jointly solve problems. I have seen a crew of a dozen ants manoeuvre a stem as tall, to them, as a tree to us, with about as many plausible false starts as a similar crew of schoolboys might make, before finding which end to insert at which angle. *If this is instinct,* it resembles intelligence in finding a particular method to solve a particular problem. M. Michelet in his recent book, *L'Insecte,* has a most elegant passage on the response to the plundering attacks of a

lumbering moth, Sphinx Atropos, imported into France at the
time of the American Revolution, probably as the caterpillar on
the potato plant, protected and promulgated by Louis XIV. M.
Michelet writes eloquently of the terrible appearance of this
'sinister being', 'marked fairly precisely in wild grey with an ugly
death's-head'—it is our Death's-head Hawk Moth, in fact. It is
a glutton for honey, and pillages the hives, consuming eggs,
nymphs and pupae in its depredations. The great Huber decided
to protect his bees and was told by his assistant that the bees had
already solved the problem either with, for instance, a variety of
experimental barriers—by building new fortifications with narrow windows which would not admit the *fat* invader—or by
making a series of barriers with successive walls zigzagging behind narrow entries, making a kind of twisting maze into which
the Death's-head could not insert its bulk. M. Michelet is delighted by this—it proves the bees' intelligence, to him, conclu-
sively. He calls it 'the *Coup d'État* of the beasts, the insect
revolution', a blow struck not only against the Death's-head but
against thinkers like Malebranche and Buffon who denied bees
any power of thought or capacity to divert their attention in new
directions. Ants too can both make mazes and learn man-made
mazes—some ants better than others. Do these things prove the
little creatures are capable of conscious development? The order
of their societies is infinitely more ancient than our own. Fossil
ants are found in the most ancient stones; they have conducted
themselves as they do over unimaginable millennia. Are they set
in their ways—however intricate and subtle these may be—do
they follow a driving force, an instinctual pattern rigid and
invariable as stone channels, or are they soft, ductile, flexible,
malleable by change and their own wills?

Much, so much, almost all, depends on what we think this
force, or power, or indwelling spirit we call 'instinct' is. How
does 'instinct' differ from intelligence? We must all admire the
miracle of *inherited aptitudes, inherited knowledge* in a founding
Queen of a new ant-colony who has never been outside her
parent-nest, who has never been digging, or food-gathering, yet

is able to nourish her young, feed and care for them, construct her first home, open the pupal shells. This is inherited intelligence, and is part of the general thoughtfulness and intelligence diffused through the whole society, which gives to all a knowledge of how to answer the needs of all in the most suitable way. The debate between the proponents of instinct and the proponents of intelligence is at its sharpest in its consideration of the Vigilance on the part of the whole community which makes decisions as to how many workers, how many soldiers, how many winged lovers or virgin Queens a community may need at any given time. Such decisions take into account the available food, the size of the nursery, the strength of the active Queens, the deaths of others, the season, the enemies. If these decisions are made by Chance, then these busy, efficient communities are ruled by a series of happy accidents, so complex that Chance must appear to be as wise as many local deities: if this is automatic response, what would intelligence be? The intelligence that directs the activities of the founding Queen, or those of the mature worker, is the intelligence of the City itself, of the conglomerate which cares for the wellbeing of the whole, and continues its life, in time and space, so that the community is infinite and eternal, even if both Queens and workers are mortal.

We do not wholly know what we mean either by the word 'instinct' or by the word 'intelligence'. We divide our own actions into those controlled by 'instinct'—the sucking of a new-born infant at the breast, the swerve of the runner to avoid danger, the sniffing at our bread and meat to detect signs of dangerous putrefaction; and those controlled by 'intelligence'— foresight, rational analysis, reflective thought. Cuvier and other thinkers compared the workings of 'instinct' with those of 'habit', and Mr Darwin has finely observed that in human beings 'the comparison gives a remarkably accurate account of the frame of mind under which an instinctive action is performed, but not of its origin. How unconsciously many habitual actions are performed, indeed not rarely in direct opposition to our conscious will! yet they may be modified by the will or reason.'

Are we to see the actions of the ants and bees as controlled by a combination of instincts as undeviating as the swallowing and swimming motions of the amoeba, or are we to see their behaviour as a combination of such instincts, acquired habits, and a directing intelligence, not residing in any particular individual ant, but accessible by these, when needed? Our own bodies are controlled by such a combination. Our own nerve-cells respond to stimuli and respond very strongly to the excitements of great fear, love, pain or intellectual activity, often arousing in us the possibility of new exercises of our skills previously unheard of. These are deep questions, pondered by every generation of philosophers, answered satisfactorily by none. Where do the soul and the mind reside in the human body? Or in the heart or in the head?

And do we find the analogy with our individual *selves* more useful, or that with the co-operative cells of our bodies, when understanding the ants? I believe I have been able to observe individual ants who habitually moved more vigorously and nervously, explored farther, approached other ants to interest them in new activities or to exhort them to greater efforts. Are these restless and inventive individual *persons* in the society, or are they large and well-fed cells in the centre of the ganglia? My own inclination is to wish to think of them as individual creatures, full of love, fear, ambition, anxiety, and yet I know also that their whole natures may be changed by changes in their circumstances. Shake up a dozen ants, in a test-tube, and they will fall on each other and fight furiously. Separate a worker from the community, and she will turn in aimless circles, or crouch morosely in a coma and wait to die: she will not survive for more than a few days at most. Those who argue that ants must blindly behave as 'instinct' dictates are making of 'instinct' a Calvinist God, another name for Predestination. And those observing similar reactions in human creatures, who may lose their wills and their memories after physical injuries or shocks, who may be born without the capacity to reason which makes us human—or may lose it, even, under the pressure of extreme desire, or extreme fear of death—are substituting the Predestination of body and instinct for the iron control of a loving and vengeful Deity on a golden immutable Throne in a Crystal Heaven.

The terrible idea—terrible to some, terrible, perhaps, to all, at some time or in some form—that we are *biologically predestined* like other creatures, that we differ from them only in inventiveness and the capacity for reflection on our fate—treads softly behind the arrogant judgement that makes of the ant a twitching automaton.

And what may we learn, or perhaps fear to learn, or draw back from learning, in a comparison between our own societies and those of the social insects?

We may see their communities as the true individuals, of which the independent creatures, performing their functions, living and dying, are no more than cells, endlessly replaced and renewed. This would fit with Menenius' fable in *Coriolanus* of the commonweal as a body, all of whose members help its continued life and wellbeing, from the toenails to the voracious belly. Professor Asa Gray, in Harvard University, has argued persuasively that in the case of the vegetable world, as in the branching animal communities of corals, it is the *variety* that is the individual, since the creatures may be divided and propagated asexually, without loss of life. The ant community is more varied than the corals, in the division of labour, and the variety of forms taken by the creatures, but it is possible to believe that its ends are no more complex and do not differ. They are the *perpetuation of the city, the race, the original breed*.

I made a Belgian friend in my travels on the Amazon, who was a good naturalist, a poet in his own language, and much given to meditation on the deeper things in life. He wrote despondingly of the effects on social animals of the *very high elaboration* of the social instinct which developed, he claimed, for the most part, from the family, the relations of mother and child, the protective gathering of the primal groups. He was in the jungle because he was not a social being, but a natural solitary, a romantic would-be Wild Man, but his observations on these matters are not uninteresting. The more perfected the association, he said, the more probability there is of a development of severe systems of authority, of intolerance, constraints, proliferated rules and regulations. Organised societies, he said, tended to the condition found in factories, in barracks, in the galleys, without leisure, or relaxation, using creatures pitilessly for their *functional benefit,* until they were exhausted and could be cast aside. Such social being he characterised memorably as 'a kind of common despair' and he saw the cities of the termites, in which fellow creatures are rationally turned to food when no longer useful, as a parody of the terrestrial Paradises towards which the social designers of human cities and communes are working so hopefully. Nature, he said, does not desire happiness. When I retorted that Fourier's communities were based upon the rationally indulged pursuit of pleasures and inclinations (1,620 passions, to count exactly), he said gloomily that these groups were doomed to failure, either because they would disintegrate into combative chaos, or because the rational organisation would substitute militarism for Harmony, sooner or later.

I retorted at the time that Réaumur claimed to have observed ants at play like ancient Greeks, indulging in wrestling-bouts without harm, on sunny days. I have since, I must confess, several times observed what I believed to be this playful phenomenon, only to conclude on closer inspection, that what I was watching was not play, but war in earnest, fought, as ant-wars usually are, for limited objectives and without wholesale berserker bloodlust. Alfred Wallace, who was travelling in the same parts at that time, and is a convinced Socialist, much affected by the vision and practical success of Robert Owen's successful experiments at New Lanark, attempted to put the problem in a kinder and milder light. Owen, he argued, had proved by his social experiments that environment can greatly modify character *for the good*—'that no character is so bad that it may not be greatly improved by a really good environment acting upon it from early infancy and that Society has the power of creating such an environment'. Owen's limited extension of *individual* responsibility to his workers, his care for their *individual* education, improved their wills, which were their individual natures. Wallace wrote (I quote an unpublished letter), 'Heredity, through which it is now known that ancestral characteristics are continually reappearing, gives that infinite diversity of character which is the very salt of social life; by environment, including education, we can so modify and improve that character as to bring it into harmony with the possessor's actual surroundings, and thus fit him for performing some useful and enjoyable function in the great social organisation.'

I have digressed far, you may think, from Elm Tree Bole and Osborne, the Red Fort and Stonewall City. In fact, these fundamental questions, of the influence of heredity, instinct, social identity, habit and will, arise at every moment of our study. We find parables wherever we look in Nature, and we make them more or less wisely. Religious thinkers have seen in the love of mother and infant, of Father and Son, a reflection of the eternal relations of the Prime Being with the Created World and with Man himself. My Belgian friend saw that love, on the other hand, as an instinctual response leading to the formation of societies which gave even more restricted and functional identities to their members. I have mentioned the role of Instinct as Predestination, and of Intelligence as residing in communities rather than individuals. To ask, what are the ants in their busy world, is to ask, what are we, however we may answer . . .

William stared at his page. He had argued round and round, not really thinking of publication, for if he had been, he thought, ruefully, at least for the large, young audience envisaged by Matty Crompton who might read for improvement, he would have had to pay more attention to the religious susceptibilities of their parents and guardians. He thought of appending that useful tag from Coleridge's *Ancient Mariner*

> He prayeth well, who loveth well
> Both man and bird and beast.

He decided to give his pages to Miss Crompton, and gauge her response, if he could. It struck him that he knew nothing of her own religious views. A friend of Charles Darwin had once told him that almost no women were prepared to question the truths of religion. He thought, then, that the whole of what he had just written was somehow set against what Harald Alabaster was trying to say—more so than appeared on the surface of the writing, for like almost all his contemporaries, he was half afraid to give full expression, even to himself, of his very real sense that Instinct *was* Predestination, that he was a creature as driven, as determined, as constricted, as any flying or creeping thing. He wrote about will and reason, but they did not *feel* to him, in his bones, in his sense of his own weight in the mass of struggling life on earth, to be very powerful or important entities, as they were for a seventeenth-century divine under the Eye of God, or a discoverer of new stars exulting in his power. His nerve-cells pricked, his hand ached, his head was full of crawling black fog. He felt his life as a brief struggle, a scurrying along dark passages with no issue into the light.

When he gave his final musings to Miss Crompton to read, he found himself waiting anxiously for her opinion. She took the pages away one day, and brought them back the next, saying that they were exactly what was required, just such scrupulous general considerations were what would greatly increase the appeal of the book to a wide audience and lead to its discussion in all circles. She added, 'Do you think it conceivable that there may be future generations who will be *happy* to believe that they are finite beings with no afterlife—or that their natures may be fully satisfied by the part they play in the life of the whole community?'

'Such beings exist now, I believe. It is a curious outcome of travel that all beliefs come to seem more—more relative, more tenuous. I was much struck by the universal incapacity of Amazon Indians to imagine a community which did not reside on the banks of a vast river. They are not capable of asking, "Do you live near a river?" only "What is *your* river like? Is your river quick or slow, do you live near rapids or possible land avalanches?" They picture the Ocean as a river, I know, no matter how we may try to describe it vividly and accurately. It is like trying to tell a blind man the principles of perspective, which I once attempted. And it led me to wonder what do *I* not reflect upon, of what important facts am *I* ignorant in my picture of the world?'

'Many—most—would not have your intellectual carefulness and humility.'

'Do you think so? Those who will not accept Mr Darwin's findings are divided between those who are very angry and quite sure they are right—who kick imaginary stones like Dr Johnson refuting Berkeley—and those, like Sir Harald, whose quest for assurance—reassurance—of Faith is shot through with trouble, indeed anguish.'

'The wisdom of the serpent might suggest strengthening your case for a possible explanation that might square with Providence.'

'Do you think I should do that?'

'I think a man must be truthful, as far as possible, or the whole truth will never be found. You must say nothing you do not think.'

There was a silence. Matty Crompton ruffled through the pages. She said, 'I liked your passage from Michelet about the depredations of the Sphinx Atropos. It is amazing how much—how much of mystery, of fairy *glamour*—is added to the creatures by the names bestowed upon them.'

'I used to think of Linnaeus, in the forest, constantly. He bound the New World so tightly to the imagination of the Old when he named the swallowtails for the Greek and Trojan heroes, and the Heliconiae for the Muses. There I was, in lands never before entered by Englishmen, and round me fluttered Helen and Menelaus, Apollo and the Nine, Hector and Hecuba and Priam. The imagination of the scientist had colonised the untrodden jungle before I got there. There is something wonderful about *naming* a species. To bring a thing that is wild, and rare, and hitherto unobserved under the net of human observation and human language—and in the case of Linnaeus, with such wit, such order, such lively use of our inherited myths and tales and characters. He wished to call the Atropos the Caput mortuum, you know, the Death's Head exactly—but the system of nomenclature requires a monosyllable.'

'So he chose the blind Fury with the abhorred Shears. Poor innocent insect, to have its small life burdened with so large an import. I was partly struck by Sphinx Atropos because I too have been writing—and what I have been writing has become strangely involved in just these names selected by Linnaeus—I have derived much instruction both from the *Systema Naturae* and from the copy of Thomas Mouffet's *Theatrum Insectorum* which is in Sir Harald's library.'

'I am amazed at your accomplishments. Latin, Greek, draughtsmanship of a high quality, a thorough knowledge of English Literature.'

'I was educated with my betters, in the schoolroom of a Bishop. My father was the tutor and the Bishop's lady was kindly-intentioned. I would be grateful,' she said, seeming to hurry on past any further personal questions, 'if you would cast your eye over this writing when you have a spare moment. I meant it for no more than an illustratory fable—you will see—I amused myself by tracing the etymology of Cerura vinula and another Sphinx, Deilephila elpenor, and thought I would write an *instructive fable* around these strange beasts—and found I had got rather carried away, and written something longer than I intended and perhaps, for a simple puzzle-tale, *over-ambitious*—and now I am puzzled what to do with it.'

'You should publish on your own behalf—a whole volume of such tales.'

'I did not believe I had an inventive nature. It is the chronicle of our insect cities that has stirred me up to authorship. But I do not think there is much merit in it. I count on you to be ruthlessly honest about its failings.'

'I am sure I shall be full of admiration,' said William, honestly, if vacantly. Matty Crompton looked thoughtfully downwards, not meeting his eye.

'I have already said, in another context, you must say nothing you do not think.'

He read her tale in bed that night, by the light of a new candle. On the other side of the door between his room and his wife's he could hear a new, regular, comfortable sort of sound—Eugenia's recent snoring, a ruffling, like a wood-pigeon, a squeak like fingernails on silk, and then a snort like a hungry foal.

THINGS ARE NOT WHAT THEY SEEM

There was once a farmer, who had a hard time tilling his land, which was full of thorns and thistles. He had three sons, too many to inherit his difficult plot, so the youngest, Seth by name, was sent out into the world with a bundle of food and clothing, to seek his fortune. He travelled far and wide, crossing and recrossing the Oceans, until one day he was shipwrecked in earnest, and cast up on a sandy shore with a few companions. They had no idea where they were—they had been blown very far off course—but they put together packets of salvaged rations, and set off to walk up the beach and into the extensive woods which lay before them. They heard the laughter of birds and monkeys, and saw the secret flashings of myriads of wings in the treetops, but they met no sign of human dwellings and were just about to decide that they were the new rulers of an uninhabited island when they found tracks and a pathway, which opened into a wide ride between the trees, which they followed.

After a time they came to a smooth high wall, too high to see over, with a gate in it, which was locked. They debated a moment or two between themselves, and knocked, and the door swung open before them on smooth, oiled hinges, and swung to behind them with the same facility, although there appeared to be no one there to control it. And they heard the bolts and tumblers fall into place inside the great lock. One was for turning back, at this, and one was for scattering and hiding, but the rest—including Seth—were for continuing boldly forwards. So they walked on, across marble floors, through great cool halls, and heard splashing fountains in courtyards, and spoke in whispers of the sumptuousness of the architecture and domestic appointments.

And finally they found themselves in a banqueting hall, with a great ebony table spread with a fine feast—tasty pies and pastries, fine jellies and blancmanges, heaps of fruit with the bloom on it, and vessels full of sparkling wine. Their mouths watered so at this sight that they sat down without more ado and helped themselves, eating untidily until the juices ran out of the corners of their mouths, for they were half-starved. Only Seth did not partake, for his father had told him always to be sure never to eat anything that was not freely offered. He had been soundly beaten as a boy for trespassing in neighbouring orchards, and he was wary.

When they had been eating for some time, and were half stupid with good feeding, they heard a sound of tinkling bells and harpstrings, and a door at the far end of the hall swung open, and admitted a strange gathering of folk. There was a major-domo, who looked more like a goat than a man, and a very pretty milk-white heifer with roses wound in her horns, and a procession of herons and geese, all wearing collars studded with rubies and sapphires, and some very very pretty

fluffy kittens, silver-blue and rosy-fawn, and an elegant little
silver greyhound, with bells round its neck, and the loveliest
King Charles spaniel, with long silky russet ears and huge,
appealing brown eyes. And in the midst of these was a cheerful, *comfortable*-looking lady, dressed a little like a shepherdess, in a frilly cap and a delightful embroidered apron, with
beautiful white ringlets falling to her shoulders. In her hand
she carried the prettiest shepherd's crook, decorated with
ribbons, silver and rose and sky-blue, and she had the sweet-
est smile, and the most dancing eyes. All the shipwrecked
mariners were immediately enchanted by her presence and
began to smile fatuously amidst the grease and fruit juice on
their lips and chins. It was easy to see she was no working
shepherdess, but a great lady who chose to dress as one, out
of condescension or simplicity of spirit.

'How *lovely*', she cried, 'to have unexpected visitors. Eat
your fill, help yourselves to wine till your cups run over. I *love*
to have visitors.'

And the mariners thanked her, and set to again, for their
hunger had been mightily restored by her words, all except
Seth, who, it is true, was now invited, so was not breaking his
father's prohibition. But he still had no appetite for the feast.
The delectable lady saw that he was not eating, and the goat
held a chair for him, so that he was more or less obliged to
sit down. And when she saw that he was not eating, the lovely
lady came near with a rustling of her pretty skirts and pressed
on him dishes of all manner of dainties, pouring him glasses
of cordial julep and fragrant syrups, which looked like dancing flames in the crystal.

'You must eat,' she said, 'or you will be faint with hunger,
for I can see you have had a terrible journey, and are salt-
stained and gaunt with weariness.'

Seth said he was not hungry. And the lady, without losing
her smiling good temper, sliced him a salad of delicate fruits
with a silver knife, and laid them out in a fan, like a flower,

shavings of melon, circles of glistening orange, fragrant black grapes and crisp white apples, and slices of crimson pomegranates studded with ebony seeds.

'I shall think you most obdurate and ill-mannered,' said she, 'if you will not taste even a sliver of apple, even a grape with its bloom on it, even a sip of pomegranate-juice.'

So for very shame he took up a slice of pomegranate, which seemed less substantial than the crisp apple-flesh, and ate three of the black seeds in their sweet, blood-coloured jellies.

One of the companions hiccuped and said, 'You must be some great Fairy, ma'am, or Princess, to have all this plenty in the midst of this wilderness.'

'Indeed I am,' she said. 'I am a Fairy who likes to make things pleasant for mortal men, as you see. My name is Mrs Cottitoe Pan Demos—which means, "for all the people", you know, and that is what I am. I am for all the people. I keep open house for everyone who comes. You are all so very welcome.'

'And can you do Magic?' asked the ship's Cook, who was no more than an overgrown Boy, and associated Magic with tricks and disappearances and feather dusters and bouquets appearing from nowhere.

'Indeed I can,' she said, with a silvery laugh.

'Show us, show us some Magic,' said the Cook, licking his lips.

'Well,' said she, 'I can make this feast vanish in a twinkling.' And she touched the table with her silver crook, and all was gone, though the scent of the fruit, and the savour of the meat, and the tang of the wine still hung in the air.

'And I can chain you in your chairs without chains,' she said, smiling more happily, and she gave a little imperious wave of the crook, and the seamen found they could no longer rise to stand, or lift their hands from the chairs.

'That is not very nice,' said the Cook. 'Let us go, ma'am. We thank you for our good meal—we must go back to mend our ship and move on.'

'How ungrateful men are,' said the lady. 'They will not stay, whatever we give them, they will not rest, they *will* sail away. I thought you might like to stay and make part of my household, for a time. Or forever. I keep an open house for everyone who comes.'

'No thank you kindly, ma'am,' said the Cook. 'I'd like to go now.'

'I don't think so,' said she, and touched him on the shoulder with her silver crook, which lengthened itself for the purpose. And immediately, with a strange half-human cry, the Cook became a great hog, at least as to his head and shoulders, with a damp snout, and great tusks and bristles. Only his poor hands, clamped to his chair, were still hands, hands hard as hoofs, and hairy, and clumsy. And the lady went round the table and touched every one of the sailors, and each of them became a different kind of pig, from the great White Boar to the dapper Black and Tan, from French *sanglier* to Bedford Blue. Seth was interested in the variety of the pig-forms, despite his own great danger. He was the last to be struck by the crook, which sent a kind of electric shock through his whole body, stinging like a snake. He put up a hand to his head to feel his snout and was surprised to find that, unlike his fellows, he could do so. His face felt much the same, his nose, his mouth, his eyebrows. But there was a kind of itching and rushing in his head, and he felt upwards and there was his hair, springing outwards like water from a fountain, into a kind of prancing mane.

Mrs Cottitoe Pan Demos laughed heartily at this sight.

'I *never* can tell what the effect of my magic will be on those who eat only frugally,' she said. 'Your head of hair is very handsome, I think, much more handsome than tusks and bristles. But you must still make one of our *party*, you know. I shall set you to work as my swineherd—my swine are kept deep in the rocky caverns below this palace, for pigs have no need of daylight, and I shall show you how to arrange their fodder, and clean out their sties, and I am very much afraid you will be horribly punished if you do not do it well. For we must all co-operate, you know, for the good of the household. Come with me, my dear.'

And she drove all the creatures—the new swine and the geese and the herons, the little heifer and the old goat—at a spanking trot through the corridors, laughing musically when they slid about on their awkward hoofs, waving her pretty crook, which stung mercilessly wherever it touched hide or fur. And under the palace they found an enormous succession of pens, caverns and cages, in which languished all sorts of creatures, docile rabbits, gentle palpitating hares, drooping draggle-tailed peacocks, a few donkeys, a few Barbary ducks, even a nest of white mice.

'You need not listen to the noises they make,' said Mistress Cottitoe Pan Demos, 'unless you wish to, and I do advise against it, for they make a very *miserable* mixture of grunting, squealing, braying and honking, which it is best to ignore. I'm afraid I must close you in with them—you may sleep in this fresh straw, and here is a delicious loaf, only a week old, and some excellent spring water to drink, so you will have no reason to grumble about your entertainment. There is *nothing* more wholesome than good bread and clean water, I'm sure you'll agree. From time to time I shall send you messages by one of the *house* creatures—the geese can carry little baskets, and the spaniel has been trained to bear letters safely in her mouth. You need not worry over how to answer. You *must* do as I say—that is the rule here—and unfortunately any infringement meets—every time I'm afraid—with the most terrible consequences. I will leave those to your imagination. I find that imagination feeds wonderfully well on bread and water in the darkness—quite like little seeds sprouting under the soil—you may imagine *all sorts* of consequences, my dear. I hope your dreams are pleasant.'

And with that, she swept through the cellar gates, going tap, tap, tap, in her little diamond pumps with her great cap nodding on her snowy curls. And the unfortunate Seth was left in almost darkness, surrounded by staring, mournful eyes, half-human eyes in furry faces, or peering between wrinkles of pigskin, glistening with bright tears.

Poor Seth had a hard time of it in those miserable caverns. He did his best to make things easier for the creatures, partly because he feared the vindictive power of the Fairy, but also because he pitied their hopeless state. He wiped their tears, and tended their sores, and changed their water, and listened to their sobs and moans, which he felt painfully, perhaps the more because he could not translate them into the words they wished to be. From time to time he formed plans of escape. He would rush the gate. He would suborn the King Charles spaniel. One day he did try to speak to the little dog. He said, 'I suppose you are also an enchanted human being—no doubt a very handsome person, to judge by your present lustrous hair and eyes. I beg you to nod your head if you are prepared to help me to think of a way out of this servitude, which can no more be agreeable to you than to me, even if your lot is easier.'

But the little animal only began to tremble all over: its hair stood on end, and it whined to get out of the gate and back into the corridors. When he approached it, it snarled, still shaking, and bit at his hand.

After this failure, he went into his corner, and sat down on his straw, and wept bitterly. His tears fell rounder and faster, damping the dust at his feet, and trickling darkly away into corners. Suddenly he realized that for the past few moments a small, scratchy voice had been crying out, in a bubbling way, 'Stop, you are drowning me, stop.' He looked all round for the invisible speaker, but could see no one.

'Where are you?' he finally said.

'Here, at your feet, in all this salt water.'

So he looked down, and there was a rather large Jet-black Ant, rolled up in one of his tears, with all its thread-like legs soaked to its body, and its antennae drooping. He broke the tear with a straw and held the straw for the creature to climb on to.

She said, 'Why are you making all this mud and mess?'

'Because I am a prisoner, and will never get out of this dark place. My life has come to a stop.'

'*I* can get in and out.'

'So I see. But you are a minute creature and I am a great useless lump. It is all quite hopeless.'

'Don't start weeping again. I can do you a good turn, for you saved my life, even if it was yourself who put it in jeopardy. Wait there.'

And the little creature ran busily away, and vanished through a crack in the rock of the cavern. So Seth waited. There was not much else he could do, whatever he thought of the capacity of the ant to render him any material assistance. After a considerable time, he saw her waving her feelers agitatedly at the edge of the crack, and then she worked her way through, accompanied by two of her fellows. They were carrying between them a package the size of a large crumb of bread—a good featherbed, by their measure—which they dragged on to his feet, and laid down. Something almost invisible was wrapped very neatly in a fragment of dark leaf, sewn, or tied, with nearly invisible thread.

'There,' said the ant. 'This will help.'

'What do I do with it?'

'Eat it, naturally.'

'What does it contain?'

'Three fernseeds. Particular fernseeds. Collected beyond-the-wall, of course.'

He hesitated. He was about to say, 'What will the effect of this be?' when the ant said, 'Hurry!' in a voice quite as determined as that of Dame Cottitoe Pan Demos.

So he put it on the edge of his tongue, where it dissolved, with a taste of woodland shadow, and he felt something like pins and needles run through his veins, and a terrible giddiness, and the next he knew he was standing next to the ant and was now only about twice her height. She appeared much more menacing and mysterious when she was larger, or he was smaller. Her huge black eyes considered him out of their dark shiny windows. Her shear-like mandibles opened and shut.

'I am worse off than before,' he said. 'I am even more helpless now. Any of the pigs and donkeys here can crush me thoughtlessly. The hens and doves can eat me. Please restore me.'

'I told you,' said the ant, in what now was a crackling boom. 'I can get in and out of here. If I can, you can. Please follow me.'

And so he began a terrible journey, through earthy tunnels, that twisted and turned every which way, with the spokes-woman ant leading, and the others helping Seth along in the absolute darkness by holding on to his limbs and pushing and pulling, gently and precisely. They trod delicately, and he slid, and stumbled, and after some time they came out, quite suddenly, round a very sharp corner, into very bright sun-light, which he had not seen for so long that he blinked and blinked and his eyes filled with tears.

He could not see where he was, for he was down among the roots of a large grassy lawn, and his view was restricted to some rocky gravel and the waving forest roof of the grasses. The ants suggested he should climb a rose-bush which stood near, so he did that, standing carefully on the largest thorns like a robber climbing over the defences of a castle. And when he was up in the air, and could see a long way, he saw he was in some kind of high-walled garden, with pleached fruit trees growing in the sun along the bricks, and with lawns, and stone benches, and flowerbeds, and beds of vegetables and herbs and soft fruits stretching as far as he could see. But everything was so much too much for his new vision that he became very giddy, and had to hold tightly to a leaf and close his eyes briefly against the terrible crimson of the rose petals as large as Persian carpets, or the glitter of the grass forest, as wide as the English Channel.

Imagine to yourself a red apple, hard and shiny and heavy as the Albert Hall, hung on a cable and swinging over your defenceless head. Imagine then how much more terrible must appear the veined spherical mountain, wonderfully streaked with rich purple, soft and green-ridged and folded with crevices and crannies, which is a gleaming cabbage, bursting with strength and just ready to pick. Seth was overcome with a mixture of awe, and apprehension, and admiration of the huge force behind all this burgeoning. He climbed down again to the earth, and thanked the ants for their kindness. He thought he might try to live in the garden until he could find a way of restoring himself to his original form, and rescuing his comrades. He thought he could hide well enough from Dame Cottitoe Pan Demos, unless of course she knew a magic that would reveal him to her. This thought cast him down a little. He began to hurry across the lawn forest, away from the wall of the castle, as though there was any use in distancing himself from her sphere of influence. The ants had helped him. He might meet other helpers, he told himself, to keep his spirits up.

He could hear all sorts of sounds around him. Some of them he would have heard in his natural state—the liquid warbling of the birds, now an orchestra singing in a waterfall, and the huge hum of bees, darting from flower to flower. He heard also sounds he would never have heard with unsharpened ears—the mumbling, and champing and sawing, and munching of thousands and thousands of busy mouths eating away at leaf and flower, fruit and flesh and bone. He could hear worms sliding by like slimy trains and thirsty mouths in the soil, sucking up dew and juices. After a time he got used to all these sounds, like a man walking easily in the bustle of a great city, and began to look about him more confidently. He came out of a tunnel in the grass, and on to the edge of a bed of raspberry canes. He thought he might manage to pull off a raspberry and eat part of it—he was suddenly hungry—and began to climb up the stem of one, hand over hand, as he used to do in the days of his sailing. By this method he managed to approach the sun-baked top of a low brick wall, against which the canes were springing, and he was about to reach out for the fruit, when, from amongst the leaves, he heard a slow, menacing hiss. And from along the wall he heard a kind of threatening coughing growl, like the voice of an angry crocodile.

Along the branches of the raspberry poured the most terrible creature, a loathsome, blunt-snouted dragon, with a horrible bloated head, and huge staring eyes. And along the wall, making the growling noise, advanced another, waving a forked tail like a whiplash, rearing up a huge cavernous mouth, snarling loudly. This one had a wine-coloured back and bright green head and tail. It moved slowly, in a swaying way, whilst the more serpentine beast *oozed* over the branch.

Seth backed away, looking frantically for a weapon. He found a flake of slate on the wall that might, at a pinch, cut or stab, and he picked up a handful of fragments to throw.

'Get away—' he cried. 'Go back.'

The serpent in the branches swayed to and fro. It spoke in a thick, bloated kind of voice, as though its mouth was full of nasty things.

'I—am—very—unpleasant—indeed. I—will—hurt—you —very—badly. I—am—very—dangerous. You—should— not—approach—me.'

And the one on the path said, 'I—am—very—cruel. I—am—the—eater. I—pick—you—to—the—bones.'

'Go back,' said Seth. He could smell their hot breaths, all fleshy and full. He threw a pebble at the forked-tailed one, which stopped and twitched its skin, and then came on again. Seth thought his last moment had come: he could not run away because there was a sheer rising wall behind him, and the fat-headed serpent in front. He was trapped between the two.

And just at that moment, out of the sky, someone descended very fast on the end of a long silken rope, which did not appear to be attached to anything. Two shiny black shoes arrived, with a little skip, and above them someone long and thin and black—a four-limbed creature, which resolved itself into a human shape, female, with a long black skirt and a white bonnet, shading a little white face with large horn-rimmed glasses on a sharp nose. She was wrapped in a long, silvery cloak. This person rolled in the silk rope out of the blue, and coiled it at her feet.

'Good morning,' she said. 'You appear to be troubled.'

'I am about to be eaten alive by dragons and serpents.'

'I don't think so,' she said. 'These are my friends, Deilephila Elpenor, and Cerura Vinula. They are quite as much afraid of you as you are of them. They tell terrible lies about themselves, and blow themselves up to horrify those they think might hurt them. I don't think this creature will hurt you,' she said to the dragons. 'You have frightened him very efficiently. That is enough for now. You must hurry, and eat more. There is not long to go.'

Seth said, 'They look very terrible and dangerous.'

'They will be pleased to hear that. Won't you, Elpenor? Won't you, Vinula? Look closely at Vinula, Sir, and you will see that his *real* jaws occupy a small space underneath that great Mask he shows the world. And watch Elpenor deflate himself, and you will see that his terrible eyes are only the spots on his saddle, puffed out to dwarf his real head, which is small enough. Really, he has a dear little snout, more like a piglet than a great Dragon. Things are not always what they seem, you know. May I know your name?'

'It is Seth.'

'And I am Mistress Mouffet.' She held out a thin hand. 'Would you like to share my picnic? I think you must have escaped from the Sties, and I may be able to help you, if you will trust me.'

So Seth sat down with Mistress Mouffet on the top of the wall, and she gave him bread and cheese and apples from her basket, all of which were the right size for him in his present state, and for her too. And she looked at him kindly with her shining eyes behind her spectacles, and told him about the Garden.

'It belongs to Dame Cottitoe Pan Demos, who uses it to ripen fruit and vegetables for her table, and flowers to decorate her boudoir and her drawing-room, and likes to walk about in it, as you see, for Dame Cottitoe is a good gardener, and her plants flourish mightily. But there are other creatures who spend time here, and are not subject to the rule of Dame Cottitoe—who came from beyond-the-wall, and have other purposes. Elpenor and Vinula are such creatures in a sense, or will *become* such creatures, as I hope you may see, for although they were born in this Garden, and have no memory of any other place, they are not subject to the laws of the Garden and will leave it. And many other creatures sail into the Garden on umbrellas of silk, or long threads as I do. And many more come in through burrows and cracks in the earth, for the Garden is part of the realm of a much more powerful Fairy than Dame Cottitoe, who allows her to tend it, but likes to see how its creatures fare, and to send and receive messages from within the wall. Look at the grass, and you will see that it is all laced over and over with silken ropes, such as I came on—each belonging to a spiderling, who will make her nest here, and spin her web, and keep watch. And the birds too, and the winged seeds of the trees, which spin in and out, and the clouds of pollen from others, and the parasols of the cow parsley and the dandelion, all carry messages.'

'And who is this Fairy? And would She help me, and my poor enchanted companions? And who are *you*?'

'I am the Recorder of this Garden, or you might say the Spy, for Dame Cottitoe does not know of my existence. I look after creatures such as Elpenor and Vinula, and yourself, as it turns out. A relation of mine, in another world, was one of the great Namegivers, one of the great historians of this Garden. It was he, indeed, who named Elpenor and Vinula, and their names are like delightful poems, you know. I got into a poem myself—"Little Miss Muffet" my poem is entitled—but it is a garbled thing, associating me with spiders, it is true, but suggesting that I, the cousin of the author of *Theatrum Insectorum sive Animalium Minimorum* might be *afraid* of a spider, when I am in fact a recorder of their names and natures, and their good friend.'

'Tell me about the poetic names of Elpenor and Vinula, Mistress Mouffet. For I too come from a country family, where namegiving is a family occupation.'

'Elpenor, you must know, was the name of a Greek sailor, who was turned into a swine by a relative of Mistress Cottitoe, named Circe, and my father chose this name for him because of the snout-like nature of his ordinary nose. He has a junior relative called Porcellus, a pigling, for the same reason. And Vinula's name is Cerura Vinula—Cerura for two Greek words, κέρας (keras) a horn, and οὐρά (oura) a tail, for his tail, you see, is forked like two horns, and hard into the bargain. And my relative called Vinula "an *elegant* caterpillar, by Jove, and beautiful beyond belief". Names, you know, are a way of weaving the world together, by relating the creatures to other creatures and a kind of *metamorphosis,* you might say, out of a *metaphor,* which is a figure of speech for carrying one idea into another.'

'Of course,' said Seth, who was pursuing his own ideas. 'Of course, they are *caterpillars.* I took them for terrible snakes, or lizards.'

'So do full-grown humans and hungry birds. That is their cleverness. And like all true caterpillars, they will change into winged beings. And then their names are added to and changed again. I know where some of Elpenor's brothers and sisters are just about to burst out of their hiding places. Will you come and see them? I think they may help you. For they carry very particular messages to the Fairy beyond-the-wall, and are named for Her, in some ways, and might consent to carry you to Her, if you have the courage.'

So they went along the top of the wall, accompanied by the caterpillar-dragons, who rippled along very busily. And after a time they came down, in a far corner of the garden, where a graceful willow-tree overshadowed pots of herbs, and a vegetable-bed, with solid rows of leeks like green cathedral-pillars, and ferny carrot-tops, like luxuriant palm-trees, and bowers of potato-leaves, in which a large caterpillar could be seen crunching up vast mouthfuls, ripping and tearing with great force.

'This is a relative of Elpenor,' said Mistress Mouffet. 'His name is Manduca, which means simply a Glutton, in Latin, which is not very nice, but appropriate, you know; because he is so large, and must grow so much, he has to eat very quickly. He is very handsome, I think, despite his nasty name. Over here are some of Elpenor's relations, feeding on the rosebay willow-herb, which is *not* one of Dame Cottitoe's nurslings, but one who flies in on silky floss on every breeze and can make a rooting-place in any nick or cranny. And Vinula's relations can be seen all over the tree here, for they love willow. If you come near the tree, I will show you the chrysalis woven by Vinula to rest in for the winter. Look, there, in that crack in the bark.'

Seth looked, but could see nothing.

'He is due to hatch any moment,' said Mistress Mouffet. 'I am here to record the date of his transfiguration.'

'I can see nothing at all,' said Seth.

'And yet there is his house, or cradle, or even coffin, however you wish to name it,' said Mistress Mouffet. 'It is woven tightly of lovely silk—he curls up and spins his own soft shroud from his own substance, using his little head as a shuttle. Each makes his own characteristic house. Manduca does not weave silk, but builds himself a horny carapace, like an Egyptian mummy-case, in darkest mahogany, and buries it far beneath the soil, where it lies quietly in waiting. And Elpenor makes a similar case—only paler—and hides it on the surface of the soil. You must have seen these things, when you were—larger. You may even have broken into one, whilst digging in your garden. Your father must turn them up, often and often, in his thorny soil. And if, by accident, you break open the coffin during the sleep of its builder you will not find either a grub or a folded moth, but a yellow soup, like egg-yolk, which looks like the decay of putrefaction and is the stuff of life and rebirth itself. For things are not what they seem, as you must always remember.'

'I will,' said Seth, and guided perhaps by this excellent principle, or perhaps by a preliminary shudder of changes, he was suddenly enabled to see the chrysalis of Vinula, which was a huge tent, or nest, on the bark of the tree, woven so wonderfully with bits of bark and sawdust, and wood, that it seemed to be an outgrowth of the tree itself, and nothing to do with caterpillars, or moths. But from within it appeared the soft head, and then the thin shoulders, and then the clinging wet, trembling wings of the moth, which clung with its fine feet to the bark of the tree, limp and exhausted.

'He will dry out his fur, and wait for his wings to harden in the air and the light,' said Miss Mouffet, obviously a person who took great pleasure in instructing others. 'Meanwhile, here is a brother of Elpenor, who has already found his way out, and is waiting for the evening. He is very handsome, I think, with his rosy body and wings, striped with the loveliest mossy-green. He is like a moss-rose-bud, though he is not named for that. He is a Large Elephant Hawk Moth.'

'Those are strange names,' said Seth, considering the beautiful rosy creature, with its pointed wings and its furry breast. 'For there is no resemblance between an elephant and a hawk, so how may Elpenor resemble both at once?'

Mistress Mouffet was momentarily puzzled at this. Then she said, 'His *family* are Hawk Moths. The gluttonous Manduca is a Hawk Moth, too. They are named for the sharpness and darting of their flight, and the pointed nature of their heads. I suppose the "elephant" is a reminiscence of his snout in the caterpillar state. His *scientific* name is Sphinx Deilephila Elpenor. Deilephila is a beautiful word, meaning "lover of the evening", for he likes to fly at dusk.'

'And Sphinx?' said Seth.

Miss Mouffet lowered her voice.

'Sphinx is one of the names of the great Fairy. It means, in part, the asker of riddles. And the answer, too. She loves these moths because they are riddles, like herself.'

'What is an elephant and a swine and a lover of twilight and a desert monster all at once?' said Seth, helpfully.

'That sort of riddle, but not only that sort,' said Miss Mouffet.

'And what is the true name of Cerura Vinula?' asked Seth, watching with fascination as the wings dried into the most beautiful floating silver, spangled with gold and smoky grey, and the damp body puffed itself out into soft grey fur.

'He is the Puss Moth, as you can see, and his family are the Notodonta, from νῶτος *(nōtos)* the back, and ὀδόντος *(odontos)* tooth—as you see, he has sharp points on his upper wings. He too is a kind of mimic dragon, at rest, though soft and delicate.

'But now, evening is approaching, and the greatest of the Moths, the Sphinx, whose larva was Manduca, the hungry one, will be stirring, and ready to sail beyond-the-wall. I might ask him to bear you with him, for he goes into her Presence. But the journey is fearful, and the place where She is is not for the faint-hearted. For you must go into the Shadows and beyond, and few return from there.'

'Will she help me?'

'She helps all of us, though some of us do not recognise her help for what it is.'

'Will she restore me to my former shape?'

'She will change you, for that is her work. It may be that the change will be a restoration.'

'I will go,' said Seth. 'Take me to the Moth.'

When he first saw the great Sphinx, he thought it beautiful, and restful, for its wings were dappled with rich shades, umber and charcoal, dark rose and silver, beautifully veined. It had long feathery antennae, gently moving in the darkening air, and its voice was soft and dreamy. Miss Mouffet stood before it, and asked it if it would carry this metamorphosed Human into Her kingdom and it answered, in soft syllables, 'If that is what he wishes, I am willing.'

'Let him see his saddle,' said Miss Mouffet, who seemed taller and darker and straighter of a sudden, and her silvery cape more mysterious and moony.

And the great Moth spread its wings—its underwings were moon-gold, fringed with soot—and there, on its back, spun in its very hair, was a staring mask, which could be read as a jackal, or a demon, or a human death head, with cavities of bone that had once held eyes. And Seth had a moment of terror, to think of riding into the dark on the back of a death's head, and thought even, 'Things are indeed not what they seem, and perhaps Miss Mouffet is a witch and perhaps Madame Sphinx is simply terrible and devouring.'

'What is *this* Moth's true name?' he asked, knowing the answer in his soul.

'It is the Death's-head Hawk, Sphinx Acherontia Atropos,' said Miss Mouffet. 'And Acheron is the River of Pain in the Underworld, where you must go, and Atropos is the Fate who snips the thread of life with her terrible shears, but fear nothing, and answer the Fairy's Question, and you will come out of it well. Hold tight to the Sphinx, no matter what forms flow past you, and remember, things are not what they seem, and the death's head is not Atropos's *face,* but a soft nest where you may lie in safety, if you dare.'

So Seth climbed up on to the great back—from where he could no longer see the deathly sockets, for they were soft brown pillows—and said goodbye to Miss Mouffet.

'You said nothing about a question.'

'I said She was the source of riddles, but also of answers,' said Miss Mouffet. 'And if you do not fear, and remember things are not what they seem, you will very likely find the answer—'

'And if I don't find it?' asked Seth.

Miss Mouffet's reply was lost in the whirring of the great wings, as the Moth rose from the earth, with steady beats, and went swiftly out, over the wall, into the dark beyond.

The journey was full of terrors and delights, which you may imagine for yourself. Sometimes the moon was obscured by great hooked leathery wings, and sometimes the earth shone silver and peaceful beneath. They flew on, and on, over oceans and cities, rivers and forests, and then began a long, slow descent in a ravine between rocks that went on, and on, so deep, that above them the stars appeared to vanish. And as the sky and the moon and the stars vanished, another world was revealed by another light, a black world washed by flickering silvery fires, and shot with rainbow colours whose source he could not see. And finally the Moth alighted on what seemed to be the steps of a temple cut in a rock face, surrounded by a thick grove of silent, watching black trees. On the step of the temple was a much smaller Hawk Moth, or Sphinx, grass-green in colour, with a gold underwing, and a look of earthly leaves in that dark place.

'This is a relative of mine,' whispered Acherontia Atropos. 'Her name is Proserpinus Proserpina, and she and her family wait constantly upon the Lady. She will take you to the Cave, through the Garden, if you wish to go.'

So Seth dismounted, and followed the small flying green moth. Inside the Temple gates was a closed and dreaming garden, where everything was asleep. Lawns of closed daisies lay in that strange even light surrounded by trellises of closed columbine where sleeping birds nested, and drowsy trees under which slept curled-up snakes, and lambs with their noses between their hooves, and many other creatures, all still and calmly waiting. Only the moths moved, silver wings, soft brown wings, chalky wings, visiting the flowers, stirring the quiet air with noiseless plumes.

In the end they came to a cavern, out of which the light seemed to be flooding, now white, now broken into many colours. Moths danced before the light, and behind the moths was a thick veil of living silk threads, moving busily, about and about. And over the cavern was written, 'I am all that hath been, and shall be, and my veil hath no mortal yet uncovered.' And Proserpinus Proserpina danced before the golden silk which seemed to spin out of the light inside. And inside stood a Figure who held a high staff, or spindle, and who could not be seen because of all the living stuff She spun into the light. But Seth thought he saw a face of great beauty, illuminated with gold, and then he thought he saw a lion, hot and ruddy with snarling lip and bloody teeth. And he fell to the earth, and said, 'I beg you to help me. I have come all the way to beg for help.'

A small dusky brown moth, with what appeared to be hieroglyphic scribbles on its draggled forewing, said, 'I am Noctua Caradrina Morpheus, and I serve the maker of dreams. You are commanded to lie down before the threshold and sleep in the dust, and take what dreams may come to you, good or ill.'

And Seth said, 'Sleep will be very welcome. I already feel drowsy. I should like to sleep here, even on the bare earth.'

So he lay down in the dust, at the sill of the Fairy's Cave, and Caradrina Morpheus flew heavily to and fro over his eyelids, dusting them with a brown, sooty dust, and he fell into a deep sleep. He dreamed of kind hands touching his brow, and of hot, bloody breath in his ears, and he heard a voice crying, 'Fear no more,' and another saying, 'I care for nothing, all must go,' and he saw in his dream everything that was, like a great river hurrying to the lip of a huge fall, and going over, in one great rush of mingled matter, liquids and solids, blood and fur and feather and leaf and stone, and he awoke with a terrible cry, and the even light was as it had been.

And then the Figure behind the veil addressed him directly in a low voice, neither male nor female, which asked him who he was, and what he desired.

So he explained, and asked for help for himself and his comrades.

And the voice said, 'Before you can be helped, you must answer my question.'

And Seth said, 'I will try. I can do no more.'

'My question is: What is my name?'

And many names murmured together in his mind, names of fairies and goddesses, and monsters too, like the sound of waters in his ear. And he could not choose. So he was dumb.

'You must speak, Seth. You must name me.'

'How can I name you, who have more names than all the creatures, when they have so many each, and Elpenor is Elephant, Hawk, Pig, Twilight Lover and Sphinx and he is only one tiny rosy moth? How can I name you, when you are hidden behind a veil, and you spin your own hiding-place, and make your own light? What would any name I choose be, to you? I cannot name you, and yet I believe you will help me, for Mistress Mouffet said you would, if you wished to, and I do believe, I do believe you are kind—'

And at that all the moths danced furiously and the light inside the silk moved with laughter, and the voice said, 'You have solved the riddle most excellently, for I am indeed kind, and that is one of my names, one of the best of them. I am known as Dame Kind in many places, and you have answered my riddle by trusting me. So I will help you—I will send you back to Dame Cottitoe Pan Demos's garden and I will send Caradrina Morpheus with you, who can creep into the palace and the garden and with his magic dust cast everyone into a deep sleep. And some of them will see sweet things and some of them will see terrors, for although Caradrina Morpheus appears to be an insignificant, dingy creature, he has another name, and another aspect, for he too is not what he seems, and is also Phobetor, the Terrifier. He is ally enough for you, although his power over

Dame Cottitoe cannot last long, for she has great strength of will, and will snap his spell even within her dark dreams. So you must hurry to rescue the enchanted creatures, which you will do by touching them with this insignificant little herb, whose name is Moly. And you may restore yourself, on your return, by the same means. Here, as you may have noticed, you have many forms and many sizes, for you are what you are as reflected in the pupil of my Eye, which you cannot see, for it is behind the veil and shrinks and grows huge like a dark moon, like the pupil of a great cat. And what I see and what my Eye reflects is your outward case, containing what you may become, like Atropos's pupa, which is named for a carved doll, or a small girl child, ready to grow. I hold you small in my gaze, Seth, and you may grow in it, or shrink in it, or vanish, if I blink. You may see my pupil, or my puppet, as you choose well or ill. Everything is single and double. Things are not what they seem.'

And then the person behind the veils laughed briefly and gave a little sigh, and must have blinked, for Seth was able to turn his own gaze away, and there was soft, humming Atropos, waiting to bear him back, with Caradrina Morpheus flittering beside them.

And it all fell out as Kind had predicted. They waited by the wall for the evening shadow, and then Morpheus fluttered away, like a blown leaf across the lawn, and over the threshold into the large *salon,* where he spread his wings, and became a monstrous creature, the size of a great eagle, and shook his wings and filled the room with a sifting cloud of dark brown dust. And the goat and the heifer and the spaniel stood like blocks of ice or marble where they were, and Dame Cottitoe stretched out her silver crook to strike at the monster, and sneezed on the dust, like an old woman taking too much snuff, and was frozen there. And Seth came in then, through a side door, and hurried to the Sties and released his comrades, who looked around and blinked and nearly killed him in their excitement for he had forgotten to restore his own shape. So he did this, appearing amongst them as if by magic, that is to say, *by magic,* to their great pleasure and amazement.

And as they hurried away from the palace to begin a new adventure, Seth heard a buzzing in his ear, and there, floating on the end of a silver rope, no bigger than his little finger, was the long thin black figure of Mistress Mouffet, borne up by her grey silk cloak like wings, with her spectacles gleaming with pleasure. And Seth thanked her, and hurried on, for he needed to be miles away before the garden resounded to the wrath of Dame Cottitoe Pan Demos.

William was much surprised by Miss Crompton's flight of imagination. It made him uneasy, in ways he could not quite analyse, and at the same time his own imagination could not quite see her *writing* this story. She had always seemed dry, and this tale, however playful, was throbbing with some sort of emotion. He waited a day or two before giving it back to her; during this time, she appeared to be avoiding him. Finally he took his courage in his hands, along with her boldly written pages, and waylaid her in the morning-room.

'I have been wanting to return your work to you. I am full of surprise and admiration. It is all very lively and vivid. Really very— full of surprises.'

'Ah,' she said. And then, 'I am afraid I got rather *carried away.* Something that rarely happens to me, or never. I became intrigued by the caterpillars—do you remember little Amy bringing in the Large Elephant Hawk Moth and saying she thought it was some kind of lizard? And I thought that the thing was a kind of *walking figure of speech*—and began to look up the etymologies—and found it was all running away from me. It was as though I was dragged along willy-nilly—by the *language,* you know—through Sphinx and Morpheus and Thomas Mouffet—I suppose my Hermes was Linnaeus—who does not appear.'

'It is all extremely ingenious, certainly.'

'I am afraid,' said Miss Crompton carefully, 'that it is too didactic. That there is too much *message*. Did you find that there was too much message?'

'I don't think that is true, no. The impression I got from it was one of thickening *mystery*, like the riddle of the Sphinx herself, a most portentous person. I think childish readers will find both instruction and delight in it.'

'Ah,' said Miss Crompton. Then, 'I had meant to write a fabulous Tale, not an allegory, it is true.'

'I wondered if Dame Cottitoe was the Church, at one point. Bishops, you know, with crooks. There have been very pretty religious allegories using butterflies, since Psyche is the Soul and the Greek name for butterflies—'

'I had no such grand aims, I assure you. My message was linked to my title.'

' "Things Are Not What They Seem," ' said William. 'Well, that is certain at least. That is a good lesson. You could have included the mimicry of poisonous butterflies by harmless ones, observed by Bates—'

'I could indeed. But the work was already too long for what it was. I am glad to have it back.'

'I think you should write much more in that vein. Your imagination is most fertile.'

'Thank you,' said Miss Crompton, with an inappropriate final sharpness.

In the Spring of 1863 Eugenia was brought to bed with Meg and Arabella, two soft, pale little creatures, as like as two white peas in a pod. In the Summer, with scientific precision, William checked and elaborated his observations of the ant colonies, managing to observe the mating of the *sanguinea* this year, as well as that of the Wood Ants, which gave rise to the experiment which provided his *coup de théâtre*. He introduced into the glass nest of Wood Ants in the schoolroom two or three *sanguinea* Queens, presumably newly fertilised, which he had collected after their nuptial flight.

What follows is a tale of patience and subterfuge, determination and racial power. The small Queen waited patiently outside the Nest, offering no resistance to workers of the Colony who attacked her, but bowing her head submissively and retiring from combat, returning only when the guardians of the city had gone about their business. Little by little she made her way along the narrow tunnels towards the centre of the Nest. Once or twice she was challenged and crouched back, like a rabbit before an oncoming hound. Once, a more agitated, or wiser defender of the city made a determined attack on her, grasping and biting, attempting to bring her sting to bear on the young Princess's new ruddy armour. At this the young intruder roused herself, and fought back, seizing the head of her attacker, and severing it neatly with her jaws. What she did then was truly amazing, considering that she had barely emerged from the shelter of her cocoon and hardly had sight of other ants, friend or enemy. She gathered up the sad remains of her gallant opponent, and crept on her way, always inwards, bearing the dead body before her. This must so have confused the inhabitants of the nest—must so effectively have masked her strangeness, her foreign odour, that this Medea was able to insinuate herself into a crevice adjoining the very bedchamber of the Queens of the Glass Nest themselves. There she lay, with the enemy corpse across her door, motionless and watching. Hungry too, we fear—we did not observe her to feed during this time. And then one day she began to burrow again, obeying some inner informant as to what was beyond the thin wall of soil she was destroying, until finally she burst into the chamber of the Rulers, where their slaves were licking their large bodies, and carrying away their eggs to the nursery. The Red Queen looked about her, and advanced to the attack. The black Queens were swollen with eggs and sweltering in luxury in their harem. They did not expect to have to fight, and did not retaliate with any fury concomitant to the power put into the assault of the aggressor, who was soon straddling one unfortunate and cutting off her head with one exact movement of her mandibles. There was some confused agitation amongst the nurserymaids and the ladies' maids, but no one confronted the regicide, who lay exhausted for a time, without relaxing her deadly hold on her adversary.

And for many days more, she did not relax her hold. She began to move more and more freely about the bedchamber, but always riding, as it were, upon the dead husk of her rival, as though she were a ghost, or a possessing demon, animating a puppet-queen. And then she laid her own first eggs, which were slavishly seized upon, and carried away to the cradle by the Wood Ant slaves, quite as though this cuckoo, this impostor, were a true heir to the slain. The eggs differ considerably in appearance from her rivals', but this appears to make no difference to the nurses, who 'recognise' them by whatever traces of the scent of the poor dead mother still cling to her murderer. And the red children will spring up amongst the black, and for a time they will work together—and who knows, they will come to outnumber the Wood Ants, and the palace may change shape, and the colony die out in its present form. Or maybe the line will fail, and the Glass Nest will return to its previous rulers? We shall watch, year by year, season by season, for the Kingdom underground to give up its secret history—

In the early days of that Autumn, as the activity in the nest died down, the book was brought to its end, and the pages, William's science, William's brooding, Miss Crompton's exact demonstrative drawings, all neatly heaped together, and copied in Miss Crompton's firm handwriting. William wrote to a friend in the British Museum asking casually about publishing houses for a possible future project, and Miss Crompton packed up the manuscript and went to the nearest market town with it, on the pretext of looking for new winter boots.

'For I do not trust the village postmistress not to tell *everyone* that such and such a fat packet has gone off—to where it has gone—and we do not wish to attract attention to what may be a completely unfruitful endeavour, do we? When the book is handsomely bound, and ready for review, *then* we must be open. But that time is not come.'

'I had thought we were to include some of your stories in the text. As it is, we have a few illustrative verses—Clare and Wordsworth and Milton and so on—but none of your fables.'

'I was a little discouraged by the nature and *length* of "Things Are Not What They Seem". And then I gathered myself, and thought I would try to put together a *collection* of such tales. I should dearly love to have an income of my own. Is that a shocking thing to say? I cannot tell you how dearly.'

'I cannot help wishing—for your sake—you had taken up the pen a little earlier.'

'Oh, I waited for my Muse. Our ants, you know, were my muses. They inspired me.'

When the letter from Mr Smith came, the time did not still seem quite ripe for explaining to the Alabasters that he had turned author. Matty Crompton brought the letter to him in his workroom, where he was mounting a very *fiddly* birdskin from Mexico. He had never seen her so full of life—her sallow cheeks were hot, and her breath uneven. He realised she had been watching the postman come and go, like a hawk, for weeks. She stood in the doorway, her fists clenched in her skirts, all tense muscles and angles, whilst he read the letter, at first to himself, and then, in a half-whisper, aloud.

Dear Mr Adamson,
   You are to be heartily congratulated upon your ingenious Natural History, which is just the kind of book of which the world of letters, at

present, cannot have enough. It has everything that could be desired—facts in abundance, useful reflections, drama, humour, and fun. We are very happy you have chosen our house as its publishers and hope we may come to a happy arrangement for what will, I am quite sure, be a most fruitful partnership.

Matty Crompton let out a great sigh, and leaned weakly against the doorpost.

'I knew it. From the start, I knew it. But I was so *afraid*—'

'I can hardly believe—'

'You must not be over-sanguine. I have *no idea* of the profit from a successful book—'

'Nor I. Nor I.' He paused. 'I hardly like to mention it to Sir Harald. He is in a very bad way with his own project. He has torn up several sheafs of writing, only yesterday. I feel I have not given him the support he needs—'

'I understand—'

'Perhaps, after all, it is not certain enough yet to be revealed? Perhaps we should keep our own counsel a little longer? We have done so well—so far—'

'I am quite happy to go on as we are. The shock—the surprise, I should say—will be the more complete when we come to reveal what has been in the making—'

There was also, though William could not mention this, the embarrassment, in Alabaster company, of his latest contretemps with Edgar. For he had noticed—it had impinged very slowly, too slowly, on his preoccupied consciousness—that his little beetle-sprite, Amy, was no longer trotting along the corridors with her buckets, no longer creeping out into the paddock on her day off. In fact, he slowly came to see, Amy was no longer there at all. He had asked Miss Crompton if she knew where Amy was, and Miss Crompton replied tersely that she believed Amy had been dismissed. William had not liked to investigate further, but casual questioning of Tom, the gardener's boy, had produced a sudden outburst, choked off, equally suddenly, by caution.

'Amy's in the workhouse, with a baby, Sir, or will be any day, and she no more than a baby herself. And *without a character,* Sir— what will she do, I don't know, I can't tell, poor little creature—'

Something in William boiled over, remembering Edgar in the scullery, remembering Amy's submissive droop of the spine. He went out, without reflection, to the stableyard, where Edgar was saddling Ivanhoe.

'I wish to say something to you.'

'What then?' without even turning his head.

'I hope this about poor Amy is nothing to do with you.'

'I know nothing, and care nothing, about "poor Amy".'

'I think you are lying. The poor girl is in trouble, and you are the cause.'

'You jump very early to conclusions. And in any case, I do not see what business it is of yours.'

Edgar let go of the girth he had been steadily tightening round Ivanhoe's belly, straightened himself, and looked at William with a very slight smile on his pale face.

'What *is* your interest in the matter?' he said slowly and deliberately.

'Common humanity. She is only a child. And one I like, one I care for, one whose childhood has been drudgery—'

'Ah. A Socialist. Who "cares for" little drudges. I could ask, where has your "care" led you? No one looking at the two of us would be in doubt which of us had spent more time with the little woman. Would he? Think about what people would make of your concern. Think about that.'

'That is ridiculous. You know it is.'

'And I answer the same, your accusations are ridiculous. The girl has not complained, and you cannot do anything to disprove what I *state*.'

'Why can I not? I can find Amy and ask her—'

'That would do no good, I assure you. And you should think what Eugenia might think. Of what I might choose to say to Eugenia.'

Edgar looked so pleased with himself that William was momentarily confused, and could feel the blood banging in his head.

'I could bang you against the wall,' said William. 'But that would not help Amy. She should be provided for.'

'And you should let those who are able to do that,' said Edgar, '—who do not include *you*—take care of that as they see fit. My mother will send some sort of present. It is her place. You yourself have found us generous enough, I trust.'

'I shall see that something is done.'

'No, *I* shall. The girl was in *our* service and unless you want to brandish your *care* for her in Eugenia's face—'

He turned back to his horse, led him out, and mounted.

'Good day, brother-in-law,' said Edgar, and dug his heels into Ivanhoe, who gave a startled bound and trotted away.

He could not bring himself to discuss Amy with any of the women, neither with Lady Alabaster, nor with Eugenia, nor with Matty Crompton. Edgar had aroused in him some disproportionate and inhibiting male shame at his own powerlessness and impotence. He thought of collecting what pitiful sum he might collect and asking Tom to give it to May, and then thought of the uselessness of such a sum, of the misconstructions that might be put on his action, and did nothing. Here and there in Brazil, it might well be, were pale-eyed dark-skinned infants with his blood in their veins, to whose support he did not contribute, who knew nothing of him. Who was he to judge so righteously? It *was not his place* to care for Amy, Edgar was right about that. And so he wavered, and did nothing, whilst Amy's biological time, presumably, moved sweetly or painfully along its inevitable track.

In the Winter of 1861 and 1862 Edgar had spent much of his time riding to hounds, or out with a gun, and the family indoors had been even more sedentary and female than in the Summer. In this Winter of 1863, whilst the Ant History was going through the press, Robin Swinnerton asked William rather diffidently if he cared to hunt, for he had a horse that needed the exercise, and could mount him. No Alabaster had proposed this, or supposed William might be interested, and perhaps other circumstances, tact or delicacy towards the family—his family—might have led him to decline Robin's offer. But he was angry with Edgar, and full of nervous energy over his book and its progress. He did not want to stay still in the house. So he accepted, and rode out once or twice on Robin's mare, Beauty, who jumped neatly, like a cat, but was not the fastest horse in the field. He was almost happy, going out across crisp English fields in the grey morning, smelling the polished leather, and the warm mane and glossy neck of Beauty, and beyond these animal smells, the whole Autumn and stubble and bracken, a whiff of woodsmoke, a sharpness of crushed hawthorn leaves that suddenly and surprisingly, as Beauty pricked her ears and rose in a rush of air and a suck of mud beneath her feet, reminded him of Matty Crompton's secret smell, her sharp armpits, the acrid touch amongst lavender and lemon.

Hounds met one day outside the Bay Tree Inn, in a neighbouring village. Edgar and Lionel rode off immediately after the Master, in the place that was usually theirs. They did not acknowledge William's presence at the Meets, as though some rule of minimal courtesy, which obtained in Bredely Hall, did not need to be kept in the outer world. They did acknowledge Robin, when he was not with William, and this led William to hold back, as the Hunt followers pressed forward, and to set off in the rear. On that day the field spread out quickly and over a distance: William could hear the horn vanishing, and the faint echo of galloping whilst he himself was still negotiating a quiet, rutted lane between high hedges. It was here that a Bredely stable lad, whom he knew only by sight, caught up with him, riding a stolid cob, and said, 'Mr Adamson, Sir. You are asked to come back to Miss Eugenia, please.'

'Is she ill? Is anything wrong?'

'I couldn't say, Sir. I don't think it can be anything bad or them as gave me the message'd've said, but that was all. You are asked to come back to Miss Eugenia.'

William was irritated. He turned back, listening to the horn and the hounds baying, and set off at a good trot—Eugenia *never* commanded his presence, so the matter must be urgent. The hedges slipped by, he galloped peaceably across a few fields and turned in at the stable gates. The ostler took his bridle and William hurried into the house. No one was around. On the stairs, he met Eugenia's maid.

'Is my wife well?'

'I think so, Sir.'

'Where is she?'

'In her room, Sir, I think,' said the young woman, unsmiling. 'I brushed her hair, took away her breakfast, and she told me she was not to be disturbed until after dinner. But that is where she is, I believe.'

There was something odd about the girl's manner. Something furtive, apprehensive, and also excited. She lowered her eyes demurely and went on down the stairs.

William went up, and knocked at Eugenia's door. There was no reply. He listened, his ear to the wood. There was movement inside, and, he could sense, a listening watchfulness which became still, reflecting his own. He tried the door, which was locked. He listened again, and then went quickly round, through his own room and the dressing-room, opening that door without knocking.

Eugenia was lying back in her bed, largely naked, though a kind of wrapper was still clinging to her arms and shoulders. She was much plumper now, but still silky-white, still sweet. As she saw who it was, she blushed, over face and neck and breasts, a great flood of furious rose. Standing next to the bed, clothed in a shirt and nothing else, was a man, a large man with his back to William. Edgar. The room was full of an unmistakable smell, musky, salty, aphrodisiac, terrible.

William did not know what to feel. He felt revulsion, but no primeval awe. He felt a kind of grim laughter rising in him, at Edgar's grotesque appearance, at his own open-mouthed idiocy. He felt humiliated, and simultaneously he felt hugely empowered. Edgar gave a kind of stifled bellow, and for a moment William sensed Edgar's thought, that it would be simplest for Edgar to kill him, now, quickly, before any more could be known or could happen. He was to think later that Edgar *might* have killed him, if he had not been caught with his tail between his legs. For a naked prick which was power two minutes ago, in the presence of the female, is vulnerability and ridicule when three are in the room. He said, tersely, to Edgar, 'Get dressed.'

Edgar fumbled obediently to obey. William became slowly decisive. He said, 'Then go. Go *now*.'

Neither brother nor sister could say, 'It is not what you think.' Neither tried. Edgar's feet would not find the outlets in his breeches. He flapped and swore to himself. William continued to watch Edgar intently and did not look at Eugenia. When Edgar bent to put on his boots, William, feeling sick and trembling with some powerful feeling said, 'Just take those, take them, in your hand, and anything else, and get out of here.'

Edgar opened his mouth, said nothing, and closed it. William nodded at the door. 'I told you to *go*.'

Edgar picked up his boots, and his jacket, and his whip, and went.

William looked at his wife. She was panting. It was no doubt from fear, but it resembled closely enough the pants of pleasure, which he knew.

'You too. Dress yourself. Cover—*cover up.*'

Eugenia turned her head on her pillows towards him. Her lips were parted. Her limp legs were still parted. She lifted a tremulous hand and tried to touch his sleeve. William sprang away as though he had been stung. He repeated, with an edge in his voice, 'Dress yourself.'

She rolled herself very slowly out of the bed, and gathered up her clothes. They were cast down here and there in the room. Stockings on the carpet, drawers on a chair, her corset draped over a stool.

'It is like a whorehouse,' said William, simply telling the truth, and betraying himself into the bargain, which went unnoticed. He remembered, then, thinking he might smutch her, God help him. His sickness increased. She ran around, curved on herself, cradling her breasts in her arms, moaning.

'I can't put this on without Bella—help me.'

'I shan't touch you. Leave it off. Hurry. You are horrible to see.'

She obeyed, and put on a white dress, which hung oddly on her uncompressed flesh. She sat down at the mirror and made one or two automatic passes with the hairbrush. When she saw her own face, a few tears fell between the pretty lashes. She sat, lumpish, in front of her mirror.

'What will you do?'

'I don't know,' William said truthfully. He was looking back, with difficulty. 'I don't want you to think you must lie to me, Eugenia. This—this has been going on all the time, hasn't it? All the time I've been here?'

He could see the lies pass over her face, like clouds over the moon. Then she shuddered, and nodded. 'Yes.'

'How long?' said William.

'Since I was very little. Very little, yes. It began as a game. You cannot possibly understand.'

'No. I cannot.'

'At first it seemed—nothing to do with the rest of my life. It was just something—secret—that *was* you know—like other things you must not do, and do. Like touching yourself, in the dark. You don't understand.'

'No. I don't.'

'And then—and then—when I was going to marry Captain Hunt—he saw—he saw—oh, not so much as *you* have seen—but enough to guess. And it preyed on his mind. It preyed on his mind. I swore then, I would stop it—I *did* stop it—I wanted to be married, and good, and—like other people—and I—I did persuade him—he—was mistaken in me. It was so hard, for he would not say what he feared—he could not speak it out loud—and that was when I saw—how very terrible—it was—I was.

'Only—we could not stop. I do not think—he—' she choked on Edgar's name, 'meant even to stop—he—he is—*strong*—and of course Captain Hunt—someone led him to see—he saw—not *much*—but enough. And he wrote a terrible letter—to—to both of us—and said—oh—' she began to weep rapidly suddenly, 'he could not live with the knowledge even if *we* could. That is what he said. And then he shot himself. In his desk there was a note, to me, saying I would know why he had died, and that he hoped I would be able to be happy.'

William watched her weep.

'But even after that—you went on.'

'Who else could I turn to?'

She went on weeping. William looked back over his life. He said, 'You turned to me. Or made use of me, anyway.' He began to feel very sick indeed. 'All your children, who revert so shockingly to the ancestral type—'

'I don't know, I don't know. I made sure I don't know,' cried

Eugenia, on a new high frantic note. She began to sway to and fro, exaggeratedly, banging her head on the mirror.

William said, 'Make less noise. You cannot wish to attract any more attention.'

There was a long silence. Eugenia moaned, and William stood, paralysed by conflicting furies and indecisions. He said, when he felt he could not protract this unbearable scene a moment longer, 'I shall go now. We will talk again later.'

'What will you do?' asked Eugenia, in a small toneless voice.

'I don't know what I shall do. I shall tell you, when I do know. You may wait for my decision. You need not be afraid I shall kill myself.'

Eugenia wept quietly.

'Or him,' said William. 'I want to be a free man, not a convicted murderer.'

'You are cold,' said Eugenia.

'I am now,' said William, lying at least in part. He retreated into his own room, and locked the door on his side.

He lay down on his own bed, and, to his later surprise, fell immediately into a deep sleep, from which he woke, just as suddenly, and unable for a moment to remember *what* had happened that was terrible, only that something had. And then he remembered, and felt sick, and over-excited, and restless, and could not think what to do. All sorts of things went through his mind. Divorce, flight, a showdown with Edgar, making him promise he would go away and never return. Could he? Would he? Could he himself stay in that house?

Nevertheless, he stood up and changed into his house clothes and went down to dinner, where, apart from the absence of both Edgar and Eugenia, things were as they were every night, with Grace from Harald, bickerings amongst the younger girls, and a kind of ruminative supping noise from Lady Alabaster. The servants brought the dishes, and removed them again, silently, unobtrusively. After dinner card-games were proposed, and William thought of declining, but Matty Crompton said to him on their way through the corridors to the parlour where tea was served, 'O what can ail thee, knight-at-arms,/Alone and palely loitering?'

'Do I look as though something ails me?' asked William, forcing himself to speak lightly.

'You have a brooding look,' said his friend. 'And you are distinctly pale, if you do not mind my observing it.'

'I missed my gallop,' said William. 'I was called back—' He paused, considering for the first time the strangeness of that calling-back. Miss Crompton appeared not to notice. She enlisted his support for a game of Anagrams, with Lady Alabaster and the elder children and Miss Fescue, who was always enlisted to help Lady Alabaster. They arranged themselves around the card-table, in the light of an oil-lamp. They all looked so comfortable, William thought, so innocent, so much at home.

The game consisted of making words out of alphabet cards, prettily decorated with pictures of harlequins, monkeys, columbines and devils with forks. Everyone had nine letters, and could give any complete word they could make secretly to anyone else, who must change at least one letter, and pass it on. The game was not to be left with the letters with demons on, which were, rather at random, some of the awkward letters, like Q and X, and some of those in demand, like E and S. William played with half his mind, pushing on easy words like 'was' and 'his' and 'mine' and accumulating demons. At one point, finding himself with PHXNITCSE, he suddenly woke up, and found himself able to present Matty Crompton with INSECT even though that left him with an X with a demon on it. Miss Crompton, her face heavily shadowed in the lamplight, gave a small snort of laughter at this word, considered it for some time, rearranged the cards, and pushed it back to him. He was about to point out that the rules did

not allow of returning the same word, without adding or subtract-
ing a letter, when he saw *what* she had sent him. There it was, lying
innocently in his hand. INCEST. He shuffled the evidence hastily,
looked up, and met the dark intelligent eyes.

'Things are not what they seem,' said Matty Crompton amiably.
William looked at his cards, and saw that he could make another
word, *and* get rid of the X, and answer her message. So he pushed
his word back, and she gave another snort of laughter, and the game
went on. But now, his eyes met hers, from time to time, and hers
gleamed with knowledge and—yes—excitement. And he did not
know if he was more comforted or alarmed that she knew. How
long had she known? How? What did she think? Her smile was not
commiserating, nor was it prurient, it was somehow satisfied and
amused. The luck of the letters was uncanny. It gave him the
feeling that occasionally comes to most of us, that however we
protest we are moved by chance, and struck by random shocks and
blows, in fact there *is* Design, there is Fate, it has us in its grip.

It was possible, of course, that *she* had somehow shaped his cards.
She liked riddles. He watched the flick of her precise, thin wrists
as she passed PHOENIX on to Elaine, neatly getting rid of the
dangerous X. Did she see him as a dupe, as a poor victim? Had she
always seen him that way? Things were not what they seemed,
indeed.

At the end of the game, he managed to say to her under his
breath, 'I must speak to you.'

'Not now. Later. I will find a time. Later.'

He found it hard to sleep, that night. On the other side of the
locked door was Eugenia. He could not hear her snore, and he did
not hear her move, and once or twice resisted a compulsion to go
in and see if she had killed herself. He thought she would not do
that; it was not in her nature; though of course he knew nothing
about her nature, after this morning. Everything he had thought he

knew was overturned. Or maybe not. He had partly known that he did not know Eugenia. Either she had *no* inner life, he had thought, or it was locked away, inaccessible to him. Something terrible had been done to him. And to her, he thought. He should perhaps wish to kill Edgar. Except that even Edgar was in some ways less simply hateful, in this hellish plight. He was more driven, less complacently, ordinarily brutal and overbearing than he had seemed.

William heard a tap on his outer door, which then opened quietly, to admit a dark figure. It was Miss Crompton, still in her day clothes, which consisted of a long black silk skirt, and a grey poplin shirt. She stood inside his door, and beckoned, without speaking. William got out of bed and wrapped himself in his dressing gown. He followed her silently along the corridor and up another flight of stairs, on to a long landing carpeted serviceably in cord, and through a door into what he saw immediately was her bedroom. She put her candle down on the little dressing-table. The room was narrow, like a high box, with one hard upright chair and a narrow bed with a cast-iron bedhead, and a precisely folded white dimity bedspread. There was a tiny bookcase, in dark oak, and books everywhere there could be, under the chair, sticking out in boxes under the bed, under the dressing-table. On the back of the door were hooks, where there hung the small wardrobe he knew so well. Under the window was a small chest of drawers, on which stood a glass, with a few teazles and poppyheads in it. That was all.

'Please take a chair,' said Miss Crompton. 'I hope you don't think this is too conspiratorial.'

'No,' he said, although he did, in part. He was troubled to be closed away with her, in her private place.

'You wished to talk,' she said, sitting down on the edge of the bed and seeming a little at a loss for how to begin.

'You sent me a word, tonight,' he said. 'And *someone* sent for me to come back to the house, today, when I was not wanted. When I was anything but wanted.'

'*I* didn't send for you,' she said. 'If that is what you are thinking. There are people in a house, you know, who know everything that goes on—the invisible people, and now and then *the house* simply decides that something must happen—I think your message came to you after a series of misunderstandings that at some level were quite deliberate—'

There was another silence. They were very awkward together, now they were on her territory, the little territory she commanded.

'But you know what I saw,' he said.

'Yes. There are people in houses, between the visible inhabitants and the invisible, largely invisible to *both,* who can know a very great deal, or nothing, as they choose. I choose to know about some things, and not to know about others. I have become interested in knowing things that concern you.'

'I have been used. I have been made a fool of.'

'Even if that is so—it is not the most important thing. I want to know—what you feel. I need to know what you will do.'

The oddness of her way of putting it struck him, but he did not remark on it. He answered heavily, as best he could, 'I find that—my most powerful feeling—is that I am free. I ought to feel—shocked, or vengeful, or—or humiliated—and from time to time, I do feel all these things—but mostly, I feel—I can go now, I can leave this house, I can return to my true work—

'I cannot, of course. I have five children and a wife, and no income—though I might seek employment—'

'There was talk of equipping a further Amazon venture—'

'I cannot *now* take one Alabaster penny. *You* must see that, you see everything, I begin to think. I must go away, and soon. And never return. Retribution is not my business. I will—I will ask Edgar for money, for Amy—I do not care how that may appear, I will ensure that Amy has an income for life—and then I will go. And never return. And never return.'

The phrase was exciting him. He said, 'You are all I shall miss here. I have never felt—not in my heart of hearts—any warmth to all those—white children—'

'This may be of the moment.'

'No, no. I can go. I shall go. My book—our book—will provide a little—more can be earned.'

'I have sold my Fairytales,' said Matty Crompton.

'I cannot take—you were not offering—I am sorry—'

'I have taken certain steps,' said Miss Crompton, in a tense voice. 'Entirely subject to your approval. I—I have a Banker's Draft from Mr George Smith that should be more than sufficient—and a letter from Mr Stevens offering to negotiate the sales of specimens as before—and a letter from a Captain Papagay, who sails from Liverpool for Rio in a month's time. He has two berths free.'

'You are truly a good Fairy,' said William with an edge of rebellion. 'You wave your wand, and I have everything I desire before I can think of desiring it.'

'I watch, and contrive, and write letters, and consider your nature,' said Matty Crompton. 'And you *do* desire it. You have just said so.'

'*Two* berths—' said William.

'I shall come with you,' said Miss Crompton. 'You have filled me with a great desire to see all those Paradisal places and I shall not rest until I have seen the great River and felt the air of the Tropics.'

'You cannot do that,' said William. 'Think of the fever, think of the terrible biting creatures, think of the monotonous insufficient food, of the rough men out there, the drunkenness—'

'Yet you wish to return.'

'*I* am not a woman.'

'Ah. And I am.'

'It is *no place* for a woman—'

'Yet there are women there.'

'Yes, but not of your kind.'

'I do not think you know what kind of woman I am.'

She rose, and began to pace, like a prisoner in a cell, in a little room. He was quiet, watching her. She said, 'You do not know that I am a woman. Why should that not continue as it is? You have *never seen me.*'

Her voice had a new harshness, a new note. She said, 'You have no idea who I am. You have no idea even how old I am. Have you? You think I may be of an age between thirty and fifty, confess it.'

'And if you know so precisely what I think, it is because you must have meant me to think it.'

What she said was nevertheless true. He had no idea, and that was what he had thought. She paced on. William said, 'Tell me then, since you invite the question, how old are you?'

'I am twenty-seven,' said Matty Crompton. 'I have only one life, and twenty-seven years of it are past, and I intend to begin living.'

'But not in the rainforest, not in the Amazons. There is Esmeralda, which looks like Paradise on Earth, until you see that all the houses are closed, that all the life is vegetable, not animal, that a poor man's face is crusted with Mosquitoes, and his food is alive with them, and his hands running blood. The place is in many ways an *Inferno*—'

'But you will go back there.'

'My work is there. And I know how to live that life.'

'I will learn. I am strong. I have not lived softly, contrary to appearances. I am resourceful. You need not heed me, once the voyage is over.'

'It is a daydream.'

'No. It is *what I will do.*'

He hardly recognized the ironic practical Miss Crompton of earlier times. She paced and turned. She swung on her heel, with her hand on her hip.

'Miss Crompton, Matty—'

'My name', she said, 'is Matilda. Up here at night there is no Matty. Only Matilda. *Look at me.*'

And she put up her hands to her head and undid the plaits of her hair over her ears, and shook it out, and came and stood before him. And her face between the dark tresses was sharp and eager and hungry, and he watched how trimly she turned and said, 'I have seen your *wrists*, Matilda. I dreamed about them now and then. You have—remarkable—wrists.'

'I only wanted you to *see me*,' said Matilda, less confidently, once she saw that he had indeed seen her. He saw that her cheekbones were high and sharp, and her mouth was hard, not soft, but full of life. He saw how quick she turned at the waist, and thought quickly of a greyhound. He said, 'I don't think that was all you wanted.'

'I want you to be happy,' said Matilda, fiercely.

William stood up, and looked her in the eye, and put his hands on her waist.

'I will be,' he said. 'I will be.'

He pulled her against him, the unyielding Matty Crompton, the new hungry Matilda.

'Shall I stay here?' he said. 'Or shall I go back, now?'

'I should like you to stay,' said Matilda. 'Though it is not comfortable here.'

'If we are to travel together, you will find we look back on this as a Paradise of comfort.'

And in a way, in many ways, they did.

Two more pictures. William went to see Eugenia to communicate to her his decisions. She had put it about that she was ill, and had her meals brought to her in her room, which was not unusual enough to cause any comment in the household. He sent her a message by her maid, saying that he wished to discuss certain arrangements with her. When he came in, he saw that she had paid great attention to her toilette. She was dressed in silvery-grey silk, with bright blue ribbons, and had a posy of rosebuds at her breast.

She looked older; the calm glaze had gone from her look, and was replaced with a new softness, a new overt sensuousness.

'So you have decided,' she said. 'What is to be my fate?'

'I must confess I am more interested in my own. I have decided to leave you. I shall set out on an expedition to explore the further reaches of the Rio Negro. I have no intention of returning to this house.'

'I suppose you will wish me to write a cheque for your passage, for your expenses and so on.'

'No. I have written a book. The money from that will suffice.'

'And—shall you speak to anyone—shall you—tell?'

'Who can I tell, Eugenia, whom I should not destroy in the telling? You must live with yourself, that is all I can say, you must live with yourself as you can.'

'I *know* it was bad,' said Eugenia. 'I know it was bad, but you must understand it didn't *feel* bad—it grew little by little, out of perfectly innocent, natural, *playful* things—which no one thought wrong—I have never been able to speak to any other living soul of it, you must forgive me for speaking to you—I can see I have made you angry, though I tried to make you love me—if I could have spoken to anyone, I might have been brought to see how wrong it was. But—*he* thought it wasn't—he said—people like making rules and others like breaking them—he made me believe it was all perfectly *natural* and so it was, it was *natural,* nothing in us rose up and said—it was—*un*natural.'

'Breeders know', said William curtly, 'that even first-cousin marriages produce inherited defects—increase the likelihood—'

Eugenia cast down her lashes. 'That is a cruel thing to say.'

She was clasping her own hands nervously in her lap. She had the curtains half-drawn against the sunlight and to hide the shadows of tearstains. She was lovely, and complacent, and amoral, and he sensed that she was now waiting for him to go, so that she could

resume her self-nurture and self-communion. At some level, what
had happened was *inconvenient* to Eugenia, and he was about to
remove the inconvenience, himself. He said, 'Morpho Eugenia.
You are very lovely—'

'It has not done me good,' said Eugenia, 'to look pretty, to be
admired. I would like to be different.'

But William could not take that seriously, as he watched her
compose her mouth, and open her wide eyes, and look hopefully
up at him.

'Goodbye, Eugenia. I shall not come back.'

'You never know,' she replied vaguely, her attention already
sliding away from him, with a pretty little sigh of relief.

And the second picture is very different. Imagine the strong little
ship, *Calypso*, rushing through the mid-Atlantic night, as far from
land as she will be at any point on this voyage. The sky is a
profound blue-black, spattered with the flowing, spangled river of
the Milky Way, glittering and slippery with suns and moons and
worlds, greater and smaller, like spattered seed. The sea is a deep
blue-black, ribbed with green, crested as it turns, with silver spray
and crinkled crests of airy salt water. It too is swarming, with
phosphorescent animalcules, the Medusae, swimming with tiny
hairs, presenting a kind of reverse image of the lavish star-soup.
William and Matilda are standing on deck, leaning over the rails,
watching the ship's nose plunge down and on. She is wearing a
crimson shawl, and a striped scarf in her hair, and the wind stirs her
skirts round her ankles. William's brown hand grips her brown
wrist on the rail. They breathe salt air, and hope, and their blood
swims with the excitement of the future, and this is a good place
to leave them, on the crest of a wave, between the ordered green
fields and hedgerows, and the coiling, striving mass of forest along
the Amazon shore.

Captain Arturo Papagay, whose first command this is, comes

past, and smiles his rich, mixed smile, white teeth in a golden-brown face, laughing dark eyes. He has brought Mr Adamson a curiosity. It is a butterfly, found by a midshipman in the rigging. It is amber-gold, with dusky borders to its wings, which are a little dishevelled, even tattered. It is the Monarch, says William, excited, Danaus Plexippus, which is known to migrate great distances along the American coast. They are strong fliers, he tells Matilda, but the winds can carry them hundreds of miles out to sea. Matilda observes to William and Captain Papagay that the wings are still dusty with life. 'It fills me with emotion,' she says. 'I do not know whether it is more fear, or more hope. It is so fragile, and so easily crushed, and nowhere in reach of where it was going. And yet it is still alive, and bright, and so surprising, rightly seen.' 'That is the main thing,' says Captain Papagay. 'To be alive. As long as you are alive, everything is surprising, rightly seen.' And the three of them look out with renewed interest at the points of light in the dark around them.

The Conjugial Angel

I

Lilias Papagay was of imagination all compact. In her profession this was a suspect, if necessary, quality, and had to be watched, had to be curbed. Sophy Sheekhy, who saw with her eyes, and heard in her ears, the unearthly visitants, was apparently more phlegmatic and matter-of-fact. They made a good pair for this reason, as Mrs Papagay had intuited they might, when her next-door neighbour, Mrs Pope, had flown into strong hysterics on hearing her new nursery-governess talking to Cousin Gertrude and her infant son Tobias, both drowned many years ago. They were sitting at the nursery table, Sophy Sheekhy said, and their clothes, though perfectly fresh and dry, gave off an odour of salt water. They wanted to know what had become of the grandfather clock that used to stand in the nursery corner. Tobias had liked the way the sun and moon followed each other with smiling faces on its dial. Mrs Pope, who had sold the clock, wanted to hear no more. Mrs Papagay offered asylum to the composed little Miss Sheekhy, who packed up her few belongings and moved in. Mrs Papagay herself had never progressed beyond passive writing— admittedly voluminous—but believed Sophy Sheekhy might work marvels. She did from time to time astonish and amaze, though not frequently. But this parsimony itself was a guarantee of authenticity.

On one late, stormy afternoon in 1875 they were proceeding along the Front, in Margate, to take part in a séance in Mrs Jesse's parlour. Lilias Papagay, a few steps ahead, wore wine-dark silk with a flounced train and a hat heavy with darkly gleaming plumage, jet-black, emerald-shot, iridescent dragonfly blue on ultramarine, plump shoulders of headless wings with jaunty tail-feathers, like the little wings that fluttered on the hat or the heels of Hermes in old pictures. Sophy Sheekhy wore dove-coloured wool with a white collar, and carried a serviceable black umbrella.

The sun was setting on the grey water, a great dusky rose disk, the colour of a new burn-mark, in a bath of ruddy gold light poured between the bars of steely cloud, like firelight from a polished grate.

'Look,' said Lilias Papagay, waving an imperious gloved hand. 'Can't you just see the Angel? Clothed with a cloud and with a rainbow on his head, and his face as it were the sun, and his feet as pillars of fire. And in his hand a little book open.'

She saw his cloudy thews and sinews bestride the sea; she saw his hot red face and his burning feet. She knew she was straining. She desired *so* to see the invisible inhabitants of the sky sail about their business, and the winged air dark with plumes. She knew that that world penetrated and interpenetrated this one, grey solid Margate equally with Stonehenge and Saint Paul's. Sophy Sheekhy observed that it was indeed a spectacular sunset. One of the angel's fiery legs flared and extended, leaving momentary rosy ripples on the dull water. His swollen grey trunk bowed and twisted, wreathed with gold. 'I never tire of looking at sunsets,' said Sophy Sheekhy. She had a pale face like a full moon, a little pitted with craters from a mild attack of pox, and shadowed here and there with freckles. She had a large brow, and a full, colourless mouth, the lips habitually lying restfully together, like the folded hands. Her lashes were long, silky, and almost invisible; her veined ears could be seen in part, under heavy wings of hay-coloured hair. She would have been unsurprised to be told that the sun and moon are constant sizes to the apprehension of the human eye, which confers on them bearable dimensions, roughly the size of a guinea coin. Whereas Mrs

Papagay, with William Blake, would have divined an innumerable company of the Heavenly Host crying, 'Holy, Holy, Holy, is the Lord God Almighty.' Or with Emanuel Swedenborg, who saw great companies of celestial creatures sailing through space like flaming worlds. A gathering of angry gulls was disputing a morsel in mid-air; they rose together, screaming and beating, as Mrs Papagay's angel dislimned and grew molten. His last light cast a momentary flush across Sophy's white face. They quickened their step. Mrs Papagay was never late.

The usual gathering was assembled in Mrs Jesse's parlour. It was not a comfortable room; Mrs Jesse had not the knack of comfort; it was a bit dusty, the polish a bit scratched, the lace curtains a little frayed. There were many books, in glass-fronted cases, and various collections of stones and shells gathering dust in bowls and boxes. A telescope stood in the window, its brass excellently polished, and various other nautical instruments, a sextant, a chronometer, compasses, occupied a cabinet of their own. There was also, bright on crimson velvet, Captain Jesse's *Médaille de Sauvetage en Or,* specially struck for him by the Emperor Napoleon III, and the Silver Medal of the Royal Humane Society, a moony dinner-plate-sized object. Captain Jesse had won both these awards since his retirement to Margate, where he had, no less than three times, in the absence of a regular lifeboat, roused the fishermen, and launched a boat, himself taking the tiller, to rescue ships foundering in gales and high seas. He had saved the entire crew on each occasion, a French ship, an English ship, and a Spanish ship. This was before Mrs Papagay had made his acquaintance, but she never tired of hearing the details of these wholly practical and wholly romantic rescues. She saw it all, she lived it all, the turmoil of the waters with their lashing crests and their howling, dissolute walls, the scream and roar of the gale, the points of stars amongst racing storm-clouds, the pinpricks of lantern lights in the furious dark, the steadfastness of Captain

Jesse, making fast wet ropes with expert hands, clambering here and there on streaming, tilting decks, descending a watery staircase to a bubbling, swirling cabin to rescue the tiny French cabin boy, making the light, semi-conscious body safe in his own lifebelt, although, like too many captains, he was unable to swim. 'Richard does not know what fear is,' Mrs Jesse would say, in her resonant solid voice, and the Captain would nod shyly and murmur that it did seem to have been left out of his makeup, he just did what seemed best at the time without counting the cost, he had no doubt but that fear was useful to the majority of men, but it did seem to have been left out of his makeup, he could claim no credit for it, indeed, true courage was only possible to those who felt fear, but he was like the prince in some fairy story or other, he couldn't remember which, and didn't rightly know what such a thing was, though he supposed he had observed its operations in others, when he stopped to think about it, which he perhaps didn't do often enough, no, he didn't think often enough. Captain Jesse's conversation was copious and indiscriminate, surprising in so statuesque a man of action.

He was standing in front of the chimneypiece, tall and upright with his white hair and full white beard, talking to Mr Hawke, who combined many offices, deacon in the New Jerusalem Church, editor of the *Spiritual Leaflet,* agent for the Seamen's Relief Fund, co-ordinator of the evening meetings. Mr Hawke had nothing hawk-like in his appearance; he was a little round man, an *appley* man, Mrs Papagay thought, with a spherical belly and spherical shining red cheeks, over which waved tufts of tawny hair under a round pink bald cranium. He was in his fifties, she judged, and unmarried. Both he and Captain Jesse were men who kept up a steady flow of talk, without too much listening to the responses of the other. Mr Hawke was a theological connoisseur. He had been a Ritualist, a Methodist, a Quaker, a Baptist, and had now come to rest, permanently or temporarily, in the Church of the New Jerusa-

lem, which had come into being in the spiritual world in the year
1787 when the old order had passed away, and that Spiritual Columbus, Emanuel Swedenborg, had made his voyages through the
various Heavens and Hells of the Universe, which he was shewn
was in the form of a Divine Human, every spiritual and every
material thing corresponding to some part of this infinite Grand
Man.

Captain Jesse and Mr Hawke were both drinking tea. Captain
Jesse was speaking about the cultivation of tea on the mountain
slopes of Ceylon, describing tea as he had drunk it, 'aromatic and
fresh-tasting, Sir, like an infusion of raspberry-leaves here, tea trans-
ported in lead-lined caskets has always a *musty* overlay to its taste
for those who have experienced it where it is grown, out of simple
terra-cotta bowls no bigger than this salt-cellar, it tastes of the *earth*,
Sir, and of the sun, a true nectar.' Mr Hawke was speaking simultaneously of Swedenborg's incessant coffee-drinking, to the noxious
effects of which some less than glorious spirits had ascribed his
visions.

'For coffee, acting on a pure temperament, will they say produce
excitability, sleeplessness, abnormal activity of mind and imagination and fantastic visions—also loquacity. I credit these effects of
coffee, I have observed it to be so. But he is a medical pedant who
would try to pour the *Arcana* or the *Diarium* out of a coffee pot.
Nevertheless a truth may be hidden here. God made the world, and
therefore everything in it, including, I suppose, the coffee-bush and
coffee-bean. If coffee disposes to clear-seeing, I do not see that the
means injures the end. No doubt seers are as regular fabrics as
crystals, and not a drug or berry is omitted from their build, when
it is wanted. We live in a material time, Captain Jesse—apart from
metaphysics, the time is gone by when anything is made out of
nothing. If the visions are good visions, their material origin is also
good, I think. Let the visions criticise the coffee and vice versa.'

'I have known hallucinations to be brought on by green tea,' replied Captain Jesse. 'We had a Lascar seaman who regularly saw demons in the rigging until he was induced by a mate to curtail the quantity he imbibed.'

Mrs Papagay moved towards Mrs Jesse, who was sharing the sofa with Mrs Hearnshaw, and handing out tea in cups garlanded with fat rosebuds and bright forget-me-nots. Mrs Hearnshaw was in deep mourning, all black silk, with a black lace cap on her abundant chestnut hair, and a large ebony locket dangling from a chain of carved jet links on to her rounded bosom. Her skin was creamy and her eyes large and limpid brown, but there were blue-grey hollows round them, and her mouth was both pinched and drooping. She had just buried the fifth little Amy Hearnshaw in seven years—they had had brief lives ranging from three weeks to eleven months, and were survived by little Jacob, a sickly pretty boy of three years. Mr Hearnshaw allowed Mrs Hearnshaw to come to the séances, but would not attend himself. He was headmaster of a small school, and held solid Christian beliefs of a gloomy kind. He believed that his daughters' deaths were tribulations sent by God to test him and punish him for his shortcomings of faith. But he did not go so far as to suggest that there was anything essentially wrong or untoward in the spiritualist activities—angels and spirits thronged the pages of the Old and New Testaments. Mrs Papagay believed that he allowed his wife to come to the séances because otherwise he found the rich violence of her grief intolerable and embarrassing. It was his nature and his profession to repress displays of excessive emotion. If Annie were comforted, his house was calmer. Or so Mrs Papagay, a great weaver of narratives from tenuous threads of looks, words and feelings, supposed he might reason.

Mrs Papagay liked stories. She spun them from bobbins of gossip or observation; she told them to herself at night, or when walking in the streets; she was tempted constantly to step too far in tittle-tattle in order to receive reciprocal nuggets of other lifelines, other chains of cause and effect. When she found herself a widow, without means, she had considered writing stories for a living, but her skills in language were unequal to it, or the movement of the pen in purposeful public writing inhibited her—for whatever reason, what she wrote was stilted, saccharine rubbish, not of interest even to her own eagerness, let alone any anonymous reader's. (The automatic writing was different.) She had married Mr Papagay, a master mariner of mixed racial origin, because, like Othello with Desdemona, he entranced her with tales of his deeds and sufferings in faraway places. He had been drowned ten years ago, in the Antarctic, or thereabout, or so she believed, since the *Calypso* had never been seen since, and nor had any of its crew. She had attended her first séance really in order to find out whether she was or was not a widow, and had been answered, as is so often the case, ambiguously. The medium on that occasion, an amateur, flushed with the recent discovery of her powers, had dictated a message from Arturo Papagay, identifying his black wavy hair, his gold tooth, his cornelian seal-ring, and claiming to tell his dearest darling love that he was at rest, and wished her to be calm and glad as he was that the time was coming when the first heaven and the first earth should pass away, and there would be no more sea, and God should wipe away all tears from their eyes.

Mrs Papagay was not quite sure that this message did emanate from Arturo, whose endearments were briefer and cruder and naughtier, and who would have been quite unable to be complacently happy at rest in a world where there was no more sea. Arturo had to be doing, and the sea drew him like a magnet, its smell, its breath, its shifting, dangerous weight, going down and down. When Mrs Papagay tried the automatic writing on her own for the first time, she received, she thought, indisputable messages from Arturo, then or now, alive or dead, tangled in seaweed or in her memory. Her respectable fingers wrote out imprecations in various languages she knew nothing of, and never sought to have translated, for she knew well enough *approximately* what they were, with their *f*s and *co*ns and *cu*ns, Arturo's little words of fury, Arturo's little words, also, of intense pleasure. She said dreamily, 'O, are you dead or alive, Arturo?' and the reply was 'Naughty-lus tangle-shells sand sand break break breaker c.f.f.c. naughty Lilias, infin che'l mar fu sopra noi richiuso.'

From which she concluded that on the whole he was probably drowned, not without struggle. So she put on mourning, took in two lodgers, tried her hand at a novel, and lived more and more in the passive writing.

Little by little she had made herself part of the community of those who sought to make contact with the spirit world. She was a welcome addition to séances in private houses, for in her presence the unseen visitors always rapped more busily and sent messages both more detailed and more surprising than the vague assurances they were given to. She began to be able to go into trance, an experience somewhat like a fainting-fit, hot, cold, clammy, nauseous and distressing in its lack of control to someone as sharp and orderly as Mrs Papagay. She was aware, from the other end of some cream-coloured, maggot-coloured, reticulated tunnel, of her own boots thrashing the carpet, of her poor throat-strings straining as harsh voices spoke through her. She realized that she had not until now been *quite sure* that the passive writing was not done by some other part of her coherent Self. Through her a good spirit called Pomona and a mischievous and interfering one called Dago spoke alternately. She went into trance less often now she had Sophy Sheekhy as a companion, for Sophy seemed to slip easily into some other world, leaving behind her a creature clay-cold, whose breath barely misted a silver spoon. She reported strange visions, and strange sayings, she was able to tell, with astonishing exactness, where lost objects and lost relations were to be found. Mrs Papagay was convinced that Sophy could make the spirits materialise if she chose, like the famous Florence Cook and her control Katie King. Sophy, who was slow to evince curiosity, and slow to see her own interests, said, 'Why?' and added that she could not imagine why the dead should want to have their bodies back, it was so much better to be as they were. They didn't exist to perform circus tricks, said Sophy Sheekhy. That would *hurt* them. Mrs Papagay was too intelligent not to take her point.

They had now insensibly, with a certain small cunning, slipped from the world of the purely amateur and private experiment to the delicately arranged world of the paid mediums. Nothing vulgar— 'gifts' from the gentlemen who arranged these matters, fees for consultations ('It is my *right*, Mrs Papagay, if I call upon your skills as I might upon those of a minister of the Church, a great musician, or a healer. We must all of us have the wherewithal to keep body and soul together, until the blessed moment when we step over the bourne to join those Others, Beyond').

Mrs Papagay was an intelligent, questioning kind of woman, the kind who, in an earlier age, would have been a theologically minded nun, and in a later one would have had a university training in philosophy or psychology or medicine. She asked herself from time to time large questions, such as *why* had the Dead just now, just recently, with such persistence, chosen to try to break back into the land of the living with raps, taps, messages, emanations, materialisations, spirit-flowers and travelling bookshelves? She did not know much history, though she had read all the novels of Walter Scott, but she imagined that there must once have been a time when they went further away, and stayed there. In the days of the Disciples and of the Prophets before them, it was true, the lovely angels had sailed in and out of people's lives, bringing with them bright soft lights, heavenly music, and a rush of mysterious importance. The Church Fathers too had seen them and some had seen unquiet spirits. Hamlet's father had walked and the sheeted dead had squeaked and gibbered in the streets of Rome—there had always been, Mrs Papagay was quite sure, odd little local apparitions in highways and byways and old dwellings, things that went bump, or gave off disagreeable smells or enchanting twangs, things that came and stared gruesomely or made you feel chilled to the bone and mournful, the boggart, the bogle, the tenacious presence of some cross dead farmer or young woman in terrible pain.

But these recent armies of the night, uncles and aunts, poets and painters, innocent infants and uproarious drowned sailors, who stood it seemed behind every chair and were imprisoned in every cupboard, who congregated thickly in the garden and trooped together up the stairs, where had they suddenly come from, what did they require? On the walls of old churches, behind the altar in the Sistine Chapel, they could be seen in their old accustomed places sitting in serried ranks in the gold-crowned heavenly congregation, moaning and writhing in the arms of black goat-foots with hot red tongues on their way down to the nether pit. Were they displaced now by new knowledge? The stars rushed and shone in vacant spaces, they were suns which could engulf this little world in fire, like an orange-pip on coals. Below the pit were the green fields of New Zealand and the red deserts of Australia. Mrs Papagay thought, we *know* that now, we imagine that it is so, up and down are losing their grip on us. And yet we cannot bear the next thought, that we become nothing, like grasshoppers and beef-cattle. So we ask them, our personal angels, for reassurance. And they come, they come to our call.

But it was not for that, she knew in her heart of hearts, that she travelled to séances, that she wrote and rapped and bellowed, it was for *now,* it was for more life *now,* it was not for the Hereafter, which would be as it was, as it always had been. For what had lain in wait for her, a dubious widow, in straitened circumstances, but constriction and tedium? She could not bear to sit and gossip of bonnets and embroidery and the eternal servant problem, she wanted *life.* And this traffic with the dead was the best way to know, to observe, to love the living, not as they were politely over teacups, but in their secret selves, their deepest desires and fears. They revealed themselves to her, to Lilias Papagay, as they would never have done in usual society. Mrs Jesse, for instance, was not rich, but she was a gentlewoman, Captain Jesse's family were landed gentry. Mrs Papagay would not have mixed socially with the Jesses if it were not for the democracy of the Spirit World.

II

Mrs Jesse was a small, handsome woman in her early sixties, with an imposing head which sometimes appeared too large for her slight body. She had very clear blue eyes in a deep-lined, brown-skinned gipsyish face, with a strong profile. Her fine dark hair, streaked with grey, was still abundant; she wore it in delicate bandeaux, falling at the sides of her face. She had bird-hands and a bird-sharp look, and a surprisingly deep resonant voice. Mrs Papagay had been much surprised by its strong Lincolnshire accent. Mrs Jesse was given to emphatic pronouncements—on the first occasion Mrs Papagay had met her, there had been a discussion of the process of grief, and Mrs Jesse had nodded sagely, 'I know that. I have felt that,' like a kind of tragic chorus. 'I have felt everything; I know everything. I don't want any new emotion. I know what it is to feel like a stoän.' If this vatic, repetitive note reminded Mrs Papagay of Mr Poe's terrible Raven with his 'Nevermore', this was partly because Mrs Jesse was always accompanied by her own pet raven, Aaron, who was secured to her wrist by a leather leash and was fed from a sinister little pouch of raw meat which travelled with it. Aaron came to the séances, as did Pug, an elephant-coloured beast, with tiny ivory teeth resting on his drooping lips, and intelligent, bulging brown eyes. Pug was insensible to the fluctuations of emotion round the table, and tended to lie snoozing on the couch, occasionally even snoring, or emitting other wet, explosive animal noises at the most sensitive moments. Aaron too provided occasional distractions at times of intense concentration—a rattle of claws, a sudden raucous cry, or the rustle of his feathers as he shook himself.

Mrs Jesse was the heroine of a tragic story. In her youth, when she was nineteen, she had loved and been loved by a brilliant young man, a university friend of her brother's, who had visited the Rectory where the family lived secluded, and had almost immediately seen that they were soul-mates, and asked her to be his wife. Fate, initially in the shape of the young man's worldly and ambitious father, had intervened. He was forbidden to see her, or to form an engagement to her, until his twenty-first birthday. This day had come and gone: despite continuing absence and opposition the lovers had persisted faithfully in their truth to each other. The engagement had been announced—the young man had spent a family Christmas with his beloved and her family. Devoted letters had been exchanged. In the Summer of 1833 he had travelled abroad with his father, and had written to her—Ma douce amie— from Hungary, from Pesth, on the way to Vienna. Early in October Mrs Jesse's brother had received a letter from the young man's uncle. Mrs Papagay knew its beginning by heart. She had heard it in Mrs Jesse's deep melancholy voice; she had heard it, word for word, in Captain Jesse's light ruminative babble.

My dear Sir,

At the desire of a most afflicted family, I write to you, because they are unequal, from the Abyss of grief into which they have fallen, to do it themselves.

Your friend, Sir, and my much loved Nephew, Arthur Hallam, is no more—it has pleased God to remove him from this his first scene of Existence, to that better World, for which he was Created . . .

Poor Arthur had a slight attack of Ague—which he had often had— Order'd his fire to be lighted—and talked with as much cheerfulness as usual—He suddenly became insensible and his Spirit departed without Pain—The Physician endeavour'd to get any Blood from him—and on Examination it was the General Opinion, that he could not have lived long—

She had come downstairs, the young woman, hearing the post arrive, hoping, and had had that read out to her by her stricken brother, and the world had gone from her darkened eyes, she had fallen in a deep faint from which the awakening had been more terrible, more shocking, than the first blow, so she told it, and so Mrs Papagay believed it, even experienced it, so intense was the telling. 'It appears', Mrs Jesse would narrate, 'that he went so quietly, so imperceptibly, that his father was able to sit by the fire with him, supposing they were both companionably reading, until it struck him that the silence was too prolonged, or maybe that something was amiss, we do not know, and *he* does not remember. For when he touched my dearest Arthur, his head was not in a wholly natural position—and he did not reply—so a surgeon was sent for, and a vein opened in his arm and another in his hand—all to no avail, he was gone forever.'

For a year after this black day she had kept herself closed in her bedchamber, prostrated with pain and shock, reappearing to her family and friends—Mrs Papagay imagined the scene not from within the young woman's body, as she did the first shock, but through the wondering eyes of the assembled company, as she crept

into the room, painfully and proudly erect, in the deepest mourning, but with one white rose in her hair, as her Arthur loved to see
her. She was back in the world but not *of* the world, she was
soul-sick and dwelt in shadows. Too late, too late, as is always the
case in tragic tales, the harsh father repented his cruelty, and his
son's beloved was invited to that house where she had never come
with her lover, became the bosom friend of his sister, the 'widowed
daughter' of his sorrowing mother, the recipient, so it was put
about, of a generous annuity of £300 per annum. These things are
always secret and are always known, gossip whispers from drawing-
room to drawing-room, generosity is praised and at the same time
questioned sneeringly for motive—to buy affection? to alleviate
guilt? to ensure perpetual devotion? This last had clearly not been
wholly or perfectly achieved, for there had been Captain Jesse.
Quite how or where he had come into the picture Mrs Papagay did
not know. Gossip put it about that the marriage had been a cruel
disappointment both to old Mr Hallam and to Mrs Jesse's brother,
Alfred, Arthur's great friend. Mrs Papagay had been shown—in the
strictest confidence—a letter from the poetess Elizabeth Barrett
(before she became Mrs Browning and before she herself joined the
happy band of Spirits) in which she characterised Mrs Jesse's behaviour as a 'disgrace to womanhood' and 'a climax of *badness*'. Miss
Barrett referred contemptuously to Captain Jesse—then in 1842,
Lieutenant Jesse—as a 'lubberly Lieutenant'. She despised both
bride and groom for accepting the continuation of the annuity
which old Mr Hallam had with great generosity not withdrawn.
And she rose to a climax of indignation over what Mrs Papagay was
sometimes disposed to think was a poetic and romantic touch, the
naming of the first son, Arthur Hallam Jesse. 'That last was a
desperate grasp at a "sentiment"—and missed!' pronounced Miss
Barrett, all those years ago. Perhaps *Mrs Browning* would have been
more charitable? Mrs Papagay wondered. Her sympathies were so
wonderfully enlarged by her own flight and marriage.

Mrs Papagay herself liked to think of this naming as a gage of perpetuity, a Life-in-Death for the dead lover, an assertion of the wondrous community of the Spirit World, for believers. For had not the Lord himself said, 'In Heaven there is neither marriage nor giving in marriage.' Though again, Emanuel Swedenborg, who had been there, had seen the marriages of the Angels, which corresponded to the Union between Christ and His Church, and so knew differently, at least could expatiate on *why* Our Lord had said that, when conjugial love was so important to Angels. To be called Arthur Hallam Jesse had not been entirely fortunate for the elder son, as it turned out. He was some kind of military man, but seemed to live in a world of his own, perhaps because, like Captain Jesse's, his bright blue eyes saw very little beyond his nose. He had, like his father and brother, a face both romantically handsome and gently amiable. Old Mr Hallam was his godfather, as he was also godfather to Alfred's elder son, also piously named in memoriam, though this was not disapproved of in the same way, since Alfred Tennyson had written *In Memoriam,* which had made Arthur Hallam, A. H. H., an object of national mourning nearly twenty years after his death, and had later caused the nation somehow to confound his young promise with the much-mourned Prince Albert, let alone the legendary King Arthur, the flower of chivalry and soul of Britain.

Sophy Sheekhy knew large runs of *In Memoriam* by heart. She liked poems, it appeared, though she could never get interested in novels, a curious quirk of taste, Mrs Papagay thought. She said she liked the rhythms, it put her in the mood, the rhythms first, then the meanings. Mrs Papagay herself liked *Enoch Arden,* a tragic tale of a wrecked sailor who returned to find his wife happily married, with children, and died in virtuous self-abnegation. The plot resembled the plot of Mrs Papagay's aborted novel, in which a sailor, having been the single survivor of a vessel burned in mid-ocean, and having been rescued after many weeks floating on a raft under the hot sun, imprisoned by amorous Tahitian princesses, taken off by pirates, pressed by a man-of-war who had overcome the pirates, wounded in a great battle, returned to his Penelope only to find her the wife of his hated cousin and mother of many little ones with his features but not his. This last Mrs Papagay thought was a fine, tragically ironic touch, but her imagination was not equal to fire, slavery, Tahiti or the press-gangs, although Arturo had often enough made these live vividly for her as they walked the Downs or sat by the fire by night. She missed Arturo still, the more so because no second lover had presented himself to distract her. She was particularly fond of one of the Laureate's lyrics about the dangers of the return of the dead.

That could the dead, whose dying eyes
Were closed with wail, resume their life,
They would but find in child and wife
An iron welcome when they rise:

'Twas well, indeed, when warm with wine,
To pledge them with a kindly tear,
To talk them o'er, to wish them here,
To count their memories half divine;

But if they came who past away,
Behold their brides in other hands;
The hard heir strides about their lands,
And will not yield them for a day.

Yea, though their sons were none of these,
Not less the yet-loved sire would make
Confusion worse than death, and shake
The pillars of domestic peace.

Ah dear, but come thou back to me:
Whatever change the years have wrought,
I find not yet one lonely thought
That cries against my wish for thee.

' "Ah dear, but come thou back to me," ' Mrs Papagay murmured
to herself, along with the Queen and countless other bereaved men
and women, in one great rhythmic sigh of hopeless hope. And so
she felt too, it was certain, Emily Tennyson, Emily Jesse, the love
the young man had tasted with half his mind and not touched, for
she called on him at their meetings, she desired to see and hear
him, he was alive to her, though gone for forty-two years, almost
twice the length of his stay on earth. They had never succeeded
unambiguously in communicating with him—not even Sophy
Sheekhy—and Mrs Papagay, a connoisseur of self-deception and
vain images, could only admire the integrity with which Mrs Jesse
refused squarely to be seduced by simulacra, or peevish spirits, to
drive tables with her own knees or to urge herself and Sophy to
greater efforts. 'He has gone a long way away, I think,' Sophy had
said once, 'he has a lot to think about.' 'He always had,' said Mrs
Jesse. 'And we are told we do not change beyond the grave, only
continue in the path we are in.'

III

The sofa on which Emily Jesse sat with Mrs Hearnshaw was high-backed and ample, covered with a printed linen designed by William Morris, which showed a trellis of dark boughs, at once randomly crossing and geometrically repeating, on a mysterious deep green ground, the colour, Emily thought, with the inveterate romanticism of her family, of deep forests, of holly thickets, of evergreen glades. The boughs were studded with little star-like white flowers, and between them loomed pomegranates, crimson and gold, and small crested birds in blue and rose, with creamy speckled breasts and crossed bills, a kind of impossible hybrid of exotic Amazonian parrakeets and the English mistle thrush. Emily was not houseproud—she believed there were higher things in life than crockery and Sunday roasts—but she took pleasure in the sofa, in Mr Morris's weaving of a kind of formal, solid series of magical objects which recalled to her childhood days in the white Rectory in Somersby, when the eleven of them had played at the Arabian Nights and the Court of Camelot, when her tall brothers had fenced on the lawn with foils and masks crying, 'Have at thee, toad-spotted traitor!' or defended the little bridge over the subsequently immortalised brook with staves against the village boys, like Robin Hood. Everything was double there, then—it was real and loved, here and now, it was glittering with magic and breathing out a faint cold perfume of a lost world, a king's orchard, the garden of Haroun al-Raschid. The windows of the Gothic dining-room which their furiously energetic father, the Rector, had built with his own hands and the help of his coachman Horlins, could be seen doubly by the active imagination, embrasures to frame ladies in the latest modes, ready to slip away to trysts, or magic casements behind which Guenevere and the Lily Maid waited with beating hearts for their lovers. Mr Morris's sofa acknowledged both worlds; it could be sat on, it hinted at Paradise. Emily liked that.

There had been a yellow sofa in the Somersby sitting-room where Mrs Tennyson sat with her mending and the little ones tumbled like a basket of puppies or waves on a choppy sea, surging round her. Here Emily had sat alone with Arthur, that one Christmas visit, beautiful Arthur with his carved features and his air of knowing about the vagaries and coquetries of the female sex. He had put his arm round her shoulder, her accepted lover, and his fastidious mouth had brushed her cheek, her ear, her dark brow, her lips. She could remember to this day how he had trembled, ever so slightly, as though his knees were not quite controlled, and she herself had been stricken by fear—of what, she could not quite remember now, of being overwhelmed, of responding inappropriately or inadequately, of losing herself? His lips were dry and warm. He had written often about the yellow sofa, after that, it had loomed in his letters, a mysterious solid object of oblique import, mixed with Chaucerian sighs out of some ideal Romance.

> Alas min Emilie
> Alas departing of our compagnie
> Alas my hertes quene.

He had missed both beginning and end of this lamenting cry:

> Allas, the deth! allas, myn Emelye!
> Allas, departyng of our companye!
> Allas, myn hertes queen! allas, my wyf!

which she said to herself still, from time to time. ' "Allas, myn hertes quene, allas, myn wyf," ' which she had never become. Poor Arthur. Poor vanished Emily with her long dark ringlets and her white rose. After this delicate embrace she had been so agitated in body and mind that she had kept her bed for two days though his scanted visit was a bare two weeks. She had written him from her seclusion little notes in charmingly inept Italian (or so he pronounced it) which he corrected for her, patiently, and returned, with the page marked where he had kissed it. Poverina, stai male. Assicurati ch'io competisco da cuore al soffrir tuo. A verray parfit gentil knight, Arthur.

Mrs Hearnshaw was not noticing the sofa. She was speaking her grief to Emily, to Sophy Sheekhy, who had settled on a footstool near them.

'She seemed so *strong,* you know, Mrs Jesse, she waved her arms so lustily and kicked with her little legs and thighs, and her eyes saw me so quietly, all swimming with life. My husband says I must learn not to attach myself so to these tiny creatures who are destined to stay with us so briefly in time—but how can I not, it is natural, I think? They have grown under my heart, my dear, I have felt them stir there, with fear and trembling.'

'We must believe they are angels, Mrs Hearnshaw.'

'Sometimes I am able to do so. Sometimes I imagine horrors.'

Emily Jesse said, 'Speak what is in your mind, it will do you good. Those of us who are *wounded to the quick,* you know, we suffer for all the others, we are appointed in some way to bear their grief too. We cry out *for them.* It is no shame.'

'I give birth to death,' said Mrs Hearnshaw, speaking the thought she walked about with, constantly. She could have added, 'I am an object of horror to myself,' but forbore. The mental image of the mottled limbs, after convulsion, of the rough, musty clay bed, was always with her.

Sophy Sheekhy said, 'It is all one. Alive and dead. Like walnuts.'

She saw very clearly all the little forms, curled in little boxes, like the brown-skinned white lobes of dead nuts, and a blind point like a wormhead pushing into light and airy leafage. She often 'saw' messages. She did not know whose thoughts they were, hers or

another's, or whether they came from Outside, or whether everyone saw similar messages of their own.

They were joined by Captain Jesse and Mr Hawke.

'Walnuts?' said Captain Jesse. 'I have a great partiality for walnuts. With port wine, after dinner, they can be most tasty. I also like
green, milky ones. They are said to resemble the human brain. My
grandmother told how they were used in certain country remedies
which might be closer to magic than to medicine. Would that be
a correspondence that might interest Emanuel Swedenborg, Mr
Hawke? The encephaloform walnut?'

'I do not remember having seen any animadversion on walnuts
in his writings, Captain Jesse, though they are so voluminous, some
reference may indeed be hidden away there. The thought of walnuts always makes me think of the English mystic, Dame Julian of
Norwich, who was shewn in a vision *all that is* like a nut in her own
hand, and told by God Himself, "All shall be well, and thou shalt
see thy self that all manner of thing shall be well." I think what she
may have seen may have been the thought of some Angel, as it
appeared in the world of Spirits or in the world of men. She may
have been in a sense a precursor of our spiritual Columbus. He
relates, you know, how he himself saw a beautiful bird in the hand
of Sir Hans Sloane, in the Spirit World, differing in no least detail
from a similar bird on earth, and yet being—it was revealed to
him—none other than the affection of a certain Angel, and vanishing with the surcease of the operation of that affection. Now, it
appears that the Angel, being in Heaven, would not be aware of this
indirect forthgoing in the world of Spirits, for the angels see all in its
highest Form, the Divine Human. The highest angels, we are told,
are seen as human infants by those approaching them from below—
though this is not how they appear to themselves—because their
affections are born of the union of the love of *good*—from an
angel-father—and of *truth*—from an angel-mother—in conjugial
love.

'And Swedenborg himself saw birds during his sojourns in the Spirit World and it was revealed to him that—in the Grand Man— rational concepts are seen as birds. Because the head corresponds to the heavens and the air. He *actually experienced in his body* the fall of certain angels who had formed wrong opinions in their community about thoughts and influx—he felt a terrible tremor in his sinews and bones—and saw one dark and ugly bird and two fine and beautiful. And these solid birds were the *thoughts* of the angels, as he saw them in the world of his senses, beautiful reasonings and ugly falses. For at every level everything corresponds, from the most purely material to the most purely divine in the Divine Human.'

'Very strange, very strange,' said Captain Jesse, somewhat impatiently. Himself a great talker he could not listen passively whilst Mr Hawke unravelled for the assembled company all the threads of connection between the Divine Human and local lumps of clay. Once started, Mr Hawke was driven to go on, expounding the Arcana, and the Principia, the *Clavis Hieroglyphica Arcanorum Naturalium et Spiritualium,* the mysteries of Influx and Vastation, Conjugial Love and Life After Death, for it was only in the act of exposition that Mr Hawke could hold all the balls of his system, so to speak, up in the air at once, an arc of theological tumbling and juggling, which Sophy Sheekhy saw briefly, during his excursus on birds, as a flurry of pouter pigeons and collared doves.

'In that world, in the spiritual world,' said Mr Hawke, 'they have their light from the spiritual sun, and cannot see our corresponding material sun, from our dead world. It appears to them as thick darkness. There are also some quite ordinary spirits who cannot bear material things, for instance, those from the planet Mercury, who correspond in the Grand Man to the memory of things, abstracted from material things. Swedenborg visited them and was allowed to show them meadows, fallowlands, gardens, woods and streams. But they hated that, they hated their *solidity,* they like abstract knowledge, so they meticulously filled the meadows with snakes and darkened them, and turned the streams black. He had more success with showing them a pleasant garden full of lamps and lights, because those appealed to their understanding, as lights represent truths. Also lambs, which they accepted, as lambs represent innocence.'

'Not unlike some preachers,' said Mrs Jesse. 'The spirits of the planet Mercury. Only able to think in abstractions related to abstractions.'

'Not unlike some savages,' said her husband. 'Those who sailed with Captain Cook used to tell how the savages in New Zealand seemed unable to see the ship anchored in the harbour. They went about their business as though it wasn't there, as though everything was the same as ever, fishing and swimming, you know, making their fires to roast their catch and all that, whatever they get up to. But the moment boats were lowered and put off from the ship the men became as it were *visible,* and caused great agitation, great lining-up on the beach and waving, great shrieking and dancing. But the ship they just couldn't *seem to see.* You'd think analogy might have operated, they might have thought it was some great white winged thing, some spirit power or what not, if they couldn't see it as a ship, but no, they couldn't see it all, it appears, not at all. Now this tends, to my mind, to support the theory that the spirit world may be juxtaposed with this, may riddle it through and through like weevils in bread, and we might just *not see it* because we haven't developed a way of thinking that allows us to see it, d'you see, like your Mercurials or Mercurians, who didn't want to know about fields and things, or like the proper Angels, who can only see the sun as thick darkness, poor things.'

Aaron the raven, perched on the arm of the sofa, chose this moment to raise both his black wings in the air, almost clapping them, and then to settle again, with a rattling of his quills and various stabbing motions of his head. He took two or three sideways steps towards Mr Hawke, who retreated nervously. Like many creatures who cause fear, Aaron seemed to be animated by signs of anxiety. He opened his thick blue beak and cawed, putting his head on one side to observe the effect of this. The lids of his eyes were also bluish and reptilian. Mrs Jesse gave an admonitory tug on his leash. Mr Hawke had once asked the origin of his name, supposing it to have something to do with Moses' brother, the High Priest who wore the god-designed bells and pomegranates. But Mrs Jesse replied that he was named for the Moor in *Titus Andronicus,* a play of which Mr Hawke had no knowledge, not having the Tennysons' erudition. 'A sable creature, rejoicing in his blackness, Mr Hawke,' she had said, shortly. Mr Hawke had said that ravens were generally birds of ill omen, he believed. Noah's raven, in Swedenborg's interpretation of the Word, had represented the wayward mind wandering over an ocean of falses. 'Gross and impenetrable falsities,' he said, looking at Aaron, 'are described in the Word by owls and ravens. By owls because they live in the darkness of the night, by ravens because they are black, as in Isaiah 34, 11, "the owl also and the raven shall dwell in it".'

'Owls and ravens are God's creatures,' Mrs Jesse replied on that occasion with some spirit. 'I cannot believe that anything so delightful and soft and surprised as an owl can be a creature of evil, Mr Hawke. Look at the screech-owls who cried back to Wordsworth's Boy, and his mimic hootings. My own brother Alfred was most successful in that line as a boy, he could imitate any bird, and had a whole family of owls who came to his fingertips for food when he called, and one who became a member of our household and travelled about on his head. He had a room under the roof of the Rectory, under the gable.' Her face softened at the thought of Somersby as it always did. She took out a little leather bag and offered the raven a small scrap of what looked like liver, which he took with another quick stab, tossed, turned, and swallowed. Mrs Papagay was fascinated by Mrs Jesse's scraps of flesh. She had seen her covertly put away the remnants of the roast meat from the dinner table into her pouch for the bird. There was something unsavoury about Mrs Jesse, as well, of course, as something pure and tragic. Sitting there with the staring bird and the sharp-toothed, bulge-headed monstrous little grey dog, she was like a weathered, watching head between gargoyles on a church roof, Mrs Papagay momentarily thought, over which centuries of wind and rain had swept as it stared, fretted and steadfast, out to the distance.

Mr Hawke proposed that if they were ready, they should constitute their circle. A round table, covered with a fringed velvet cloth, was pulled out into the centre of the room, and Captain Jesse manhandled the chairs into position, addressing them as though they were living creatures, come along now, don't be awkward, that will do for *you*. Mrs Jesse produced a sufficiency of paper and various pens and pencils, and a large jug of water with glasses for everyone. They sat down, in semi-darkness, lit only by the flickering flames of the fire in the grate. Mrs Papagay reported that this was how it was done in the most advanced spiritualist circles. The spirits appeared to fear bright light, or to be incommoded by it—its rays were of the wrong constitution, a dead scientific gentleman had once explained through the lips of the American medium Cora V. Tappan—an ideal climate for their appearance would be soothing *violet light*. Emily Jesse liked the firelight. She did most sincerely believe that the dead lived and were eager to speak to the living.

Like her brother Alfred, like the thousands of troubled faithful for whom he partly spoke, she felt a pressing and threatened desire to know that the individual soul was immortal. Alfred as he got older got more and more vehement on the subject. If there were no afterlife, he shouted at his friends, if it were proved to him that was so, he would jump into the Seine or the Thames, he would put his head in the oven, he would take poison or fire a pistol at his own temple. She said to herself often Alfred's lines:

That each, who seems a separate whole,
Should move his rounds, and fusing all
The skirts of self again, should fall
Remerging in the general Soul,

Is faith as vague as all unsweet:
Eternal form shall still divide
The eternal soul from all beside;
And I shall know him when we meet.

She liked that. 'Is faith as vague as all unsweet' was a good line. But she liked the firelight too with part of her ancient childhood self, expecting marvels. They had played country games by the fire, the eleven children cramped into the pretty Rectory, had told each other terrifying tales and magical visions. The old man, their father, had been half-mad with rage and disappointment and frustrated intellect. And drink, if the record was kept truly. Half the children had suffered from melancholia—one, Edward, never mentioned, was permanently confined in an asylum in York. Septimus lay in the hearth and sorrowed and Charles had taken to opium dreams. Yet they had been happy, she remembered, they had been happy. They had taken pleasure in the dark. They had seen strange things and recounted them with gusto. Horatio, her youngest brother, walking home in the dusk past the Fairy Wood, between Harrington and Bag Enderby, had seen a ghastly human head, apparently severed, running along inside the wood, staring at him over the hedge. Alfred himself had slept with some ceremony in his father's own bed, less than a week after his father's death, desirous, he said, of seeing his ghost. The Rectory had been so unaccountably quiet without his father's howling and crashing that the girls had begged him not to attempt to arouse that perturbed spirit. But Alfred had clung to his idea, somewhere between the ghoulish and the awe-struck. He had closed himself into that stuffy room and put out his

candle. And had passed a quiet night, he reported the next morning, thinking much of his father, his bitterness, his misery, his
towering intellect, his fits of piercing reasonableness, straining to
see him stride, tall and thunderous, past the bed. 'Or clutch at your
throat,' said Horatio, 'you disrespectful creature.' 'No ghost would
appear to *you*, Alfred,' said Cecilia. 'You are too vague to see one,
you are not receptive.' 'Ghosts do not appear to men of imagination, I believe,' said Alfred, and went on to tell of a cowman who
had seen the ghost of a murdered farmer, with a pitchfork protruding from his ribcage. Arthur Hallam had described to her how
Alfred had read his one and only paper, entitled *Ghosts*, to the
Apostles in Cambridge, that learned society of young men who
were going to change the world into something altogether more
just and delightful. 'You should have seen him, dearest Nem, so
abominably handsome and so abominably shy and hang-dog, prop-
ping up the fireplace and peering at his pages, and then putting on
the voice of the tale-teller by the chimney-corner in Sidney and
frightening the life out of us with his gruesome visage.' He had
once read the first part of the paper to the assembled Somersby
Tennysons.

He who has the power of speaking of the spiritual world, speaks
in a simple manner of a high matter. He speaks of life and death,
and the things after death. He lifts the veil, but the form behind
it is shrouded in deeper obscurity. He raises the cloud, but he
darkens the prospect. He unlocks with a golden key the iron-
grated gates of the charnel house, he throws them wide open.
And forth issue from the inmost gloom the colossal Presences of
the Past, majores humano; some as they lived, seemingly pale,
and faintly smiling; some as they died, still suddenly frozen by the
chill of death; and some as they were buried, with dropped
eyelids, in their cerements and their winding sheets.

The listeners creep closer to each other, they are afraid of the drawing of their own breaths, the beating of their own hearts. The voice of *him* who speaks alone like a mountain stream on a still night fills up and occupies the silence . . .

Arthur had loved their story-telling circles, the crowd of them, adding a dramatic touch, a dying fall to each other's telling. Arthur's house, he said, was correct and formal. His brother and sisters and himself were the survivors of a family almost as numerous as the Tennysons. They were watched anxiously for signs of decline, they were treasured and protected, they were exercised in virtue and taught rigorously. They did not run wild in fields nor tumble in hedges, nor shoot with bows and arrows, nor ride wildly across country. I love you all, he had told the Tennysons, his thin face flushed with happiness, aware of conferring happiness, for they loved him too, he was beautiful and perfect, he was to be a great man, a Minister, a philosopher, a poet, a Prince. Matilda had called him King Arthur and crowned him with bay-leaves and Winter aconites. He was patient with Matilda, who was a little odd, a little gruff and abrupt, who had been dropped on her head in infancy and somehow damaged. Matilda, unlike Alfred, certainly saw apparitions. She and Mary had seen a tall white figure—shrouded from head to foot—progressing along the Rectory lane and vanishing through the hedge in a place where there was no gap. Matilda had been affected to tears, she had wept and howled like a dog, and rolled on her bed, in mortal terror. A few days later it was Matilda who had walked to Spilsby and collected at the Post Office that terrible letter.

Your friend, Sir, and my much loved Nephew, Arthur Hallam, is no more—it has pleased God, to remove him from this his first scene of Existence, to that better World, for which he was Created.

He died at Vienna on his return from Buda, by Apoplexy, and I believe his Remains come by Sea from Trieste.

IV

Mr Hawke arranged them. He sat between Sophy
Sheekhy and Lilias Papagay, with a copy of the Bible,
and a copy of Swedenborg's *Heaven and Hell* in front of
him. Mrs Jesse was next to Mrs Papagay and on her other side was
Mrs Hearnshaw. Captain Jesse sat between Mrs Hearnshaw and
Sophy Sheekhy, in a kind of parody of dinner-party placement
when there were insufficient men. It was Mr Hawke's custom to
begin the proceedings with a reading from Swedenborg and a
reading from the Bible. Emily Jesse was not quite sure how he had
made himself so central a figure, since he had exhibited no medi-
umistic powers up to that point. She had been glad at first, when

she told him of their promising, if alarming results from their early
cautious spiritual experiments, that he had asked to be included.
Like her eldest brother, Frederick, and her sister, Mary, she was a
dedicated member of the Swedenborgian New Jerusalem Church,
and also a convinced spiritualist. Whilst the spiritualists claimed
Swedenborg, who had made such momentous journeys into the
interior of the spirit world, as a founder of the faith, many of the
more orthodox Swedenborgians looked askance at what they saw
as the loose and dangerous power-play of the spiritualists. Mr
Hawke was not an ordaining minister in the New Church, but a
wandering preacher, ordained to speak but with no society to
govern, a grade, as he never tired of explaining, referred to by
Swedenborg as sacerdos, canonicus, or flamen. He sat with his back
to the fire and read out:

'The Church on earth before the Lord is One Man. It is also
distinguished into societies, and each society again is a Man, and
all who are within that Man are also in Heaven. Every member
of the Church also is an angel of heaven, for he becomes an angel
after death. Moreover, the Church on earth, together with the
angels, not only constitutes the inward parts of that Grand Man,
but also its outward parts, which are called cartilaginous and
osseous. The Church brings this about because men on earth are
furnished with a body in which the spiritual ultimate is clothed
with a natural. This makes the conjunction of Heaven with the
Church, of the Church with Heaven.

'Today's reading from the Word,' he went on, 'is taken from the
Book of Revelation, the twentieth chapter, verses 11 to 15.

'And I saw a great white throne, and him that sat on it, from
whose face the earth and the heaven fled away; and there was
found no place for them.
    And I saw the dead, small and great, stand before God; and the

books were opened: and another book was opened, which is the
book of life: and the dead were judged out of those things which
were written in the books, according to their works.

And the sea gave up the dead which were in it; and death and
hell delivered up the dead which were in them: and they were
judged every man according to their works.

And death and hell were cast into the lake of fire. This is the
second death.

And whosoever was not found written in the book of life was
cast into the lake of fire.'

The passage from Revelation sent a frisson of accustomed delight through the frame of Mrs Papagay, who loved its sonorous
booming and its lurid colours, scarlet, gold, white and the black of
the Pit. She loved too, and had loved since childhood, all its strange
visions and images, the angels rolling up the scroll of the heavens
and tidying them away forever, the stars falling out of the sky into
the sea like a rain of golden fiery globes, the dragons and swords,
the blood and the honey, the swarms of locusts and the hosts of
angels, those creatures at once pure white and fiery-eyed, casting
down their golden crowns around a glassy sea. She had asked herself
often and often why everyone loved the ferocious Saint John and
his terrible vision so, and had answered herself variously, like a
good psychologist, that human beings liked to be terrified—look
how they enjoyed the nastier Tales of Mr Poe, pits, pendulums,
buried alive. Not only that, they *liked to be judged,* she considered,
they could not go on if their lives were not of importance, of
absolute importance, in some higher Eye which watched and made
real. For if there were not death and judgement, if there were not
heaven and hell, men were no better than creepy-crawlies, no
better than butterflies and blowflies. And *if this was all,* sitting and
supping tea, and waiting for bed-time, why were we given such a
range of things guessed at, hoped for and feared beyond our fat
bosoms confined in stays, and troubles with stoves? Why the white

airy creatures towering, the woman clothed with the sun and the Angel standing in it?

Mrs Papagay was not good at giving up thinking. Their practice was to sit in silence, composing the circle, holding hands lightly, to join them into one, waiting, passive mind for the spirits to use, to enter, to speak through. At first they had used a system of raps and answers, one for yes, two for no, and every now and then they were still startled by great peals of banging from beneath the table, or shakings of the surface below their fingers. But mostly now they waited until the spirits gave signs of their presence, and then proceeded to automatic writing—all might hold pencil over paper, all, except Captain Jesse, had produced scripts, long or short, which they had studied and interrogated. And then, if it was a good day, the visitors would speak through Sophy, or more rarely, through herself. And once or twice, Sophy could see them, she could describe what she saw to others. She had seen Mrs Jesse's dead nephew and nieces, the three children of her sister Cecilia—Edmund, Emily, and Lucy, dead at thirteen, nineteen, and only last year at twenty-one. So slow, so sad, Mrs Papagay thought, though the spirits said how happy and busy they were in a land of Summer amongst flowers and orchards of wonderful light. It was the marriage of this sister, Cecilia, which had been celebrated at the end of *In Memoriam* as the triumph of Love over Death, with the bride's little slippered feet, Mrs Papagay could just see them, tripping on the tablets of the dead in the old church. But we live in a Vale of Tears, Mrs Papagay had to conclude, we need to know that there is Summerland. The unborn child who was the future hope of the Laureate's poem had come and gone, like A. H. H. himself. With whom, for some reason, they were none of them, not even Sophy Sheekhy, able to establish communication.

The firelight made shadows on walls and ceilings. Captain Jesse's mane of white hair stood out like a crown, his beard was god-like, and Aaron's smooth black head appeared in a smoky and wavering silhouette. Their hands were fitfully lit. Mrs Jesse's were long and brown, gipsy hands with glinting red rings. Mrs Hearnshaw's were softly white, covered with mourning rings containing the hair of the lost in littler caskets. Mr Hawke's were muddy, with a few gingery hairs on them. He took good care of his nails, and wore a little signet ring with a bloodstone. He was given to making little pats and squeezes of encouragement and reassurance to his neighbours. Mrs Papagay could also feel his knees, which occasionally rubbed her own, and, she was sure, Sophy Sheekhy's. She knew, without having to think about it, that Mr Hawke was an excitable man in *that* way, that he liked female flesh, and thought much and very frequently about it. She knew, or thought she knew, that he liked the idea of the cool pale limbs of Sophy Sheekhy, that he imagined undoing that smooth unornamented bodice, or running his hands up those pale legs under the dove-coloured dress. She knew, with slightly less assurance, that Sophy Sheekhy did not respond to this interest. She saw Sophy's pale hands, creamy-pale even under the nails, motionless and at rest in his grip, with no answering sweat, Mrs Papagay was sure. Sophy seemed to have no interest in that kind of thing. Part of her spiritual success might be due to this intact quality of hers. She was a pure vessel, cool, waiting dreamily.

Mrs Papagay also knew that Mr Hawke had considered her own possibilities as a source of creature comfort. She had caught his eye on her breast and waist, involuntarily speculative, she had felt his warm fingers massage her palm, at moments of excitement. She had met his eye, once or twice, as he weighed up her full mouth and her still-youthful coils of hair. She had never offered him any voluntary encouragement, but she had not, as she could have done, repelled him once and for all when he looked too long or brushed against her. She was trying to weigh it all up. She believed any woman who put her mind to it could *have* Mr Hawke for the asking, if only that woman were reasonably buxom and inclined to

him. Did she want to be Mrs Hawke? The truth was she wanted
Arturo, she wanted what Swedenborg would call the 'conjugial
delights' of her married life. She wanted to sleep with male arms
round her in the scent of marriage-sheets. Arturo had taught her
much and she had been an apt pupil. He had gained courage to tell
his wide-eyed wife of what he had seen in various ports, of women
who had entertained him—he went so far, and further, as he saw
that his surprising wife did not take umbrage, but evinced detailed
curiosity. She could teach Mr Hawke, or some other man, a thing
or two, could Lilias Papagay, that would surprise him. If she could
bring herself to it, after Arturo. She had a terrible nightmare once,
about embracing Arturo and finding herself engorged with a great
sea-eel, dragon or sea-serpent, which had somehow half-absorbed
or half-extruded parts of him. Though the occasional dream in
which he returned, as it were, 'to the life' hurt almost more, on
waking. ' "Ah, dear, but come thou back to me," ' said Mrs Papagay to herself, to her dead man. Her outside thumb found itself
measured, and rubbed, by Mr Hawke's stiff outside thumb. She
tried to compose her mind to the purpose of the meeting. She
reproached her own backsliding by looking at the expectant strain
on Mrs Hearnshaw's large soft face.

Sophy Sheekhy was much better at emptying her mind than Mrs
Papagay. Indeed, before Mrs Papagay had led her to make a profession of it, she had been constantly delighted, alarmed and embarrassed by slipping and sliding in and out of different states
of consciousness as she might slip and slide her body in and out of
its various garments and coverings, or in and out of warm water
or cold Winter air. One of her favourite biblical readings, and one
of Mr Hawke's too, because it allowed him to reflect on the
experiences of Swedenborg, was Saint Paul's anecdote in II Corinthians 12.

I knew a man in Christ above fourteen years ago, (whether in the body, I cannot tell; or whether out of the body, I cannot tell: God knoweth;) such an one caught up to the third heaven.

And I knew such a man, (whether in the body, or out of the body, I cannot tell: God knoweth;)

How that he was caught up into paradise, and heard unspeakable words, which it is not lawful for a man to utter.

Of such an one will I glory: yet of myself I will not glory, but in mine infirmities.

She liked the equivocal repeated phrase 'whether in the body, I cannot tell; or whether out of the body, I cannot tell: God knoweth'. It described many of her own states and could be used, like poetry, with its repeated hum of rhythm, to induce such states. You went on saying it to yourself until it became at first *very strange,* as though all the words were mad and bristling with shiny glass hairs, and then very simple and meaningless, like clear drops of water. And you were there and not there. Sophy Sheekhy sat there like a grey nun with her face turned down, and something saw. Saw what? Sophy herself did not feel there was a great discontinuity between the creatures and objects met in dreams, the creatures and objects glimpsed through windows, or out over the sea-wall, the creatures and objects called up by poems and the Bible, or the creatures which came from nowhere and stayed awhile, could be described to other people, seen, smelled, heard, almost touched and tasted—some were sweet, some were smoky. Lying in bed at night, waiting for sleep, she saw processions of all kinds, sometimes in the dark air, sometimes bringing with them their own worlds, strange or familiar, desert dunes, scrubby heaths, the interior of dark cupboards, the heat of fires, orchards heavy with fruit. She saw flocks of birds and clouds of butterflies, camels and llamas, little naked black men and the sheeted dead with bound jaws, bolt upright and shining. She saw burning lizards and families of golden balls, large and infinitesimal, she saw transparent lilies and walking pyramids of glass. Other indescribable creatures wandered through her consciousness—something like a purple firescreen with fringed silvery arms came by, open and shut, emitting a feeling of great contentment, and a kind of orange hedgehog of agony blew up and exploded in front of her. Many of these she never tried to describe to anyone else. They were her world. But some of the things which came, or could be called up, were whole human beings, with faces and histories, and she had learned slowly and painfully that she was required—from both sides it seemed—to mediate between these and those others who neither saw nor heard them. The more the weight of hope, the more the sucking whirlpool of grief *here* that called and called, the harder it became for Sophy Sheekhy to do as she was asked, to invite these *particular* comers among all others to make their stay and speak. They strangled her, she felt sometimes, the living not the dead.

Today she sensed, composing herself, that the room was full of activities. It was her habit to look slowly round the circle, 'seeing' the members of it in an abstracted way, weighing up as it were in her blood and bones their preoccupations and motions of the mind, and then to cast off, and listen. Often outside the living circle she saw another, of creatures pressing in, desiring and hearing, desiring an audience, ready to give a whirligig performance or to chuckle or to howl. She looked calmly at her hands, at Mr Hawke's finger stroking the web between hers, and made hers chill as the dead, cold as stone, so she was sitting there with a heavy marble hand, its life shrunk back to her heart. She looked at Mr Hawke and saw in his place, as she often did, a kind of flayed terracotta red creature, somewhat resembling Pug, or a glazed statue of a Chinese lion, or a satin pincushion with glass-headed pins in it, a thing the colour of the angrily shining tip of that Part of Mr Pope which he had held straining stiffly upwards in front of him, the day he sleepwalked into her garret making husky little groans before she left her body entirely cold like a dead fish, cold like a marble peach when he put his hot hand on it, and jumped back, burnt by ice.

Mrs Papagay she saw as Mrs Papagay, because she loved her as she was, though she saw her head all crowned with the feathers of peacocks and lyrebirds and whitest ostriches, like a South Seas Queen. Mrs Hearnshaw she often saw all wet and gleaming with water on fat rolls as a mermaid risen from the waters, as a huge sealion on a rock, wailing to the sky. Sometimes she seemed to see through Mrs Hearnshaw as through a huge vase or calyx in which forms faintly struggled like peaches in a jar. And next to Mrs Hearnshaw, holding her own other hand, Captain Jesse. Once, looking at him, she had seen a great white plumed creature, a creature with huge powerful wings and a fierce beak confined inside his body, compressed inside his ribs, like something caged, staring out with golden inhuman eyes. Later, she was sure it was later, Captain Jesse had shown her his engravings, of the great white Albatross which he had seen on his Polar explorations. He had told her a great deal about the wastes of snow and the dogs who pulled the sleds and had pale blue eyes and were eaten when they were exhausted. He had told her about crevasses where men sank without trace in sheets of green ice like emeralds—the Poet was right, Captain Jesse told Sophy Sheekhy, it is just such a green, the emerald, that is scientifically *exact,* my dear, and very creditable.

As for Mrs Jesse, Sophy Sheekhy saw her sometimes young and beautiful, in a black dress, with a white rose in her raven hair, as *he* loved to see her. A disinterested stare at almost anyone, she had discerned, could reveal the ghost of the girl they had once been, and simultaneously the old crone they were to become. She saw Mrs Jesse as a witch, too, wrapped and hooded in black black rags and tatters, with a pointed chin and a sharp nose and a toothless crumple of a mouth. The girl waited and waited, and the old woman's wrinkled hands lay beside the raven's claws or caressed the flaccid roll of fat on Pug's neck.

*   *   *

'Shall we try singing a little?' Mrs Papagay suggested. It fell to her
to conduct the approach to the Spirit World after Mr Hawke had
asserted the authority of the Word. Her own favourite hymn was
Bishop Heber's 'Holy, Holy, Holy', a taste she shared with the
Laureate and with Sophy Sheekhy, who felt transfixed with glass
spears of pure joy at the verse

> Holy, Holy, Holy! All the Saints adore Thee
> Casting down their golden crowns around the glassy sea;
> Cherubim and Seraphim, falling down before Thee
> Which wert, and art, and evermore shall be.

Mrs Hearnshaw however had a predilection for 'There's a home for
little children' and

> Around the Throne of God a band
> Of glorious angels ever stand
> Bright things they see, sweet harps they hold
> And on their heads are crowns of gold.

So they sang both of those, lifting their joined hands rhythmically
in a circle, feeling the power run from finger to finger, an electric
pulse along which the lines of communication could open to the
land of the dead.

The fire died a little. The dark thickened. Sophy Sheekhy said,
clear and cool, 'There are spirits here, I feel them, also I can smell
roses. Is anyone else aware of a strong perfume of roses?'

Mrs Papagay said she believed she also caught their scent. Emily
Jesse drew in a great breath in her nostrils and thought she detected
the ghost of roses across the livery breath of Aaron and the lingering
residues of one of Pug's farts, which everyone was far too well-bred

to remark upon. Mr Hawke was going, 'Sniff, sniff, sniff,' and
Sophy told him gently to be still, that things would not be manifest
if he strained, that he must give way, be passive, receive. And
suddenly Mrs Hearnshaw cried out, 'Oh, I have it, I have it, it came
wafting by me like gardens in Summer.' Mrs Papagay said, 'It is
given to me that we are to imagine a rosegarden with hedges of
roses, and arches of roses, and soft lawns, and great beds of roses of
every colour, red and white and cream-coloured and all the pinks,
and golden-yellow, and colours never imagined on earth, roses
blushing like fire, roses with hearts of heavenly blue and gleaming
black velvet—'

They imagined. The delightful odour was now perceived by
everyone. The table beneath the circle of hands began to thrum and
shift. Mrs Papagay said, 'Is there a spirit there?'

Three quick, affirmative raps.

'Is it a spirit we know?'

A whole plethora of raps.

Captain Jesse said, 'I make that fifteen. Fifteen. Five times three.
Five spirits we know, you know. It may be your little ones, Mrs
Hearnshaw.'

Sophy was invaded by Mrs Hearnshaw's pain and hope and fear,
like a great beak tearing at her. She cried out, involuntarily.

'It may be an evil spirit,' said Mr Hawke.

Mrs Papagay said, 'Do you wish to speak to us?'

Two raps for indecision.

'To *one* of us, maybe?'

Fifteen raps again.

'Is it to Mrs Hearnshaw you wish to speak?'

Three raps.

'If we hold the pens, will you guide them? Will you tell us who
you are?'

'Who shall write?' Mrs Papagay asked the visitors. She went
through the circle in turn, and the spirits fixed upon her, Mrs

Papagay, as she had hoped and believed they might. She could feel the pull between Mrs Hearnshaw and Sophy, a pull of pure pain and a kind of glittering emptiness, and she knew instinctively she must take a hand, if the hunger was to be met and not magnified. She wanted a *good* message for the poor bereft woman, she put up a little prayer to the Angels for comfort, let her be comforted, she said to them in her mind, before taking up the pen and dutifully emptying her mind for the messages to run through to her fingers.

There was always a moment of fear when her hand began to move, without any volition on her part. Once, visiting a cousin on the South Downs, she had been taken to see a water-diviner at work, who had held a forked hazel-twig over a meadow, which had suddenly risen and writhed under his hands. He had looked at the dark girl between her sceptical town parents, and held the thing out to her, saying, 'Try, you, try it.' She had looked at it as though it was a knife, and her father had laughed and said, 'Go on, Lilias, it's naught but a twig of wood.' And at first it had been wood, cut wood, dead wood, and she had begun to advance woodenly across the grass, feeling foolish. And then suddenly something had poured along it and in it, had caused it to rear and buck and writhe in her hands and she had screamed out in such real fear, that everyone had believed, no one had thought of mocking. This experiment it was easy now to adduce as an early knowledge of the powers of animal magnetism. Mrs Papagay recounted it in spiritualist circles as a moment of spiritual force, pouring through her fingers, an early indication of what powers she might have. But at the time it had made her sick with fear, and now, always, taking up the pen, however full of prayer and hope, she was sick also with a kind of animal fear. For pens could take over as hazel twigs did. The hazel twig bucked and twisted between the child's hands and what? Running unseen channels of cold water under the earth. And the pen, the pen bucked and twisted between her passive fingers and what letter-forming force?

Mrs Papagay's passive writing tended to begin with a kind of hither and thither searching among strings of words which as it were *hooked into each other,* until out of the scribbling rose a message or a face, as a rambling pencil might slip into the depiction of speaking eyes under a broad brow, might change tempo from aimless marks to urgent precise depiction. The pencil wrote:

Hands hands across hands hand over under above between below hands little pudy hands pudy plumpy hands Ring a Roses hands tossed with tangle on a bald on a bald street skull not skull soft head heaven gates opened in small head cold hands so cold such cold hands no more cold ring a roses AMY AMY AMY AMY AMY love me I love you we love you in the rosy garden we love you your tears hurt us they burn our soft skins like ice burns here cold hands are rosy we love you.

'Speak, Mrs Hearnshaw,' said Mrs Jesse.
'Are you my children? Where are you?'

We grow in a rose garden. We are your Amys. We watch you we watch over you we watch everything you do you shall come to us not soon not soon.

' 'Shall I know you?' the woman asked. She said to Emily Jesse, 'I remember the scent of their little heads.'

We are older now. We grow we learn wisdom. The angels smile on us and teach us wisdom.

'Have you any particular advice for your mother?' said Mrs Papagay.
The pen took a long scrabbling curve across the paper and

suddenly began to write incisively, not in the rounded childish script it had so far used.

We have seen a new brother or sister take form as an earthly seed growing in the dark, we rejoice in the hope for that child in the dark earth and in this rose garden. We wish you to wait for her with hope and love and trust and without fear, for if it is willed for her to come quickly to this summer land she will be happier and you will bear the pain in that certainty as you may bear the pain of her coming bear the pain of her going our death dear Mother death dear we love you and you must love her. You must not give her Our Name. We are here and we live forever and we share Our Name but that suffices. We are five fingers of one rosy hand.

Mrs Hearnshaw appeared to be in the process of dissolution. Her flesh quaked and shook, her large face was slippery with a warm sheet of tears, her neck was damp, her great breasts quivered, her arms enclosed patches of wetness. She said, '*What* shall I call her? What name?'

There was a pause. Then painfully, in capital letters, '*ROSA*'. A longer pause. '*MUNDI*'.

Then, in the incisive hand,

Rosamund, Rose of this Earth so we hope she may stay with you a little and make you happy on your dark Earth dearest Mama it is not given to us to know if it will be so and we shall love to have a new Rose in our Ring if it must be but she will be strong if you are strong she will live in your earth many years we trust and hope dearest death Mother.

It was a quirk of Mrs Papagay's automatic writing to form the word 'death' when it clearly meant 'dear', and vice versa. It ran away with itself, and the sitters had decided not to attach too much significance to it, apart from Mr Hawke, who had wondered whether there was a hidden meaning or intention in the closeness of the two words. Mrs Papagay was somewhat appalled at the certainty with which the spirits had proclaimed both that Mrs Hearnshaw was expecting another little one and that this little one would be a girl. She *preferred* the messages to be more tactfully ambiguous, like those of the Delphic Oracle. Mrs Jesse was mopping up Mrs Hearnshaw with a crumpled handkerchief which had also been used to wipe her own fingers after feeding Aaron. Sophy Sheekhy had gone a kind of opaque pearly colour, and was immobile as a statue. Mr Hawke picked, as he *would,* on the scientifically verifiable aspect of all this so sweetly touching writing.

'This is a genuine prophecy, Mrs Papagay. Which may be either true or false.'

Another salt flood overwhelmed Mrs Hearnshaw. 'Oh, Mr Hawke, but that is just the *heart* of the matter. What they say is so. I have known for only a week with any certainty—and I have said nothing to anyone, not even to my dear husband—but it is certainly as they say, I am expecting another child, and to be truthful I was in a state of much greater dread than hope, which after my experience is to be understood, I think, and not blamed, and the dear little ones have seized on my fear and understood it and tried to console me.' Great sobs clucked in her large white throat. 'I did all I could—to prevent—I had quite given up *hoping*—I felt only dread, only dread—'

Mrs Papagay's irrepressible imagination rushed into Mrs Hearnshaw's conjugal bedroom, aghast, prurient, excited. She saw the large weeping woman brushing her hair—she would have a rather good ivory brush, yes, and a little cheval glass, and would be wearing a kind of black silk peignoir, a *mourning* peignoir, she would be brushing her thick hair and would have taken off all that jewellery, those jet and ebony crosses and lockets, the mourning rings and bracelets, they would be lying sadly in front of her between the candles, like a little shrine to the five Amys. And he would come in, little Mr Hearnshaw, he was a little man, like a black wasp, with a lot of black stiff whiskers to make him look bigger, to puff him out, and a crest of coarse black hair like a horse's hogged mane on his head. And he would have a sort of little sign that *that* was what he wanted. Perhaps he would come up quietly and lift a tress or two and kiss the nape of her sad neck, or massage it with his fingers, if he had the imagination. And the poor woman's head would droop lower and lower, for she wanted to do her conjugal duty but she was afraid, she was afraid right at the beginning, of the seed rushing in . . . Mrs Papagay rapped her rampant imagination severely on the head but it rushed on. Mr Hearnshaw clutched Mrs Hearnshaw and propelled her towards the bed. Mrs Papagay constructed the bed, gave it red velvet curtains and then made them vanish on grounds of inverisimilitude. It was a big *dark* bed, she was sure, and ample, like Mrs Hearnshaw; it had a purple silk eiderdown and fresh lavender-smelling linen sheets. It was a bed that had to be climbed, and Mrs Hearnshaw climbed slowly, having taken off the peignoir and being clad now in white cotton, with broderie anglaise trimmings, threaded with black ribbons. Her big breasts swung inside the bell of this as she leaned over the bed, climbing in, with him close behind her, holding on to her big haunches, that was how Mrs Papagay saw it, the little prickly man, *pushing her in* like a sow into a sty. She saw his white legs below his striped nightshirt, covered with criss-crossing black hairs, like scribbling. They were thin, strong, *angular* legs, not comfortable.

And then the dialogue.

'My dear, I *must* . . .'

'No, please. I have a headache.'

'I must, I must. Be kind to me, dear. I *must*.'

'I cannot bear it. I am afraid.'

'The good Lord will take care. We must do His Will and trust in His Providence.'

With his whiskers bristling on her face, and the little hands pulling at her ample flesh, and the little sharp knees working closer to the white flanks.

'I do not know if I—'

Mrs Papagay, in a rush of indignation saw the little man mount and pump, pump, possessed in a male way, unregarding. Then she was contrite and angry with herself for her own dramaturgy, which had provoked her indignation, and tried to imagine it otherwise— two disconsolate people, who loved each other, turning to each other in the dark, out of their separate griefs, holding each other for comfort, and out of the warmth of comfort, naturally enough, the prick of desire. But that didn't feel natural as the first scene did. Mrs Papagay returned to the present of the séance—all this action having flickered into life and out of it in a brief minute—and wondered whether other people told themselves stories in this way in their heads, whether everyone made up everyone else, living and dead, at every turn, whether this she knew about Mrs Hearnshaw could be called knowledge or lies, or both, as the spirits had *known* what Mrs Hearnshaw had confirmed, that she was indeed *enceinte*.

V

'There is something in the room,' Sophy Sheekhy announced dreamily. 'Between the sofa and the window. A living creature.'

All looked towards this dark corner—those opposite Sophy

Sheekhy, especially Emily Jesse, who was directly opposite her, turning their heads and craning their necks, seeing only the dim outlines of Mr Morris's pomegranates and birds and lilies.

'Can you see it clearly?' asked Mrs Papagay. 'Is it a spirit?'

'I can see it clearly. I don't know what it is. I can describe it. Up to a point. A lot of the colours don't have names.'

'Describe it.'

'It is made up of some substance which has the appearance of—I don't know how to say this—of—*plaited glass*. Of quills, or hollow tubes of glass all bound together like plaits of hair or those pictures you see of the muscles of flayed men all woven together—but these are like molten glass. It appears to be very hot, it gives off a kind of bright *fizzing* sort of light. It is somewhat the shape of a huge decanter or flask, but it is a living creature. It has flaming eyes on the sides of a high glassy sort of head, and it has a long, long beak—or proboscis—its long neck is slightly bent and its nose or beak or proboscis—is tucked into its—into the plaits of—what in a way is its fiery breast. And it is all eyes, all golden eyes, *inside* . . . it has in a way plumes, in three, in three layers, all colours—I can't do the colours—it has plumes like a great mist, a ruff under its—head—and a kind of cloak round its centre—and I don't know if it has a train or a tail or winged feet, I can't see, it's all stirring about all the time, and shining and sparking and throwing off bits of light and I get the feeling, the sensation, it doesn't like me to describe it in demeaning human words and comparisons—it didn't like me saying "decanter or flask", I felt its anger, which was hot. It does wish me to describe it, I can tell.'

'Is it hostile?' asked Captain Jesse.

'No,' said Sophy Sheekhy, slowly. She added, 'It is irritable.'

' "Skirted his loins and thighs with downie Gold / And colours dipt in Heav'n," ' said Mrs Jesse..

'Can you see it too?' said Sophy Sheekhy.

'No. I was quoting the description of the Archangel Raphael in

Paradise Lost. "A seraph winged; six wings he wore, to shade/His lineaments divine".'

Captain Jesse said, 'It is interesting about the wings of an angel. It has been pointed out that an angel would need a protruding breastbone of several feet to counterbalance the weight of its wings, like a bird, like a big bird, you know, an arched breastbone.'

Mrs Jesse said, 'My brother Horatio was once observing a lady sculptor making a carved reredos for a church and disconcerted her by observing, "Angels are only a clumsy form of poultry." '

'Levity, Mrs Jesse,' said Mr Hawke, 'at such a moment—'

'The good Lord makes us as we are, Mr Hawke,' replied Mrs Jesse. 'He knows that a little levity is in its way an expression of awe, of our own inadequacy to ingest marvels. Are we to suppose that Miss Sheekhy is at this moment contemplating the pure Form of an angel? An angel made of air, like Dr Donne's— "Then as an Angell, face, and wings / Of aire, not pure as it, yet pure doth weare . . ." Can an angel be compared to a glass bottle with a proboscis?'

The séance, even at its most intense, visionary and tragic, retained elements of the parlour game. It was not that Mrs Jesse did not believe that Sophy Sheekhy saw her Visitor; it was patently clear that she did; it was more that there were all sorts of pockets of disbelief, scepticism, comfortable and comforting unacknowledged animal un*awareness* of the unseen, which acted as checks and encouraged a kind of cautious normalness.

Mr Hawke said judiciously, 'It is possible that what Miss Sheekhy sees is the form taken by the thought of an angel in the lower world of the Spirits. Swedenborg has many curious things to tell us of angelic offgivings, reliques of past mental states stored up inwardly for future use. He believed for instance that such *offgivings* were inserted into infants in the womb as reliques of past states of angelic conjugial love—an affection is *an organic structure having life*—so we may in certain circumstances be made sensuously aware of it.'

Mr Hawke, Mrs Papagay thought, would theorise if a huge red Cherub with a fiery sword were advancing on him to burn him to the bone; he would explain the circumstances, whilst the stars fell out of the sky into the sea like ripe figs from a shaken fig-tree.

Sophy Sheekhy watched the living creature simmer in its brilliant fronds. It was making her feel alternately hot and cold; her skin pulsed crimson and then the hot tide dipped and she was again pale and clammy. The flask or vase that was the creature seemed to be full of eyes, to be made up of huge golden eyes the way a mass of frogspawn is made up of jelly. She had the idea nevertheless that all this mass of burning vision did not exactly see her, that the creature's awareness of the room they were in, and of its inhabitants, was less acute, vaguer, than hers of it. It hummed at her on various painful notes, that hurt cords in her hearing.

'It says, "Write!" ' she said, in a strangled voice.

Mrs Papagay looked up, all concern, and saw that Sophy Sheekhy was in real distress.

'Who shall write?' she asked, helpfully.

Sophy took up a pencil. Mrs Papagay could see the tendons rigid on her neck. She said to the others, 'Be very careful. This communication is dangerous and painful to the Medium. Keep very still, and concentrate on helping her.'

The pen took a little rush, and produced a neat, elegant handwriting, not at all like Sophy's large schoolgirl spherical characters.

Thou art neither cold nor hot. I would thou wert cold or hot.

> *Your silliness o'ercasts me much with thought.*
> *You have a bounden duty and you ought*
> *Never forget our Lady who is dead:*

Laodicea Laodicea

The pen wavered and then went back, crossing out 'Laodicea' and writing, very slowly and carefully,

Theodicaea Noviss Novissima. Lost Remains, his loved remains sail the placid ocean-plains thy dark freight. Lost, lost.

Thy dark freight a vanished life.

Mrs Papagay could feel the separate yet fused emotion of all the company. Mrs Hearnshaw was awestruck, her breathing laboured. Mr Hawke was alert, his mind trying to decipher. He said, 'Revelation 3, 15 to 16. The writing commanded to the Angel of the Church of the Laodiceans. "I know thy works, that thou art neither cold nor hot: I would thou wert cold or hot. So then because thou art lukewarm, and neither cold nor hot, I will spue thee out of my mouth." We are reproached for lack of zeal. Theodicaea I do not know—it may be that we are not zealous enough in promoting the Kingdom of God in Margate. But the words are not cognate.'

Captain Jesse said, 'One of the lines of poetry is from *In Memoriam,* I believe. It is one of the lines about the ship that bears the dead man home. "Thy dark freight, a vanished life." It is a line I have always particularly admired, since the *weight* of the freight, so to speak, is the weight of absence, of what is vanished, a lost life. It is not what remains that is heavy, but what is not there, what is dark, what I believe is a figure called a paradox, is it not? The ship sails in an ominous calm across the *placid* ocean-plain, it glides like a ghost, the ship bearing . . .'

'Richard, stop talking,' said Mrs Jesse. 'Everyone knows that line is from my brother's poem. The spirits often speak to us through that poem, it seems to be a particular favourite with them, and not only in this house, where it has its natural central place in our thoughts, but in many others, many others.'

She turned her dark, fierce face in the half-light on Sophy Sheekhy. At her side the raven rattled his quills, and the little dog showed his sharp little teeth.

'To whom is this message addressed, pray? To whom and from whom?'

'Who is "our Lady who is dead"?' added Mr Hawke, helpfully, concentrating his agile mind on the spiritual conundrum.

Sophy Sheekhy stared at the Visitor whose eyes were boiling in a kind of immaterial convection current. She took up the pen again:

> Thy voice is on the rolling air
> I hear thee where the waters run
> Thou standest in the rising sun
> And in the setting thou art fair.
> —Revelation 2, 4

Mr Hawke pounced. 'The angel standing in the sun is indeed in Revelation, but he is not Revelation 2, 4, he is in chapter 19, verses 17 to 18 "And I saw an angel standing in the sun; and he cried with a loud voice, saying to all the fowls that fly in the midst of heaven, Come and gather yourselves together unto the supper of the great God; That ye may eat the flesh of kings and the flesh of captains—" '

'We all know that text, Mr Hawke,' said Mrs Jesse. 'And it is, as you say, Revelation 19, 17 to 18.'

Captain Jesse had picked up the Bible from the table, and read out helpfully, 'Here is the verse from chapter 2, verse 4. It is addressed to the Angel of the Church of Ephesus. "Nevertheless I have somewhat against thee, because thou hast left thy first love." Dear me. How interesting. What can that mean?'

'Who is our Lady who is dead?' persisted Mr Hawke.

'It is a translation from the Italian, from one of the sonnets of Dante's *Vita Nuova*,' said Mrs Jesse, tartly. 'The dead Lady is Beatrice, who died at the age of twenty-five and inspired the *Divine Comedy*. The poet met her at the age of nine and remained faithful to her memory, though he married, after her death. Will our visitor not reveal, Miss Sheekhy, to whom these warnings are addressed?'

Sophy Sheekhy looked at the boiling eyes and the feathery fringes.

'He is growing fainter,' she said.

The pen wrote: '*Allas the deeth. Allas min E. Allas.*'

'It is for you, Mrs Jesse,' said Mrs Hearnshaw, who was less knowledgeable about Mrs Jesse's history, and therefore less alarmed by the faintly threatening nature of the messages, interpreted in terms of Mrs Jesse.

'So I supposed,' said Mrs Jesse. 'But we do not know from *whom*. Many spirits, living and dead, may enter the circle, as we all know.'

She put up her two hands, round her head, with its silver-dark wings of hair, breaking the circle. Stirred by this movement, the raven suddenly put up his great wings and clapped them together, over his head, opening his black beak to show a black, pointed, snaky tongue, and uttering a series of harsh, grating cries. Dark feathered shadows flailed across the ceiling. Pug rose from his slumbers and made a noise, half throaty growl, half strangled snort, followed by an explosive rumbling in his belly. A Lilliputian Vesuvius of coals collapsed in the grate, flaring fitfully scarlet and then crimson, with a puff of gas. Sophy Sheekhy's visitor was only a few bright lines on the dark, a diagram paler than the golden fruit and the starry white flowers on the sofa behind him, and then nothing. Mrs Papagay drew the proceedings to an end. She would dearly have loved to question Mrs Jesse closely about the meaning of the visitor's messages, for it was clear to her that they had meaning for Mrs Jesse, very precise meaning, that the spirits had somehow hit home, and that Mrs Jesse was not inclined to share her understanding with the rest of them. They usually took a cup of tea, or of coffee, after their exertions, and discussed the meaning of what had transpired, but on this occasion Mrs Papagay observed that Mrs Jesse was tired and that it would be best if they left.

Mrs Jesse did not thank her. Captain Jesse began a long rambling speech about the Laureate's depiction of the sea in his great poem. He pronounced the stanzas about burial at sea to be particularly fine. 'You might think it was a landsman's understanding of that ceremony, and you would be right, of course, a landsman is affected differently from a sailor by the ocean. I believe the sea is both more matter-of-fact and more ever-present and dare I say more *mysterious* to a sailor than to a landsman; it is borne forcibly home to a sailor how far below and around him at all moments is shifting salt water in which he cannot survive, and this perhaps causes him to view our human existence as something precarious and temporary in the nature of things; the landsman has more the illusion of stability and permanences, you know, the landsman is more struck by the disappearance of the corpse in the water, though I have never myself seen a body sink with its white trail of bubbles, the air going so far in the water, you know, and then rising again, being forced to rise, as the body goes more and more slowly into its other element where it will rest—I have never seen this without a constraint of pain and moment of terror—all sailors are afraid of that element, rightly so—and you would be surprised too how many naval men murmur to themselves those lines about the mother who prays God will save her sailor son, whilst that exact moment "His heavy-shotted hammock-shroud/Drops in his vast and wandering grave." "Vast and wandering" is very good, very good indeed. They keep that book under their pillows, these naval men, you know, they appreciate the understanding . . .'

'Stop talking, Richard,' said Mrs Jesse.

VI

A cab bore Mrs Hearnshaw away. Mr Hawke offered to accompany the other two ladies to their home—it was on his way, it was dark, the walk would benefit all of them. Out on the pavement he attempted to take the arms of both ladies, but Sophy Sheekhy drew back, and they somehow found themselves progressing along the Front with Mr Hawke and Mrs Papagay in front and Sophy walking a few paces behind, like a dutiful child. There were gaslights along the Front, whose yellow flames danced and shimmered. Beyond, the sea was ink-black, with occasional curls of white crests in the small wind. A vast and wandering grave indeed, Mrs Papagay thought. Arturo must be ground white bones by now. It was probable that there had been no one to sew him neatly into a weighted hammock. Ah dear, but come thou back to me. Nevermore, her mind muttered.

Mr Hawke said, 'I *detest* that bird, Mrs Papagay. I think its presence most inappropriate on such occasions. I have tried to point this out, but Mrs Jesse does not choose to hear. The little dog is not an agreeable little dog, it is a smelly little dog, to be blunt, Mrs Papagay. But I sometimes believe that bird is possessed of a malignant spirit.'

'It reminds me irresistibly of Edgar Allan Poe's raven, Mr Hawke.

'Ghastly grim and ancient raven wandering from the Nightly
    shore—
Tell me what thy lordly name is on the Night's Plutonian shore!'
    Quoth the raven, "Nevermore." '

'It is hard', said Mr Hawke, 'to divine whether that poem is designed as some macabre exercise of humour, or a genuine response to the sense of loss we feel for the beloved Departed. It has a tantivy tantivy sound that is hard to take seriously in such a melancholy and sinister circumstance.'

'It is very easy to learn,' said Mrs Papagay, 'and hard to get out of the mind once it is lodged there.'

She pulled her feather scarf tighter round her neck with her free hand, and recited at random.

'But the raven still beguiling all my sad soul into smiling,
Straight I wheeled a cushioned seat in front of bird and bust and
    door;
Then, upon the velvet sinking, I betook myself to linking
Fancy unto fancy, thinking what this ominous bird of yore—

What this grim, ungainly, ghastly, gaunt and ominous bird of yore
Meant in croaking "Nevermore."

This and more I sat divining, with my head at ease reclining
On the cushion's velvet lining that the lamp-light gloated o'er,
But whose velvet violet lining with the lamp-light gloating o'er,
She shall press, ah, nevermore!'

'It is certainly *vivid,*' said Mr Hawke dubiously. 'It portrays
obsessive grief, of which *you,* in your profession, with your gifts,
Mrs Papagay, must see more than enough. I was much struck with
the apposite nature of some of the communications this evening to
the situation of Mrs Jesse. "Because thou hast turned from thy first
love." There is a certain delicacy often felt as to the advisability of
second marriages, particularly now it is known that the integral
human partner survives the Grave, as spirit. It may be felt that to
take a second partner is wrong. What is your opinion on this
matter, Mrs Papagay?'

'In India,' said Mrs Papagay, 'I believe it is enjoined on widows
to place themselves beside their dead masters on the funeral pyre,
and voluntarily submit themselves to incineration. I find that hard
to imagine, yet it is done, it is even, we are told, usual.'

She had *tried* to imagine, the silk-robed woman, exalted, stepping up the heap of scented wood to embrace the embalmed dead
flesh. She tried to imagine the flames. She imagined quite successfully the frantic involuntary struggle of the unwilling, whose young
life revolted, and the dark hands and severe faces that brought
down, that bound, that overcame.

'But in a Christian society,' persisted Mr Hawke. 'Mrs Jesse, for
instance, did she do well, or ill?'

'Mrs Jesse was only *betrothed* to the young man,' Mrs Papagay
demurred. 'There had been no marriage.'

'As to that,' said Mr Hawke, 'Swedenborg teaches, as you know,
that true conjugial love comes to us all but once, that our souls have

one mate, one perfect other half, whom we should seek ceaselessly. That an angel, properly speaking, joins two parts in one, in *conjugial love*. For in a heavenly Marriage, and Heaven *is* a Marriage, of and in the Divine Human, truth is conjoined with good, understanding with will, thought with affection. For truth and understanding and thought are male, but good, will and affection are female, we are taught.

'So two married partners in Heaven are not called two, but one angel, and this is what is meant, Swedenborg tells us, by the Lord's words: "Have ye not read, that he which made them at the beginning made them male and female. And said, For this cause shall a man leave father and mother, and shall cleave to his wife: and they twain shall be one flesh? Wherefore they are no more twain, but one flesh. What therefore God hath joined together, let no man put asunder." '

'That is very beautiful and very true,' said Mrs Papagay, vaguely. Her imagination could not hook itself into good and will and truth and understanding; these were cold null little words, like identical sixpences, dropped, chink, chink, in the collection dish on a Sunday. She could imagine 'one flesh', the beast with two backs, Arturo had said, and a delicious sensation of melting and vanishing in warmth all down the front, from the breast to the key in the lock that held them.

Mr Hawke patted her hand, as it lay demurely on his arm, with his free hand. He said, 'Swedenborg describes the conjugial blisses of the Heavens in the most delightful, the most—iridescent way. He tells us that in the innermost heaven conjugial love—which is a state of innocence, Mrs Papagay—is represented by various beautiful objects, such as a lovely virgin in a bright cloud, such as atmospheres bright as diamonds, and sparkling as though with carbuncles and rubies. All the angels, Mrs Papagay, are clothed, corresponding to their natures, as all things in heaven correspond.

The most intelligent angels have garments which glitter as with flame, and some are resplendent as with light, while the less intelligent have garments of clear or opaque white without splendours, and the still less intelligent have garments of various colours. But the angels of the innermost Heaven are naked.'

Mr Hawke, a little out of puff, paused for effect, and patted Mrs Papagay's gloved hand, where it lay on his arm, with his own. Mrs Papagay was distracted by the word 'carbuncles', which she always, when reading or hearing about Heaven, saw in their earthly or fleshly sense, as distended, painful lumps of hard flesh on foot or nose or buttock. So there are carbuncles on the Divine Human, something irrepressible in her—something to do with Arturo— tried to say.

'Swedenborg,' said Mr Hawke portentously, 'was the first religious founder to give to the expression of sexual delight the central place in heaven that it holds in many of our hearts on earth—to divine, and to constate, that earthly love and Heavenly Love, are truly One, at their highest. This is a noble, a daunting understanding, of our nature and our true *duty* do you not think?'

'Better to marry than burn,' said Mrs Papagay reflectively, quoting the gloomy admonition of the misogynist Saint Paul, but thinking of her own state of mind and body. Mr Hawke made her aware of his own discreet burning at her side.

'And yourself, Mrs Papagay. For yourself, would you consider at any point a second marriage? Does your spiritual nature feel itself in search of its soul-mate? I hope you do not consider the question impertinent. I do not mean it so. It comes from a lively—a very lively—concern for your welfare, your nature—to which mine is drawn, as you, with your sensitivity, will already have perceived.'

And that, thought Mrs Papagay, was well negotiated. She said, 'Bravo' to him in her mind, for that. He was asking her for something, but leaving open a decent retreat into the purely spiritual for both of them. He was frank, and he was devious. 'Bravo', Mrs Papagay said to herself, looking at the dark sea, and thinking of Arturo under it. Was Arturo her soul-mate, the other half of her angel? She did not know. She only knew that Arturo had satisfied her body in ways to her previously unimaginable, had touched her with a thousand delectable flames, that she missed daily his smell, male, salt, tobacco, dryness, desire, inside her nostrils and her belly. And the body which had given her such delight was washing in shreds and fragments somewhere in all that cold weight of water. The automatic writing had used some of his private nonce-words, 'little pudy hand,' it had said. 'Look at your pudy hands and feet, little Lilias,' Arturo had said. She did not know if 'pudy' was a mis-translation of a word from one of his many tongues, or a word made up for what he liked to lick and stroke. She supposed it was almost certain that some quirk of her own mind had put Arturo's word into Mrs Hearnshaw's Amys' message. But maybe it had been Arturo, telling her he was there.

'I hardly know, Mr Hawke,' said Mrs Papagay. 'I was happy with Captain Papagay, and I grieve for him, and I am resigned to a lonely life on this earth. I make do as best I can. I try to be good and active. It is true that I miss the married state. Most women do, I suppose. Most human beings; it is after all natural. I do not know about "soul-mates". I have seen men and women *consumed* by love for each other, and I do not aspire to that state, I cannot imagine what it might be like. But the comfort of a shared hearth—of a shared life—of mutual affection—I do confess to desiring, however hard I try to be satisfied with my present lot.'

'I have never experienced that happiness and comfort, Mrs Papagay. Once it seemed I might—but the cup was taken from me at the last moment, as my lips approached its brim. I too became resigned to the half-life of solitude. I do not think that at that time I had found my one soul-mate, though it appeared to me then that this was so. Swedenborg says that the Lord in His Divine Human understands that men may make many earthly marriages in a sincere search for the One true soul-mate, and does not condemn these marriages, as he condemns adulteries undertaken in levity of spirit.'

Mrs Papagay found this hard to answer. She said, 'Do you suppose there could be uncertainty, Mr Hawke, as to the identity of . . . such a person?'

'I think there could, Mrs Papagay. I think a man may look at many women and wonder, is it she, is it she? and be in true doubt. I have certainly *wondered*. I have never *recognised*.'

They walked on in silence, and Sophy Sheekhy glided behind them in her dove-coloured boots.

They reached Mrs Papagay's house, where they were accustomed, all three, to take a glass of port or sherry, before Mr Hawke went on his way. It was a tall, thin, terrace-house, with a door-knocker in the shape of a fat fish, which Arturo had liked, and of which Sophy Sheekhy was fond. Betsy, the maid-of-all-work, was instructed to light a fire for them on cold Winter evenings when they came back exhausted from the seances. It burned brightly in the grate of the parlour, which was on the first floor, behind tall, narrow windows, a tall narrow room. Mrs Papagay busied herself with glasses and decanters. Mr Hawke stood in the hearth and warmed his legs. Sophy Sheekhy sat at a distance from the fire and the other two, leaning back in her chair, and closing her eyes. Mr Hawke addressed her.

'Are you much fatigued, my dear, by your experiences today? The creature you described was certainly strange—too strange to be a product of the imagination, a wonderful gift.'

'I *am* very tired,' said Sophy Sheekhy. 'I do not think I shall be able to digest a glass of port. I will take a little milk, if I may, Mrs

Papagay, and retire early. I am very uneasy. Something is *unfinished*. I feel weighed upon. I need to be calm and still.'

Indeed, she could hardly raise her eyelids to accept the milk, and her limbs were marbly weight. She sipped, and Mr Hawke savoured his port, and the fire flared up a little, dispelling the mixture of smokiness and sea fret that seemed to hang in the room.

Sophy Sheekhy rose dreamily and went away to bed. Mr Hawke sat in an armchair facing his hostess. Mrs Papagay, moving to replenish his glass, caught sight of herself in the mirror over the table, and thought she had not wholly lost her looks. Her colour was high, but lively, healthy, her large dark eyes were still shaded by good black lashes, her nose was sharp and arched but within the bounds of elegance, and she had not put on, or lost, too much flesh. She met her own eye, challenging, questioning, and glimpsed Mr Hawke behind her, sizing up her waist, her hips, with a look she knew. He is going to speak, she was suddenly convinced. He is going to commit himself and require an answer.

She took her time with the decanter, thinking what to say. She would be much better off as a respectable married woman. She did need company, she needed gossip, someone to concern herself with, and Sophy Sheekhy had no social ways or curiosity; she lived in another world, very precisely. Mr Hawke might be trained to laugh a little, to relax his solemnity, a lascivious man like that could not be all pure sermonising behind the closed doors of a good home. I hold back, she told herself, from what may be my best chance. I must at least be moderately encouraging, I must respond with cautious warmth, that will be best, give him space and see what he is and does.

Mr Hawke cleared his throat with a loud 'Hem'. 'I should like to revert to the subject of our previous talk, Mrs Papagay. I should like to make it—in a hypothetical way—more personal. Here we do sit by a fireside, very easy in each other's company, I would say, very natural, enjoying the good things of life and sharing also high ideals, high intuitions, pressing intimations—' He was carried away in a direction in which he had not meant to go, but his preaching style was too much for him, '—pressing intimations of the unseen, the spirit world, crowding upon us on every side, close and wonderful.'

'Indeed,' said Mrs Papagay. 'It is so, and we should give thanks.' That rang a little *untrue,* she thought.

'I have hoped', said Mr Hawke, 'that I have lightened your loneliness a little with my—concern—with my—*understanding*—with my affection, may I say, Mrs Papagay?'

'I have felt it,' said Mrs Papagay with deliberate solemn vagueness. He doesn't know if he's in a church or a drawing-room, she thought. Will he ever? In a bedroom, will he distinguish? Would he—and his wife—pray lengthily at the bedside, or even—her imagination was setting off again—during the act?

'Lilias,' said Mr Hawke. 'I should like to feel I had the right to call you Lilias.'

'It is a long time since anyone has called me Lilias,' said Mrs Papagay.

And then Mr Hawke did a terrible thing.

'Job,' he said, 'my name is Job,' and cast himself bodily at Mrs Papagay as she sat on her cherry-coloured velvet sofa, missing his footing perhaps, she thought afterwards, perhaps he only meant to sit at her feet, or to kiss her hand, but as it was he cast his small rotund person more or less into her black silk lap, like Mrs Jesse's Pug suddenly taking a lumbering leap on to the sofa, so that his hands scrabbled at her bosom, and his breath, heavy with port wine, invaded her lips and nostrils. And Mrs Papagay, that cautious woman of the world, screamed out and pushed automatically at him with strong rejecting hands, so that he bounced back on his bottom on to the hearthrug, clutching at her ankles, and making a wheezing noise from a purply face.

VII

Emily Jesse lit the oil-lamp and considered the automatic writing. The servant, a blowsy, self-assertive, hysterical girl, with a tendency to faint in a haze of sherry fumes and a daemonic capacity to cause the evaporation of whisky in decanters and silver teaspoons in boxes, cleared away the teacups and poked the dying fire. Captain Jesse paced up and down in the window, looking out at the stars, and murmuring about the weather, as though he were trying to steer the house to some distant port across deep gulfs. You could not see the sea from this window, but you might have thought you could, the way he looked out. He murmured mathematical observations, and commented to himself on the visibility of Sirius, of Cassiopeia, of the Pleiades. 'Stop talking, Richard,' said Emily automatically, frowning over the papers. She had once overheard her sister-in-law, Emily Tennyson, telling someone that Alfred absolutely *had* to leave home, on some excuse or other, if he had warning that Captain Jesse was coming, for Captain Jesse babbled indiscriminately and Alfred had need of *absolute calm* in order to compose his poetry. 'She wraps Alfred up like a mummy and does his buttons like a baby,' Emily Jesse would say to herself uncharitably, but only to herself, for the Tennysons were close, close, and fiercely attached to each other, all of them, except poor Edward in his lunatic asylum, and they had tried their best to love and encompass him too, until it became clear they couldn't. Alfred had composed well enough, and better than now, in the cramped and inventive racket of the Rectory, which had so delighted Arthur in 1829, in 1830, those few weeks, when their angry father had been away in France, and they had all been in blossom, expansive and playful. Alfred had been a great poet then, and was a great poet now, and Arthur had recognised that fact early, and with a delightful, strengthening and calm certainty.

She considered the handwriting of the messages, so unlike Sophy Sheekhy's innocent loops and circles. It was somewhere between Arthur's small quick hand, and Alfred's, also small and quick, but less pinched. It staggered a little, here and there. It had Arthur's characteristic small *d,* hooked backwards at the top, but not always. It had such a *d* in both *d*s of 'dead'—'Never forget our Lady who is dead'—and also in the controversial and troubling Theodicaea. The messages were all undoubtedly to do with Arthur, and perhaps she should have cried out, in pain and longing, as Mrs Hearnshaw had, as she saw his words, in a passable rendering of his hand. But she had not. She had questioned. She had dissembled. She knew, for instance, she the Lady of her Arthur's eternal devotion, Monna Emilia, min Emilie, dearest Nem, dearest Nemkin, that these lines of Dante were not only from the *Vita Nuova,* but from Arthur's own translation of Dante's poems of devotion to his dead Lady, Monna Beatrice, done so little before his death. '*L'amaro lagrima che voi faceste*' he had given her to translate, teasing her for her bad memory, her faulty constructions. 'The bitter weeping you made', addressing the poet's own eyes, which had briefly rested on another maiden, when they 'had a bounden duty and they ought / Never forget our Lady who is dead'. The spiritualist newspapers, the members of the New Jerusalem Church, would be overwhelmed that any message so pretty, so private, so appropriate, could be sent to one mourner. But there was more—beside the by now habitual citation of *In Memoriam*, there was the Theodicaea. A. H. H. had written the 'Theodicaea Novissima' for those exclusive intelligences the Cambridge Apostles, who pronounced it wholly original and very fine. He had argued that the reason for evil was God's need for love—for the *passion of love*—which had caused Him to create the finite Christ as an object of desire, and a Universe, full of sin and sorrow, to provide an adequate background for this passion to work itself out in. The Incarnation, Arthur had argued, had made human love—'the tendency towards a union so intimate, as virtually to amount to identification'—one with Divine Love, so that Christ's loving death was a way to God. Here it became obscure, to Emily, how evil was so necessary to this Love, how Arthur could be so sure. The essay was abstract and boiled with human passion. Arthur had wished she had not read it.

> *I was half inclined to be sorry that you looked into that Theodicaea of mine. It must have perplexed rather than cleared your sight of those high matters. I do not think women ought to trouble themselves much with theology: we who are more liable to the subtle objections of the Understanding, have more need to handle the weapons that lay them prostrate. But where there is greater innocence, there are larger materials for a single-hearted faith. It is by the heart, not by the head, that we must all be convinced of the two great fundamental truths, the reality of Love, and the reality of Evil. Do not, my beloved Emily, let any cloudy mistrusts and perplexities bewilder your perception of these, and of the great corresponding Fact, I mean the Redemption, which makes them objects of delight instead of horror.*

'I do not think women ought to trouble themselves much with theology.' She had found that sentence chilling and rebuffing at the time—she had put a lot of work, in a desultory way, into under-

standing the involutions and niceties of the Theodicaea, only to
arouse one of Arthur's most *lordly* letters, which always made her,
conscious of her provincial lack of social grace, her female lack of
educated talk, wince a little with anxiety and some other, unde-
fined feeling. It was hard now, at sixty-four, to remember that
Arthur had been only twenty when he wrote that, and twenty-two
when he died. He had seemed like a young god. Everyone he knew
had known he was a young god. He had not been so lordly when
they were face to face, he had been flushed—partly because of the
circulatory problem which made him ill, even then—and his hands
had been damp, and his narrow mouth anxious. But they had been
face to face, in all, for only four weeks before their engagement,
and three more short visits before his death. He had treated her like
a mixture of a goddess, a house-angel, a small child and a pet lamb.
This was, she supposed, not unusual. It had not seemed unusual.
She had loved him passionately. She had thought of him most of
the time, most days, after that first nervous embrace on the yellow
sofa.

She turned back to the spirit writings. They were all, all reproaches, bitter reproaches, aimed to hurt. They were pointed.

Nevertheless I have somewhat against thee, because thou hast left thy
first love.
Your silliness o'ercasts me much with thought.
Lost Remains.

People are always angry and disappointed, thought Emily Jesse.
She had wanted so much to speak to lost Arthur, to be reassured
that she was forgiven for not having been able to be what Arthur's
sister Julia Hallam called a 'dedicated *Nun*'. But it might be that
Arthur, too, like his family, like Alfred, did not really forgive. She
had a letter in her bureau from her nephew, Hallam Tennyson,
named like her own son, Arthur Hallam Jesse, for lost Arthur, and

like him, godson to old Mr Hallam, who had been so excessively kind to herself, as a memorial, in memoriam.

> *My dear Aunt,*
>
> *You may imagine my surprise when it was brought to my attention that a copy of Arthur Hallam's* Remains, *inscribed to you by his Father, had been offered for sale by a bookseller in Lyme Regis. My Father and I assume that the Volume was sold* inadvertently—*though how that could happen is not clear to him or to me—and have immediately secured its safety. It is here in our Library, where we shall keep it, until you advise us differently. You will understand my Father's feelings on making this unhappy discovery . . .*

She was convinced that it was the sale of the *Remains* that had attracted the spirit displeasure. It might even be Arthur's own displeasure, though she wanted to hope that Sophy Sheekhy had, through some process of animal magnetism and aethereal telegraphy, managed to communicate the buzzing of Hallam Tennyson's disapproval, of Alfred's disappointment. It was true that she should not have sold the *Remains.* It was in execrable taste to have sold the *Remains,* of which old Mr Hallam had had only a hundred copies privately printed, for his son's close friends and family, the testimony to his genius, tragically cut off. There were writings in there about Dante and divine Love, about sympathy and Cicero. There was the spirited review of Alfred's *Poems, Chiefly Lyrical* (1830), which had aroused the sneers of the tetchy Christopher North at the young critic's 'superhuman—nay, supernatural—pomposity' and caused a flurry of impotent protective rage in all the Tennysons for both the young men, Alfred, morbidly sensitive to criticism, and Arthur, only apparently, proudly, more robust. There were also poor Arthur's poems, including those reverently breathed to herself, and some to one of his previous loves, Anna Wintour, whose graces, as young men will, he had enumerated to his Emily,

sitting on the yellow sofa, offering her himself, and all that he had
so far become in his short life. Anna's poems, Emily thought, were
on the whole better than her own, more lively, less full of sweet
incense and the thrill of sanctification. There was also a poem
inviting her, Emily, to enter the Temple of Italian poetry, assuring
her that the feast of music, 'this pleasure thou dost owe me', would
not wrong her gentle spirit

> or make less dear
> That element whence thou must draw thy life;—
> An English maiden and an English wife.

This poem reminded her of her struggles to master Italian, to
please him. It was odd that the spirits should have cited with such
precision one of his translations from the *Vita Nuova*. He had
shown her them with such pride, but they were not in the *Remains*.
Old Mr Hallam had taken it upon himself to burn them, finding
them 'rather too literal and consequently harsh'. She had rather
liked the harshness—it had a kind of male forcefulness, a kind of
directness she had been taught to value. Old Mr Hallam had taken
much upon himself, including the guilt of having separated the
lovers, and the care of Emily's sad future, which was to be beside
his own sad future. She had tried, she thought. She was not brought
up to find the rigorous formality of the Hallams easy. She liked
Ellen, the younger sister, who was like Arthur, without the dramatic tension of sexual difference, but with a kind of sympathetic
ease. But the friendship had not really survived. Had not survived
her marriage, that was.

She had not exactly taken a decision to sell the *Remains*. The
house was full of books, and now and then she, or Richard, shipped
off a basket or two, to make room for new ones. She remembered
now perhaps glimpsing the binding of the *Remains* between other
books shifted from the same shelf. She had seen, and pretended not

to see. She hoped Arthur might forgive her. She found the objects which attracted the devotion of his worshippers—including herself, including that desperate fainting girl—almost too much to bear. She was not at all sure Arthur would forgive her. His writings were the best part of himself. His truncated future. She should not have sold the *Remains*, intentionally or unintentionally. She was at fault.

She had never liked the *Remains*, partly at least because it reminded her, always and sickeningly, of that terrible Letter.

'*He died at Vienna on his return from Buda, by Apoplexy, and I believe his Remains come by Sea from Trieste.*'

She had not liked, in those early days, to think of the terror of the fate of those flesh and blood Remains, and yet had been drawn to do so. The body decayed in earth, the spirit went free. Someone told her Arthur's heart had been shipped in a separate iron casket. There had been an Autopsy. He had been cut up and wounded, poor Arthur, dead and unfeeling—'*the Physician endeavour'd to get any Blood from him—and on Examination it was the general Opinion, that he could not have lived long*'. He had been dismembered and searched as he began on the process of his dissolution. She had spent his absence imagining his return—the outstretched hands, the smiling eyes, the large brow with the 'bar of Michelangelo' of which he was so proud, in the bone over the eyes. She could not in those days stop herself imagining what was to come of all that. She had not lived next to a churchyard for nothing. The Thing coming so slowly across the sea filled her with horror, which she never expressed to a soul. Arthur himself might have understood. He had introduced a joke about the stinking corpse of the fair Rosamond into his criticism of Alfred's use of 'redolent' to describe the perfumes in the garden of the Arabian Nights. 'Bees may be redolent of honey; spring may be "redolent of youth and love"; but the absolute use of the word has, we fear, neither in Latin nor in English any better authority than the monastic epitaph on Fair Rosamond: "*Hic jacet in tomba Rosa Mundi, non Rosa Munda, non redolet, sed olet, quae redolere solet."* ' Or perhaps he wouldn't have. You have to be touched to the quick, to touch dead flesh with the imagination and rest there, as she had done in all those months of illness and grief. Alfred too had been there. Alfred too had said nothing, but it was clear throughout *In Memoriam* that his imagination had faced and probed what remained, or ceased recognisably to remain, of that much-loved form.

> Old Yew, which graspest at the stones
> That name the under-lying dead,
> Thy fibres net the dreamless head,
> Thy roots are wrapt about the bones.

Now *that* was both gruesome and in some way beautiful, making the dead a part of nature. Worse, more savage, was

> I wage not any feud with Death
> For changes wrought on form and face;
> No lower life that earth's embrace
> May breed with him, can fright my faith.

The breeding of 'lower life' had also haunted her own dreams— indeed had begun to cease to do so only shortly before *In Memoriam,* published in 1850, seventeen years after Arthur's death and eight years after her own marriage, which should have purged some of the horrors. *In Memoriam* had reawakened much that had lain quiet. Alfred's mourning had been long and steadfast. It put hers, however fierce, however dark, however passionate, ultimately to shame. Nevertheless she had moments of violence. On receiving Hallam Tennyson's letter, alone in her drawing-room, she had strode up and down as though the room were too small, and cried out to emptiness, 'Let him buy it back then and scent it with violets!' Violets budded all over *In Memoriam*. 'My regret / Becomes an April violet / And buds and blossoms with the rest."

Arthur had written, in that savaged review, of Alfred, 'When this Poet dies, will not the Graces and the Loves mourn over him, *"fortunataque favilla nascentur violae"*?' and Alfred had turned the compliment on dead Arthur, mourning him in violets. In grim moods, of which she had her share, Emily Jesse had compared the *Remains* to Isabella's pot of basil, which produced balmy perfumed leafits because it was watered by grieving tears and drew

> Nurture besides, and life, from human fears,
> From the fast mouldering head there shut from view.

It was wrong, she knew it was wrong, to see Arthur in terms of mouldering heads and moral oppression. When he came to Somersby he had made it into a real Summerland of its own, a land of Romance. She could see him now, leaping down out of the gig into the lane, under the trees, embracing Alfred, Charles, Frederick, his Cambridge friends, smiling amiably at the younger boys and the assembled garden of girls, Mary the beauty, Cecilia the intelligent, Matilda the damaged innocent, Emilia, Emily, the wild and shy. 'I love you all,' he had told them, sitting out on the lawn in the evening light, 'I am in love with every one of you, however romantic, however prosaic, however strange and fantastic, however resolutely down-to-earth." He had put up his arms in a great circular gesture embracing them all, which echoed, or more properly was echoed, in the gestures of the witch-elms, in *In Memoriam*, the trees who 'Laid their dark arms about the field'. She remembered them reading Dante and Petrarch aloud, she remembered singing and playing the harp, and Arthur's watching, delighted, ear and eye, gave the music a kind of perfection of intention and resonance they never had when the family played and sang only to itself. And this too, Alfred had captured perfectly, perfectly, in the poetry of memory, in memoriam, so that though her own phantom voice still sounded in phantom moonlight in her private recollection, it was always accompanied by his words.

> O bliss, when all in circle drawn
> About him, heart and ear were fed
> To hear him, as he lay and read
> The Tuscan poets on the lawn:
>
> Or in the all-golden afternoon
> A guest, or happy sister, sung,
> Or here she brought the harp and flung
> A ballad to the brightening moon.

She thought Arthur had at first been undecided whether he was to be in love with Mary or with herself. She was quite a sharply *noticing* girl when not bursting with passionate feeling, and she herself at first had only shared the general Tennyson-worship of this bright being. He sat down and wrote poems to both of them, to Emily and Mary, he admired both pairs of dark eyes, he brought back little posies of wild flowers for both girls from his ramblings with Alfred in the woods. He had a kind of accomplished town-flirtatiousness with women, which alarmed Emily more than the composed Mary, and caused her to see herself as a country-mouse, though before his arrival she had seen herself, particularly on horseback, as a wild Byronic heroine, only waiting for her elegant Prince to remove her to her proper sphere. She quite decided he would love Mary, whom she also loved, and loved to this day, sharing with her the visionary hopes and delights of the New Jerusalem Church and the spiritualist discoveries.

And then they had come upon each other in the Fairy Wood, he and she, when the whole rambling family had somehow become separated. It was April 1830 and the weather was all watery and silver-gold light, and the sky was full of movement, long racing ribbons of clouds, and veils of water, and rainbow-flashes, and the trees were both sombre-stemmed and alive with a veil of bright green buds, and the earth smelled mouldy and was spattered all over with pale windflowers and glossy yellow celandine. And she had stood at one side of the glade, breathing fast because she had been running, and he had stood at the other, with the light behind him like a halo and his face in shadow, Alfred's friend, Arthur, and he had said, 'You look, you really look, like a wandering fairy or dryad. I never saw anything so beautiful in my life.' Some women, remembering this scene, might have remembered a vision of themselves to fill the space at her side of the glade, or to balance his eager, smiling one at his, but Emily was not a mirror-gazer, she carried no such self-image. She could not even remember what she had been wearing. Only the energy of his pleasure at seeing her, and her stepping towards him, for this moment not Alfred's friend, but a young man who *saw her* and was full of equally balanced apprehension and anticipation. So she had walked towards him across the flower-carpet, in the smell of leaf-mould, and he had taken both her hands and said, 'You know I have been falling in love with you for what seems like forever, and can only really have been four weeks?'

She always thought of the centre of her love for Arthur in this way, of two creatures joining hands in a leafy, flowery thicket. Such a thicket, Arthur said, for he shared, indeed created the sacredness of that moment, as was the English type, such as might have been met in Malory or Spenser, of the eternal sacred groves of Nemi and Dodona. He addressed his letters to Nem, to dearest Dod, a childish lisping of something daemonic, or so she hoped. He compared her to the Fair Persian in Alfred's *Recollections of the Arabian Nights,* 'tressèd with redolent ebony, / In many a dark delicious curl'. He compared their grove in the Fairy Wood to the 'Blackgreen bowers and grots' of that rich vision, and recited, in his clear, modulated voice, higher than Alfred's rich grumble, the vision of the Nightingale in the grove.

The living airs of middle night
Died round the bulbul as he sung;
Not he: but something which possessed
The darkness of the world, delight,
Life, anguish, death, immortal love,
Ceasing not, mingled, unrepressed,
Apart from place, withholding time . . .

Somersby in those days was a place created and rendered timeless by the imagination, which sang like the Nightingale. Alfred's *Ode to Memory*, like the *Recollections of the Arabian Nights*, was a young man's first recording, he said, of the sense that he already had an irrevocable Past of his own, his childhood reading, the earthly Paradise he made out of the garden. As they got older the Tennysons more and more remembered the Rectory garden in his words:

Or a garden bowered close
With plaited alleys of the trailing rose,
Long alleys falling down to twilight grots,
Or opening upon level plots
Of crownèd lilies, standing near
Purple-spikèd lavender:
Whither in after life retired
From brawling storms,
From weary wind,
With youthful fancy re-inspired,
We may hold converse with all forms
Of the many-sided mind,
And those whom passion hath not blinded,
Subtle-thoughted, myriad-minded.

My friend, with you to live alone,
Were how much better than to own
A crown, a sceptre, and a throne!

Emily Jesse shuffled the spirit papers in her gipsy hands as she found herself caught again in the thicket of thoughts that surrounded timeless Somersby, made by men, made for men. There was Alfred, desiring to live alone with his friend, to whom he gave, without irony, Coleridge's epithet of high praise for Shakespeare, 'myriad-minded'. It was not that she was *jealous of Alfred*—how could she be? It was she, Emily, Arthur meant to marry, it was her approach that made him catch his breath, it was on her lips that he pressed those nervous, urgent kisses. He was eager for marriage, he burned for it, that was clear enough. Alfred was different. Alfred had most terribly tried the patience of Emily Sellwood, sister to Charles's much-loved wife, Louisa. He had teased out their engagement, on, off, on, off, over twelve long years, marrying her finally in 1850, the year of *In Memoriam,* when she was thirty-seven, and her youth was irrevocably gone. Emily Jesse had received desperate letters in her time from Emily Sellwood, begging her for some assurance of continuing love and friendship, whilst Alfred gloomed and equivocated, and went away, and wrote. It was curious, Emily Jesse always thought, that Emily Sellwood would tell again and again the story of meeting Alfred in Holywell Wood, when she was walking there with Arthur.

'I was wearing my light-blue dress,' Emily Sellwood would say, 'and Alfred suddenly appeared through the trees in a long blue cloak, and said to me, "Are you a dryad or a Naiad or what are you?" And I was suddenly quite sure that I loved him, and I have never wavered in that love, whatever the temptations, whatever the pain.'

Emily Jesse imagined the young men talking together in the room they shared at night. She imagined Arthur telling Alfred, as they lay smoking on the two white couches in the attic room, about his vision of her in the Fairy Wood, and Alfred turning it into a kind of poem in his head, which he found himself suddenly enacting, faced with another Emily, in another blue dress, on

Arthur's arm. Alfred *diffused* everything so fast into poetry. He never had been very able to distinguish one human being from another—Jane Carlyle, one of his most intimate friends, meeting him at one of Dickens's theatrical parties in 1844, had found herself taken by the hand and told earnestly, 'I should like to know who you are—I know that I know you, but I cannot tell your name.' Emily Jesse thought that Emily Sellwood's response to the dryad-greeting had brought a hard fate on her, though in the end she had a sort of happiness. Two sons, and a devoted Laureate-husband, who drew her about his grounds in an invalid-carriage.

Women gossiping together, she knew, made love-affairs thrilling. What a man said, how he looked, what he dared, his masterfulness, his charming timidity, all this stuff of Romance was woven and knitted delightfully in quiet talk, so that a woman again alone with her professed lover after she had most thoroughly talked him over with her sisters and friends would feel a sudden shock, perhaps exciting, perhaps daunting, perhaps disappointing, at his *difference* from this created figure. She did not know what men made of women when they talked of them. Conventionally, it was believed that they had different, and higher topics to engage them. 'Subtle-thoughted, myriad-minded.' Arthur and Alfred had discussed herself and Emily Sellwood. In what terms?

If she was wholly truthful with herself, she remembered the sight of those two male backs, those two pairs of eagerly climbing legs, going up to the attic with the white beds, with the sensations of one excluded from Paradise. They talked away about love and beauty, sometimes till dawn; she caught the echoes of the indecipherable flow of words, the ruminative grumble, the quick, decisive, leaping voice. From time to time she could hear recitation. The 'Ode to a Nightingale'. 'On a Grecian Urn.' 'Thou still unravish'd bride of quietness'—she knew the words, she could add the rest, as the rhythm hummed. Arthur had praised Alfred's poems by comparing him with Keats and Shelley. He called him a 'poet of sensation', he quoted the letters of the tragically dead young poet. 'O for a life of sensations rather than thoughts!' he echoed, approvingly, praising Alfred for reaching the ideas of good, perfection, truth, suffused by the colouring of 'the energetic principle of love for the beautiful'. Arthur's God, in the 'Theodicaea', he had claimed, had created the Universe full of sin and sorrow, in order to experience Love, for His Son, as he redeemed the fallen world and made it beautiful.

She had once come upon those two, sitting out on the lawn, reclining in wicker chairs with their heads thrown back on battered cushions, discussing, in a male way, the Nature of Things. Alfred's pipe-smoke curled up into the air and diffused itself. Arthur stabbed at the lawn with a kind of prong with which the gardener—obstructed and protested against by the weed-loving Tennysons—tried ineffectively to grub up daisies and clover.

'It all comes out of the old Neoplatonic mythic belief,' Arthur said. 'The Mind, the higher Mind, Nous, immerses itself in inert Matter, Hyle, and creates life and beauty. The Nous is male and the Hyle female, as Ouranos, the sky, is male, and Ge, the earth, is female, as Christ, the Logos, the Word, is male, and the soul he animates is female.'

The young Emily Tennyson, carrying her basket of books, Keats and Shakespeare, *Undine* and *Emma,* passed in front of them and peered between her veils of dark hair at them. They lay back and looked up at her contentedly. Between the sagging wicker arms their two hands almost touched on the turf, one stretched towards the other, one dirty-brown, one well-tended and white.

'Why?' said Emily Tennyson.

'Why what, my dearest?' said Arthur. 'What a picture you make, against the roses, with the wind in your hair. Don't move, I love to see you.'

'Why is inert Matter female and the animating Nous male, please?'

'Because earth is the Mother, because all beautiful things spring from her, trees and flowers and creatures.'

'And Nous, Arthur?'

'Because Men busy their foolish heads with notions, half of which are mere chimaeras, unnatural nonentities, and lead themselves astray.'

Arthur was not good at teasing. He spoke too decisively, as though beginning a lecture.

'That isn't the answer,' she persisted, flushing.

'Because women are beautiful, my little one, and men are mere *lovers* of the beautiful, because women are naturally good and *feel* goodness in the chambers of their sweet hearts as their pure blood goes in and out, and we poor male things only apprehend truth because we are able to *feel* your virtues, to hold our soaring fantasies down to earth.'

'That isn't the answer,' Emily persisted.

'Women shouldn't busy their pretty heads with all this theorising,' he said, beginning to be fatigued. Alfred had abstracted himself; his long black lashes rested on his cheeks. There were the two fingers of their trailing, relaxed arms, touching earth, pointing quietly at each other.

VIII

The fire was sinking, and Pug had gone to sleep and was snoring and bubbling. Aaron was not asleep—he moved sideways along the table towards her, his shoulders hunched, one black eye glittering at her. 'Nevermore,' Emily Jesse said to the bird, with a certain grim wit, and reached into her leather pouch for another morsel for him. He sidled round, peering, and opened his beak. The bit of flesh, roasted but red-raw at the edges, with a slippery fringe of fat, went in, came out, was rearranged, and swallowed in a gulp. Emily watched the throat muscles push. The bird shook himself and looked at her, hoping for more. 'You have terrible fierce crooked claws,' Emily told him, touching his head with a finger. 'You have left your mark on every good chair in this house. There is no virtue in you. We are old and tough and shabby, you and I.'

They had been bred to be generous in spirit. Resentment was ignoble, and Emily hoped she didn't feel it. But she could never be wholly easy about the way in which Alfred's mourning had overtaken her own. Had not only overtaken it, she told herself in moments of bleak truthfulness, had undone and denied it. It had been she, Emily, who fainted, she, Emily, who had lived incarcerated, entombed in grief, for a year, she, Emily, who had reduced the assembled company to tears with her appearance in black, with the one white rose in her hair, as he liked to see her. Alfred had not attended the funeral, and had begun to write again, to go about his life, whilst she lay in her bed of pain and anguish. She remembered her face in the wet pillows, wet through the cotton to the damp feathers inside. She remembered swollen eyelids, uneasy sleep, and terrible wakings to the truth of loss. Her grief for poor Arthur, his bright mind, his young bones, his lecturing and his bodily need of her was confused with her terror over her own now empty future, and she was ashamed of this, she tried to push such thoughts away, so fiercely that they crowded back in moments of slack consciousness, drowsy awakenings, midnight eye-openings in ghastly moonlight.

Alfred's dream Somersby, Arthur's visited garden Paradise, wild wood, and family hearth, with its laughter and its singing, depended on their presence, depended, in a way, on their creation of them. It was different—it had been different before Arthur and was different again after his death—in the long Winter months—for a young girl with no chance of any journey, or occupation, or festivity, except waiting for a husband or mourning a dead lover. She had wanted to get out—and like a woman, a contradictory creature, had been terrified of coming out, so that when a family visit had finally been made by the Tennysons, it had been Alfred and *Mary* who had visited Wimpole Street, whilst she, the chosen one, had lurked in the depths of Somersby, in an agony of social terror over her unpresentable clothes and Lincolnshire accent, in a genuine physical agony of pains in the liver and constrictions of the blood that had left her lying in a nest of sheets and coverlets, warmed with hot stones, and fed with delectable sips of brandy and water, reading Keats and the books Arthur had sent her, *Undine,* whom he said she resembled, and Miss Austen's *Emma,* 'Quite a woman's book—(don't frown, Miss Fytche, I mean it for compliment)—none but a woman and a lady could possess that tact of minute observation, and that delicacy of sarcasm.' She had been so ill, all those young years, she had written such pathetic and pleading letters to the Old Man of the Wolds, her autocratic grandfather, disinheritor of her father and source of cash, begging to be given sufficient money to travel to Europe, or to some spa, where her symptoms might be relieved and her black despair lightened by a little cheerful company. But he had remained obdurate, and she had remained in Somersby, a beloved prison. The pains had been real enough. She had imagined herself as she lay curled about her own tender, swollen belly, like a female Prometheus, whose liver was regularly ripped at by a huge, rapacious dark bird. It drained her life. She could scarcely bring herself to walk out of doors; a kind of dizziness overtook her on the lawn, as though a cloud of wings beat about her head, clapping and humming in her ears, making the air in front of her eyes undulate and buzz. She remembered, half a century ago, standing there and swaying, and groping her way back to the safety of the bedclothes and the reduced glimmer of light from the window. Arthur had offered a way out of all that, half desired, half feared, and had remonstrated with her weakness in letter after letter, enquiring tenderly after her health, urging her to grow better, stronger, readier, more cheerful, more confident.

> And therefore it is, Emily—even because my love for you is part of my religion—that no faults I may discover in you will lessen, but on the contrary will stimulate and exalt it. For your faults, which arise from an overwrought sensibility, too much concentrated by circumstances on itself, have in some degree the complexion of virtues, especially when accompanied with humility to confess, and endeavour to amend them.

His death, ironically, had accomplished what his life could not, had brought her out of her thicket and into polite society. Old Mr Hallam had entertained her with kindness, Arthur's sister Ellen had become her friend, to whom she had written, with a delicious new ease and edge, descriptions of her unpoetic world.

> Remember such icons as Wordsworth and Coleridge etc are never seen in our part of the world—scarcely ever any thing comes over our black wolds, but bleak winds, upon bleak-feeling people; sometimes indeed, a determined hunter is seen swiftly crossing the field at the bottom of the garden, but these eager, life-taking beings, you must own, are even worse than nothing.

She had even denied the Nightingale and its eternal preamble in the thicket, at least in Somersby.

Have the nightingales commenced their warblings yet?—thou art mistaken in supposing there are any in Somersby, no such birds are ever seen with us—Once on a time indeed a solitary one came to Lincoln and trilled for some time in a poor man's garden. Of course, crowds came to see and hear it. The man, becoming quickly aware that his vegetables were getting completely trodden down ("For cabbage he sow'd, and when it grew, / He always cut it off to boil!") had the unheard of barbarity, to shoot this adventurous songster. Dreadful, unmusical clodhopper!— what are all the cabbages in the world to one nightingale.

She had been able to laugh a little with Ellen, as she had not, for fear, for love, for humility, with Arthur. She had sparkled a little— meekly, always mindful of her great grief—at the Hallams' dinner-table, where, one evening, she had been observed by the tall young Lieutenant Jesse. She had mourned nine years, Emily thought. She had known Arthur, alive, for four years, of which she had spent no more than a few weeks in his company. *She had mourned him nine years.* She had hoped that the Hallams would understand, would be kind—she could not, knowing the depth of their grief and the concentration of their lost hopes in Arthur, exactly expect them to be *happy*. They had—or at least old Mr Hallam had—been most correctly, most civilly gracious, had continued her money, which she had confusedly become accustomed to think of as her independence, had not severed relations, though she knew that Julia at least said unkind things of her behind her back—quite as though I was a *heartless flirt* or worse, a *bought woman*, the savage Emily asserted, when she momentarily overcame the meek one. Relations had stiffened, had even soured. She made small talk, never a Tennyson competence, where once she had made quiet jokes that were accepted. She had been trapped in, and sustained by, their grieving affection; she was trapped in, and suffocated by, their quiet, implacable disapproval.

She had spirit enough, she thought, to deal with the Hallams, if only by unmaking them now and then in her mind, as though they had not been. She had travelled since her marriage, had been in Paris during the excitement of the Commune, had roamed the Apennines and seen the Brownings in their Florence home. She had mixed with many kinds of people in London, and if she chose to be thought a little eccentric, she did it, she believed, with a kind of abrupt charm. She could make people laugh, and talked with spirits. But she had not spirit enough, she thought in the dark hours, to bear certain wounds, certain unmentionable pains, inflicted by Alfred's masterpiece and Arthur's monument, *In Memoriam*. Which she admired and idolised, the Lord knew, as much as anyone alive, for it expressed *exactly* the nature of her own shock and sorrow, the very structure and slow process of pain, and the transformations and transmutations of grief, like rot in the earth-mould, like roots and other blind things moving in the grave. Other things also, it expressed, the desire for the presence of the dead, the hand to clasp, the bright eye, the voice, the thoughts spoken and unspoken. It made an eternal world of the bounds of the vicarage lawn and the flat Lincolnshire horizon, over the wold or the sea. It spoke to God and expressed doubt and terror as to His purposes. It felt its way into the thick of her heart fibres and crept in her blood, 'a mass of nerves without a mind' as she had feared to remain.

But Alfred had lived with his grief, and worked upon it, for another eight years after her nine. She had married Richard in 1842 and closed her mourning. Alfred had grieved and written, worked and brooded, from the day of that terrible letter to the day, almost, of his own wedding, ending his solitude in 1850, and putting out *In Memoriam* in that year, with no poet's name on the title page, a book for Arthur, *In Memoriam A. H. H.* Alfred had been faithful, as she had not. He had given her away at her wedding, so quiet, so secret, grumbling a little as he used to do, and had gone on writing those chill, terrible little lyrics, accounts of loss, of defeat, of unappeasable longing.

She believed that in that poem she stood accused. She had not read it at first, as she did later, in the way the wife, or child, or friend or enemy of a novelist riffles through the pages of the latest stories looking for traces of their own existence, anything from a particular lace collar to a secret defect of character they had believed successfully suppressed or cloaked. She had read it with love and tears, as she read all Alfred's poetry, tears for Arthur, tears at its sheer beauty. The young women had had a secret poetry society in the Somersby days, which they had called the Husks—they 'shucked' the seed-corn of the poetry in passionate debates, they read Alfred's and Arthur's prescribed 'sensuous' poetry—Arthur himself claimed credit for the reintroduction of that useful word into the English language. Keats, Shelley, Alfred Tennyson. Their highest term of approbation was 'wicked', by which they meant 'thrilling', disturbing, passionate. Emily Jesse wondered sometimes, as tremulous Emily Tennyson had not, what had possessed them to choose such a dry, lifeless name for themselves, the papery container that held the ripe grain. They had read with love, and so she had read—and could still read—*In Memoriam*. It was, she knew and said often, the greatest poem of their time. And yet, she thought in her bursts of private savagery, it aimed a burning dart at her very heart, it strove to annihilate her, and she *felt* the pain of it, and could not speak of that pain to a soul.

Her small ghost appeared from time to time in the poem. She saw herself early on, in the sixth lyric, the lyric of the drowned sailor, when Alfred likened his own waiting for Arthur's return to a young girl, a 'meek, unconscious dove'. 'Poor child, that waitest

for thy love!' choosing a riband or a rose to please him, turning
back to the mirror 'to set a ringlet right' whilst at that very moment
her future Lord

> Was drowned in passing through the ford,
> Or killed in falling from his horse.

> O what to her shall be the end?
> And what to me remains of good?
> To her, perpetual maidenhood,
> And unto me no second friend.

The ringlets and the rose were hers, though Alfred had made the
meek dove's hair golden, not raven. Arthur had once compared her
voice to that of the Lady in *Comus,* 'stroking the raven down / Of
darkness till it smiles' and had stroked her wild ringlets as he spoke.
She had not been able to manage perpetual maidenhood, whatever
Alfred had supposed or desired. And in some curious way, which
could be poetic tact, the poem had made *Alfred* into Arthur's
widow, even here.

> Two partners of a married life—
> I looked on these and thought of thee
> In vastness and in mystery,
> And of my spirit as of a wife.

And

> My heart, though widowed, may not rest
> Quite in the love of what is gone,
> But seeks to beat in time with one
> That warms another living breast.

The dust of him I shall not see
Till all my widowed race be run.

Alfred had taken Arthur and bound him to himself, blood to
blood and bone to bone, leaving no room for her. It was true that
late in the poem, reference was made to her love and her loss, but
that too was painful, most painful. Alfred had allowed his fantasy to
imagine Arthur's future, Arthur's children, Alfred's nephews and
nieces, mixing their blood.

Thy blood, my friend, and partly mine;
For now the day was drawing on
When thou shouldst link thy life with one
Of mine own house, and boys of thine

Had babbled 'Uncle' on my knee;
But that remorseless iron hour
Made cypress of her orange flower,
Despair of Hope, and earth of thee.

I seem to meet their least desire,
To clap their cheeks, to call them mine.
I see their unborn faces shine
Beside the never-lighted fire.

And these unborn children, with terrible energy, haunted her
and her own two sons, named as they were for the dead, the
younger, Eustace, for her uncle Charles's lost son, and the elder,
Arthur Hallam Jesse, for Arthur. But it had not come about as she
had hoped. Those shining unborn angel-faces were brighter in
the world's eye—and in her own, in dark moments—than the
poor, mundane, anxious little face of Arthur Hallam Jesse, handsome though he was. He was an awkward living evidence of the
failure of perpetual maidenhood, and she herself was uneasy with
him and knew that he knew it, that he thought her cold. Alfred's

poem had no place for Arthur Hallam Jesse, though it ended with a celebration of a wedding, an ambiguous assertion of the power of life over death, an invocation to a new soul to 'draw from out the vast / And strike his being into bounds'. Alfred had passed over her own inconvenient wedding to celebrate that of her sister Cecilia to Edmund Lushington, an Apostolic friend of himself and Arthur,

> worthy; full of power;
> As gentle; liberal-minded, great,
> Consistent; wearing all that weight
> Of learning lightly like a flower.

Here too, she and Arthur had been briefly united in Alfred's words

> Nor have I felt so much of bliss
> Since first he told me that he loved
> A daughter of our house; nor proved
> Since that dark day a day like this.

He could hardly have celebrated her own wedding-day, which preceded Cecilia's by a few months, with such roundness and perfection. But he had somehow managed to undo it completely, as though it had not been, as though *these* vows had not been spoken, and *those* children not engendered in which A. H. H.'s soul might possibly find a convenient new house.

> Now waiting to be made a wife,
> Her feet, my darling, on the dead;
> Their pensive tablets round her head,
> And the most living words of life
>
> Breathed in her ear. The ring is on,
> The 'wilt thou' answered, and again

The 'wilt thou' asked, till out of twain
Her sweet 'I will' has made you one.

. . .

Nor count me all to blame if I
Conjecture of a stiller guest,
Perchance, perchance, among the rest,
And, though in silence, wishing joy.

She loved Cecilia too. Cecilia's lost children approached from
the spirit world through the voices of Sophy Sheekhy and Mrs
Papagay. Cecilia's marriage had been happy, but the boy Edmund,
the child invoked into being in the poem, had died long ago, aged
thirteen, followed by his two sisters Emily and Lucy, over the slow
years, at nineteen and twenty-one, breaking poor Cecilia's heart.
But even Cecilia, kind Cecilia, conventional Cecilia, had not
managed to love Richard, had been heard, after one of his visits, to
express fear that he would become a 'permanent fixture'. Just as
Richard the sailor had a strangely simple absence of fear, so Richard
the social being had a strangely simple unawareness of other people's sentiments, or irritability, or reserve. He talked on, saying
what he thought, what he felt, as though everyone lived comfort-
ably in some open, bright, evenly lit place where things were
exactly as they appeared to be, and he drove people mad. Or so
Emily observed when she chose to. Mostly, she didn't. She encased
herself in her private aura of mixed eccentricity, lingering tragedy,
and finicking attention to Pug and Aaron.

If it had not been for Richard's unawareness and absence of fear,
perpetual maidenhood might well have been her fate and future,
and she would have been hallowed and cherished. She had not
'fallen in love' with Richard all at once, as she had in a sense with

bright Arthur in the Fairy Wood. Arthur compared her to 'a trembling flower, or a being, like Undine herself, composed of subtler elements than common earth'. Richard sat opposite her in the Hallams' dark, panelled dining-room, like a young man turned to stone by a genie, his heavy silver knife and fork suspended between his mouth and his fricassee of chicken, staring abstractedly, as though, she told him later, he was trying to work out a difficult equation. Someone said, 'What has caught your attention, Mr Jesse?' and he answered simply, 'I was thinking how very lively and handsome Miss Tennyson looks in the candlelight. I never saw a more interesting face.'

'That is a compliment indeed,' the someone said. It was Julia Hallam, and it was said with a touch of lemon-juice, Emily thought, remembering how she had turned her own eyes down towards her own chicken, wondering if she had smiled too broadly, or been forward in some way.

'Not a *compliment*,' persisted Richard. 'What I think. What I really think. I'm not in the habit of paying compliments.'

And he went back to his attitude of contemplation, to the suppressed amusement of his neighbours, so that his chicken was quite cold, and the other guests had to wait for him to finish. Ellen and Julia quizzed Emily later in the evening, about 'having made a *conquest,* my love, of that gawping Midshipman,' and Emily giggled with them, and said that making conquests was not in her thoughts. But she liked Richard for admiring her—how could she not—even if his admiration was an embarrassment. She was pleased one day when he came up behind her in Wimpole Street, and fell into step with her, talking peacefully about the difficulties of life in London compared to his Devonshire home, putting a large, firm hand under her elbow, saying, as they parted at the door of the circulating library where she had been going, 'I didn't mean to embarrass you, Miss Tennyson, at dinner. I didn't, truly. I said what came into my head. I do that, it causes me no end of trouble in my life, always in scrapes and talking myself out of muddles I need never have got into, but it was true what I said, I do most greatly admire you, and I am not given to complimenting ladies. I don't see many, and to tell you the truth, none has ever much interested me before. But you do. You do interest me.'

'Thank you, Mr Jesse.'

'No, don't look all prim and confused, now, I didn't mean to put you in a twitter. Why are simple things always such an intricate muddle, I wonder? I wanted to tell you, simply, I do admire the way you have overcome your great grief—'

'I fear I have not, nor shall not.'

'Not *overcome*, exactly, that was the wrong word, no, but how much you are alive and—and *vital*, Miss Tennyson, it is an inspiration.'

'Thank you.'

'You don't seem to understand. I didn't mean to speak so much so soon, but there I go, rushing on, like the North Wind, can't stop—have you ever felt that someone *was to do with you*, when you saw them, quite simply, just that, that there are people all over the place with noses like dough-buttons and eyes like currants and other people like Roman busts, you know, and then suddenly you see a face that's *alive*—for you—and you know it's to do with you, that that person is a part of your life, have you ever felt that?'

'Once,' said Emily. 'Once, I believe.' Had she? They stood in the street and looked at each other. Richard's bland, amiable brow was crumpled with his puzzled attempt to make her share what was perfectly plain to him. He made an awkward movement with his arms, half a salute, half the prelude to enfolding her, and drew back.

'I'm crowding you, Miss Tennyson, I'll go now, I hope you'll talk later and not hold my awkwardness against me. If I'm right, we do have things to say to each other, and if I'm not, it will become clear enough, no bad feelings, won't it? So I'll bid you goodbye for the present, Miss Tennyson. It's been a pleasure.'

And he strode off, very fast, down the street, leaving her not knowing whether to laugh or cry.

He had persisted, single-minded, and apparently oblivious of anything ridiculous in his courtship. He had accompanied Miss Tennyson to museums and parks, had sat, too large for his chair, manhandling china teacups, listening to the Hallams discussing what Arthur would have been, and nodding sagely, and staring at Emily. Emily herself had looked back between the ringlets, still glossy and multitudinous. Ellen and Julia characterised the long face as vacuous, stupidly amiable. Emily was principally struck by its kindness. There appeared to be no malice in Richard Jesse, which made other people's minor mockeries of him seem to her cruel and disproportionate. She found also, as she looked, that she liked parts of him in a *bodily* way that it was not decent to speak of. He had good brows. His mouth was a good shape. His tall back and long taut legs were elegant and *strong*. There was something strong also about the hands which chattered teacups in their saucers but which were doubtless—she had begun to try to imagine his life—different with ropes in a blizzard. She told herself he was a man of action, not of words, despite the constant steady flow of his undirected talk, and compared him to Miss Austen's naval heroes. Arthur had sent her *Emma,* which she loved, but her secret favourite among Miss Austen's works was *Persuasion,* the story of a woman not in her first youth, set aside as an old maid, who loved a sea captain, and declared, 'All the privilege I claim for my own sex (it is not a very enviable one: you need not covet it) is that of loving longest, when existence or when hope is gone!'

He proposed to her in the Hallams' house, untroubled by any feeling of delicacy about choosing ground on which Arthur might have walked, or addressing a lady who sat in a dark leather armchair in which Arthur might have sat. Old Mr Hallam's history books loomed above them, dusky, leathery and dark. A wintry light came in from the street, Alfred's 'long unlovely' Wimpole Street, where he had waited with beating heart for 'a hand that can be clasped no more'. Richard pulled his chair nearer to Emily's, making a grating sound on the polished floor. She clasped her hands together on her knee, feeling Arthur's ring cut her fingers.

'I have something to ask you,' said Richard Jesse. 'I don't find it easy to see you alone, and I am oppressed by the idea that the ladies of the house might return at any moment. So I will be brief—don't laugh, I am able to be brief when it's a question of urgent action, I can be quick enough when a ship's going aground, or a squall's setting in—'

'A curious metaphor,' said Miss Tennyson, looking at him with her head on one side. 'Are we going aground or in danger of shipwreck?'

'I hope not. There I go again. You *know* what I have to say, don't you? I want to ask you to be my wife. No, don't rush into speaking, I know what *you* have to say, too. But I do believe you could be happy, with me. And I know I could, with you. You are *not* a comfortable person, I wouldn't say that, you are all full of fits and starts and little dramas, and I don't believe you have all that much *commonsense,* to be truthful, but, you know, I think we go well together, I think we are what each other needs. If a member of the Tennyson family can bear to hear a proposal from anyone who can commit that gawky kind of sentence. Maladroit,' he said, finding a better word. She opened her mouth.

'No,' he said, 'don't speak. I know you are going to say no, and

I can't bear it. Think, please, consider it, think, and you will see it will do capitally. Oh please, Miss Tennyson, *think of me.*'

Emily was touched. She had a prepared little speech, truthful as far as she had thought it out, about how a great love burns one out. She even had a line of Donne, 'But after one such love, can love no more.' She believed it. She believed it. Richard Jesse put one great hand over her two hands and one finger of the other to her lips.

'Don't speak,' he said.

She could not lift her hands to move his finger. When she tried to move her lips to speak she found she was in some way kissing the large forefinger. She opened her eyes very fiercely and stared into his, intent, blue, determined. She wanted to say, 'You look like a pirate boarding a brig,' but couldn't speak. She shook her head angrily from side to side. Her hair rustled silky on her shoulders. He picked up a tress of it, with the offending hand. 'Lovely,' he said. 'The most beautiful I've ever seen.'

'You are very foolish,' said Emily, shaken and disturbed. ''I am over thirty years old. I am not a young girl. My days of loving are over. I am resigned to a single life. I am—I am unable to feel.'

'I don't think so.'

'All those years, I have felt like a *stone.* I am worn out with feeling. I do not want to feel any more.'

'I don't think so. I know you're not a young girl. You're older than I am, we both know that, no need beating about the bush. Young girls are boring, fizzing kinds of things, all froth and fuss and romantic notions. Whereas you are a real woman, Miss Tennyson. You ought to be a wife. You aren't cut out to be a maiden aunt, I know, I've watched you ever so sharply. I know you think you *ought,* but you haven't thought of me, have you? You didn't expect *me,* did you?'

'No,' said Emily, in a small voice. 'I didn't.'

Something black and cruel in her wanted to puncture his precarious self-confidence, to slap him down, to mock, to hurt. And something else wanted to make him happy, to protect him from just such savagery, of which he seemed so blithely unaware. She said, 'My heart was sealed up, Mr Jesse, when Arthur died. I loved him completely and lost him. That is my history. There can be no more, for me as for him.'

'I don't mind your having loved him,' said Richard Jesse. 'If you loved him so well, it only proves you can love well and be faithful—as I know I can, though untested as yet. We will not forget him, Miss Tennyson, if you marry me—the love can persist. I honour you, I truly honour you, for its depth and constancy.'

'Maybe you only want to marry me because of that, because of him. Maybe you see me as an object of pity—I know you are kind, I do know you are kind. I don't require to be rescued.'

'Damn it, it isn't rescue. Can't you see that? I told you, if you would listen, I know we could be comfortable together, I know it in my bones—and my heart and liver and all my nerve-endings. Why can't I get you to hear the plain truth?'

She was silent. He said, 'I want so much to take you in my arms. I know I could make you feel the rightness of it. These damned chairs—and all these fusty books—they aren't right—I should like to be able to walk along the beach with you, and listen to the gulls—you'd feel it, then—I'm not in my usual state of mind, I've been sleeping badly, working up to this—to this—it's worse than a battle, any day.'

'I can't,' she said, in a whisper.

'If you can't, if you are quite sure you can't, say it again, and I'll go, now this minute, and never come back, never see you again. Do you understand? Do you believe me? I mean it. If you can really tell me you won't—you can't—you don't wish to—I'll go. It will be that hard, I won't wish to see you again. Do you hear me?'

'Don't shout, Mr Jesse. They will all come.'

'What do they matter?' he mistakenly demanded. Emily, half-pleased nevertheless at his daring, rose abruptly to her feet, a preliminary perhaps to bidding him farewell. But she said nothing and went nowhere. She stood mute. He took a step towards her—he was taller even than her tall brothers, and darkly handsome, as they were, too—and put his large hands on her shoulders. Then he lifted her from the ground, holding her against his shirt, laying his face gently against hers. His hands and skin spoke to her, he pulled like a magnet, he was strong as a tree, a tree in summer the poet in her head hummed, and she laid her own head on his shoulder, listening to their blood banging and leaping.

'You are—choking me—I cannot breathe. Mr Jesse. I cannot breathe.'

'Answer me *now*—'

'Put me down. I will. I cannot resist you, I see. Put me down. Restore me to equilibrium.'

'I should like to roar like a lion,' he said, quietly enough. 'But that can come later, we may do as we like when we are married.'

'I don't know about that,' said Emily, on her feet again, with sudden caution.

They had not, of course, done as they liked, though they had done many things together she would never have done as a maiden aunt and the Hallams' pet. She had allowed, she thought, for the effect of her defection on the Hallams, but not for the consternation and disapproval of the Tennysons, or of the social world. They stood ranged against her in her dark dreams, accusing, hurt and angry. And with them in the dreams stood also a separate creature, the girl in black with a white rose in her hair, as he liked to see it. You are accompanied through life, Emily Jesse occasionally understood, not only by the beloved and accusing departed, but by your own ghost too, also accusing, also unappeased.

IX

Sophy Sheekhy stood in front of her mirror in her white shift. She stared at herself and herself stared back at herself. The mirror on the pine chest reflected the cheval glass by the door so that she stood behind and behind herself on a series of thresholds going white-green into diminishing infinity. She put a finger to the violet shadow under her staring eyes, and her simulacra simultaneously touched their glassy skins. She touched her lips, and leaned forward and breathed on the mirror, and all their faces were misted at once, grey-white mists crowned with pale hair which could have been called colourless, though that would have been wrong, it was hair for which there was no good word, none of the soft beasts, mouse, or dove, none of the harvest, corn or hay, no metal, gold or bronze, and yet immediately recognisable, ordinary, archetypal, pale hair. So many was no one. She was everywhere and nowhere. She stared into the pupils of her eyes, Sophy Sheekhy's eyes, all those eyes, into the velvety black point where there was nothing, and there was nothing, there was no one there.

Once she had hypnotised herself this way, and had been found by Mrs Papagay, rigid as stone, standing and staring, cold and clammy to the touch. Mrs Papagay had clasped her in warm arms to a generous bosom, had flung a quilt round her, had fed her on broth when she woke with a start and could not say where she had been. Mrs Papagay had a warm heart, like a comfortable brown thrush in a soft nest. She had felt its flutter and come back unafraid. There had been times in childhood when she had provoked such absences and been less lucky. She had had *ways* of going outside herself which as a very small child she had supposed were quite natural, ways available to anyone, in the course of daily life, natural as sipping water, or using the chamber-pot, or washing the hands. By holding her breath, in certain ways, or arching her body on the bed and letting it fall again, rapidly, rhythmically, she could find a kind of flying Sophy, hovering mildly near the ceiling and placidly observing the husk, the still pallid husk she had left behind, with its parted lips and closed eyelids. Only her mother, an impatient woman with rough red hands like nutmeg-graters, had brought her back sharply by slapping and shaking, after which Sophy had vomited for a good month, and almost died for lack of nourishment. So she learned to be careful, and to control her outgoings and returns.

Behind her the room was full of rustling, as though it was packed with birds. It was fatigue rushing in her ears, it was white wings she would see if she turned to look. She saw in her mind's eye doves with golden eyes, doves all over, doves preening themselves on the bedhead and windowsill. She saw their little pink feet, so vulnerable, so naked, so scratchy, strutting and curling, open and shut. She began to hear their liquid voices bubbling amongst the rustling. If she turned round, the room might or might not be full of white wings. She did not know if she made the doves by expectation, or sensed their presence and brought them with her mind to her vision, or whether the doves were there and she merely happened to be able to see them. She could not change them to parrots, or oysters, or roses, with any effort of will, she knew now. They were loose from her, they were talking to each other in their different garglings, comforting, irritable, puffed out, smoothed.

She looked into her eyes, and said, not to herself, 'Are you there?' She called on him often, and many times she had sensed him, anxious and elusive, the young man, behind her in the room, like the doves, or the other creatures who from time to time prowled, or slid, or strode there. She could not see him, and he did not speak, but she sensed him there. He wanted to break through, he wanted to make a communication, she believed, using the language she had been taught, since she took up the profession. She believed sometimes that if she were less afraid of him, he might have come long ago. She sensed he was far away, and cold, and lost, but maybe all this was not so, maybe so good, so perfect a young man would not be cold and lost but would know how to ascend the heavens Mr Hawke described so confidently. She wanted to be of use, to open a gate for him, but he did not come. Only a current of cold air, a space between the warm birds and their peaceful busyness, which made her ask again, 'Are you there?' and believe she had been answered in the affirmative.

As a child, too, she had called people up. She had called up people from stories—Rapunzel's pitiful blinded Prince, poor murdered Abel in the Bible, a child called Micky who had been her closest friend until Mrs Papagay, who appeared in every state, from a sensed air of presence, through an imagined gipsyish, dark-skinned boy, to a more or less flesh-and-blood acquaintance, sitting on the edge of the dresser and drumming it with his heels, whose broken fingernail, or scratched lip, she could from week to week simply see with her eyes. He just was. At other times he *almost* was, and she bent her will to pull him into being. She told him things which he seemed to understand. He did not tell her things. Sometimes her efforts to conjure up Micky or other desired presences brought unwanted and unexpected visitors. An angry female baby that howled and would not be comforted, a towering cold male presence who wanted to pull at her—Sophy—but who could not see her, she sensed, as well as she saw him, with his blue beard-stubble and protuberant eyes. These were denizens of a different world from the stolidly solid visitors—only five or six altogether—like the drowned relations she had entertained at her first employer's, or the stout matron looking desperately for a lost watch in Crimond Wood, or the costermonger's boy who told her he missed his horse although it had kicked him to death, for it had been no fault of old Whitey's, he had been maddened by pain in his fetlock. None of these solid revenants had ever put their nose inside a séance, to her knowledge, where the visitors were either willed into apparition by their common desire, or half-glimpsed by her own strenuous desire to be of help, or inhabitants of some other dimension, partly apprehended, like today's wine-bottle Creature with its boiling eyes, much the most vivid so far, but still not solid as apples.

Sophy Sheekhy combed her hair, and the doves rustled and cooed. She wanted so much to find the dead young man for Mrs Jesse, as she wanted to find Captain Papagay for Mrs Papagay, but in some way the very strength of her desire to help held them off. Creatures came, spirits came, wandering into sloppiness and slippage, into emptiness of mind, not into the strain of attention. Yet she sensed he was not far off. There was a cold space amongst the doves where he perhaps waited. She had no idea what he looked like but imagined him pale, with golden curls, a wide brow, craggy,

and a Greek sort of mouth. (She knew about the 'bar of Michelangelo' both from Mrs Jesse and from *In Memoriam*.) Mrs Jesse once
claimed to have detected his spirit form in a photograph taken of
herself in Bristol, but Sophy Sheekhy, who had pored over the
blurred figure in a tall hat behind Mrs Jesse's caped shoulders, could
see little more than chalk-white skin and eye-sockets like dark
coals. It could have been anyone at all, Sophy Sheekhy thought,
though Mrs Jesse's sister Mary agreed that it was uncannily like
Arthur, the face and stance were strikingly like what she remembered of him.

Sometimes she could produce the necessary vague, floating state
of mind by reciting poetry to herself. She had not known much
poetry before her work at Mrs Jesse's house, but had taken to it
there like a duck to water, which was an apt metaphor; she floated
on it, she ducked and dived in its strong flow, it bore her up.
Séances, not only at Mrs Jesse's house, frequently opened with
poetic evocations of those gone before. A favourite was Dante
Gabriel Rossetti's *Blessed Damozel*. It was so beautiful and so sad,
Sophy Sheekhy concurred with other readers, the solitary blessed
angel leaning out, yearning, over the bar of Heaven, whilst all
around her, the pairs of lovers were conjoined in bliss, all their tears
wiped away, conjugial angels two-in-one, as Mr Hawke was fond
of pointing out, as though Mr Rossetti was an instinctive Swedenborgian. Sophy Sheekhy's mind was like a river, in the depths of
which strong and uncontrollable currents pulled and drove, but was
frilled and feathered on the surface with little tossing waves of
ordinary female sentimentality. She looked at her own face in the
mirror and imagined the face of the Damozel, with her one white
rose of Mary's gift, her corn-yellow hair, her bosom which made
the bar she leant on warm. Sophy Sheekhy could see the passionate
girl in the tart, etched Mrs Jesse, with her lined hands and folded
neck, though she sensed other presences too, something feline,
something scissor-like. But it was really the Damozel who en-

tranced her, sometimes literally, in Rossetti's poem. It was the distances. He knew something she knew. She stared into her eyes in the mirror and recited his Heavenly House.

> It lies in Heaven, across the flood
> Of ether, as a bridge.
> Beneath, the tides of day and night
> With flame and darkness ridge
> The void, as low as where this earth
> Spins like a fretful midge.
>
> Around her, lovers, newly met
> 'Mid deathless love's acclaims,
> Spoke evermore among themselves
> Their heart-remembered names;
> And the souls mounting up to God
> Went by her like thin flames.
>
> . . .
>
> The sun was gone now; the curled moon
> Was like a little feather
> Fluttering far down the gulf; and now
> She spoke through the still weather.
> Her voice was like the voice the stars
> Had when they sang together.
>
> . . .
>
> 'I wish that he were come to me,
> For he will come,' she said.

Sophy Sheekhy's arms were wrapped about herself and she was swaying slightly, like a lily on its stalk, like a snake before the charmer, back and forth, her hair lifting and slipping on her shoulders. Her voice was low and pure and clear. As she spoke, she saw the thin flames, the moon curled like a feather, and felt herself spinning away from herself, as sometimes happened, as though she had applied her huge eye to the orifice of a great kaleidoscope where her face whirled like a speck of tinsel amongst the feathery flakes, snow-crystals, worlds. She heard herself saying, as though in answer,

> 'He will not come,' she said.
> She wept, 'I am aweary, aweary,
> O God, that I were dead.'

That was another poem entirely. Reciting that made her cold all over. She held tighter to herself for comfort, cold breast on cold ledge of arms, little fingers clasping at her ribs. She was sure, almost sure, sure, that something else breathed amongst the floating feathers behind her. Poems rustled together like voices. She felt a stab of pain, like an icicle between the clutched ribs. She heard the rattle of hail, or rain, suddenly in great gusts on the windowpane, like scattered seed. She felt a sudden weight in the room, a heavy space, as one feels tapping at the door of a house, knowing in advance that it is inhabited, before the foot is heard on the stair, the rustle and clink in the hall. She knew she must not look behind her, and knowing that, began drowsily to hum in her head the richness of 'The Eve of St Agnes':

> Out went the taper as she hurried in;
> Its little smoke, in pallid moonshine, died:
> She clos'd the door, she panted, all akin
> To spirits of the air, and visions wide:
> No uttered syllable, or, woe betide!
> But to her heart, her heart was voluble,
> Paining with eloquence her balmy side;
> As though a tongueless nightingale should swell
> Her throat in vain, and die, heart-stifled, in her dell.

Whatever was behind her sighed, and then drew in its breath, with difficulty. Sophy Sheekhy told him dubiously, 'I *think* you are there. I should like to see you.'

'Perhaps you wouldn't like what you saw,' she heard, or thought she heard.

'Was that you?'

'I said, perhaps you wouldn't like what you saw.'

'It isn't my habit to like or dislike,' she found herself answering.

She took her candle and held it up to the mirror, still filled with the superstitious sense, like those poetic ladies, Madeline, the Lady of Shalott, that she must not look away from the plane of glass. The candle caused a local shimmer and gloom in the depths in which she thought she saw something move.

'We cannot always help ourselves as to that,' he said, much more clearly.

'Please—' she breathed to the glass.

She felt him move in on her, closer, closer. She heard the words of the poem spoken in an ironic, slightly harsh voice.

> 'Into her dream he melted, as the rose
> Blendeth its odour with the violet,—
> Solution sweet:'

Her hand shook, the face behind her bulged and tightened, sagged and reassembled, not pale, but purple-veined, with staring blue eyes and parched thin lips, above a tremulous chin. There was a sudden gust of odour, not rose, not violet, but earth-mould and corruption.

'You see,' said the harsh, small voice. 'I am a dead man, you see.'

Sophy Sheekhy took a breath and turned round. She saw her own little white bed, and a row of doves preening themselves on the cast-iron bedstead. She saw, briefly, a parrot, scarlet and blue, on the windowsill. She saw dark glass, and she saw him, struggling, it seemed to her, to keep his appearance, his sort-of-substance, together, with a kind of deadly defiance.

She knew immediately that he was the man. Not because she recognised him, but because she did not, and yet he fitted the descriptions, the curls, the thin mouth, the bar on the brow. He wore an ancient high-collared shirt, out of fashion when Sophy's mother was a small child, and stained breeches. He stood there, trembling and morose. The trembling was not exactly human. It caused his body to swell and contract as though sucked out of shape and pressed back into it. Sophy took a few steps towards him. She saw that his brows and lashes were caked with clay. He said again, 'I am a dead man.'

He moved away from her, walking like someone finding his feet after a long illness, and sat down on the seat in the window, displacing a number of white birds, who ran fluttering and resettled at the foot of the curtains. Sophy followed him, and stood and considered him. He was very young. His lovers on earth watched and waited for him like some wise god gone before, but this young man was younger than she was herself, and seemed to be in the last stages of exhaustion, owing to his state. She had been told, in the Church of the New Jerusalem, of Swedenborg's encounters with the newly dead, who refused to believe that they were dead, who attended their own funerals with indignant interest. Later, Swedenborg taught, the dead, who took with them into the next world the affections and minds of this terrestrial space, had to find their true selves and their true, their appropriate companions, amongst spirits and angels. They had to learn that they were dead, and then to go on. She said, 'How is it with you? What is your state?'

'As you see me. Baffled and impotent.'

'You are much mourned, much missed. More than any being I know.'

A spasm of anguish twisted the dull red face, and Sophy Sheekhy suddenly felt in her blood and bones that the mourning was painful

to him. It dragged him down, or back, or under. He moved his
heavy tongue in his mouth, unaccustomed now.

'I walk. Between. Outside. I cannot tell you. I am part of
nothing. Impotent and baffled,' he added, quick and articulate
suddenly, as though these were words he knew, had tamed
doggedly in his mind over the long years. Which might not, of
course, appear to him to be years. A thousand ages in thy sight are
but an instant gone. She spoke from her heart.

'You are so *young*.'

'I am young. And dead.'

'And not forgotten.'

Again, the same spasm of pain.

'And alone.' The pure self-pity of the young.

'I would like to help you, if I could.'

It was help he appeared to need.

'Hold me,' he said. 'I imagine—you cannot. I am cold. It is dark.
Hold me.'

Sophy Sheekhy stood, white.

'You cannot.'

'I will.'

She lay on the white bed, and he walked across to her, in his
hesitant, imperfect step, and lay beside her, and she cradled his head
and his stench on her cold bosom. She closed her eyes, the better
to bear it, and felt his weight, the weight, more or less, of a living
man, but a man not breathing, a man inert like a side of beef.
Perhaps it would kill her, Sophy Sheekhy thought on the surface
of her mind, where the ripples crisped away from the dark pool in
a flurry of terror. But the depths of the pool bore her up, her and
him both, Sophy Sheekhy and the dead young man. With her
chilly lips, carefully, she kissed his cold curls. Could he feel her kiss?
Could she warm him?

'Be still,' she said, as she would to a fractious child.

He put a kind of hand on to her shoulder, where it burned like ice. 'Speak. To. Me.'

'What? What shall I say?'

'Your name. John Keats.'

'My name is Sophy Sheekhy. I can—I can say the 'Ode to a Nightingale'. If you would like—'

'Say that. Yes.'

> 'My heart aches, and a drowsy numbness pains
> My sense, as though of hemlock I had drunk,
> Or emptied some dull opiate to the drains
> One minute past, and Lethe-wards had sunk.'

'He knew,' he said. 'The energetic principle of love for the beautiful. I remember. I restored a word to life, for him. Sensuous. My word. Not sensual. Sensuous.' The husky voice faltered and then took on strength: ' "O for a life of sensation rather than thought." Both gone. Here, both gone. Sophy Sheekhy. Pistis Sophia. Poems are the ghosts of sensations, Pistis Sophia, the ghosts of thoughts, they move in the mind, my dear, and are also thoughts and sensations, both at once. Your bosom warms me, Pistis Sophia, as a frozen snake is warmed. It was Pistis Sophia, the gnostics said, who sent the first snake into Paradise.'

'Who is Pistis Sophia?'

'Why, my dear, the Angel in the Garden, before Man. The energetic principle of love for the beautiful. They were young men, Keats and Shelley. I felt kindly to them, they were so young. Speak more. Darkling I listen. Darkling.'

> 'Darkling I listen; and, for many a time
> I have been half in love with easeful Death,
> Call'd him soft names in many a mused rhyme,
> To take into the air my quiet breath;

> Now more than ever seems it rich to die,
> To cease upon the midnight with no pain,
> While thou art pouring forth thy soul abroad
> In such an ecstasy!
> Still wouldst thou sing, and I have ears in vain—
> To thy high requiem become a sod.'

'The feel of not to feel it,' whispered the creature in her arms. It was growing heavier. Breathing was harder. Sophy Sheekhy faltered.

> 'Thou wast not born for death, immortal Bird!
> No hungry generations tread thee down . . .'

Her companion exhaled. She felt his icy breath pass her ear.

> 'Not he: but something which possessed
> The darkness of the world, delight,
> Life, anguish, death, immortal love,
> Ceasing not, mingled, unrepressed,
> Apart from place, withholding time . . .'

She saw, in the middle of the room, a hand, a long, brown hand, no longer young, tentatively and awkwardly buttoning a nightshirt. She saw the row of buttons. They were wrongly aligned. The hand fumbled at them. It clasped the pleated front of the neck to its chest, as though it sensed, briefly, the cold of their presence.

' "Mingled, unrepressed," ' said the cold, dull voice in Sophy's ear. 'Good, lively words. I knew he would be as great as Keats, as Coleridge saw in Wordsworth the greatest poet since Milton. I loved him for it, you must believe me, Pistis Sophia.'

'Oh, I do. I do.'

'I cannot see . . . I cannot see . . . Sophia, I cannot see . . . can you?'

'Not very well. A little. A hand. An old man, in a nightshirt, in a room with a candle . . . he is holding his hand up to his face, and—and sniffing at it . . . he has a beard—shaggy, partly grey—stained at the mouth—he is a handsome old man . . . I know who he is . . .'

'I cannot see.' The thick, cold fingers were touching her eyelashes as though to feel her vision. 'He is old, I cannot see him. I partly think I snuff his tobacco. He walked about in a cloud of it, burning and fragrant, and the stale remnants of its old ashes, its dottle . . . What is he doing?'

'He is sitting on his bed, turning his hand over and over. He looks puzzled. And very handsome. And a bit absent-minded.'

'You would think I could hear his thoughts. But I cannot.'

X

Alfred Tennyson did feel something stir in his room. He felt that mixture of excessive atmospheric stillness and pricking in the skin which he was accustomed to refer to as 'an angel walking on my grave' though he knew very well he was conflating two superstitions, the angels whose silent passage overhead caused table chatter to cease at twenty minutes before or after the hour, and the prescient shiver induced by someone treading the clay which at some inexorable future moment would be grubbed up to make space for his mortal remains. He also felt attention somehow on his hand, so that he stopped trying to do up his buttons and held it up as though it was some strange, separate creature he had got hold of. Its fingers were long and brown and still sinewy. There was no puffiness or plumpness, though he had overheard Emily Jesse observing tartly that since he married he had never lifted a finger to help himself. Some of the fingers were stained mahogany by his smoking. He was afraid he perhaps carried its powerful aroma with him unnoticed. His nostrils would never again be innocent of it, as an ostler's nostrils no doubt perceived everything through a warm haze of hair and sweat and horse-piss and horse-dung. It was a good smell when it was, so to speak, alive, and less good when it was cold. Like the pillar of fire by night and the pillar of cloud by day, he thought, burning and fragrant, then stale remains, old dottle, a good word, 'dottle'. Perhaps he stank? He lifted the ends of his fingers to his nostrils. He heard the buzzing of little flying fragments of language that hung around his head all the time in a cloud, like the veils of living and dead smoke, like the motes of dust that hung in shafts of sunlight, 'thick-moted' as he had so beautifully described them. 'Let me kiss that hand,' he heard, and answered, 'Let me wipe it first. It smells of mortality.' Or if not Lear, Lady Macbeth. 'All the perfumes of Arabia will not sweeten this little hand.' Or John Keats. 'When this warm scribe my hand, is in the grave.' Or worse, that fragment of his:

> This living hand, now warm and capable
> Of earnest grasping, would, if it were cold
> And in the icy silence of the tomb,
> So haunt thy days and chill thy dreaming nights
> That thou wouldst wish thine own heart dry of blood
> So in my veins red life might stream again,
> And thou be conscience-calm'd—see here it is—
> I hold it towards you.

He remembered Arthur frightening him with that in the owl-dark moon-glimmered bedroom at Somersby, with its two little white beds. 'That makes life worth living,' Arthur had cried in his enthusiasm, 'that a man should write so well, with death staring him in the face, such a defiance is noble—' He had made his own image of the dead hands, in Arthur's poems, that he was proud of. It had the cheating life of the lifeless, his image.

> And hands so often clasped in mine,
> Should toss with tangle and with shells.

Hands moving, like weeds, like flotsam, the tumble of drowned flesh, he had caught the rhythm of the tumble. It was Arthur's hands he had remembered most sharply, afterwards, of Arthur's life. Arthur's handclasp had faded on him like a diminishing, then guttering, candle, over forty years. He looked at the old pads on his fingertips and touched them with his other hand. A curious smoothness had glossed his knuckle-skin, the lines of life effaced, the opposite of what had happened to his mouth and brow. He had remembered the feel of Arthur's palm warm against his own, Arthur's eager grip. This was where Arthur met and temporarily mixed with him, in the English gentleman's grip. Manly, alive, a renewal of touch. Meeting and

parting. After the terrible letter, he had been savagely tormented by
the fact that his hand still anticipated that grip. He had made fine
poetry of that haunting, too, fine poetry. He had hundreds of letters.
'I too have had *exactly* that sensation, I must tell you, Sir: "I should not
feel it to be strange." Your percipience is a great comfort, I thought
you would wish, perhaps, to know.'

That had been early, when it had been impossible for his body
and feelings to know what his poor brain had instantly accepted.
He had imagined the ship touching land and the passengers descending.

> And if along with these should come
> The man I held as half-divine:
> Should strike a sudden hand in mine,
> And ask a thousand things of home;
>
> . . .
>
> And I perceived no touch of change,
> No hint of death in all his frame,
> But found him all in all the same,
> I should not feel it to be strange.

That was accurate enough, but long ago, long gone. Arthur had
died inside his own body and soul, gradually, gradually, like the
slow death of a tree, an inch here, a string of cells there. When
Arthur was first dead, the sudden recall of his bodily presence, an
impatient motion, an alert look, had been pure torment. And then,
perversely, in proportion as flesh and blood gave way to shadow,
he had tried to hold his friend back, to flesh out his imaginings, to
see the unseen. But Arthur had gone on dying.

> I cannot see the features right,
> When on the gloom I strive to paint
> The face I know.

Frederick and Mary and Emily invoked lost forms and spirits, but he himself was afraid and repelled, afraid of being cheated by flecks of canker on the matter of his own brain, repelled by morbidity. 'I shall not see thee,' he had asserted once or twice, firmly and terribly, taking toll of his loss. Some kind of mystic union, light in light, ghost in ghost, might be possible beyond the veil, but his hands would remain empty, feeling blindly for absence.

He remembered a day when he and Arthur had talked all day long on the lawn at Somersby, of the nature of things, of creation, of love and art, of sense and soul. Arthur's hand had been a few inches from his own, on the warm grass among the daisies. Arthur had talked of Keats's sensuous imagination, which created beauty, and Keats said might be compared to Adam's dream of the creation of the Woman from his own bloody ripped-out rib, 'he awoke and found it truth'. And he, Alfred, had seen in his mind's eye, not Milton's Adam, but Michelangelo's, with his limp hand livening at the power, the electric power, that arched across from the fingertip of the clouded God to his own. Arthur had said how *daring* that was, how shocking, and how right. ' "O for a life of sensation rather than thought!" ' Arthur had said, in the Somersby sunlight, and had gone on to read out of the wonderful letter:

'It is "a Vision in the form of Youth", a shadow of reality to come— And this consideration has further convinced me,—for it has come as auxiliary to another favourite speculation of mine,—that we shall enjoy ourselves hereafter by having what we called happiness on Earth repeated in a finer tone . . .'

Arthur had gone on talking of Dante and Beatrice and the making sensuous of Heaven in the journeyings of the *Divine Comedy*—'we must surely, in the very different cases of Keats and Dante, Alfred, take the pulsions of earthly Love as a faint figur-

ing—a faint prescience—a faint foreshadowing—of Divine Love—
do you not think?'

And he himself had lain back in his creaking chair, leaving his
trailing hand where it was, imagining Paradise and loving Arthur,
and feeling such happiness, such unaccustomed happiness for a
blackly morbid Tennyson, in his skin and flesh and bones, that he
could only smile, and hum assent, and hear the air full of singing
words that were the unformed atoms of his own creation to come.

Michelangelo had been a lover of other men. He himself had
told Arthur, more than once, jokingly, that he loved him as Shakespeare had loved Ben Jonson, 'this side idolatry', and both of them
had found in Shakespeare's sonnets line after line that could be
offered to the other as a gift, or a grace, or an assurance. He knew
the fruitless fire they flew round, without burning their wings,
without being shrivelled, and he knew too the terrible miscon-
struction to which his exact exposition of the full extent of his pain
and longing in Arthur's poems had laid him open. Arthur's father
had disliked their love and had written slightingly, after Arthur's
death, and before Alfred had ventured to let Arthur's poems see the
light, of Shakespeare's sonnets.

> Perhaps there is now a tendency, especially among young men of poetical
> tempers, to exaggerate the beauties of these remarkable productions
> . . . An attachment to some female, which seems to have touched neither
> his heart nor his fancy very sensibly, was overpowered, without entirely
> ceasing, by one to a friend; and this last is of such an enthusiastic
> character, and so extravagant in the phrases that the author uses, as to
> have thrown an unaccountable mystery over the whole work. It is true
> that in the poetry as well as in the fictions of early ages, we find a more
> ardent tone of affection in the language of friendship than has since been
> usual and yet no instance has been adduced of such rapturous devoted-
> ness, such an idolatry of admiring love, as the greatest being whom nature
> ever produced in the human form pours forth to some unknown youth in
> the majority of these sonnets . . . Notwithstanding the frequent beauties

of these sonnets, the pleasure of their perusal is greatly diminished by
these circumstances; and it is impossible not to wish Shakespeare had
never written them.

Henry Hallam had destroyed Alfred's letters to Arthur. He knew
very well what Arthur's father feared and suspected, though he had
never once allowed Arthur's father to see in his face, or hear in his
voice, any acknowledgement of his suspicions, any disquietude. He
had learned young and early to cloak everything he felt, every
uncomfortable perception of his own or others, with an impenetrable mist of vagueness. For eight years he had squirted black vague
ink at his dearest Emily, like a retreating squid. He had never by any
the smallest twitch of irritation replied to the personal message he
detected in Henry Hallam's magisterial dismissal of the sonnets,
though he had told others, repeatedly, that the sonnets were noble.
He was doubly cloaked, now, in the distracted vagueness of genius
and in the thick cloak of the respectability of his Age, of which he
had somehow or other become an exemplary citizen. There had
been bad moments when he was younger, when critics had
mocked his unwary phrases, his description of his 'darling room
. . . with thy two couches soft and white.' When Arthur's poems
had first appeared, anonymous as they still, in a sense, were since
he had never allowed his name to appear on the title page, one
critic had written that he had spent 'much shallow art' on 'an
Amaryllis of the Chancery Bar'. There was now almost more
liveliness in the salted rawness of the wound that slick phrase had
inflicted than in the remembered touch of Arthur's hand. He had
never—however great his success—got over his wincing despon-
dency over harsh criticism. Another reviewer had thought he was
a woman. "These touching lines evidently come from the full heart
of the widow of a military man.' It was true, it was true, he had
called himself, over and over, Arthur's widow, but that was only in
the spiritual sense in which his soul, his *anima,* was bereaved. He

believed that all great human beings encompassed both sexes, in some sense. Christ, the Son of God, the object, in Arthur's 'Theodicaea Novissima,' of the Creator's Divine Love and Longing, was both male and female, in that he was God incarnate, he was Wisdom and Justice, which were male, and Mercy and Pity, which were female. He and Arthur both, this was his conception, had their womanly aspects, for 'pitee renneth soone in gentil herte,' which only increased their poetic sensibility, their manly energy. But there were things he abominated. Things Arthur abominated. Things he was sure secretly appealed to the diagnostician of the Amaryllis of the Chancery Bar. Men should be androgynous and women gynandrous, he had noted felicitously, *but* men should not be gynandrous nor women androgynous.

He had made an epigram 'On One Who Affected an Effeminate Manner':

> While man and woman still are incomplete,
> I prize that soul where man and woman meet,
> Which types all Nature's male and female plan,
> But, friend, man–woman is not woman–man.

Pretty neat, he thought, deftly put. An epigram was a kind of bonbon, one moment it wasn't there, the next it was popped into your mouth and turning round and round, smooth and sweet. People thought he was an innocent old creature, he was well aware. They humoured him, they protected him. But he knew more than he said, that was a politic way of going on in this straitlaced time, and he was a child of an altogether less innocent time. He and Arthur both knew of the proclivities, and more than proclivities, of the elegant Richard Monckton Milnes, their Cambridge contemporary, whose interest in beautiful boys kept bubbling to the surface of his and others' talk. He knew, too, from Arthur, of the carnal passions that drove William Gladstone to prowl the streets at night in search of *those* women, and to repent in agony afterwards. A sensual man, Arthur had said of Gladstone, who had loved bright Arthur at Eton, as Alfred had loved him at Cambridge. Arthur was not a sensual man. He loved in a romantic glow. He had written in Arthur's poems

> He tasted love with half his mind
> Nor ever drank the inviolate spring

and he believed that was a pretty fair assessment, he believed he should have known if Arthur had ever, so to speak, stepped over the threshold of imagination into fleshly fact.

He himself was not, he considered, a passionate man, his sensuous apprehensions were, so to speak, diffused and mingled throughout the creation, in little bursting buds and the rolling of the sea. He had found the act of love—he pushed the button in and out of its slit, and found another, still not the appropriate one, making a kind of loop of fabric—anyway it was long ago, now, Emily had long been an invalid, there was no need to think. He thought he had acquitted himself well enough, he thought he had. He had felt a suffusion of affection and companionable calm, which he suspected was less than what others felt, somehow, but not unpleasant, not inadequate. To Emily's taste, he was sure. If he was truthful, there was more excitement in the space between his finger and Arthur's, with all that implied of the flashing-out of one soul to another, of the symmetry and sympathy of minds, of the recognition they had both felt, that they had in some sense *always known* each other, they did not have to learn each other, as strangers did. But this did not make them men like Milnes. They were like David and Jonathan, whose love to each other was wonderful, passing the love of women. And yet David was the greatest lover of women in the Bible, David had despatched Uriah to his death to possess Bathsheba, David was manly beyond all heroes. Arthur's cold completeness, his air of carved, self-contained sufficiency, attracted more agitated, more stressful souls. Alfred knew that William Gladstone still in some sense envied him the completeness of his relations with their common object of worship. They were uneasy in each other's company, though drawn together as much by their great loss as by the fact that they were the twin eminences of their time. Gladstone was a David-type. But Arthur had loved Alfred. He remembered Arthur showing him the draft of a letter he had despatched to Milnes, who had made a wild plea for an exclusive friendship, in Milnes's own emotional way. It must have been 1831. Poor Arthur had less than two years of life in him at that time. He had held out his letter to Alfred and said, 'I don't know if it's right to show one man's letter to another. But I want you to see this, Ally, I want you to read what I have frankly written to Milnes. Don't say anything, don't comment, it would be wrong. Just read what I have written, and then it shall be sealed and sent, to have whatever effect it may. I hope you will feel my frankness is justified—'

I am not aware, my dear Milnes, that, in that lofty sense which you are accustomed to attach to the name of Friendship, we ever were, or ever could be friends. What is more to the purpose, I never fancied that we could, nor intended to make you fancy it. That exalted sentiment I do not ridicule—God forbid—nor consider as merely ideal: I have experienced it, and it thrills within me now—but not—pardon me, my dear Milnes, for speaking frankly—not for you. But the shades of sympathy are innumerable, and wretched indeed would be the condition of man, if sunshine never fell upon him save from the unclouded skies of a tropical summer.

Their eyes had met. 'You *see*, Alfred,' Arthur had said. 'You do see?' He saw. He had written in the poems, advisedly,

> I loved thee, Spirit, and love, nor can
> The soul of Shakespeare love thee more.

He believed that was true.

He sat down on his bed and began again to fumble at his mismatched buttons. His legs were cold and goosefleshed; he shivered inside his nightshirt. He was aware of his own body, with an appalled pity he might have felt for some dumb ox doomed to be slaughtered, or heavy, cunning-eyed porker, whose vast throat was appointed to be slit in the fullness of its grunting and chuckling. When he was younger, when Arthur was only dead as it were yesterday, he had felt the unnaturalness of that vanishing in every ending of his own live nerves. Now he was an old man, he saw that the young man he was had felt himself eternal in his noonday strength, in his grip and his stride and his inhalation and his exhalation, all of them now problems. He was approaching annihilation, however temporary he trusted it would be, step by step, and at every step, he saw his poor flesh as another creature he was responsible for. And at every step the terror of being merely snuffed out, like a mere creature, was greater. When they were young they had chanted in church that they believed in the resurrection of the body and the life everlasting. He imagined that there might have been a time when the whole body of the Church believed triumphantly and unquestioningly in the reconstitution of atomies of dust, the flying together of chips of bone and flakes of fallen hair at the last Trump, but that was now past, and men were afraid. As a young man he himself had once, walking in London, nearly fainted and fallen under the sudden realisation of the *whole* of its inhabitants lying horizontal a hundred years hence. Men now saw what he saw, the earth heaped and stacked with dead things, broken bright feathers and shrivelled moths, worms stretched and chewed and sliced and swallowed, stinking shoals of once bright fish, dried parrots and tigerskins limply and glassily snarling on hearths, mountains of human skulls mixed with monkey skulls and snake skulls and asses' jawbones and butterfly wings, mashed into humus and dust, fed on, regurgitated, blown in the wind, soaked in the rain, absorbed. You saw one thing, nature red in tooth and claw, the dust, the dust, and you believed another, or said you believed, or tried to believe. For if you did not believe, where was the point of it all, of life or love or virtue? His dearest Emily was appalled that he should ever entertain such doubts. He had put his pretty compliment to her into Arthur's poems.

> You say, but with no touch of scorn,
> Sweet-hearted, you, whose light-blue eyes
> Are tender over drowning flies,
> You tell me, doubt is Devil-born.

He had gone on again to praise Arthur's direct struggles with his Doubt:

> Perplext in faith, but pure in deeds,
> At last he beat his music out.
> There lives more faith in honest doubt,
> Believe me, than in half the creeds.

But he himself watched the drowning flies in anguish of his own. They were alive, they struggled and whirred, they were dead. They were bodies and life was in them, they circled the edge of the jug of water, they buzzed, they were nothing. And Arthur, so bright with life? If he had known Arthur's death, truly known the death of Arthur's body, at the time when he had known Arthur's life, he could not have loved him, they could not have loved each other. He had found that, not by thinking it out, but by *writing* it. He was not clever, like Arthur. He couldn't write out an argument to save his life, he couldn't build up a theory or defend a position. He had been a dumb member of the Apostles, he had decorated the chimneypiece and made sly, quiet jokes, and recited verses and accepted homage for his great gift, which seemed only partly to belong to himself, whoever he was. But he had thought it out, love and death, those pitiless abstractions, in that cunningly innocent form he had found for Arthur's poems, a form that seemed so straightforward, primitive songlets or chants of grief, but could *feel* its way through an argument, through shifts and shifts of ideas and feelings, stopping and starting, a rhyme closed in a rhyme, and yet moving quietly and inexorably on. In this case, from abstract personified Love to pure animal sensuality, still sweetly singing on.

> Yet if some voice that man could trust
> Should murmur from the narrow house,
> 'The cheeks drop in; the body bows;
> Man dies: nor is there hope in dust:'
>
> Might I not say? 'Yet even here,
> But for one hour, O Love, I strive
> To keep so sweet a thing alive:'
> But I should turn mine ears and hear
>
> The moanings of the homeless sea,
> The sounds of streams that swift or slow
> Draw down Æonian hills, and sow
> The dust of continents to be;
>
> And Love would answer with a sigh,
> 'The sound of that forgetful shore
> Will change my sweetness more and more,
> Half-dead to know that I shall die.'
>
> O me, what profits it to put
> An idle case? If Death were seen
> At first as Death, Love had not been,
> Or been in narrowest working shut,
>
> Mere fellowship of sluggish moods,
> Or in his coarsest Satyr-shape
> Had bruised the herb and crushed the grape,
> And basked and battened in the woods.

Since he had become an eminence he had taken, somewhat
awkwardly, and particularly when he had taken too much port, to
making pronouncements. He liked to say—watching his friends,
his visitors, his devoted son, reach for their notebooks and pencils—things like, 'Matter is a greater mystery than Mind. What such
a thing as spirit is apart from God and man, I have never been able
to conceive. Spirit seems to me to be the reality of the world.' He
got in an awful mess if he tried to elaborate on that kind of
oracularity, and would say, with what he hoped was an engaging
shaggy evasiveness, that he was no theologian. Spirit was a slippery
word and a slippery thing. He liked the rotundity of ghost, the
good old English word, the ghost in man, the ghost that once was
man, the Holy Ghost, the ghosts he had written his Apostolic essay
on, but spirit ran into all sorts of quibbling trouble. He nodded
sagely when his friends castigated the crass materialism of the Age,
but his imagination was stirred by matter, by the thick solidity of
the hugely redundant quantity of flesh and earth and vegetation that
either was or wasn't informed by spirit. 'The lavish profusion too
in the natural world appals me,' he had written, 'from the growths
of the tropical forest to the capacity of man to multiply, the torrent
of babies.' If man was not an angelic intelligence, his own thoughts
were mere electric sparks emitted by a pale, clay-slimy mass of
worm-like flesh.

> I trust I have not wasted breath:
> I think we are not wholly brain,
> Magnetic mockeries; not in vain,
> Like Paul with beasts, I fought with Death;
>
> Not only cunning casts in clay . . .

He knew well enough what it was like to feel he *was* his body.
Be near me, he had urged his dead friend, when my light is low,

when the blood creeps and the nerves prick. He knew what could
be done with words like 'creep' and 'prick', he knew how to make
solid the horrid vision of the nightmare world where

> shoals of puckered faces drive . . .
> Dark bulks that tumble half alive,
> And lazy lengths on boundless shores;

Lovely *thick* words, 'puckered', 'bulk', 'lazy'. Like 'bruised' and
'crushed' and 'basked' and 'battened'. Fearful and enticing. But the
other, the world of spirit, of light, resisted language and remained
more ephemeral than ethereal. 'Who will deliver me from the body
of this Death?' Saint Paul had asked wildly. Paul was a man who
knew well about the mass of the nerves and the ghost trapped in
their too-solid meshes. Saint Paul had written of the man caught up
to the Third Heaven, 'whether in the body, I cannot tell; or
whether out of the body, I cannot tell'. He himself could escape
from himself into a kind of waking trance, and by the strangest of
methods, the steady repetition to himself of two words, his own
name, until the pure concentration on his isolated self seemed
paradoxically to destroy the bounds of that self, that consciousness,
so that he was everything, was God, and this not a confused state,
but the clearest of the clearest, the surest of the surest, the weirdest
of the weirdest, utterly beyond words, where death was an almost
laughable impossibility, the loss of personality (if so it was) seeming
no extinction but the only true life. He knew loss of sharp consciousness in many forms, had feared the family epilepsy in youth,
had wandered in a mist like the hero of his own *Princess* or the
battling armies in the *Morte d'Arthur,* but this loss of self by chanting
the name of self was different. He had tried to write it in Arthur's
poems, hoping, like Dante at the opening of the *Paradiso,* to speak
to those who had some idea of what it was to go out of oneself.

Trasumanar significar per verba
Non si porìa: però l'esiempio basti
A cui esperienza grazia serba.

He felt a kind of dissatisfaction with the *transcendental* aspects of
Arthur's poems which was at one simple level craftsman-like—they
did not afford him the sense of rightness, so intimately connected
with sensuous pleasure, that the grim bits did, or the accurate trees
and birds and gardens and seashores which appeared and disappeared like precise visions. He had written and rewritten his attempt to convey the 'waking trance'.

So word by word, and line by line,
The dead man touched me from the past,
And all at once it seemed at last
The living soul was flashed on mine,

And mine in this was wound, and whirled
About empyreal heights of thought,
And came on that which is, and caught
The deep pulsations of the world,

Æonian music measuring out
The steps of Time—the shocks of Chance—
The blows of Death. At length my trance
Was cancelled, stricken through with doubt.

Vague words! but ah, how hard to frame
In matter-moulded forms of speech,
Or even for intellect to reach
Through memory that which I became:

Till now the doubtful dusk revealed
The knolls once more where, couched at ease,
The white kine glimmered, and the trees
Laid their dark arms about the field:

He had been considerably perplexed about how to put those two lines about the mingled souls. When he had first given the poem to the world it had read differently.

> The dead man touched me from the past,
> And all at once it seemed at last
> *His* living soul was flashed on mine,
>
> And mine in *his* was wound . . .

He had changed it. He had felt the first reading gave a wrong impression. He believed his trance *did* mean that he was whirled up and rapt into the Great Soul, of which perhaps both Arthur and himself were a part. They had talked together of the reasons why Dante's *Inferno* was so much more compelling than the *Paradiso,* and had decided that it was to do with the inescapably sensuous nature of language, of words, which were breath, and tongue, and teeth, and the motions of this warm scribe my hand over the white paper, leaving its black trail. He *wanted* Arthur to be like the Beatrice of Dante's Paradise. He imagined Arthur saying,

> ' 'Tis hard for thee to fathom this;
> I triumph in conclusive bliss,
> And that serene result of all.'

And quickly, quickly, the life of the poem itself slipped into the truth of qualification.

> So hold I commerce with the dead;
> Or so methinks the dead would say;
> Or so shall grief with symbols play
> And pinning life be fancy-fed.

But it was not Beatrice, but the doomed lovers, Paolo and Francesca, whose intertwined souls in their glimmering hellish flame had roused such pity, such sensuous pleasure, in generations of Dante's readers.

The life of his poem was in the ease of the white cows and the field in the dark arms of the trees. He was proud of the good phrase 'matter-moulded forms of speech'—that said in a nutshell what he wanted to say about the stubborn body of language, and so of his poem, Arthur's poems. Now '*mould*' was a good word, it made you think. It made you think of the body of this death, of clay, of things mouldering away. It was art, it was decay. Not only cunning casts in clay, he had written in his moments of doubt about the magnetic tics of the fleshly brain, though elsewhere he had added to his idea of 'what *is*' a pair of potter's hands:

> And what I am beheld again
> What is, and no man understands;
> And out of darkness came the hands
> That reach through nature, moulding men.

Mould, mouldering. God livening the clay, God, or whatever it was, breaking it all down again.

> And if that eye which watches guilt
> And goodness, and hath power to see
> Within the green the mouldered tree,
> And towers fallen as soon as built—

That was a wonderful line, he thought, the terror of that eye seeing simultaneously the mould from which the green tree was moulded which contained the seeds of its own mouldering; there was in a few words the terror of mortality and meaningless eternity. 'And lo, thy deepest lays are dumb / Before the mouldering of a yew . . . Whose fibres net the dreamless head, / Whose roots are wrapt about the bones.' He had made some delightfully poignant images of his own poetic cries of grief as things natural as birdsong, the trill shaped in the feathered throat, 'short swallow-flights of song that dip / Their wings in tears and skim away.' 'I do but sing because I must, / and pipe but as the linnets sing.' One step away, the song of the creatures, from the despair of an infant crying in the night, and with no language but a cry.

He made yet another stab at the buttons, moving his beard out of his own way, where hairs were caught in his blunt fingers, in the white bone of the button. The spirit does but mean the breath. It was a long time since he had been moved to go over all that in his head like that, fighting old battles, suffering old pains. O last regret, regret can die. Regret was like himself, it stiffened and ached, it responded less quickly to stimuli; Arthur was gone so far away, and his regret and himself were moving towards Arthur, or towards annihilation, *pari passu,* less fluent than they had been, more sullen when they heard the call. That wasn't the whole truth, the truth was that both he and Arthur had seeped into his poem, had become parts of its fabric, a matter-moulded kind of *half-life* he sometimes thought it was, something not independent, but not part of each, not a handclasp, but a kind of vigorous parasite, like mistletoe on dying oaks with its milky berries and its mysterious evergreen leaves. He had had all sorts of worries and wicked thoughts about his poem. Perhaps he was using it to keep alive a memory and a love it would have been stronger and more manly to let lie. Perhaps he was in some wrong way *using* his beloved to subserve his own gain, his own fame, or more subtly, making something fantastically beautiful out of the horror of Arthur's dissolution, which it would have been wiser, more honest, to stare at in dumb and truthful uncomprehending pain, until its hurtful brightness either faded like a fire eaten away, or caused him to drop his own eyes. You could not make a man into a poem, neither the singer nor the sung, neither the rippling throat nor the still corpse.

And yet, and yet, and yet, if there was one thing he knew, it was that his poem was beautiful and alive and true, like an angel.

days. That was one of the sources of his interest in mould and moulding. There were others, of course. Watching his father preside grimly, trumpet-tongued and not always uninflamed by brandy, at burials in Bag Enderby and Somersby. The clay on the walls of the graves, sliced by the sextons' shovels, wet with rain. (He himself had added the tears of the angels.) Now there was Darwin, grubbing away at the life of the earthworm, throwing up mould and humus all over the place. Of the earth, earthy, humankind. But also, all the same, the round of green, the orb of flame, existed. Arthur had liked the Nightingale in his poem on the *Arabian Nights,* 'Apart from place, withholding time' in its singing. And the Nightingale had found its defiant voice in his poem for Arthur. It was there in opposition not only to the birds drawn down by the charming serpent, but to the nicely innocent, 'I pipe but as the linnet sings,' or the idea of language and song as a sad narcotic, dulling pain.

The Nightingale was the secret voice of the Art Trench had told him he could not live in. Now he was old, he was somehow more tempted to live in it again, as the child had lived in the *Arabian Nights.* Sometimes he saw dearest Emily and dutiful Hallam and his thousands of admirers and sycophants and people *asking for things* as shadows racing on a hillside, and heard the voices of the invisible as the only reality.

> Wild bird, whose warble, liquid sweet,
> Rings Eden through the budded quicks,
> O tell me where the senses mix,
> O tell me where the passions meet,
>
> Whence radiate: fierce extremes employ
> Thy spirits in the darkening leaf,
> And in the midmost heart of grief
> Thy passion clasps a secret joy:
>
> And I—my harp would prelude woe—
> I cannot all command the strings;

> The glory of the sum of things
> Will flash along the chords and go.

'The glory of the sum of things' was a good phrase. He had written rhetorically—a *Shakespearian* touch—to Arthur of his

> knowing Death has made
> His darkness beautiful with thee.

But he had made his poem beautiful with Arthur's death, and was afraid that that very beauty was something inhuman, animal and abstract at once, matter-moulded and shadowy.

A long thought, along accustomed tracks, can pass in a flash, as though the images and conjunctions and hurtful memories and brightnesses of which it is made up are wound into a tight ball, not strung out on thread like a necklace, and are then rolled at speed all at once, through the tunnels of the brain. He had still not manipulated the button into the hole, and now gave up trying and approached the mirror with his candle, though he knew mirror-images of buttonholes could be as confusing as feeling them out. The flame, in front of the black pool of glass, bellied and flared, white and murky yellow in an unexpected draught, and he saw a dark smear of smoke running backwards over his shoulder. He put the candlestick down on the dressing-table and saw himself like a bearded demon, his eyes glittering under bushy brows, his yellow teeth bared between tendrils of hair. He saw his own skull shaping his soft flesh and its covering of stretched wrinkled skin. He saw the huge bone-pits inside which his eyes were dark reflecting brilliants—wet jellies, he said to himself, pitying his thinning lashes, studying the caverns of his nostrils. He saw his invisible breath curl out of his mouth, and disturb the candle-flame, send wavering loops into its stream of smoke. It came in uncontrolled flickerings and jets, the little light. The spirit does but mean the breath.

This decaying, handsome face peers at me. He touched its cheek. Icy. The body of this death. He said to it, 'Alfred Tennyson, Alfred Tennyson.' Neither of them, the looker inside his warm motion, the ghostly cold starer, were what everyone thought of as Alfred Tennyson. 'Alfred Tennyson, Alfred Tennyson, Alfred Tennyson,' he said, and then faster, more nervously, 'Alfred Tennyson, Alfred Tennyson,' unmaking both of them with every naming of this nothing, this incoherent and terribly brief concatenation of nerves and mind. Pitying his white throat, the skin as innocent as a baby's below the shirtline, he finally did up the button, with peg-fingers that no longer belonged to him. The whole room, all space, was turning vertiginously round him. He fended off himself with a movement of his arms, flattening the flame with the sleeves of his nightshirt, making a stink of singed cloth and wax-fall. He staggered across to his bed and fell awkwardly into it, aware that he was not losing consciousness but was losing himself. His feather mattress shifted and billowed under his bones, his brain-box sank into the feathers of his pillow that shifted and sighed. He was a sack of bones borne up on a sack of plucked plumes. He was light as air, he was light and air. The voices sang and sang. He had been afraid, sickly afraid of this loss of coherence in youth, had suffered fit after fit of falling-sickness. First the too-bright aura, then the dizzying fall and the howling, like the Soul in the Palace of Art. He had written a poem, *The Mystic,* in 1830. He remembered, line by line:

> Angels have talked with him, and showed him thrones . . .
> Always there stood before him, night and day,
> Of wayward varycoloured circumstance
> The imperishable presences serene
> Colossal, without form, or sense, or sound,
> Dim shadows but unwaning presences
> Fourfacèd to the corners of the sky:
> And yet again, three shadows, fronting one,

One forward, one respectant, three but one; . . .
One shadow in the midst of a great light,
One reflex from eternity on time,
One mighty countenance of perfect calm,
Awful with most invariable eyes. . . .
He often lying broad awake, and yet
Remaining from the body, and apart
In intellect and power and will, hath heard
Time flowing in the middle of the night,
And all things creeping to a day of doom.

Sophy Sheekhy saw the terrible face, with its flaring lights, and its smoke and its bone-pits peering as it were through an invisible window into her room. The dead cold weight was heavier on her each moment, pinning her down so that she could move not the smallest muscle, not an eyelid, not her dry throat to swallow. The thick, mumbling tongue asked with difficulty, next to her ear, 'What do you see?' and she saw, as though through very thick glass, the old figure in its nightshirt stumble towards its bed, and stretch itself out under the folds of its sheets, and then she saw a kind of haze of spinning threads emanating from it, as though it were some white grub making a cocoon. The shining threads emanated from the mouth and wound about the face, transparent at first, then denser, leaving only a craggy profile, smoothing steadily, and the spinning went on until the whole form was bound into a kind of long bundle of bright woven matter, still, yet glowing and moving and busy and shining.

'I can't say what I see.'

'Everything is—dim. I—cannot—see.' She felt him grasp at her with disintegrating fingers that tried to pry into her flesh like roots searching for a vantage. She thought she had been afraid in trances before, but that that fear had been nothing compared to this, pity and fear, fear and pity, each making the other harder to bear. He wanted to feed off her life, and was invading the very fibre of her nerves with his death. The surface of her thought was that she would never again, never again try to come into the presence of the terrible dead, and this time too the depths of the still dark places of her were stirred with terror too, his terror, her terror, the terror of the tearing-out of life from flesh and of the energy of love for whatever remained when that was gone. He was being unmade, undone, and she could not, lying there, hold him together with her arms, or hear his voice any more in her ears, he had no more face, or fingers, only clay-cold, airless, stinking mass, plastering her mouth and nostrils.

XI

The day of the Angel was heavy with approaching storm. Mrs Papagay and Sophy Sheekhy, proceeding along the Front, trod between shining dark wind-ruffled puddles and patches of dull grey. There were gusts of wet, slaty wind in their skirts and they had to hold on to their hats, which threatened to take wing and bowl out to sea. White birds swooped and screamed and cackled, bobbed negligently on slaty waves streaked with sand, or strutted arrogantly in the puddles. Sophy looked at their cold feet in the cold water, clawed and wrinkled, and shuddered. Mrs Papagay sniffed the salt and asked Sophy if she felt ill. 'You look grey, my love, there is a grey tinge to your skin I do not like, and you have become very subdued.'

Sophy said guardedly that she did not, in fact, feel very well. She said, almost in a whisper, her words carried away by the wind, that she was not sure she was equal to the stress of the séance. Mrs Papagay cried bravely, 'I will take care of you, I will rescue you the moment I perceive you in any distress.' Sophy muttered that it was not too easy to rescue anyone from spirits. It was a weight on her mind, she said, gripping the brim of her struggling hat with white knuckles. 'It may be,' she said to Mrs Papagay, stopping her and peering into her face, with the movement of the sea behind it, 'it may be we are not *meant* to spend our time trying to make contact with *them*, Mrs Papagay. It may be against Nature.' Mrs Papagay replied robustly that it was, as they were taught, a natural aptitude of human beings in most societies to wish to speak with the dead. Look at Saul and the Witch of Endor, said Mrs Papagay, look at Odysseus offering Tiresias beakers of blood, look at the Red Indians, who live peaceably among the spirits of their ancestors. Spiritualists were always being exhorted to look at the Red Indians, whose English-speaking souls were regular guests to many British drawing-rooms, among antimacassars and stuffed parrots they must have had trouble in understanding. Mrs Papagay was worried that Sophy, usually so placid, should stop in a storm to express doubt. She peered under Sophy's hat and saw that her eyes were full of standing tears. 'Dearest Sophy,' said Mrs Papagay, 'you must *never* be led into doing anything against your own nature, anything you are not equal to. We can make our living in some other way, we can take in lodgers and do fine sewing. We will talk of this.'

Sophy stared through her tears at the iron water, at the rocking line of the horizon, at the iron sky. White spume, white birds, white fringes of fast cloud, sailing on grey. She said, 'You are very kind, and I am very grateful, indeed I love you for your kindness, and I do *not* intend to let you down. I feel less afraid, now I have spoken. I am happy to go on.'

The wind squealed past, mocking these sober words of human trust with its whining. The two women took each other's arms, and leaned into each other, then proceeded united through the gusts and into the town.

Inside the house, there was an atmosphere of ill-temper and constraint which daunted Mrs Papagay immediately she entered. She had not seen Mr Hawke since the ill-fated discussion of marriage in Heaven, and feared that at the very least his ruffled feathers would need smoothing. She saw immediately that it was worse than that. He was seated in a corner, lecturing Mrs Jesse and Mrs Hearnshaw on Swedenborg's physical apprehension of evil spirits, who persisted in thinking that their smoky darkness and foul odours were clearest air, and their loathsome appearance beautiful, who '*clung* to the corresponding part of him of their own place in the Divine Human and emitted sensations of anguish—'. He had brought Mrs Jesse a large, pallid bouquet of hothouse roses, which the maid had arranged in a silver rose-bowl in the centre of the table. He acknowledged the arrival of Mrs Papagay and Sophy Sheekhy with no more than a cursory nod. Mrs Hearnshaw's condition made her nauseous. She put a lace handkerchief frequently to her lips, and kept her left hand clasped to her ribs under her bosom, as though holding her emotions, and her unborn child, together in her body. Mrs Jesse herself seemed edgy and tired. Captain Jesse was for once not talking. He was standing in the bay of the window, his white mane rimmed with reflected light from the oil-lamp, staring into the thickening gloom, as though, Mrs Papagay thought, his right place was out there, in the weather.

They sat round the table in an apprehensive silence. Mr Hawke's face was red anyway, and was further reddened, a shiny apple, an angry cherub, by the reflected firelight. He offered no opening to Mrs Papagay, but said he had solemn matters to impart to them, as they settled their spirits to receive messages from the world of spirits and angels. He had been thinking, he said, about the peculiarly *material* nature of the Swedenborgian witness, and its relation to the spiritualist faith. He had been much struck, when he first read Swedenborg's accounts of his journeys to Heaven and Hell, by the sage's claims to have taught the angels in heaven many truths. But why should this not be so? A man who lived in two worlds at once would, by his very doubleness, learn and teach something that no single-world denizen could suspect. The angels *did not know,* until Swedenborg's visit, what matter was, or that it was distinct from spirit. It was only when a man came, who embraced at once matter and spirit and the difference between them, that an experience was given which taught what the difference is. You might argue that Swedenborg's visit was in the way of a scientific *experiment* for the angelic hosts, a *positive experience,* as needful for archangels and angels as for chemists, philosophers and mechanics. In fact, in all wisdom, there is no substance but *fact,* nothing so divine as experience. This is why the Divine Human is higher than the Angels, because His nature is Human, and corresponds perfectly to the human doubleness, matter and spirit.

There were things moreover, it was needful to know, about the material nature of the Divine Human. It was rightly said that even as the angels in heaven, joined in conjugial love, were both male and female, so was the Divine Human Himself. True it was, as Swedenborg had borne eloquent witness, that at one particular moment and spot in time and space, on one planet of all the inhabited planets, the Divine Human had taken on a particular human form and become an *earthly man,* of the earth earthy, as Saint Paul had written. True it was, that the heavens were male and female, for they proceeded from mankind, which was male and female, 'in the image of God created he him; male and female created he them' (Genesis 1, 27). But there was a further Doctrine of Swedenborg's about the Humanity of the Lord which it was essential to know and understand. Whilst He was incarnate here on earth, the Lord had had *both* a human form from His human mother and an eternal human form from the fact of His Divine Self, the Father. And Swedenborg taught that the Lord successively *put off* the Human assumed from the mother, and put on the Human from the Divine in Himself. He had two states on earth, one called the state of humiliation or exinanition, the other the state of glorification or union with the Divine, which is called the Father. He was in the state of humiliation so far as, and when, He was in the Human from the mother; and He was in the state of glorification so far as, and when, He was in the Human from the Father. In the state of humiliation he prayed to the Father as a being distinct from Himself; but in the state of glorification he spoke with the Father as with Himself. His Crucifixion was a necessary shedding of the corrupt humanity He had from the mother, in order to experience glorification and union with the Father.

'The first man is of the earth, earthy: the second man is the Lord from heaven.

As is the earthy, such are they also that are earthy: and as is the heavenly, such are they also that are heavenly.

And as we have borne the image of the earthy, we shall also bear the image of the heavenly.

Now this I say, brethren, that flesh and blood cannot inherit the kingdom of God; neither doth corruption inherit incorruption.

Behold, I shew you a mystery; We shall not all sleep, but we shall all be changed,

In a moment, in the twinkling of an eye, at the last trump: for the trumpet shall sound, and the dead shall be raised incorruptible, and we shall be changed.

'I Corinthians 15, 47 to 52,' said Mr Hawke.

There was a glum silence amongst the predominantly female members of his audience, who felt themselves individually and generally chastised, found wanting, or rather, not wanting, but too abundantly fleshly. Mrs Hearnshaw clasped her arms tighter around the prison of whalebone that held in the surge of her flesh inside which her own bones caged her growing child, precariously alive. Mrs Papagay fingered the little purse of her flesh under her chin, looking down, not meeting Mr Hawke's eye. Sophy Sheekhy shivered and shrank further into her clothes. Mrs Jesse stroked Pug's gentle, ugly, snoring head. Captain Jesse gave a sort of snort and trumpeted inconsequentially, 'And the sons of God saw the daughters of men that they were fair.'

There was a silence. Mr Hawke said, 'Excuse me—I fail to see the relevance—'

'I just like the sound of that saying, Mr Hawke, it cheers me, it suggests a kind of happy union of the earthly and the heavenly, you know, the beauty of women, and the *admiration* of the sons of God for that, in the oldest days you know, in Paradise, I suppose.'

'That is a very wrong interpretation, Captain Jesse. Very wrong. The authorities agree that those so-called sons of God are the *fallen angels* who fell into corruption out of their lust for earthly beauty, as certain among the angels are prone to do, as Swedenborg has also revealed. Even Saint Paul, I may tell you, in a most *interesting* text, warns against the excessive angelic desire for female corporeality. He requires women to be covered in the congregation, for a reason, which is that the head of every man is Christ, and the head of the woman is the man, so the man ought not, Saint Paul says, to cover his head, forasmuch as he is the image and glory of God: but the woman is the glory of the man.

> 'For the man is not of the woman; but the woman of the man.
> Neither was the man created for the woman; but the woman for the man.

'And he continues,' said Mr Hawke excitedly, ' "*For this cause ought the woman to have power on her head because of the angels.*" Now this is a hard saying to understand, but it is thought to relate to the temptation placed before the angels when the congregation, praying, attracts their attention—those angels imperfectly in possession of their *spiritual* nature—'

'So we are to suppose that all the wonderfully confected millinery of our great ladies, all the slaughtered birds of Paradise and egrets, all the macaws and ostriches, blue jays and snow-white doves, Mr Hawke, are what you call *power* to deflect the lusts of angels?' enquired Mrs Jesse. '*Power* they are, those towers and turrets of poor dead creatures put up to terrify like savages with bird-masks and golden feathery cloaks, power of money to send out ships across the sea to slaughter poor innocent living beings to nod above dewlaps, and flutter like portative dovecots in the breeze of society chatter.'

"Saint Paul had no knowledge of such things, Mrs Jesse. He spoke out against female vanity and male lust and showed that these things were not trivial, but part of the very fabric of things, involving Beings celestial and infernal, as our great prophet, Swedenborg, has most clearly shown. Female vanity in all its forms was an abomination to him, and that would of course include modern millinery in many of its modes, as you observe.'

'He said,' remarked Captain Jesse, 'that if a woman have long hair it is a glory to her.'

'He did indeed, and continued, the verse continues, "for her hair is given to her for a covering". She should be *covered*,' cried Mr Hawke.

'When we were married,' said Captain Jesse, 'Emily's hair was below her waist, all curls, I remember. I thought it was beautiful. It was beautiful.'

'Gone the way of all flesh,' said his wife, lightly, touching the silvery wings beside her face.

'Only changed,' said Captain Jesse. 'Not exactly in the twinkling of an eye, though it can feel like that, the years race past, and where are we, the feathered feet of time flitter past us and we are changed.'

'You speak frivolously of mysteries,' said Mr Hawke.

'And you are disposed to be very severe with us,' said Mrs Jesse, 'as though we were a flock in a church, where we are not, though we are gathered together for a serious purpose. And I think we should leave off this discussion and ask Mrs Papagay to calm us, and open our hearts to what messages those who are loved and vanished may wish to impart to us. Do you think a little gentle singing would be of help, Mrs Papagay?'

'The atmosphere is a little too *electric,* I think, Mrs Jesse. I feel a great striving of angry and mischievous spirits which is dangerous. I think we should join hands and pray for calm.'

She held out her hands, to Mr Hawke on her left, and Mrs Jesse on her right. Sophy had managed to position herself between Mrs Jesse and Captain Jesse. It was more than she could do, to dip her fingers in Mr Hawke's hot wrath. Mrs Hearnshaw was between Captain Jesse and Mr Hawke. Mrs Papagay felt great waves of dull red heat, sweating heat inside broadcloth, coming off Mr Hawke. She was all contrariwise, she put it to herself, and could not collect and recognise the individual feelings as she usually did. Instead, defensively, she was *thinking,* from a distance, and the séance never went anywhere if she was thinking. They were quite interesting thoughts, about how spiritual battles could truly rage, even in quiet firelit seaside drawing-rooms, fuelled by texts flung like arrows, made of words that were there to indicate *things,* hair, feathers, angels, man, woman, God. There had been a kind of jousting with words between Mr Hawke and Captain Jesse. The words were almost things, in the sense that she had seen, as they talked, a head of hair, a hat, a winged male body burning with desire, and yet they were not things, in the way in which her knowledge of Mrs Hearnshaw's distress was a thing, or her sense of Sophy's spiritual vastation, caused by she knew not what, not last week's creature full of eyes, she thought. Sophy's state was puzzling. She turned her attention to Mrs Jesse, who was also puzzling, who had had some understanding of last week's message, which she had chosen not to share, Mrs Papagay was sure. Mrs Jesse had withdrawn a hand, and was fiddling with the leather straps around Aaron's feet. She was releasing the great bird, massaging his black skin with her fingers, as he stood on the edge of the table and bowed, and rattled his quills. He then took one or two steps towards Mr Hawke, turning his head to one side and peering out of a glittering inky eye. Mr Hawke opened his mouth to speak and then thought better of it. Aaron put his beak against his breast, hunched up his shoulders, and appeared to sleep. The room was full of powers, wrathful and yearning, disconsolate and amorous, the movement of them swayed and lapped around the heads bent over the table.

The silence thickened. A petal fell. A sudden flurry of rain lashed the windowpane—Captain Jesse turned his great head to consider the weather. Mrs Papagay proposed that they try automatic writing. She drew the paper towards herself—she did not wish to impose on Sophy. She waited. After a moment the pen wrote confidently:

Blessed are they that mourn.
For *THEY SHALL BE COMFORTED.*

'Is anyone there?' Mr Hawke enquired. 'Any message for any particular person present?'

He will not come, she said.

'Who will not come?' said Mr Hawke.

'Arthur,' said Mrs Jesse, with a little sigh. 'It means Arthur, I am sure.'

The pen wrote rapidly.

And he that shuts Love out in turn shall be
Shut out from Love and on her threshold lie
Howling in outer darkness.

The pen appeared to like this word, for it played with it, repeating it several times, 'howling', 'howling', 'howling', and then adding

those that lawless and incertain thoughts
Imagine howling—'tis too horrible . . .

'A poetic spirit,' said Mr Hawke.

'The first two are Alfred,' said Mrs Jesse. 'The pen may have hooked them, so to speak, out of my mind. The last is from *Measure for Measure,* a passage about the fate of the soul after death which Alfred was much struck by, as we all were. I have no idea who is uttering these things.'

One shall be Comforted. All tears shall be wiped away. The Bridegroom Cometh. Ye know neither the day nor the Hour when he cometh. Light the Lamp.

'Who is telling us these things?' asked Mrs Jesse.

'No, oh *no,*' said Sophy Sheekhy, in a strangled voice.

'Sophy—' cried Mrs Papagay.

Sophy felt cold hands at her neck, cold fingers on her warm lips. The flesh crept over the bones of her skull, along the backs of her fingers, under the whalebone. She began to shake and jerk. She fell back open-mouthed in her chair and saw something, someone, standing in the bay of the window. It was larger than life, and more exiguous, a kind of pillar of smoke, or fire or cloud, in a not exactly human form. It was not the dead young man, for whom she had felt such pity, it was a living creature with three wings, all hanging loosely on one side of it. On that side, the winged side, it was dull gold and had the face of a bird of prey, dignified, golden-eyed, feather-breasted, powdered with hot metallic particles. On its other side, turned into the shadow, it was grey like wet clay, and formless, putting out stumps that were not arms, moving what was not a mouth in a thin whisper. It spoke in two voices, one musical, one a papery squeak. 'Tell her I wait.'

'Tell whom?' said Sophy, in a small voice they all heard.

'Emilia. I triumph in conclusive bliss. Tell her. We shall be joined and made one Angel.'

It was hungry for the life of the living creatures in the room.

'Sophy,' said Mrs Papagay. 'What do you see?'

'Gold wings,' said Sophy. 'It says, "I wait." It says to tell you, "I triumph in conclusive bliss." It says to tell Emily—Mrs Jesse—Emily—that—they shall be joined, and made one Angel. In the hereafter, that is.'

Emily Jesse gave a great sigh. She let go Sophy's cold hand, and detached Sophy's other hand from her husband's, breaking the circle. Sophy lay inert, like a prisoner before an inquisitor, staring at the half-angel, whom no one else saw, or really *felt* the presence of, and Emily Jesse put her hand into her husband's.

'Well, Richard,' she said. 'We may not always have got on together as well as we should, and our marriage may not have been a success, but I consider that an extremely unfair arrangement, and shall have nothing to do with it. We have been through bad times in this world, and I consider it only decent to share our good times, presuming we have them, in the next.'

Richard picked up her hand and looked at it.

'Why, Emily,' he said, and then again, 'why, Emily—'

'You are not usually at a loss for words,' said his wife.

'No, I am not. It is only that—I understood—I understood you to be waiting—for some such communication. I had never supposed you would say—anything like—what you have just said.'

'It may be that you have other ideas,' said Mrs Jesse.

'You know *that* is not so. I have tried to be understanding, I have tried to be patient, I have respected—'

'Too well, too well, you tried too well, we both—'

Captain Jesse shook his head, like a surfacing swimmer.

'But all through these séances *I understood you to be waiting*—'

'I do love him,' said Emily. 'It is hard to love the dead. It is hard to love the dead enough.'

Mrs Papagay was made intensely happy by this exchange. Who would have thought it, she said to herself, and yet, *how right,* it was only when the Angel threatened her with the loss of the husband she had taken for granted that she really saw him, saw him in terms of his loss, his vanishing, that was implied, and was driven to imagine existence without him. She knew she was romanticising, but she was filled with a kind of bubbling delight at the spectacle of the looks, shrewd and wondering together, that passed between these two elderly people, who might be supposed to have no possible secrets from each other, and yet had this great one. How *interesting,* said Mrs Papagay to herself, and was brought back by a kind of choking sound from Sophy, who was turning a terrible colour, ash and plum and lapis blue together, her lips moving numbly. She snorted, she sucked desperately for breath, as though her life was being sucked out of her. Mrs Papagay stood up quietly and went round and put her own warm hands on Sophy's chilly temples. Sophy's little heels drummed on the carpet, her spine arched and jerked. Her eyes were open and unseeing. Nothing so dreadful had happened to her before. Mrs Papagay tried to pour love and holding, *withholding,* along her own fingers. Sophy lay entranced in the presence of absence, ab- sence made of dripping clay and the dust falling from drooping feathers. Sophy felt it weaken, sighed its terrible rattling sigh in her own larynx, saw it disintegrate, baleful, yearning, into the spangly gloom which frothed up, boiled, swayed and was black liquid again. She turned her head towards Captain Jesse and saw his albatross stretching its wings, its huge uncaged wings, and star- ing with its gold-rimmed eye.

'Sophy,' said Mrs Papagay.

'I am quite well,' said Sophy, 'now.'

Mrs Papagay judged it might be better to end the séance with some perhaps uplifting written messages. It was always surprising how the

living, in the presence of the dead, continued to be preoccupied
with their living concerns, great and trivial. No one but herself had
been much shocked by Sophy's state. No one had feared for her.
As though they all *knew* Sophy was acting, Mrs Papagay thought,
although they also needed to believe she was not; they believed
what they needed to believe, either way, she thought, and thus kept
the dark, the ferocious, lurching dark, in order and at bay. She
herself knew Sophy was not acting, but could not see what Sophy
had seen. Afterwards, she thought she must have been mad not to
suppose the forces in the room might be unappeased and dangerous, but then, she was like the others, she *knew* it was all a parlour
game, at one level, a kind of communal story-telling, or charade,
even whilst she held Sophy's mortally cold hands. Anyway, she
drew the paper absently towards herself, and took up the pencil,
which squirmed gleefully in her hand, and set off, possessed, across
the paper, in a fanatically neat, unhesitating hand.

Is the Conjugial Angel stone
That here he stands with heavy head
The backward-looking pillared dead
Inert, moss-covered, all alone?

The Holy Ghost trawls in the Void
With fleshly Sophy on His Hook
The Sons of God crowd round to look
At plumpy limbs to be enjoyed

The Greater Man casts out the line
With dangling Sophy as the lure
Who howls around the Heavens' colure
To clasp the Human Form Divine

Rose-petals fall from fallen hair
That in the clay is redolent
Of liquid oozings and the scent
Of the dark Pit, the Beastly lair

And is my Love become the beast
That was, and is not, and yet is,
Who stretches scarlet holes to kiss
And clasps with claws the fleshly feast

Sweet Rosamund, adult'rous Rose
May lie inside her urn and stink
While Alfred's tears turn into ink
And drop into her quelque-chose

The Angel spreads his golden wings
And raises high his golden cock
And man and wife together lock
Into one corpse that moans and sings

'Stop,' said Mr Hawke. 'There is an evil spirit present. These are filthy imaginings, which must be put an end to. Turn up the lights, *stop*, Mrs Papagay, we must be strong."

Aroused by his angry voice, Aaron sidled across the table, knocked over the rose-bowl, and took wing to the mantelshelf, leaving behind him a dark stain covered with white rounds.

'What can it mean?' said Mrs Hearnshaw, reading. 'What can it mean?'

'It is obscene,' said Mr Hawke. 'It is not fit for the eyes of ladies. I believe it is the communication of an evil spirit, to which we should give no more hearing.'

Aaron let out a loud, perhaps affirmative, croak at this, which made them all jump. And Pug, shifting in his sleep, let out a series of popping little farts, and a rich, decaying smell. Emily Jesse, her lips pinched and white, took up the offending paper and carried it over to the fire, into which she dropped it. It curled and crisped, browned and blackened, and flew on ashen wings up the chimney. Mrs Papagay, watching Mrs Jesse, knew that this was their last séance in this house, that something truly remarkable had happened, and precisely for that reason, no more attempts would be made. She was sorry, and she was not sorry. After Mr Hawke, rumbling, had left alone, and Mrs Hearnshaw's cab had borne her away, Mrs Jesse made tea for Mrs Papagay and Sophy, and said she had decided it would be wiser to have no more meetings for the present. '*Something* is playing games with much that is sacred to me, and it is not myself, Mrs Papagay, but can be no one else, and I find I do not wish to know more. Do you think I lack courage?'

'I think you are wise, Mrs Jesse. I think you are very wise.'

'You console me.'

She poured tea. The oil-lamps cast a warm light on the teatray. The teapot was china, with little roses painted all over it, crimson and blush-pink and celestial blue, and the cups were garlanded with the same flowers. There were sugared biscuits, each with a flower made out of piped icing, creamy, violet, snow-white. Sophy Sheekhy watched the stream of topaz-coloured liquid fall from the spout, steaming and aromatic. This too was a miracle, that gold-skinned persons in China and bronze-skinned persons in India should gather leaves which should come across the seas safely in white-winged ships, encased in lead, encased in wood, surviving storms and whirlwinds, sailing on under hot sun and cold moon, and come here, and be poured from bone-china, made from fine clay, moulded by clever fingers, in the Pottery Towns, baked in kilns, glazed with slippery shiny clay, baked again, painted with rosebuds by artist-hands holding fine, fine brushes, delicately turning the potter's wheel and implanting, with a kiss of sable-hairs, floating buds on an azure ground, or a dead white ground, and that sugar should be fetched from where black men and women slaved and died terribly to make these delicate flowers that melted on the tongue like the scrolls in the mouth of the Prophet Isaiah, that flour should be milled, and milk shaken into butter, and both worked together into these momentary delights, baked in Mrs Jesse's oven and piled elegantly on to a plate to be offered to Captain Jesse with his wool-white head and smiling eyes, to Mrs Papagay, flushed and agitated, to her sick self, and the black bird and the dribbling Pug, in front of the hot coals of fire, in the benign lamplight. Any of them might so easily not have been there to drink the tea, or eat the sweetmeats. Storms and ice-floes might have taken Captain Jesse, grief or childbearing might have destroyed his wife, Mrs Papagay might have lapsed into penury and she herself have died as an overworked servant, but here they were and their eyes were bright and their tongues tasted goodness.

XII

And when at last they left, they went out into the dark indeed. It was ice-cold, and gusty, with salt water flung in the air, and the sound of water distant and close at once. They thought nevertheless they would walk home, already

apprehensive about making savings. For if Mrs Jesse would hold no
more séances and Mr Hawke was angry and hostile, what was to
become of them? They hurried towards the sea-front, with the
wind behind them, preceded by a bulwark of open umbrellas. After
a time, Sophy pulled at Mrs Papagay's sleeve and tried to shout
quietly into her ear.

'I think we are being followed. There have been footsteps behind us since we left Mrs Jesse.'

'I think you are right. And now we are stopped, they are
stopped. It is only one person.'

'I am afraid.'

'So am I. But I believe we should stand our ground—here under
this gas-lamp and allow our follower to pass peaceably, or challenge
him. We are two, he is only one. I do not wish to go into the maze
of alleys behind the fish-market still with a follower. Do you feel
brave, Sophy?'

'No. But he is only flesh and blood, I think.'

'Inhabited by a *living* spirit, my dear, which can also be dangerous.'

'I know. But at the moment, I more fear the dead. Let us face
him out. He may pass by.'

They stopped, and the following footsteps stopped, and then
came on, slower, more hesitant. They stood still under their chosen
lamp, clutching their umbrellas. The steps came on, and were seen
to belong to a shaggy creature in a shapeless greatcoat and a dark
cap. When he came up to them, he stopped stock-still, and stood
and looked at them.

'Why are you following us?' said Mrs Papagay.

'Ah,' said the watcher. 'It is you. I was not quite sure in the dark,
but now I see it is you, plain as plain. I went to your house, and
all was dark and closed, but the woman in the next house told me

you would be going this way—so I set out—it being cold and wet on the doorstep—and myself having had enough cold and wet for two lifetimes. Don't you know me, Lilias?'

'Arturo,' said Mrs Papagay.

'Twice wrecked,' he said tentatively. 'Once cast away. Did you not get my letters, saying I was sailing for home?'

Mrs Papagay shook her head. She was afraid she was breaking up. Her nerves hurt, her head banged, she was like a stunned cow at the slaughterer's.

'I have given you a frightful shock,' said Captain Papagay. 'I should have waited on the doorstep.'

Mrs Papagay travelled to the mouth of the grave and was brought back on the wings of the wind. Life was pumped into her heart and lungs and she gave a great whirling cry, 'Arturo, Arturo,' and flung away her umbrella, which was caught by the wind and went floating away down the street like a giant dandelion-seed. 'Arturo,' cried Mrs Papagay. And she leaped at him, so that if he had not been there and solid to hold her up, she must have dashed herself unconscious on the wet pavement. But he was there, and Mrs Papagay came to rest in his arms, and he opened his greatcoat and pulled her in against him, and she smelled his live smell, salt, tobacco, his own hair and skin, unlike any other hair and skin in the whole world, a smell she had kept alive when it had seemed wiser to let it die in the memory of her nostrils. And he buried his face in her hair, and she put her empty arms around his fullness, lean but lively, remembering his shoulder, his ribs, his loins, crying out 'Arturo' into his greatcoat and the wind.

And Sophy Sheekhy stood under the lamp, watching the two of them becoming more and more completely entangled in one, as they clutched and touched and babbled. And she thought of all the people in the world whose arms are aching and empty to hold the dead, and of how in stories, and very occasionally in sober fact, the cold and the sea give back what they have taken, or appear to have taken, and this dark windswept conjunction became in her mind a harmonious whole with the vision of the Jesses' fireside, and the miracle of the tea. A life in death, Sophy Sheekhy thought, turning discreetly away from Mrs Papagay's dishevelled rapture to the inky black of the sky and the sea, beyond the lamplight.

ACKNOWLEDGMENTS

I should like to thank several people for their help, both practical and bibliographical. Ursula Owen and David Miller lent books on bees and angels. My French publishers, Marc and Christiane Kopylov, hunted through second-hand bookstores in Paris. Lisa Appignanesi lent the whole of Swedenborg's *Arcana Caelestia*. Gillian Beer and Jenny Uglow made crucial suggestions for reading. Chris O'Toole at the Hope Entomological Institute in Oxford and someone very patient on the entomological enquiry desk at the Science Museum were extraordinarily helpful and interesting. My daughter Isabel Duffy, Elizabeth Allen, and Helena Caletta, most resourceful of booksellers, were both practical and patient. And Jane Turner, at Chatto & Windus, hunted for illustrations with great imagination, as well as erudition.

A work of fiction doesn't need a bibliography. But I should like to thank Colonel A. Maitland Emmet, whose *The Scientific Names of the British Lepidoptera* has given me hours of happy reading and inspired much of Matty's story 'Things Are Not What They Seem'. Michael Chinery's *Collins Guide to the Insects of Britain and Western Europe* has also given me great pleasure and much information. Anyone interested in A. H. Hallam owes a great debt to the late T. H. Vail Motter, editor of *The Writings of Arthur H. Hallam,* and to Jack Kolb, editor of his *Letters*. Christopher Ricks's great edition of Tennyson's *Complete Works* is steadily inspiring. I also owe a great deal to Derek Wragge Morley's *The Evolution of an Insect Society*. Alex Owen's *The Darkened Room* is an excellent study of female mediums in the nineteenth century. And I learned much, with pleasure, from Michael Wheeler's *Death and the Future Life in Victorian Literature and Theology*.

Finally, this book could not have been written without the resources of the London Library.

Illustrations

The author and publisher would like to thank the following for permission to reproduce illustrations: Brian Hargreaves, F.R.S.A., for ten line drawings; the Courtauld Institute of Art, London, for two engravings by John Martin from Milton's *Paradise Lost;* the Fogg Art Museum, Harvard University, Cambridge, Mass., Bequest of Grenville L. Winthrop, for two drawings by Edward Burne-Jones from 'The Days of Creation' (The First and Second Days), and for the drawing by Dante Gabriel Rossetti: 'Study for The Blessed Damozel'.

About the Author

A. S. Byatt is the author of the Booker Prize–winning *Possession: A Romance*. She has taught English and American literature at University College, London, and is a distinguished critic and reviewer. Her critical work includes *Degrees of Freedom* (a study of Iris Murdoch) and *Unruly Times: Wordsworth and Coleridge in Their Time*. She is also the author of four previously published novels—*Shadow of a Sun, The Game, The Virgin in the Garden,* and *Still Life*—and a collection of short fiction, *Sugar and Other Stories*.